brick lane

a novel

monica ali

SCRIBNER

New York London Toronto Sydney Singapore

SCRIBNER
1230 Avenue of the Americas
New York, NY 10020

First Scribner edition 2003
Originally published in Great Britain in 2003 by Doubleday, a division of Transworld Publishers

Designed by Kyoko Watanabe
Text set in Aldine

Manufactured in the United States of America

1 3 5 7 9 10 8 6 4 2

Library of Congress Cataloging-in-Publication Data
Ali, Monica.
Brick Lane : a novel / Monica Ali.—1st Scribner ed.
p. cm.
I. Title.
PR6101.L45B75 2003
823'.92—dc21 2003042795

ISBN 0-7432-4330-7

For Abba, with love

brick
lane

Sternly, remorselessly, fate guides each of us; only at the beginning, when we're absorbed in details, in all sorts of nonsense, in ourselves, are we unaware of its harsh hand.

—*Ivan Turgenev*

A man's character is his fate.

—*Heraclitus*

Chapter One

MYMENSINGH DISTRICT, EAST PAKISTAN, 1967

An hour and forty-five minutes before Nazneen's life began—began as it would proceed for quite some time, that is to say uncertainly—her mother, Rupban, felt an iron fist squeeze her belly. Rupban squatted on a low three-legged stool outside the kitchen hut. She was plucking a chicken because Hamid's cousins had arrived from Jessore and there would be a feast. "Cheepy-cheepy, you are old and stringy," she said, calling the bird by name as she always did, "but I would like to eat you, indigestion or no indigestion. And tomorrow I will have only boiled rice, no parathas."

She pulled some more feathers and watched them float around her toes. "Aaah," she said. "Aaaah. Aaaah." Things occurred to her. For seven months she had been ripening, like a mango on a tree. Only seven months. She put aside those things that had occurred to her. For a while, an hour and a half, though she did not know it, until the men came in from the fields trailing dust and slapping their stomachs, Rupban clutched Cheepy-cheepy's limp and bony neck and said only "Coming, coming" to all inquiries about the bird. The shadows of the children playing marbles and thumping each other grew long and spiky. The scent of fried cumin and cardamom drifted over the compound. The goats bleated high and thin. Rupban screamed white heat, red blood.

Hamid ran from the latrine, although his business was unfinished. He ran across the vegetable plot, past the towers of rice stalk taller than the tallest building, over the dirt track that bounded the village, back to the compound, and grabbed a club to kill the man who was killing his wife. He knew it was her. Who else could break glass with one screech? Rupban was in the sleeping quarters. The bed was unrolled, though she was still standing. With one hand she held Mumtaz's shoulder, with the other a half-plucked chicken.

Mumtaz waved Hamid away. "Go. Get Banesa. Are you waiting for a rickshaw? Go on, use your legs."

* * *

Banesa picked up Nazneen by an ankle and blew disparagingly through her gums over the tiny blue body. "She will not take even one breath. Some people, who think too much about how to save a few takas, do not call a midwife." She shook her hairless, wrinkled head. Banesa claimed to be one hundred and twenty years old, and had made this claim consistently for the past decade or so. Since no one in the village remembered her birth, and since Banesa was more desiccated than an old coconut, no one cared to dispute it. She claimed, too, one thousand babies, of which only three were cripples, two were mutants (a hermaphrodite and a humpback), one a stillbirth, and another a monkey-lizard-hybrid-sin-against-God-that-was-buried-alive-in-the-faraway-forest-and-the-mother-sent-hence-to-who-cares-where. Nazneen, though dead, could not be counted among these failures, having been born shortly before Banesa creaked inside the hut.

"See your daughter," Banesa said to Rupban. "Perfect everywhere. All she lacked was someone to ease her path to this world." She looked at Cheepy-cheepy lying next to the bereaved mother and hollowed her cheeks; a hungry look widened her eyes slightly although they were practically buried in crinkles. It was many months since she had tasted meat, now that two young girls (she should have strangled them at birth) had set up in competition.

"Let me wash and dress her for the burial," said Banesa. "Of course I offer my service free. Maybe just that chicken there for my trouble. I see it is old and stringy."

"Let me hold her," said Nazneen's aunt Mumtaz, who was crying.

"I thought it was indigestion," said Rupban, also beginning to cry.

Mumtaz took hold of Nazneen, who was still dangling by the ankle, and felt the small, slick torso slide through her fingers to plop with a yowl onto the bloodstained mattress. A yowl! A cry! Rupban scooped her up and named her before she could die nameless again.

Banesa made little explosions with her lips. She used the corner of her yellowing sari to wipe some spittle from her chin. "This is called a death rattle," she explained. The three women put their faces close to the child. Nazneen flailed her arms and yelled, as if she could see this terrifying sight. She began to lose the blueness and turned slowly to brown and purple. "God has called her back to earth," said Banesa, with a look of disgust.

Mumtaz, who was beginning to doubt Banesa's original diagnosis, said, "Well, didn't He just send her to us a few minutes ago? Do you think He changes His mind every second?"

Banesa mumbled beneath her breath. She put her hand over Nazneen's chest, her twisted fingers like the roots of an old tree that had worked their way aboveground. "The baby lives but she is weak. There are two routes you can follow," she said, addressing herself solely to Rupban. "Take her to the city, to a hospital. They will put wires on her and give medicines. This is very expensive. You will have to sell your jewelry. Or you can just see what Fate will do." She turned a little to Mumtaz to include her now, and then back to Rupban. "Of course, Fate will decide everything in the end, whatever route you follow."

"We will take her to the city," said Mumtaz, red patches of defiance rising on her cheeks. But Rupban, who could not stop crying, held her daughter to her breast and shook her head. "No," she said, "we must not stand in the way of Fate. Whatever happens, I accept it. And my child must not waste any energy fighting against Fate. That way, she will be stronger."

"Good, then it is settled," said Banesa. She hovered for a moment or two because she was hungry enough, almost, to eat the baby, but after a look from Mumtaz she shuffled away back to her hovel.

Hamid came to look at Nazneen. She was wrapped in cheesecloth and laid on an old jute sack on top of the bedroll. Her eyes were closed and puffed as though she had taken two hard punches.

"A girl," said Rupban.

"I know. Never mind," said Hamid. "What can you do?" And he went away again.

Mumtaz came in with a tin plate of rice, dal, and chicken curry. "She doesn't feed," Rupban told her. "She doesn't know what to do. Probably it is her Fate to starve to death."

Mumtaz rolled her eyes. "She'll feed in the morning. Now you eat. Or you are destined to die of hunger too." She smiled at her sister-in-law's small sad face, all her features lined up, as ever, to mourn for everything that had passed and all that would come to pass.

But Nazneen did not feed in the morning. Nor the next day. The day after, she turned her face away from the nipple and made gagging noises. Rupban, who was famous for crying, couldn't keep up with the demand for tears. People came: aunts, uncles, cousins, brothers, nephews, nieces, in-laws, village women, and Banesa. The midwife dragged her bent feet across the hard mud floor of the hut and peered at the infant. "I have heard of one child who would not feed from the mother but was suckled by a goat." She smiled and showed her black gums. "Of course, that was not one of *my* babies."

Hamid came once or twice, but at night he slept outside on a choki. On the fifth day, when Rupban in spite of herself was beginning to wish that Fate would hurry and make up its mind, Nazneen clamped her mouth around the nipple so that a thousand red-hot needles ran through Rupban's breast and made her cry out for pain and for the relief of a good and patient woman.

As Nazneen grew she heard many times this story of How You Were Left to Your Fate. It was because of her mother's wise decision that Nazneen lived to become the wide-faced, watchful girl that she was. Fighting against one's Fate can weaken the blood. Sometimes, or perhaps most times, it can be fatal. Not once did Nazneen question the logic of the story of How You Were Left to Your Fate. Indeed, she was grateful for her mother's quiet courage, her tearful stoicism that was almost daily in evidence. Hamid said—he always looked away as he spoke—"Your mother is naturally a saint. She comes from a family of saints." So when Rupban advised Nazneen to be still in her heart and mind, to accept the Grace of God, to treat life with the same indifference with which it would treat her, she listened closely, with her large head tilted back and her cheeks slack with equanimity.

She was a comically solemn child. "How is my precious? Still glad you came back to life?" asked Mumtaz after she had not seen Nazneen for a couple of days. "I have no complaints or regrets to tell you," said Nazneen. "I tell everything to God."

What could not be changed must be borne. And since nothing could be changed, everything had to be borne. This principle ruled her life. It was mantra, fettle, and challenge. So that, at the age of thirty-four, after she had been given three children and had one taken away, when she had a futile husband and had been fated a young and demanding lover, when for the first time she could not wait for the future to be revealed but had to make it for herself, she was as startled by her own agency as an infant who waves a clenched fist and strikes itself upon the eye.

Her sister, Hasina, born only three days after Banesa passed away (one hundred and twenty years old then and forevermore), listened to no one.

At the age of sixteen, when her beauty was becoming almost unbearable to own or even to look at, she eloped to Khulna with the nephew of the sawmill owner. Hamid ground his teeth and an axe besides. For sixteen hot days and cool nights he sat between the two lemon trees that marked the entrance to the compound. For that time his only occupation was throwing stones at the piebald dogs that scavenged in the dump just beyond, and cursing his whore-pig daughter whose head would be severed the moment she came crawling back. Those nights, Nazneen lay awake listening to the rattling of the corrugated tin roof, starting at the owl calls that no longer sounded like owls but more like a girl felled by an axe on the back of her neck. Hasina did not come. Hamid went back to supervising the laborers in the paddy fields. But for a couple of thrashings given on only the slightest of provocation, you would not know he had lost a daughter.

Soon after, when her father asked if she would like to see a photograph of the man she would marry the following month, Nazneen shook her head and replied, "Abba, it is good that you have chosen my husband. I hope I can be a good wife, like Amma." But as she turned to go she noticed, without meaning to, where her father put the photograph.

She just happened to see it. These things happen. She carried the image around in her mind as she walked beneath the banyans with her cousins. The man she would marry was old. At least forty years old. He had a face like a frog. They would marry and he would take her back to England with him. She looked across the fields, glittering green and gold in the brief evening light. In the distance a hawk circled and fell like a stone, came up again and flew against the sky until it shrank to nothing. There was a hut in the middle of the paddy. It looked wrong: embarrassed, sliding down at one side, trying to hide. The tornado that had flattened half the neighboring village had selected this hut to be saved, but had relocated it. In the village they were still burying their dead and looking for bodies. Dark spots moved through the far fields. Men, doing whatever they could in this world.

TOWER HAMLETS, LONDON, 1985

Nazneen waved at the tattoo lady. The tattoo lady was always there when Nazneen looked out across the dead grass and broken paving stones to the block opposite. Most of the flats, which enclosed three sides of a square, had net curtains, and the life behind was all shapes and shadows. But the tattoo lady had no curtains at all. Morning and afternoon she sat with her big thighs spilling over the sides of her chair, tipping forward to drop ash in a bowl, tipping back to slug from her can. She drank now, and tossed the can out of the window.

It was the middle of the day. Nazneen had finished the housework. Soon she would start preparing the evening meal, but for a while she would let the time pass. It was hot and the sun fell flat on the metal window frames and glared off the glass. A red-and-gold sari hung out of a top-floor flat in Rosemead block. A baby's bib and miniature dungarees lower down. The sign screwed to the brickwork was in stiff English capitals and the curlicues beneath were Bengali. No Dumping. No Parking. No Ball Games. Two old men in white panjabi pajama and skullcaps walked along the path, slowly, as if they did not want to go where they were going. A thin brown dog sniffed along to the middle of the grass and defecated. The breeze on Nazneen's face was thick with the smell from the overflowing communal bins.

Six months now since she'd been sent away to London. Every morning before she opened her eyes she thought, *If I were the wishing type, I know what I would wish.* And then she opened her eyes and saw Chanu's puffy face on the pillow next to her, his lips parted indignantly even as he slept. She saw the pink dressing table with the curly-sided mirror, and the monstrous black wardrobe that claimed most of the room. Was it cheating? To think, *I know what I would wish*? Was it not the same as making the wish? If she knew what the wish would be, then somewhere in her heart she had already made it.

The tattoo lady waved back at Nazneen. She scratched her arms, her shoulders, the accessible portions of her buttocks. She yawned and lit a cigarette. At least two thirds of the flesh on show was covered in ink. Nazneen had never been close enough (never closer than this, never farther) to decipher the designs. Chanu said the tattoo lady was Hell's Angel, which upset Nazneen. She thought the tattoos might be flowers, or birds. They were ugly and they made the tattoo lady more ugly than was necessary, but the tattoo lady clearly did not care. Every time Nazneen saw her she wore the same look of boredom and detachment. Such a state was sought by the sadhus who walked in rags through the Muslim villages, indifferent to the kindness of strangers, the unkind sun.

Nazneen sometimes thought of going downstairs, crossing the yard, and climbing the Rosemead stairwell to the fourth floor. She might have to knock on a few doors before the tattoo lady answered. She would take something, an offering of samosas or bhajis, and the tattoo lady would smile and Nazneen would smile and perhaps they would sit together by the window and let the time pass more easily. She thought of it but she would not go. Strangers would answer if she knocked on the wrong door. The tattoo lady might be angry at an unwanted interruption. It was clear she did not like to leave her chair. And even if she wasn't angry, what would be the point? Nazneen could say two things in English: sorry and thank you. She could spend another day alone. It was only another day.

She should be getting on with the evening meal. The lamb curry was prepared. She had made it last night with tomatoes and new potatoes. There was chicken saved in the freezer from the last time Dr. Azad had been invited but had canceled at the last minute. There was still the dal to make, and the vegetable dishes, the spices to grind, the rice to wash, and the sauce to prepare for the fish that Chanu would bring this evening. She would rinse the glasses and rub them with newspaper to make them shine. The tablecloth had some spots to be scrubbed out. What if it went wrong? The rice might stick. She might oversalt the dal. Chanu might forget the fish.

It was only dinner. One dinner. One guest.

She left the window open. Standing on the sofa to reach, she picked up the Holy Qur'an from the high shelf that Chanu, under duress, had specially built. She made her intention as fervently as possible, seeking refuge from Satan with fists clenched and fingernails digging into her palms. Then she selected a page at random and began to read.

> To God belongs all that the heavens and the earth contain. We exhort you, as We have exhorted those to whom the Book was given before you, to fear God. If you deny Him, know that to God belongs all that the heavens and earth contain. God is self-sufficient and worthy of praise.

The words calmed her stomach and she was pleased. Even Dr. Azad was nothing as to God. To God belongs all that the heavens and the earth contain. She said it over a few times, aloud. She was composed. Nothing could bother her. Only God, if he chose to. Chanu might flap about and squawk because Dr. Azad was coming for dinner. Let him flap. To God belongs all that the heavens and the earth contain. How would it sound in Arabic? More lovely even than in Bengali, she supposed, for those were the actual Words of God.

She closed the book and looked around the room to check it was tidy enough. Chanu's books and papers were stacked beneath the table. They would have to be moved or Dr. Azad would not be able to get his feet in. The rugs, which she had held out of the window earlier and beaten with a wooden spoon, needed to be put down again. There were three rugs: red and orange, green and purple, brown and blue. The carpet was yellow with a green leaf design. One hundred percent nylon and, Chanu said, very hard-wearing. The sofa and chairs were the color of dried cow dung, which was a practical color. They had little sheaths of plastic on the headrests to protect them from Chanu's hair oil. There was a lot of furniture, more than Nazneen had seen in one room before. Even if you took all the furniture in the compound, from every auntie and uncle's ghar, it would not match up to this one room. There was a low table with a glass top and orange plastic legs, three little wooden tables that stacked together, the big table they used for the evening meal, a bookcase, a corner cupboard, a rack for newspapers, a trolley filled with files and folders, the sofa and armchairs, two footstools, six dining chairs, and a showcase. The walls were papered in yellow with brown squares and circles lining neatly up and down. Nobody in Gouripur had anything like it. It made her proud. Her father was the second-wealthiest man in the village and he never had anything like it. He had made a good marriage for her. There were plates on the wall, attached by hooks and wires, which were not for eating from but only for display. Some were rimmed in gold paint. "Gold leaf," Chanu called it. His certificates were framed and mixed with the plates. She had everything here. All these beautiful things.

She put the Qur'an back in its place. Next to it lay the most Holy Book wrapped inside a cloth covering: the Qur'an in Arabic. She touched her fingers to the cloth.

Nazneen stared at the glass showcase stuffed with pottery animals, china figures, and plastic fruit. Each one had to be dusted. She wondered how the dust got in and where it came from. All of it belonged to God. She wondered what He wanted with clay tigers, trinkets, and dust.

And then, because she had let her mind drift and become uncentered again, she began to recite in her head from the Holy Qur'an one of the suras she had learned in school. She did not know what the words meant but the rhythm of them soothed her. Her breath came from down in her stomach. In and out. Smooth. Silent. Nazneen fell asleep on the sofa. She looked out across jade-green rice fields and swam in the cool dark lake. She walked arm-in-arm to school with Hasina, and skipped part of the way and fell and they dusted their knees with their hands. And the mynah birds called from the trees, and the goats fretted by, and the big, sad water buffaloes passed like a funeral. And heaven, which was above, was wide and empty and the land stretched out ahead and she could see to the very end of it, where the earth smudged the sky in a dark blue line.

When she woke it was almost four o'clock. She rushed to the kitchen and began chopping onions with the sleep still in her eyes so that it was not long before she cut her finger, a deep cut to the left index, just below the nail. She turned on the cold tap and held her hand beneath it. What was Hasina doing? This thought came to her all the time. *What is she doing right now?* It was not even a thought. It was a feeling, a stab in the lungs. Only God alone knew when she would see her again.

It worried her that Hasina kicked against fate. No good could come of it. Not a single person could say so. But then, if you really looked into it, thought about it more deeply, how could you be sure that Hasina was not simply following her fate? If fate cannot be changed, no matter how you struggle against it, then perhaps Hasina was fated to run away with Malek. Maybe she struggled against *that,* and *that* was what she could not alter. Oh, you think it would be simple, having made the decision long, long ago, to be at the beck and call of fate, but how to know which way it is calling you? And there was each and every day to be got through. If Chanu came home this evening and found the place untidy and the spices not even ground, could she put her hands like so and say, "Don't ask me why nothing is prepared, it was not I who decided it, it was fate." A wife could reasonably be beaten for a lesser offense.

Chanu had not beaten her yet. He showed no signs of wanting to beat her. In fact, he was kind and gentle. Even so, it was foolish to assume he would never beat her. He thought she was a "good worker" (she had overheard him on the telephone). He would be shocked if she lapsed.

"She is an unspoilt girl. From the village."

She had got up one night to fetch a glass of water. It was one week since they married. She had gone to bed and he was still up, talking on the telephone as she stood outside the door.

"No," said Chanu. "I would not say so. Not beautiful, but not so ugly either. The face is broad, big forehead. Eyes are a bit too close together."

Nazneen put her hand up to her head. It was true. The forehead was large. But she had never thought of her eyes being too close.

"Not tall. Not short. Around five foot two. Hips are a bit narrow but wide enough, I think, to carry children. All things considered, I am satisfied. Perhaps when she gets older she'll grow a beard on her chin, but now she is only eighteen. And a blind uncle is better than no uncle. I waited too long to get a wife."

Narrow hips! You could wish for such a fault, Nazneen said to herself, thinking of the rolls of fat that hung low from Chanu's stomach. It would be possible to tuck all your hundred pens and pencils under those rolls and keep them safe and tight. You could stuff a book or two up there as well. If your spindle legs could take the weight.

"What's more, she is a good worker. Cleaning and cooking and all that. The only complaint I could make is she can't put my files in order, because she has no English. I don't complain, though. As I say, a girl from the village: totally unspoilt."

Chanu went on talking but Nazneen crept away, back to bed. A blind uncle is better than no uncle. Her husband had a proverb for everything. Any wife is better than no wife. Something is better than nothing. What had she imagined? That he was in love with her? That he was grateful because she, young and graceful, had accepted him? That in sacrificing herself to him, she was owed something? Yes. Yes. She realized in a stinging rush she had imagined all these things. Such a foolish girl. Such high notions. What self-regard.

The bleeding seemed to have stopped. Nazneen turned off the tap and wrapped a piece of kitchen roll around her finger. Who had Chanu been talking to that day? Perhaps it was a call from Bangladesh, a relative who did not come to the wedding. Perhaps it was Dr. Azad. Tonight he would see for himself the big forehead and too-close-together eyes. Blood spotted through from the cut. She discarded the kitchen roll and watched the red drops fall on the silver sink. The drops slid together like mercury and rolled down the drain. How long would it take to empty her finger of blood, drop by drop? How long for the arm? And for the body, an entire body? What she missed most was people. Not any people in particular (apart, of course, from Hasina) but just people. If she put her ear to the wall she could hear sounds. The television on. Coughing. Sometimes the lavatory flushing. Someone upstairs scraping a chair. A shouting match below. Everyone in their boxes, counting their possessions. In all her eighteen years, she could scarcely remember a moment that she had spent alone. Until she married. And came to London to sit day after day in this large box with the furniture to dust, and the muffled sounds of private lives sealed away above, below, and around her.

Nazneen examined her finger. The bleeding had stopped again. Random thoughts came now. She would speak to Chanu about another sari. Abba had not said goodbye. She thought he would come in the morning, before they went to Dhaka, to the airport. But when she rose, he had already gone to the fields. Was it because he cared too much or because he cared too little? She needed more furniture polish. And bleach for the lavatory. Would Chanu want his corns cut again tonight? What was Hasina doing?

She went to the bedroom and opened the wardrobe. The letter was in a shoebox at the bottom. She sat on the bed to read it with her feet almost touching the black lacquered doors. Sometimes she dreamed the wardrobe had fallen on her, crushing her on the mattress. Sometimes she dreamed she was locked inside it and hammered and hammered but nobody heard.

Our cousin Ahmed have given me your address praise God. I hear of marriage and pray many time on your wedding day I pray now also. I pray your husband is good man. You will write and telling all things to me.

I so happy now I almost scared. Hardly dare opening my eye. Why it is? What is bringing fear? God not putting me on earth only to suffer. I know this always even when days bringing no light. Maleks uncle have got for him First Class job in railway company. This uncle very High Up at railway. Malek go out early in morning and coming back late late. He not knowing much about trains and such like but he say too also that do not matter. What matter is being smart. Nobody smarter than my husband.

Can you believe? We live in block of flat is three story high. Our place have two room. No veranda but I go up on roof. There is brown stone floor it cool your feet. We have bed with metal spring a cabinet and two chairs in bedroom. I fold saris and put in box under bed. In living room we has three cane chair a rug one stool (Malek like to put feet on) a crate is only temporary before we getting table. Also kerosene stove I keep under shawl for making tidy. My pot and pans is keep inside the crate. Hardly any cockroach only one maybe two I see time to time.

Even we have nothing I happy. We have love. Love is happiness. Sometime I feel to run and jump like goat. This is how we do on way to school.

But not much room for running here and I sixteen year old and married woman.

Everything good between us now. I do not let my tongue make trouble for it as my husband say. Just because man is kind to wife it do not mean she can say what she like. If women understanding this no one will beat. Malek have First Class job. I pray for son. I pray Maleks mother forgive the "crime" of our marriage. It will come. Time comes she love me like daughter. If I wrong she is not true mother for mother love every part of son. Now I part of him. If Amma alive you think she forgive this thing Abba cannot? Sometime I think yes she do that. Many time I think no and then I angry and also too sad.

Sister I think of you every day and send love. I send respect to husband. Now you have address you will write and tell all thing about London. It make me tremble you so far away. You remember those story we hear as children begin like this. "Once there was prince who lived in far off land seven seas and thirteen rivers away." That is how I think of you. But as princess.

We see each other before long time pass and we as little girls again.

Someone was knocking on the front door of the flat. Nazneen opened it a crack, with the chain on, then closed it while she slid the chain off, and opened it wide.

"No one is saying it to his face," Mrs. Islam was telling Razia Iqbal, "but everyone is saying it behind his back. I don't like that kind of gossip."

Nazneen exchanged salaams with her visitors and went to make tea.

Mrs. Islam folded handkerchiefs, leaning over from the sofa to the low table and tucking them up the bobbled sleeves of her cardigan.

"Spreading rumors is our national pastime," said Razia. "That's not to say it is a good thing. Most of the time there's not a shred of truth in it." She gave a sideways look at Nazneen, who was setting down the tea things. "What is it they are saying this time? If I hear it from someone else I can set them straight about everything."

"Well," said Mrs. Islam slowly. She settled back against the brown upholstery. Her sleeves bulged and bagged. She had carpet slippers on over black socks. Nazneen looked through the glass at the center of the table and watched Mrs. Islam's feet twitch with an excitement that her face did not betray. "You have to bear in mind she had no children. This is after twelve years of marriage."

"Yes, that is so," said Razia. "It is the worst thing, for any woman."

"And at sixteen floors up, if you decide to jump, then there's the end to it." Mrs. Islam extracted a handkerchief and wiped away a little sweat from her hairline. Just looking at her made Nazneen feel unbearably hot.

"There's no chance of ending up a vegetable, if you jump from that high," agreed Razia. She accepted a cup from Nazneen and held it in her man-size hands. She wore black lace-up shoes, wide and thick-soled. It was the sari that looked strange on her. "But of course it was an accident. Why say otherwise?"

"A terrible accident," said Mrs. Islam. "But everyone is whispering behind the husband's back."

Nazneen sipped her tea. It was ten past five and all she had done was chop two onions. She had not heard about the accident. Chanu had mentioned nothing. She wanted to know who this woman was who had died so terribly. She formed some questions in her mind, phrased and rephrased them.

"It is a shame," said Razia. She smiled at Nazneen. Nazneen thought Razia did not look as though she really thought so. When she smiled she looked deeply amused, although her mouth turned up only slightly to indicate pity rather than laughter. She had a long nose and narrow eyes that always looked at you from an angle, never straight on, so that she seemed perpetually to be evaluating if not mocking you.

Mrs. Islam made a noise signaling that it was, indeed, a shame. She took a fresh handkerchief and blew her nose. After a decent interval she said, "Did you hear about Jorina?"

"I hear this and that," said Razia, as if no news about Jorina could possibly interest her.

"And what do you say to it?"

"That depends," said Razia, looking down her nose at her tea, "on what particular thing you mean."

"I don't tell anything that isn't known already. You can hardly keep it a secret when you begin going out to work."

Nazneen saw that Razia looked up sharply. Razia did not know the things that Mrs. Islam knew. Mrs. Islam knew everything about everybody. She had been in London for nearly thirty years, and if you were a Bangladeshi here, what could you keep secret from her? Mrs. Islam was the first person who called on Nazneen, in those first few days when her head was still spinning and the days were all dreams and real life came to her only at night, when she slept. Mrs. Islam was deemed by Chanu to be "respectable." Not many people were "respectable" enough to call or be called upon. "You see," said Chanu when he explained this for the first time, "most of our people here are Sylhetis. They all stick together because they come from the same district. They know each other from the villages, and they come to Tower Hamlets and they think they are back in the village. Most of them have jumped ship. That's how they come. They have menial jobs on the ship, doing donkey work, or they stow away like little rats in the hold." He cleared his throat and spoke to the back of the room so that Nazneen turned her head to see who it was he was addressing. "And when they jump ship and scuttle over here, then in a sense they are home again. And you see, to a white person, we are all the same: dirty little monkeys all in the same monkey clan. But these people are peasants. Uneducated. Illiterate. Close-minded. Without ambition." He sat back and stroked his belly. "I don't look down on them, but what can you do? If a man has only ever driven a rickshaw and never in his life held a book in his hand, then what can you expect from him?"

Nazneen wondered about Mrs. Islam. If she knew everybody's business then she must mix with everybody, peasant or not. And still she was respectable.

"Going out to work?" Razia said to Mrs. Islam. "What has happened to Jorina's husband?"

"Nothing has happened to Jorina's husband," said Mrs. Islam. Nazneen admired the way the words left her mouth, like bullets. It was too late now to ask about the woman who fell from the sixteenth floor.

"Her husband is still working," said Razia, as if she were the provider of the information.

"The husband is working, but still she cannot fill her stomach. In Bangladesh one salary can feed twelve, but Jorina cannot fill her stomach."

"Where is she going? To the garment factory?"

"Mixing with all sorts: Turkish, English, Jewish. All sorts. I am not old-fashioned," said Mrs. Islam. "I don't wear burkha. I keep purdah in my mind, which is the most important thing. Plus I have cardigans and anoraks and a scarf for my head. But if you mix with all these people, even if they are good people, you have to give up your culture to accept theirs. That's how it is."

"Poor Jorina," said Razia. "Can you imagine?" she said to Nazneen, who could not.

They talked on and Nazneen made more tea and answered some queries about herself and about her husband, and wondered all the while about supper and the impossibility of mentioning anything to her guests, who must be made welcome.

"Dr. Azad knows Mr. Dalloway," Chanu had explained to her. "He has influence. If he puts in a word for me, the promotion will be automatic. That's how it works. Make sure you fry the spices properly, and cut the meat into big pieces. I don't want small pieces of meat this evening."

Nazneen asked after Razia's children, a boy and a girl, five and three, who were playing at an auntie's house. She made inquiries about Mrs. Islam's arthritic hip, and Mrs. Islam made some noises to indicate that indeed the hip was troubling her a great deal but it was nothing she could mention, being in fact a stoic. And then, just when her anxiety about supper was beginning to make her chest hurt, her guests stood up to leave and Nazneen rushed to open the door, feeling rude as she stood by it, waiting for them to go.

Chapter Two

Dr. Azad was a small, precise man who, contrary to the Bengali custom, spoke at a level only one quarter of a decibel above a whisper. Anyone who wished to hear what he was saying was obliged to lean in towards him, so that all evening Chanu gave the appearance of hanging on his every word.

"Come," said Dr. Azad, when Nazneen was hovering behind the table, ready to serve. "Come and sit down with us."

"My wife is very shy." Chanu smiled and motioned with his head for her to be seated.

"This week I saw two of our young men in a very sorry state," said the doctor. "I told them straight, 'This is your choice: stop drinking alcohol now, or by Eid your liver will be finished.' Ten years ago this would be unthinkable. Two in one week! But now our children are copying what they see here, going to the pub, to nightclubs. Or drinking at home in their bedrooms, where their parents think they are perfectly safe. The problem is our community is not properly educated about these things." Dr. Azad drank a glass of water down in one long draft and poured himself another. "I always drink two glasses before starting the meal." He drank the second glass. "Good. Now I will not overeat."

"Eat! Eat!" said Chanu. "Water is good for cleansing the system, but food is also essential." He scooped up lamb and rice with his fingers and chewed. He put too much in his mouth at once, and he made sloppy noises as he ate. When he could speak again, he said, "I agree with you. Our community is not educated about this, and much else besides. But for my part, I don't plan to risk these things happening to my children. We will go back before they get spoiled."

"This is another disease that afflicts us," said the doctor. "I call it Going Home Syndrome. Do you know what that means?" He addressed himself to Nazneen.

She felt a heat on the back of her neck and formed words that did not leave her mouth.

"It is natural," said Chanu. "These people are basically peasants and they miss the land. The pull of the land is stronger even than the pull of blood."

"And when they have saved enough they will get on an aeroplane and go?"

"They don't ever really leave home. Their bodies are here but their hearts are back there. And anyway, look how they live: just re-creating the villages here."

"But they will never save enough to go back." Dr. Azad helped himself to vegetables. His shirt was spotless white, and his collar and tie so high under his chin that he seemed to be missing a neck.

Nazneen saw an oily yellow stain on her husband's shirt where he had dripped food.

Dr. Azad continued, "Every year they think, just one more year. But whatever they save, it's never enough."

"We would not need very much," said Nazneen. Both men looked at her. She spoke to her plate. "I mean, we could live very cheaply." The back of her neck burned.

Chanu filled the silence with his laugh. "My wife is just settling in here." He coughed and shuffled in his chair. "The thing is, with the promotion coming up, things are beginning to go well for me now. If I just get the promotion confirmed then many things are possible."

"I used to think all the time of going back," said Dr. Azad. He spoke so quietly that Nazneen was forced to look directly at him, because to catch all the words she had to follow his lips. "Every year I thought, 'Maybe this year.' And I'd go for a visit, buy some more land, see relatives and friends, and make up my mind to return for good. But something would always happen. A flood, a tornado that just missed the building, a power cut, some mind-numbing piece of petty bureaucracy, bribes to be paid out to get anything done. And I'd think, 'Well, maybe not this year.' And now, I don't know. I just don't know."

Chanu cleared his throat. "Of course, it's not been announced yet. Other people have applied. But after my years of service . . . Do you know, in six years I have not been late on one single day! And only three sick days, even with the ulcer. Some of my colleagues are very unhealthy, always going off sick with this or that. It's not something I could bring to Mr. Dalloway's attention. Even so, I feel he ought to be aware of it."

"I wish you luck," said Dr. Azad.

"Then there's the academic perspective. Within months I will be a fully fledged academic, with two degrees. One from a British university. Bachelor of Arts degree. With honors."

"I'm sure you have a good chance."

"Did Mr. Dalloway tell you that?"

"Who's that?"

"Mr. Dalloway."

The doctor shrugged his neat shoulders.

"My superior. Mr. Dalloway. He told you I have a good chance?"

"No."

"He said I didn't have a good chance?"

"He didn't say anything at all. I don't know the gentleman in question."

"He's one of your patients. His secretary made an appointment for him to see you about his shoulder sprain. He's a squash player. Very active man. Average build, I'd say. Red hair. Wears contact lenses—perhaps you test his eyes as well."

"It's possible he's a patient. There are several thousand on the list for my practice."

"What I should have told you straightaway—he has a harelip. Well, it's been put right, reconstructive surgery and all that, but you can always tell. That should put you on to him."

The guest remained quiet. Nazneen heard Chanu suppress a belch. She wanted to go to him and stroke his forehead. She wanted to get up from the table and walk out of the door and never see him again.

"He might be a patient. I do not know him." It was nearly a whisper.

"No," said Chanu. "I see."

"But I wish you luck."

"I am forty years old," said Chanu. He spoke quietly, like the doctor, but with none of his assurance. "I have been in this country for sixteen years. Nearly half my life." He gave a dry-throated gargle. "When I came I was a young man. I had ambitions. Big dreams. When I got off the aeroplane, I had my degree certificate in my suitcase and a few pounds in my pocket. I thought there would be a red carpet laid out for me. I was going to join the civil service and become Private Secretary to the Prime Minister." As he told his story, his voice grew. It filled the room. "That was my plan. And then I found things were a bit different. These people here didn't know the difference between me, who stepped off an aeroplane with a degree certificate, and the peasants who jumped off the boat possessing only the lice on their heads. What can you do?" He rolled a ball of rice and meat in his fingers and teased it around his plate.

"I did this and that. Whatever I could. So much hard work, so little reward. More or less it is true to say I have been chasing wild buffaloes and eating my own rice. You know that saying? All the begging letters from home I burned. And I made two promises to myself. I will be a success, come what may. That's promise number one. Number two, I will go back home. When I am a success. And I will honor these promises." Chanu, who had grown taller and taller in his chair, sank back down.

"Very good, very good," said Dr. Azad. He checked his watch.

"The begging letters still come," said Chanu. "From old servants, from the children of servants. Even from my own family, although they are not in need. All they can think of is money. They think there is gold lying about in the streets here and I am just hoarding it all in my palace. But I did not come here for money. Was I starving in Dhaka? I was not. Do they inquire about my diplomas?" He gestured to the wall, where various framed certificates were displayed. "They do not. What is more . . ." He cleared his throat, although it was already clear. Dr. Azad looked at Nazneen and, without meaning to, she returned his gaze so that she was caught in a complicity of looks, given and returned, which said something about her husband that she ought not to be saying.

Chanu talked on. Dr. Azad finished the food on his plate while Chanu's food grew cold. Nazneen picked at the cauliflower curry. The doctor declined with a waggle of the head either a further helping or any dessert. He sat with his hands folded on the table while Chanu, his oration at an end, ate noisily and quickly. Twice more he checked his watch.

At half past nine Dr. Azad said, "Well, Chanu. I thank you and your wife for a most pleasant evening and a delicious meal."

Chanu protested that it was still early. The doctor was adamant. "I always retire at ten-thirty and I always read for half an hour in bed before that."

"We intellectuals must stick together," said Chanu, and he walked with his guest to the door.

"If you take my advice, one intellectual to another, you will eat more slowly, chew more thoroughly, and take only a small portion of meat. Otherwise I'll see you back at the clinic again with another ulcer."

"Just think," said Chanu, "if I did not have the ulcer in the first place, then we would not have met and we would not have had this dinner together."

"Just think," said the doctor. He waved stiffly and disappeared behind the door.

* * *

The television was on. Chanu liked to keep it glowing in the evenings, like a fire in the corner of the room. Sometimes he went over and stirred it by pressing the buttons so that the light flared and changed colors. Mostly he ignored it. Nazneen held a pile of the last dirty dishes to take to the kitchen, but the screen held her. A man in a very tight suit (so tight that it made his private parts stand out on display) and a woman in a skirt that did not even cover her bottom gripped each other as an invisible force hurtled them across an oval arena. The people in the audience clapped their hands together and then stopped. By some magic they all stopped at exactly the same time. The couple broke apart. They fled from each other and no sooner had they fled than they sought each other out. Every move they made was urgent, intense, a declaration. The woman raised one leg and rested her boot (Nazneen saw the thin blade for the first time) on the other thigh, making a triangular flag of her legs, and spun around until she would surely fall but didn't. She did not slow down. She stopped dead and flung her arms above her head with a look so triumphant that you knew she had conquered everything: her body, the laws of nature, and the heart of the tight-suited man who slid over on his knees, vowing to lay down his life for her.

"What is this called?" said Nazneen.

Chanu glanced at the screen. "Ice skating," he said, in English.

"Ice e-skating," said Nazneen.

"Ice skating," said Chanu.

"Ice e-skating."

"No, no. No e. Ice skating. Try it again."

Nazneen hesitated.

"Go on!"

"Ice es-kating," she said, with deliberation.

Chanu smiled. "Don't worry about it. It's a common problem for Bengalis. Two consonants together causes a difficulty. I have conquered this issue after a long time. But you are unlikely to need these words in any case."

"I would like to learn some English," said Nazneen.

Chanu puffed his cheeks and spat the air out in a *fuff*. "It will come. Don't worry about it. Where's the need anyway?" He looked at his book and Nazneen watched the screen.

"He thinks he will get the promotion because he goes to the *pub* with the boss. He is so stupid he doesn't even realize there is any other way of getting promotion." Chanu was supposed to be studying. His books were open at the table. Every so often he looked in one, or turned a page. Mostly, he talked. *Pub, pub, pub.* Nazneen turned the word over in her mind. Another drop of English that she knew. There were other English words that Chanu sprinkled into his conversation, other things she could say to the tattoo lady. At this moment she could not think of any.

"This Wilkie—I told you about him—he has one or maybe two O levels. Every lunchtime he goes to the pub and he comes back half an hour late. Today I saw him sitting in Mr. Dalloway's office using the phone with his feet up on the desk. The jackfruit is still on the tree but already he is oiling his mustache. No way is he going to get promoted."

Nazneen stared at the television. There was a close-up of the woman. She had sparkly bits around her eyes, like tiny sequins glued to her face. Her hair was scraped back and tied on top of her head with plastic flowers. Her chest pumped up and down as if her heart would shoot out and she smiled pure, gold joy. She must be terrified, thought Nazneen, because such things cannot be held, and must be lost.

"No," said Chanu. "I don't have anything to fear from Wilkie. I have a degree from Dhaka University in English literature. Can Wilkie quote from Chaucer or Dickens or Hardy?"

Nazneen, who feared her husband would begin one of his long quotations, stacked a final plate and went to the kitchen. He liked to quote in English and then give her a translation, phrase by phrase. And when it was translated it usually meant no more to her than it did in English, so that she did not know what to reply or even if a reply was required.

She washed the dishes and rinsed them, and Chanu came and leaned against the ill-fitting cupboards and talked some more. "You see," he said, a frequent opener although often she did not see, "it is the white underclass, like Wilkie, who are most afraid of people like me. To him, and people like him, we are the only thing standing in the way of them sliding totally to the bottom of the pile. As long as we are below them, then they are above something. If they see us rise then they are resentful because we have left our proper place. That is why you get the phenomenon of the *National Front.* They can play on those fears to create racial tensions, and give these people a superiority complex. The middle classes are more secure, and therefore more relaxed." He drummed his fingers against the Formica.

Nazneen took a tea towel and dried the plates. She wondered if the ice e-skating woman went home and washed and wiped. It was difficult to imagine. But there were no servants here. She would have to manage by herself.

Chanu plowed on. "Wilkie is not exactly underclass. He has a job, so technically I would say no, he is not. But that is the mindset. This is what I am studying the subsection 'Race, Ethnicity, and Identity.' It is part of the sociology module. Of course, when I have my Open University degree then nobody can question my credentials. Although Dhaka University is one of the best in the world, these people here are by and large ignorant and know nothing of the Brontës or Thackeray."

Nazneen began to put things away. She needed to get to the cupboard that Chanu blocked with his body. He didn't move, although she waited in front of him. Eventually she left the pans on the stove, to be put away in the morning.

"Ish," said Chanu, breathing sharply. "Did you draw blood?" He looked closely at his little toe. He wore only his pajama bottoms and sat on the bed. Nazneen knelt to the side with a razor blade in her hand. It was time to cut her husband's corns again. She sliced through the semitranslucent skin, the buildup around the yellow core, and gathered the little dead bits in the palm of her hand.

"It's OK," he said, "but be careful, huh?"

Nazneen moved on to the other foot.

"I think it was a success this evening," said Chanu when Nazneen got into bed next to him.

"Yes, I think so," said Nazneen.

"He doesn't know Dalloway, but that's not important. He's a good man, very respectable."

"Respectable. Yes."

"I think I am certain of the promotion in any case."

"I am happy for you."

"Shall we turn out the light?"

"I'll do it."

After a minute or two in the dark, when her eyes had adjusted and the snoring began, Nazneen turned on her side and looked at her husband. She scrutinized his face, round as a ball, the blunt-cut thinning hair on top, and the dense eyebrows that crawled across his brow. His mouth was open and she began to regulate her breathing so that she inhaled as he did. When she got it wrong she could smell his breath. She looked at him for a long time. It was not a handsome face. In the month before her marriage, when she looked at his face in the photograph, she thought it ugly. Now she saw that it was not handsome, but it was kind. His mouth, always on duty, always moving, was full-lipped and generous, without a hint of cruelty. His eyes, small and beleaguered beneath those thick brows, were anxious or faraway, or both. Now that they were closed she could see the way the skin puckered up across the lids and drooped down to meet the creases at the corners. He shifted in his sleep and moved onto his stomach with his arms down by his side and his face squashed against the pillow.

Nazneen got out of bed and crossed the hall. She caught hold of the bead curtain that hung between the kitchen and the narrow hallway to stop it tinkling, and went to the fridge. She got out the Tupperware containers of rice and fish and chicken and took a spoon from the drawer. As she ate, standing beside the sink, she looked out at the moon, which hung above the dark flats checkered with lights. It was large and white and untroubled. She thought about Hasina and tried to imagine what it would be like to fall in love. Was she beginning to love Chanu, or just getting used to him? She looked down into the courtyard. Two boys exchanged mock punches, feinting left and right. Cigarettes burned in their mouths. She opened the window and leaned into the breeze.

The woman who fell, what terror came to her mind when she went down? What thoughts came? If she jumped, what thoughts came? Would they be the same ones? In the end, did it matter whether she jumped or fell? Suddenly Nazneen was sure that she had jumped. A big jump, feet first and arms wide, eyes wide, silent all the way down and her hair wild and loose, and a big smile on her face because with this single everlasting act she defied everything and everyone. Nazneen closed the window and rubbed her arms. Across the way the tattoo lady raised a can to her lips.

Life made its pattern around and beneath and through her. Nazneen cleaned and cooked and washed. She made breakfast for Chanu and looked on as he ate, collected his pens and put them in his briefcase, watched him from the window as he stepped like a bandleader across the courtyard to the bus stop on the far side of the estate. Then she ate standing up at the sink and washed the dishes. She made the bed and tidied the flat, washed socks and pants in the sink and larger items in the bath. In the afternoons she cooked and ate as she cooked, so that Chanu began to wonder why she hardly touched her dinner and shrugged in a way that suggested that food was of no concern to her. And the days were tolerable, and the evenings were nothing to complain about. Sometimes she switched on the television and flicked through the channels, looking for ice e-skating. For a whole week it was on every afternoon while Nazneen sat cross-legged on the floor. While she sat, she was no longer a collection of the hopes, random thoughts, petty anxieties, and selfish wants that made her, but was whole and pure. The old Nazneen was sublimated and the new Nazneen was filled with white light, glory.

But when it ended and she switched off the television, the old Nazneen returned. For a while it was a worse Nazneen than before, because she hated the socks as she rubbed them with soap, and dropped the pottery tiger and elephant as she dusted them and was disappointed when they did not break. She was glad when the ice e-skating came no more. She began to pray five times each day, rolling out her prayer mat in the sitting room to face east. She was pleased with the order it gave to her day, and Chanu said it was a good thing. "But remember," he said, and coughed away a little imaginary phlegm, "rubbing ashes on your face doesn't make you a saint. God sees what is in your heart." And Nazneen hoped it was true, because Chanu never to her knowledge prayed, and of all the books that he held in his hand she had never once seen him with the Holy Qur'an.

He took down his framed certificates and explained them to her. "This one is from the Centre for Meditation and Healing in Victoria Street. Basically it is a qualification in transcendental philosophy. Here's the one from Writers' Bureau, a correspondence course. I applied for some jobs as a journalist after that. And I wrote some short stories as well. I have a letter from the *Bexleyheath Advertiser* somewhere. I'll look it out for you. It says, 'We were most interested in your story, "A Prince Among Peasants," but unfortunately it is not suitable for our publication. Thank you for your interest in the *Bexleyheath Advertiser.*' It was a nice letter, I kept it somewhere.

"Now *this* is not actually a certificate as such. It's from Morley College evening classes on nineteenth-century economic thought, and it's just directions to the school, but that's all they gave out. No certificates. Here's my mathematics A level. That was a struggle. This is cycling proficiency, and this is my acceptance letter for the IT communications course—I only managed to get to a couple of classes."

He talked and she listened. Often she had the feeling that he was not talking to her; or rather that she was only part of a larger audience for whom the speech was meant. He smiled at her but his eyes were always searching, as if she were a face in the crowd singled out for only a moment. He was loud, he talked, he joked, and he sang or hummed. Sometimes he read a book and sang at the same time. Or he read, watched television, and talked. Only his eyes were unhappy. What are we doing here, they said, what are we doing on this round, jolly face?

It was when he talked about promotion that Chanu grew serious. "This Mrs. Thatcher is making more cuts. Spending cuts, spending cuts, that's all we hear. The council is being squeezed dry. Now we have to pay if we want biscuits with our tea. It's ridiculous. And it could affect my promotion." And then he was silent for a while, and Nazneen began to include the promotion in her prayers, although it came below her prayer for another letter from Hasina.

Once or twice she went out. She asked Chanu for a new sari. They looked in the shop windows on Bethnal Green Road. "The pink with yellow is very nice," she said. "Do you think so?"

"Let me think," said Chanu. He closed his eyes. Nazneen looked up at the gray towers, the blown-by, forgotten strands of sky between them. She watched the traffic. There were more cars than people out here, a roaring metal army tearing up the town. A huge truck blocked her line of vision, petrol on her tongue, engines in her ears. The people who passed walked quickly, looking ahead at nothing or looking down at the pavement to negotiate puddles, litter, and excrement. The white women wore clinging trousers, like tights with the feet cut out. They pushed prams and their mouths worked furiously. Their children screeched at them and they screeched back. A pair went by who were differently dressed, in short dark skirts with matching jackets. Their shoulders were padded up and out. They could have balanced a bucket on each side and not spilled a drop of water. They saw her looking and whispered together. They walked and laughed, and looked at her over their puffy shoulders.

"According to Hume," said Chanu, "aaah, ahem." He prepared himself. He spoke in English at some length, then screwed up his face. "It's not easy to translate. Let me try. 'All the objects of human reason or inquiry may naturally be divided into two kinds, that is, Relations of Ideas, and Matters of Fact.' Yes, I think that is a reasonable translation. He gives some examples from geometry and arithmetic of the first kind, meaning Relations of Ideas. 'That three times five is equal to the half of thirty.' Do you follow? 'Though there never was a circle or triangle in nature the truths demonstrated by Euclid would forever retain their certainty and evidence.' Are you with me? Don't worry about the circle and triangle. They are from his other examples.

"Don't be anxious, I am getting to the point shortly. 'Matters of Fact, which are the second objects of human reason, are not ascertained in the same manner; nor is our evidence of their truth, however great, of a like nature.' This he illustrates, to my mind, brilliantly. '*That the sun will not rise tomorrow* is no less intelligible a proposition and implies no more contradiction than the affirmation *that it will rise*.'

"Do you see? Two proper objects of human inquiry, and you ask me if the pink and yellow is nice? What shall I say? I can say that it is nice or not nice, and how could I be wrong?" He stopped and smiled at Nazneen. She saw that he was waiting for a reply.

"I think it is nice, but I don't mind."

He laughed and went inside the shop. He returned with the length of fabric. "Foundations of Modern Philosophy. It's a very interesting module. Here is your sari."

That night, as she lay awake next to her snoring husband, Nazneen wondered what kind of job it was that he had where the rising of the sun or the failure of the sun to rise could be a topic for serious discussion. If these were the things he had to learn to advance himself, what could he be doing? He worked for the local council. This much she understood. But whenever she asked what he did he gave such a long reply that she got lost in it and although she understood the words, they got together in such a way that their meaning became unclear, or she became confused by them. She remembered Chanu's words about the sun and wondered what he meant. If the sun did not rise tomorrow, that would be beyond everyone's understanding but God's. And to say that it will *not* rise and then that it *will* is definitely a contradiction. *As sure as when I say the bed is too soft and toss and turn all night because of it, and Chanu says it is not too soft and falls asleep immediately. But then both of us can be right in our own way about the bed, but not about the sun. Either way, what is the point in lying awake and thinking about it? Let me sleep, let me sleep, let me sleep.* And she drifted off to where she wanted to be, in Gouripur, tracing letters in the dirt with a stick while Hasina danced around her on six-year-old feet. In Gouripur, in her dreams, she was always a girl and Hasina was always six. Amma scolded and cuddled, and smelled as sweet as the skin on the milk when it had been boiled all day with sugar. Abba sat on the choki, sang and clapped. He called out to them and took them on his lap, and sent them away with a rough kiss on the cheek. Then they walked around the lake to watch the fishermen pulling in great nets of silver fish, and saw the muscles knot on their arms and legs and chests. When she woke she thought, *I know what I would wish,* but by now she knew that where she wanted to go was not a different place but a different time. She was free to wish it but it would never be.

She did not often go out. "Why should you go out?" said Chanu. "If you go out, ten people will say, 'I saw her walking on the street.' And I will look like a fool. Personally, I don't mind if you go out, but these people are so ignorant. What can you do?"

She never said anything to this.

"Besides, I get everything for you that you need from the shops. Anything you want, you only have to ask."

She never said anything to this.

"I don't stop you from doing anything. I am westernized now. It is lucky for you that you married an educated man. That was a stroke of luck."

She carried on with her chores.

"And anyway, if you were in Bangladesh you would not go out. Coming here you are not missing anything, only broadening your horizons."

She razored away the dead flesh around his corns. She did not let the razor slip.

The days passed more easily now than at first. It was just a matter of waiting, as Amma always said. She had waited and now they passed more easily. If it wasn't for worrying about Hasina, she could call herself calm. *Just wait and see, that's all we can do.* How often she had heard those words. Amma always wiped away her tears with those words. When the harvest was poor, when her own mother was taken ill, when floods threatened, when Abba disappeared and stayed away for days at a time. She cried because crying was called for, but she accepted it, whatever it was. "Such a saint," Abba said. And then she died, and in dying proved life unpredictable and beyond control.

Mumtaz found her leaning low over the sacks of rice in the store hut, staked through the heart by a spear. "She had fallen," said Mumtaz, "and the spear was the only thing holding her up. It looked . . . It looked as if she was still falling."

At the funeral, Mumtaz said, "Your mother was wearing her best sari. I think that's nice, don't you?" After a mourning period, Abba took another wife. She appeared suddenly out of nowhere and Abba said,

"This is your new mother." Four weeks later, just as suddenly, she went. She was never mentioned again.

"Your mother was wearing her best sari," said Mumtaz. "It's strange. It wasn't a special day after all."

She never spoke to Abba after that, not that Nazneen saw. She always kept back the choicest bits of meat for Nazneen and Hasina. She kissed them all the time, even though they were fourteen and twelve. And she talked about Amma, over and over, as if you could change something by talking about it. "I don't know why those spears were in the store, and wedged like that. So dangerous." Hasina always ran off when she started, but Nazneen just stayed and listened.

Razia moved to Rosemead block, two floors beneath the tattoo lady. Staying on the estate did not count as going out. Nazneen, on the short journey over from Seasalter House, began to strike up acquaintances. She nodded to the apoplectic man in undershirt and shorts who flung open his door every time she passed it in the harshly lit corridor. She smiled at the Bengali girls who chattered about boys at top volume on the stairs but fell silent as she passed. Razia introduced her to other Bengali wives on the estate. Sometimes they would call and drink tea with her. She enjoyed the company, although most times she did not mention it to Chanu. She did not look at the group of young Bengali men who stood in the bottom of the stairwell, combing their hair and smoking or making loud, sudden hoots so that their voices bounded around the concrete shell of the building and rained down on her like firecrackers. In the summer evenings they stood outside next to the big metal bins and played with the iron shutters that should have kept the bins out of sight. They rattled them up and down or kicked against them, and appeared to find pleasure in these simple activities. Nazneen did not look directly at them, but they were respectful as she passed, standing aside and extending salaam.

She enjoyed seeing Razia the most. Razia always had stories to tell. She was a mimic, a big bony clown. And there was no harm in her. She looked funny and she looked at you funny too, but really she was kind-hearted. It took Nazneen's mind off Hasina when she went to visit Razia. The last letter she got from Hasina had been nearly six months ago. It was short and it was written in a scrawl, not her usual neat hand.

My sister I have your letter. It mean so much to me know you are well and husband also. Love is grow between you I feel it. And you are good wife. I maybe not good wife but is how I try for always. Only it very hard sometime. Husband is do very well at his work. He have already promotion. He is good man and very patient. Sometime I make him lose patience without I mean to. He comes soon to home and I getting ready for him now. God bless you. Hasina

Nazneen had written three more times, but nothing came back. "It's the postal system," Chanu told her. "Maybe she doesn't get your letters either." It was beginning to eat her. Razia was a good distraction.

"You know the one—with the big puffed-up fringe that goes over to the side like this." Razia made a dramatic sweeping gesture across her forehead with her big-knuckled hand. "He hangs around the staircase on your block, even though he's supposed to be at college." She broke off to cuff Tariq around the back of the head for pulling his sister's hair, then cuffed at Shefali for trying to grab her teacup. The children ran off to console each other.

"His father saw him in a pub with a white girl. He was just walking down the street and there they were in the window, drinking and everything in full view. You'll recognize the boy next time you see him. He has two black eyes."

"These kids!" said Nazneen.

Razia smiled and looked sideways at her through narrowed eyes. Nazneen felt her neck get warm. The boys were probably her age, maybe a year or two younger.

"Well, Jorina's boy is in trouble. I heard that he drinks alcohol every day, even for breakfast. He can't get out of bed unless he has a drink first, and then he's good for nothing." Razia shivered her large bony shoulders. "It makes me fear for my own children."

"But Jorina goes out to work, and you are at home. Anyway, Tariq and Shefali are so well behaved. And only very small."

"Yes, but growing so fast. Did you see Tariq's trousers, up around his ankles?"

"Jorina has a daughter as well, I think."

"Aaah," said Razia. Her eyes lit up. She crossed one ankle over the other, both legs sticking straight out in front of her on the floor. She adjusted the folds of her sari. The folds were never right: too bunched, too loose, too far to the side, too low or too high. Razia would look better in overalls. Overalls would match her big shoes. "She does have a daughter. You met her. She was here one day when you came. She had her school uniform on—maroon sweater and gray skirt. You remember? But she won't be coming anymore. They have sent her back."

"To be married?"

"Of course, to be married and to live in the village."

"They took her out of school?"

"She is sixteen. She begged them to let her stay and take her exams. . . ." Razia went quiet and knocked her shoes together. "Anyway," she said briskly, "the son has gone bad, and they wanted to save the daughter. So there it is. Now she can't run off for a love marriage."

Nazneen put her hand on the radiator. It was off although there were icy patterns on the window. The room was almost square, like her own sitting room, with a door to the hallway and another to the bathroom. Half the space was filled with children's paraphernalia: plastic toys, colonies of dismembered dolls, a small and rusting bike, a high chair folded against the wall, two neat piles of children's clothes, an array of footballs in various states of deflation, a child-size wooden table covered in crayon scribbles. A twin-size bed stood against one wall, and the other furniture crowded together beneath the window, so that the arms of the chairs and sofa touched one another. Tariq slept in the twin bed, and Shefali still slept with her parents. There was space to grow. *Three point five people to one room. That's a council statistic,* Chanu had told Nazneen. *All crammed together. They can't stop having children, or they bring over all their relatives and pack them in like little fish in a tin. It's a Tower Hamlets official statistic: three point five Bangladeshis to one room.*

"The heating's broken. My husband called the council but no one has come." Razia shrugged and pointed to a two-bar electric heater in the corner. "That's it, for now."

"My sister made a love marriage." Nazneen looked at the lacy frost on the glass.

"Wait," said Razia. She got to her feet. "Let me check on the children. I want to hear everything. So when I come back, you can start at the beginning."

Nazneen told her everything. About Hasina and her heart-shaped face, her pomegranate-pink lips and liquid eyes. How everyone stared at her, women and men and children, even when Hasina was only six years old. And how the older women began to say, even before she turned eleven, that such beauty could have no earthly purpose but trouble. Amma would cry, and say it was no fault of hers. Abba looked grim, and said that was certainly true, which made her cry harder. And, all in all, it was a fact that being beautiful brought hardship, though nobody would think it, and it was sheer good luck that the marriage turned out all right. "Her husband has a first-class job with the railway company."

"Any children?"

Nazneen hesitated. Perhaps there was a baby. That was why Hasina was too busy to write. She might have sent another letter saying she was expecting, and the letter got lost and then she didn't have time to write again. "Perhaps. Yes, that's possible," she said, and wanted to add something more but did not.

Razia was not really listening. She sighed. "It's so romantic." She stiffened her back, then pretended to rummage in the sleeve of her cardigan and blow her nose. "But when I was a young girl," she said, making her voice hard and pumping out the words like darts from a blowpipe, "we didn't have any of this nonsense. I only left our family compound with my mother and we rode in a palanquin. Four bearers carried us to the house of my mother's father. And it was a journey of six hours. If one of them had dared lift the curtain and catch a glimpse, that man . . ." Razia made a strangled screech and slashed a finger across her throat.

Nazneen laughed. "But poor Mrs. Islam. We shouldn't make fun."

"Poor Mrs. Islam, nothing," said Razia, dabbing her eyes. "So romantic." She got up because her daughter was calling from the bedroom. "But Shefali will make a love marriage over my dead body."

Regular prayer, regular housework, regular visits with Razia. She told her mind to be still. She told her heart, *Do not beat with fear, do not beat with desire.* Sometimes she managed it, when she stopped thinking of her sister. If she wanted something, she asked her husband. But she deferred to him. Like this:

"The bed is so soft. Does it make your back ache?"

"No."

"It is not too soft for you?"

"No."

"Good."

"I am making a sketch."

"Let me see. What is it?"

"A plan for the house I will build in Dhaka. What do you think of it?"

"What shall I say? I am only a girl from the village and I know nothing of big houses."

"Do you think it is too grand?"

"I don't know anything about houses, or beds."

"What about the bed? Is it too soft for you?"

"It does not matter."

"Tell me if it makes your back hurt."

"It does not matter."

"Can't you tell me anything?"

"I don't mind. I can sleep on the floor."

"Now you are being ridiculous."

"I'll get a bedroll. That is what we village girls are used to. Of course, when our child is born, he will sleep on the floor with his mother."

"What? Are you . . . ?"

"———"

"You are?"

"Yes."

"Why didn't you say?"

"I am saying."

"It's definite?"

"I went to see Dr. Azad. Mrs. Islam took me."

"Hah. Hah. Good. Hah."

"I will put the bedroll in the sitting room. There isn't space for it in the bedroom."

"Nonsense. What are you talking about, bedroll? I'll get a new mattress. I'll fill it with bricks if you like."

"Well. I don't need anything. If you want to get it, I don't mind."

"It's settled then. What about a pond here—I'll just draw it in. And a guest bungalow in the grounds." He licked the end of his pencil and drew. "Now I have to get the promotion; they can't keep delaying. I will tell them, I will tell Mr. Dalloway, 'Look here, I am about to have a son. I am going to be a father. Give me a proper job, fit for a real man, a father.' And if he does not do it, I will tell him to go to hell."

One week later the letter arrived. It lifted up her heart and then pounded it on a rock. She did not try to calm herself.

Chapter Three

She handed him his lunch, leftover curry between two slices of white bread, and he put it in his briefcase. He zipped his anorak and pulled up the hood, which was deep with a white furry trim. From the side his face was invisible. Front-on he looked like a kachuga turtle. She watched him from the window, green shell, black legs, scuttling across the estate. The tattoo lady was still in her nightdress. From the stump of her cigarette she lit a fresh one, keeping the sacred flame alight. She was fat like a baby. Her arms were ringed with flesh and her hands seemed tiny. This woman was poor and fat. To Nazneen it was unfathomable. In Bangladesh it was no more possible to be both poor and fat than to be rich and starving. Nazneen waved. Then she put on her cardigan, took her keys, and left the flat.

She walked slowly along the corridor, looking at the front doors. They were all the same. Peeling red paint showing splinters of pale wood, a rectangular panel of glass with wire mesh suspended inside, gold-rimmed keyholes, stern black knockers. She walked faster. A door flew open and a head bobbed out in front of her. It was bald and red with unknown rage. She nodded but today the man did not acknowledge her. Nazneen passed with her eyes averted to the wall. Someone had drawn a pair of buttocks in thick black pen, and next to them a pair of breasts with elongated nipples. Behind her a door slammed. She reached the stairwell and cantered down. The overhead light was fierce; she could feel its faint heat even as the concrete cold crept into her toes. The stairs gave off a tang of urine. She bunched the skirts of her sari with one hand and took the steps two at a time until she missed a ledge and came down on her ankle against an unforgiving ridge. She caught the stair rail and did not fall but clung to the side for a moment, then continued down, stamping as if the pain was just a cramp to be marched out.

Outside, small patches of mist bearded the lampposts and a gang of pigeons turned weary circles on the grass like prisoners in an exercise yard. A woman hurried past with a small child in her arms. The child screamed and kicked its legs against the kidnapper. The woman produced a plastic rattle with which to gag her victim. Nazneen pulled the end of her sari over her hair. At the main road she looked both ways, and then went left. Two men were dragging furniture out of a junk shop to display on the pavement. One of them went inside and came out again with a wheelchair. He tied a chain around it and padlocked it to an armchair as if arranging a three-legged furniture race. Nazneen changed her mind and turned around. She walked until she reached the big crossroads and waited at the curb while the traffic roared from one direction and then the next. Twice she stepped into the road and drew back again. To get to the other side of the street without being hit by a car was like walking out in the monsoon and hoping to dodge the raindrops. A space opened up before her. God is great, said Nazneen under her breath. She ran.

A horn blared like an ancient muezzin ululating painfully, stretching his vocal cords to the limit. She stopped and the car swerved. Another car skidded to a halt in front of her and the driver got out and began to shout. She ran again and turned into a side street, then off again to the right onto Brick Lane. She had been here a few times with Chanu, later in the day when the restaurants smelled of fresh boiled rice and old fried fat and the waiters with their tight black pants stood in doorways holding out menus and smiles. But now the waiters were at home asleep, or awake being waited on themselves by wives who only served and were not served in return except with board and lodging and the provision of children whom they also, naturally, waited upon. And the streets were stacked with rubbish, entire kingdoms of rubbish piled high as fortresses with only the border skirmishes of plastic bottles and grease-stained cardboard to separate them. A man looked up at some scaffolding with an intent, almost ardent, expression as if his love might be at the top, cowering on the high planks or the dark slate roof. A pair of schoolchildren, pale as rice and loud as peacocks, cut over the road and hurtled down a side street, galloping with joy or else with terror. Otherwise, Brick Lane was deserted. Nazneen stopped by some film posters pasted in waves over a metal siding. The hero and heroine peered at each other with epic hunger. The scarlet of her lips matched the bandanna tied around his forehead. A sprinkling of sweat highlighted the contour of his biceps. The kohl around her eyes made them smoke with passion. Some invisible force was keeping them (only inches) apart. The type at the foot of the poster said: *The world could not stop their love.*

Nazneen walked. She walked to the end of Brick Lane and turned right. Four blocks down she crossed the road (she waited next to a woman and stepped out with her, like a calf with its mother) and took a side street. She turned down the first right, and then went left. From there she took every second right and every second left until she realized she was leaving herself a trail. Then she turned off at random, began to run, limped for a while to save her ankle, and thought she had come in a circle. The buildings seemed familiar. She sensed rather than saw, because she had taken care not to notice. But now she slowed down and looked around her. She looked up at a building as she passed. It was constructed almost entirely of glass, with a few thin rivets of steel holding it together. The entrance was like a glass fan, rotating slowly, sucking people in, wafting others out. Inside, on a raised dais, a woman behind a glass desk crossed and uncrossed her thin legs. She wedged a telephone receiver between her ear and shoulder and chewed on a fingernail. Nazneen craned her head back and saw that the glass above became dark as a night pond. The building was without end. Above, somewhere, it crushed the clouds. The next building and the one opposite were white stone palaces. There were steps up to the entrances and colonnades across the front. Men in dark suits trotted briskly up and down the steps, in pairs or in threes. They barked to each other and nodded somberly. Sometimes one clapped a hand on his companion's shoulder and Nazneen saw that this was not for reassurance, but for emphasis. Every person who brushed past her on the pavement, every back she saw, was on a private, urgent mission to execute a precise and demanding plan: to get a promotion today, to be exactly on time for an appointment, to buy a newspaper with the right coins so that the exchange was swift and seamless, to walk without wasting a second and to reach the roadside just as the lights turned red. Nazneen, hobbling and halting, began to be aware of herself. Without a coat, without a suit, without a white face, without a destination. A leafshake of fear—or was it excitement?—passed through her legs.

But they were not aware of her. In the next instant she knew it. They could not see her any more than she could see God. They knew that she existed (just as she knew that He existed) but unless she did something, waved a gun, halted the traffic, they would not see her. She enjoyed this thought. She began to scrutinize. She stared at the long, thin faces, the pointy chins. The women had strange hair. It puffed up around their heads, pumped up like a snake's hood. They pressed their lips together and narrowed their eyes as though they were angry at something they had heard, or at the wind for messing their hair. A woman in a long red coat stopped and took a notebook from her bag. She consulted the pages.

The coat was the color of a bride's sari. It was long and heavy, with gold buttons that matched the chain on her bag. Her shiny black shoes had big gold buckles. Her clothes were rich. Solid. They were armor, and her ringed fingers weapons. Nazneen pulled at her cardigan. She was cold. Her fingertips burned with cold. The woman looked up and saw Nazneen staring. She smiled, like she was smiling at someone who had tried and totally failed to grasp the situation.

No longer invisible, Nazneen walked faster and looked only at what she had to see to walk without falling or colliding. It occurred to her that she had, without meaning to, compared herself to God. This thought distressed her so much that tears came into her eyes and she banged into a man whose briefcase swung against her knee like a mallet. She recited in her head her favorite sura:

> By the light of day, and by the dark of night, your Lord has
> not forsaken you, nor does He abhor you.
> The life to come holds a richer prize for you than this present
> life. You shall be gratified with what your Lord will give you.
> Did He not find you an orphan and give you shelter?
> Did He not find you in error and guide you?
> Did He not find you poor and enrich you?

But the pain in her knee and her hands and her ankle destroyed the verses. *Proclaim the goodness of your Lord. Proclaim the goodness of your Lord.*

There was a patch of green surrounded by black railings, and in the middle two wooden benches. In this city, a bit of grass was something to be guarded, fenced about, as if there were a sprinkling of emeralds sown in among the blades. Nazneen found the gate and sat alone on the bench. A maharani in her enclosure. The sun came out from behind a black cloud and shone briefly in her eyes before plunging back under cover, disappointed with what it had seen. She was cold, she was tired, she was in pain, she was hungry, and she was lost.

She had gotten herself lost because Hasina was lost. And only now did she realize how stupid she was. Hasina was in Dhaka. A woman on her own in the city, without a husband, without family, without friends, without protection. Hasina had written the letter before she left.

Sister I have not know what to tell and this is how no letter is coming before. Now I have news. In morning soon as husband go out for work I go away to Dhaka. Our landlady Mrs. Kashem is only person who know about it. She say it is not good decision but she help anyway. She say it is better get beaten by own husband than beating by stranger. But those stranger not saying at same time they love me. If they beat they do in all honesty.

Mrs. Kashem have uncle in Dhaka and this uncles brother-in-law rent out property. I have saving from housekeeping. You remember Amma always tell "A handful of rice a day." I have manage it and more. Do you think Amma save? Why she did not save?

Every evening I go up on roof. There is beggar woman lie on street corner. Body is snap shut. If she sit on behind she can look only at ground. It like big big foot press on the back. Any time she wanting to look higher she roll on side. She move along with shuffling and use hands as paddle. After it get dark man come and put on handcart and take somewhere. One time he come and she do not want to go. She start shuffling back away and shout. She get so far as coconut vendor at other corner.

I like to watch this woman. She have courage.

When I get address I write again to you.

Hasina

A young man, tall as a stilt walker and with the same stiff-legged gait, came and sat on the opposite bench. He put his motorcycle helmet on the ground. He ate a sandwich in four large bites. Something in his jacket crackled like a radio. He spoke to it and it appeared to speak back. He put on his helmet and left. Nazneen needed a toilet. The baby made her want to urinate about eight or nine times in the day, two or three times at night. It was past noon, and all morning she had not thought of the toilet once.

She would have to urinate on the grass like a dog, or else wet herself and walk home in soaked clothes. But how would she go home? That was the point of being lost. She, like Hasina, could not simply go home. They were both lost in cities that would not pause even to shrug. Poor Hasina. Nazneen wept, but as the tears started to come she knew that she was weeping more for her own stupidity than for her sister. What propelled her down all those streets? What hand was at her back? It could not help Hasina for Nazneen to be lost. And it could not give Nazneen any idea what Hasina was suffering. She watched heads above the railings. The people who looked in looked away again, neither slowly nor quickly, without interest or design. Razia always said, if you go out to shop, go to Sainsbury's. English people don't look at you twice. But if you go to our shops, the Bengali men will make things up about you.You know how they talk. Once you get talked about, then that's it. Nothing you can do.

Hasina would be talked about.

The baby had taken over her bladder. The baby was not much bigger than a litchi but it was in charge of all her internal organs, particularly her bladder. Nazneen got up and began walking again. The sun had gone somewhere. It no longer peeped out from time to time from behind the clouds, which rushed at the tops of buildings as if they would smother them in a murderous rage. The buildings stood their ground, impassive as cows. And at the very last second the clouds went to pieces.

Nazneen wondered if Chanu worked in a building like these. She imagined him in a glass office, surrounded by piles of paper and talking in a big voice to his colleagues, who hurried back and forth, getting on with their jobs while he talked and talked. It was lunchtime now and the streets were busier. People carried white paper bags with sandwiches poking out. Some ate and walked to save time. She might see Chanu; he might work just here, in this building, or this. These were important buildings. They were proud of what they were. They could be government buildings. Chanu might be walking towards her now. He could be behind her. She turned around and bumped into a man carrying a plastic cup of hot tea that spilled on her arm. She turned back again and walked quickly, stepping hard on her twisted left ankle, to distract from the pain in her arm, to punish herself for being so stupid. Someone tapped her on the shoulder and she leaped like a dog away from a whip snake. He came around to the front. A brown-faced man in a dark coat and tie. He had a handkerchief arranged like an exotic flower in his breast pocket and his glasses had lenses as thick as pebbles. He said something. Nazneen recognized Hindi when she heard it, but she did not understand it. He tried again, in Urdu. Nazneen could speak some Urdu, but the man's accent was so strong that she could not understand this either. She shook her head. He spoke in English this time. His eyes looked huge behind their lenses, like they had been plucked from another, much bigger creature. She shook her head again and said, "Sorry." He nodded solemnly and took his leave.

It rained then. And in spite of the rain, and the wind which whipped it into her face, and in spite of the pain in her ankle and arm, and her bladder, and in spite of the fact that she was lost and cold and stupid, she began to feel a little pleased. She had spoken, in English, to a stranger, and she had been understood and acknowledged. It was very little. But it was something.

She got home twenty minutes before her husband, washed the rice and set it to boil, searched through a cupful of lentils for tiny stones that could crack your teeth, put the lentils in a pan with water but no salt, and put the pan on the stove. She removed her shoes and examined her blisters. She put on fresh underclothes and sari and soaped the rain-sodden one. When she had twisted the water out of it, she left it in the bath like a sleeping pink python.

She was skimming brown froth from the lentils when he came in.

"You see," he said, as though the conversation had not been interrupted by a whole day, "there's very little that I could do anyway. What your sister has done cannot be undone by me, or by anybody else. If she decides to go back to him, then that is what she will do. If she decides to stay in Dhaka, so be it. What will happen will happen."

He leaned against the cupboards. His hood was still up and he had gloves on. He folded his arms so they rested on the shelf of his belly. She could hear him breathe, and then he began to hum. It was the tune of a nursery rhyme, a silly song about going to Uncle's house for rice and milk but being disappointed. Every particle of skin on her body prickled with something more physical than loathing. It was the same feeling she had when she used to swim in the pond and came up with a leech stuck to her leg or her stomach.

"Shall I take your coat?" she said. "Would you like to go and sit down?"

"Oh, coat," he said, and carried on humming. "When my boy is born I will teach him some songs. Do you know that the child can hear even in the womb? If I sing to him now, when he is born he will recognize the tunes."

He dropped to his knees, put his arms around Nazneen's middle, and began to sing to her stomach. She held a ladle full of boiling scummy water above his head. She poured it with great care into a bowl.

"You could go there." The words burst as hot and fast as boils.

"Where?" He pulled down his hood and blinked at her.

"Where? To Dhaka. You could find her."

He got to his feet and cleared his throat. He stirred the lentils absently and lifted the lid from the rice so that the steam escaped, meaning it would not be properly cooked. "Well," he said, "yes, I could go. I could go and walk around the streets and ask for her. 'Have you seen my wife's sister? She just ran away from her husband, and she sent us this address: Dhaka.' I'm sure it would not take long to find her. Perhaps one or two lifetimes. And after all, there is very little for me to do here. I only have a degree to finish, and a promotion to get, and a son on the way.

"Shall I pack a suitcase? Perhaps you have prepared one. I shall go to Dhaka and pluck her instantly from the streets and bring her back to live with us. On the way I could pick up the rest of your family and we could make a little Gouripur right here. Is that what you have in mind?"

Anything is possible. She wanted to shout it. *Do you know what I did today? I went inside a pub. To use the toilet. Did you think I could do that? I walked mile upon mile, probably around the whole of London, although I did not see the edge of it. And to get home again I went to a restaurant. I found a Bangladeshi restaurant and asked directions. See what I can do!*

She said, "It is up to you. I was only suggesting."

Chanu took his coat off. He began to rub his hand over his face, looked at his gloves and took those off too. "You are worried. Let me tell you something. Sometimes we just have to wait and see. Sometimes that's all we can do."

"I have heard it. I know it." She put three pinches of salt in with the lentils, now that they were soft enough to break down. She stirred in chili powder, cumin, turmeric, and chopped ginger. The golden mixture blew fat, contented bubbles. Nazneen tasted some from a spoon and burned her tongue. But it was her heart that was ablaze, with mutiny.

Nazneen dropped the promotion from her prayers. The next day she chopped two fiery red chilies and placed them, like hand grenades, in Chanu's sandwich. Unwashed socks were paired and put back in his drawer. The razor slipped when she cut his corns. His files got mixed up when she tidied. All her chores, peasants in his princely kingdom, rebelled in turn. Small insurrections, designed to destroy the state from within.

Mrs. Islam took her to see Dr. Azad. The waiting room was fetid, as if to sweat the illness out of the patients. An old man with a knobbly nose sat in the corner sipping mournfully from a can of something. A large family of Africans, the color of wet river stones, with long, beautiful necks and small sloping eyes, fanned out on the front seats. The children sat on their hands and whispered to each other. The grown-ups were silent. Their faces expressed nothing other than the ability to wait. Waiting was their profession.

Mrs. Islam sucked her teeth. She shuffled her feet beneath her chair and rubbed her right heel with the toe of her left slipper. From her large black bag (it looked like a doctor's bag, but it smelled of mints and the clasp was jeweled with bright glass) she took out a polyethylene envelope of handkerchiefs. "Here, child," she said. "Take them. They're for you."

"Very pretty, very nice," said Nazneen.

Mrs. Islam snorted. "Someone gave them to me. *My* handkerchiefs are high quality. If you like *these*, I'll get more."

"No. Don't get more," Nazneen protested.

"You don't like them either." She raised a hand to ward off denials. "Give them to your husband." She leaned in towards Nazneen. The wart on the side of her nose was encircled by three stubby hairs, toughened and thickened by tweezing. "How are things now, with your husband?"

Nazneen looked away. "He is well. Not counting the corns, and a little stomach problem sometimes." From the corner of her eye she saw her companion waggle her head and purse her lips. There was a pause.

Eventually, Mrs. Islam spoke. "There is no need to tell me. I know how it is. I get to know these things."

Nazneen stared at a notice on the wall, printed in five languages.

"All the young people, they come to me. Everyone knows that what they say to me stays in confidence. But if you do not wish to speak, I do not wish to hear."

The notice said: No Smoking, No Eating, No Drinking. All the signs, thought Nazneen, only tell you what *not* to do.

"I'll tell you something instead." Mrs. Islam took Nazneen's wrist. Her hand was hot and dry. The skin was powdery, as if it would dissolve in water. "When I was a girl, the nearest well was a two-mile walk. There was a well in the village but the water had turned bad because of a curse, and the pond water was also poisoned. Two hard miles to the water, and two harder miles back. And the women got fed up. They did the fetching and the carrying, and when they complained to their husbands, what was the result?

"There was no result. Because for the men, there was no incentive. They were not suffering. Why should they act? So then the women of the village came together to discuss. First they shared their complaints. Then they sympathized, one with another. After that they berated their menfolk. Once these important things were done, they moved on to decide what to do.

"One woman, I believe it was Reba, a seamstress, said, 'Sisters, it is obvious. We must make the men suffer so that they will come to our aid and dig a new well. All we have to do is withdraw our labor. We go on strike. If they want water, let them fetch it for themselves.' This suggestion found some favor and it was discussed. But then the faults emerged. Could the men be trusted to bring sufficient water for their families? Was it possible for the women to bring only their own ration of water and not share it with the men? Would the children be the ones to suffer most? Would the men see reason and begin to dig, or would they resort to violence?

"That is when Shenaz spoke.

"Shenaz was sitting just outside the circle. So far she had been silent. After marriage, Shenaz had gone to the town but her husband abandoned her there. That is when she became a jatra girl, a dancing girl. When she came back to the village, she had to survive by selling the only thing that she had to sell. That is why she sat outside the circle.

"Anyway, now she spoke. 'There is another kind of labor we perform, and if we withdraw it that will be a discomfort only for the men.' Everyone turned to look at her, and though she could only look at the ground she was determined to press her point. 'A man cannot live without water. He cannot live without it, but he can bear the thought of no water. A man can live without sex. He can live without it, but he cannot bear the thought of no sex. This is my suggestion.'

"That's how the women in my village got themselves a new well. If you think you are powerless, then you are. Everything is within you, where God put it. If your husband does not do what is required, think what you yourself have left undone."

Mrs. Islam let go of Nazneen's wrist. She took a handkerchief and wiped her mouth, as if clearing the way for the next story. Her eyes were small and hard like a bird's; her white hair looked as if it would snap under a comb. On her face was written grandeur and weariness, and the knowledge that whatever happened she would be the one called to preside over it.

The receptionist, who had a cigarette tucked behind her ear, called Nazneen's name. "Mrs. Ahmed," she said, leaning over the counter so that her breasts threatened to roll into the waiting room.

Nazneen got up but hesitated because she was unsure if she would go in alone, or with her chaperone.

"Go. Go," said Mrs. Islam. She glared at the receptionist's breasts, and the girl withdrew them at once.

* * *

Dr. Azad sat with his feet together. His knees pressed against each other. Although his chair was large and well padded, he did not lean into it but kept his back straight, so that he appeared like a jointed doll balanced stiffly in a seat. He sat at a ninety-degree angle to his desk, facing Nazneen. On the desk were a notepad, a pen, a yellow pocket file, and a row of snowstorms. Nazneen learned about snowstorms on her first visit to Dr. Azad. They were fascinating, these sleeping underwater towns. When you shook them they were whipped with a white explosion but then, only then, you could imagine the life within. Children's things, Dr. Azad said. He didn't explain why they were on his desk.

"Any problems, any pain, any blood loss?"

"No," said Nazneen. "Everything is fine."

"Any soreness, any swellings in the hands or ankles?"

"No."

"You're having a good diet?"

"Yes."

"Then I predict that things will go smoothly, you will have a healthy child, and he will look after you in your old age." The doctor smiled. He had the most peculiar smile. His chin pushed up, the ends of his mouth turned down. But still it was a smile. You could tell by the way his eyebrows lifted that he intended some kind of merriment.

"All I have to do now is take your blood pressure and make an appointment for you at the hospital. Do you have any questions?" His voice was soft; the words opened like flowers on his lips and yet they had authority. Chanu spoke loudly. He weighed his words like gold and threw them about like a fool.

"Just one thing," said Nazneen. "My husband would like you to come to us again, for a meal."

Dr. Azad took out a black armband from a drawer and motioned for Nazneen to roll up her sleeve. She watched his face, trying to read his answer. She saw that his nose turned up at the end: a sign of weakness in a man, according to Amma. The doctor did not appear weak. His hair was like a shiny helmet, cut short and straight across the fringe and printed with a circle of light from the bulb overhead. The flesh around his eyes looked puffed and gray, and the eyes themselves were neither penetrating nor commanding. But his mouth was firm and his posture erect. He held himself like a man who knew his place in the world, and knew that the world knew it too.

"Blood pressure is perfect. Good, good." He put the armband and the little tube with the pump back in the drawer. "Yes," he said. "I accept, with pleasure. We have a conversation to pursue, your husband and I. We were most rudely interrupted by my patients. And I have some books to return. There's one I'm still reading. I have it in my bag. Do you think I may be allowed to keep it a while longer?"

Nazneen did not know about conversations interrupted and books lent. Her back was hurting. Even lying flat on the new hard mattress was no relief. She needed to urinate, and now when she urinated it burned. The rest of the time it itched. But what could be said of this to Dr. Azad? Everything is fine, she had told him. She could have mentioned the back, but what else can a pregnant woman expect if not back pain?

"Yes, your husband has been to see me once or twice." He paused. "No, let's say three or four times. I have tasted your excellent kebabs. I have signed his petition. I have been lent books. And I have engaged in literary debate. All these are fine things, but everything in its proper place. I shall, let's say, pay a home visit."

A petition? What petition is this? Nazneen had not seen any petition. She returned to Mrs. Islam, who was slumped in her chair with her head lolling back so that, but for the fact that her eyes were open, she appeared to be sound asleep. Perhaps she sleeps with her eyes open, thought Nazneen. That's how she misses nothing and knows everything. It must have been Razia, though, who told her about Chanu and Hasina and our troubles. She smiled a little at the thought of Razia, curling up her long legs and dishing gossip sideways out of her man-size mouth.

She was on her knees and her hands were flat against the mat. Midday prayer. Everything must be kept clear now. All the complaints, all the anxieties and lists that made up her life must be set aside. She could be grateful. She could flush her body and mind with gratitude. There should be no room for other thoughts. Although she could think about God. And the words of the prayer. *Glory be to my Lord, the Most High. God is greater than everything else.* And remember the baby, too, because God would not want her to forget that. Hasina, also. Because she was grateful for her safety, for the letter safely delivered. The baby she could not forget because he was scrambling around her belly, looking for footholds just beneath her ribs. She could not get her forehead down to the mat. It simply was not possible. There was a special dispensation for pregnant women. If she chose to, Nazneen could do namaz from her chair. She had tried it once and it made her feel lazy. But it was nice that the imams had thought of it. Such was the kindness and compassion of Islam towards women. Mind you, if any imam had ever been pregnant, would they not have made it *compulsory* to sit? That way, no one could feel it was simply due to laziness. *How did I come to be so foolish?* thought Nazneen. *What is wrong with my mind that it goes around talking of pregnant imams? It does not seem to belong to me sometimes; it takes off and thumbs its nose like a practical joker.*

She was half annoyed and half relieved to hear knocking, and Razia calling out, "Sister, it's just me. I've brought medicine for you."

Razia was wearing a woolen hat that came down over her ears and sat in a line with her eyebrows. Over her salwaar kameez she had a baggy sweater with some kind of animal (a deer? a goat?) knitted into the front. Her shoes were big as trucks and battered by untold collisions. She kept the hat on, and Nazneen was constantly on the brink of pointing this out.

"Dissolve the packets in water and take it twice a day. It will sort out your problem. No more burning."

"I'll do it," said Nazneen. "I've got something to show you."

The letter was longer this time. It gave an address. Hasina talked about her landlord, Mr. Chowdhury, about the job he was going to get for her in a garment factory, and about the ice cream parlor at the end of the road. She sounded excited, especially about the pistachio flavor and the little plastic spoons. It seemed she had not the least idea about the danger she was in (and she *was* in danger, a girl, a beautiful young girl, alone in Dhaka), but Nazneen hoped that Mr. Chowdhury would look out for her. Mr. Chowdhury would be responsible. A man with property will be respectable, Chanu said, she will be under his protection.

"I'm glad for you," said Razia. "And your husband is glad too, I expect."

"He didn't want to do anything, and now he doesn't have to."

"Men like to be proved right. We must go out of our way to show them how right they are. My husband is just the same."

"When he read the letter, he said, 'What did I tell you? Sometimes we must sit and wait.'"

"Did he push his lips out and waggle his head like this?" Razia made a fat bunch of her mouth, and made her eyes wide.

Nazneen was not finished. "He cannot accept one single thing in his life but this: that my sister should be left to her fate. Everything else may be altered, but not that."

Razia leaned back on the sofa. She made the sofa look small, and she knocked one of the plastic headrests to the floor. "What can we say against fate?"

"I am not saying anything against it." Nazneen thought briefly of telling the story of How You Were Left toYour Fate. It was too long to go into now. "I am just . . ." What? Angry with Chanu. But about what, exactly?

"You are just concerned for your sister. It's natural. And in your condition, things become more of a worry. You have to take care, and don't overdo things. Did you know that Nazma had her third on Saturday and he was two months early? I don't know if it's true, but Sorupa says that it was because her husband wouldn't leave her alone, and that made the baby come before it was ready."

"Ish," said Nazneen, narrowing her eyes at the thought. She rubbed her stomach and pressed on it firmly to feel around the curve of the baby's head, or his bottom. She put her feet up on a footstool. There were three footstools now, and an extra chair. (This one had things growing on it, strands of gray, moldy stuff, but Chanu said it was valuable, and when he had fixed it he was going to sell it.) It was getting difficult for her to navigate the furniture now. They were both growing, Nazneen and the furniture.

"Anyway, it was a quick labor. Not like her first. That was thirty-six hours. Mine was twenty-eight."

"When I was born, Amma thought it was indigestion. She said that some women make a big fuss."

"Hah," said Razia. She picked up one of Chanu's books from under her feet and put it on the coffee table.

"It's a natural thing, which happens to all women."

"Hah," said Razia. "I'll come with you to the hospital. Next time I come, I'll help you pack a bag for the big day."

"Amma didn't make a single sound when I was born."

"Mmmm," said Razia. She looked around the room, as if she had just stepped into it for the first time. Nazneen looked around too. A piece of wallpaper was curling back just by the window and the thin gray curtains looked like large, used bandages. It was afternoon but the light had crept away and the grayness of the curtains seemed to hang over everything.

"Did you know about Amina?"

Nazneen did not know.

"She's asking for a divorce. I heard it from Nazma, who heard it from

Sorupa. Hanufa told her about it, and she got it straight from the horse's mouth."

"I saw her with a split lip. And one time she had her arm in a sling. He must have gone too far this time."

"Not only that," said Razia. She looked at Nazneen from under her curly eyelashes and Nazneen knew she was savoring the moment. "He has another wife that he forgot to mention for the past eleven years."

"May God save us from such wicked men." *And from ourselves, too, that we should enjoy such stories.*

"Anyway, your husband has not made you a co-wife. You have something to be grateful for." Razia smiled. There was nothing feminine about her face, and with her hair tucked into her hat she could have been a laborer or a fisherman, but when she smiled her face lost its sly, sideways look and her nose seemed smaller. When she was smiling she was almost handsome. "Any news of the promotion?"

"My husband says they are racist, particularly Mr. Dalloway. He thinks he will get the promotion, but it will take him longer than any white man. He says that if he painted his skin pink and white then there would be no problem." Chanu had begun, she had noticed, to talk less of promotion and more of racism. He had warned her about making friends with "them," as though that were a possibility. *All the time they are polite. They smile. They say "please" this and "thank you" that. Make no mistake about it, they shake your hand with the right, and with the left they stab you in the back.*

"Well," said Razia, "this could be true."

Nazneen turned the words over. This *could* be true. She waited for more. Razia was unpicking a thread from her sweater.

Nazneen said, "My husband says it is discrimination."

"Ask him this, then. Is it better than our own country, or is it worse? If it is worse, then why is he here? If it is better, why does he complain?"

These were questions she had neither asked nor thought of asking. She was in this country because that was what had happened to her. Anyone else, therefore, was here for the same reason.

"I don't know if he complains," she found herself saying. "He just likes to talk about things. He says that racism is built into the 'system.' I don't know what 'system' he means exactly."

"My son's teacher, she's a good one. She helps him a lot, and he likes her. My husband has a work colleague, he gives us things. Clothes that his children have grown out of. A machine for drying hair. A radio and stepladders. All sorts of things. There are good ones, and bad ones. Just like us. And some of them you can be friendly with. Some aren't so friendly. But they leave us alone, and we leave them alone. That's enough for me."

"But the ones at my husband's work—they could be the bad ones."

"Something else: if you don't have a job here, they give you money. Did you know that? You can have somewhere to live, without any rent. Your children can go to school. And on top of that, they give you money. What would happen at home? Can you eat without working? Can you have a roof above your head?" Razia took off her hat.

Nazneen squeaked.

"I cut it," said Razia. "I was fed up with it, all that brushing and brushing." She ran her hand over her hair and pulled a piece around her face. It didn't even reach her mouth. She read what Nazneen was thinking. "He didn't say anything yet. He just looked at it like this." She let her mouth hang open and crossed her eyes. Her laugh was like a saucepan dropped on a tiled floor; the burst of it made you jump.

"He wasn't angry?" Razia's husband appeared to Nazneen to be perpetually angry. She had seen him at their flat several times, and once or twice in the courtyard. He worked in a factory that made plastic dolls. Such a big man, making little dolls. There were legs in the kitchen cupboards, heads on the windowsills, torsos down the back of the sofa. Either he brought home only parts or Tariq and Shefali were keen on dismemberment. She had never heard him speak except behind a closed door, to Razia, so she could not make out the words. Although he was silent, he had thunder in his brows and his mouth had a murderous set. So different from her own husband. Even when Chanu was ranting he seemed more bewildered by the world than enraged.

"Let him be angry," said Razia, as if it were none of her business. "Will it bring my hair back? I have to go now. Don't forget the medicine. I have to go, because I am going to college. I am going to learn English."

Nazneen struggled to her feet. She reminded Razia to take her hat. She suddenly had a picture of Hasina with short hair, striding about in a pair of men's trousers and smoking a cigarette with bright, painted lips.

"Do you know why I'm going to learn English?" said Razia as she was leaving. "So that when my children start telling dirty jokes behind my back, I'll be able to whip their backsides."

Chanu, cross-legged on the bed. Bald knees pointing blindly at the walls. Stomach growing goiterlike over his privates. Hands tucked beneath the belly folds, exploring, weighing. Thin dark arms, a cluster of pimples over the right elbow. Shoulders that are slender, correctly held, almost graceful. Above, a round, plump face. On another man, such a face would look content.

Chanu was thinking. His mouth twitched. It slid over to the left. Back over to the right, high this time, pushing up the cheek, twisting the nostril, closing the eye. For a second, the lips relaxed, and then parted, stretched, rejected a word. The eyes took over. They narrowed in concentration, parted in surprise, squinted in evaluation. They made the eyebrows work, and they gathered the marching lines at the temples to do their part. If Chanu was awake, he was thinking, and his thoughts were written on his face. He is like a child, thought Nazneen, who has learned to read but must mouth the words.

"You see . . ." He chewed for a while, as if tasting his thoughts. He cleared his throat, brought his hands out from under his stomach. "You see, Azad was implying a deception on my part, a fraud. Yes, he definitely inferred that a malpractice had taken place. That is not on. It simply isn't on."

Nazneen handed him pajamas. She slung his trousers on a hanger, without folding them properly, and put them in the wardrobe. He did not notice the dirty socks, the crumpled trousers. Her rebellions passed undetected. She was irritated by his lack of interest; she was pleased by her subtlety.

Chanu looked at his pajamas as if there were something surprising or unfamiliar about the flowered material. "But, you see, the point of the inserted clause was not deviousness but clarification. Naturally, I would be in charge of running the mobile library. Who else would do it? It was my idea, my petition, my baby, so to speak. No one could be better suited than I to bring the great world of literature to this humble estate.

"Of course, there wouldn't be much to start off with in the way of Bengali books. But I could go to Dhaka. To Calcutta, to scour the bookstalls around the university. On a sort of literary mission, I suppose." He made a satisfied noise, as though he had just finished a meal. Then his face became animated once more. He raised a finger and his voice. "But Azad said, not in so many words, that I had done something underhand. I told him, 'Look, Azad (*I was there! Don't you remember? I was there, and you always call him "Doctor"*), I asked you to sign my petition and you signed. You agreed with the idea of a mobile library for the estate. I believe you used the word "splendid." Are you now telling me that if I am in charge it will turn from splendid to sordid? (*No, you didn't. You didn't say that.*) And I hardly need to point out to you that amending the wording of the petition was an act of correction, not corruption.' And he kept quiet." Chanu put on his pajama top. He smiled. "I think that says a lot."

"When will you get it, the library?"

"Ah, it's a funding issue, of course. The cost of a van, the books, petrol. All these things. Anyway, I haven't yet finished collecting signatures."

"How many signatures do you have?"

Chanu made some reckonings, leaning his head this way and that. "Altogether, I'd say seven or eight. But I am aiming for more. Do you think Azad will put out that copy in his office?"

"I don't know," said Nazneen. "Maybe." She looked at the man in the yellow-flowered pajama top, with his bald knees splayed on the pink bedspread. She looked up at the massive black shiny wardrobe and the gold zigzag design that you could pick off with a fingernail. She looked at the brown carpet, at the patch worn through to the webbed plastic that held it together. She looked at the ceiling light that lit up the dust on the shade and bent shadows across the walls. She looked at her stomach that hid her feet and forced her to lean back to counter its weight. She looked and she saw that she was trapped inside this body, inside this room, inside this flat, inside this concrete slab of entombed humanity. They had nothing to do with her. For a couple of beats, she closed her eyes and smelled the jasmine that grew close to the well, heard the chickens scratching in the hot earth, felt the sunlight that warmed her cheeks and made dancing patterns on her eyelids.

"Maybe, maybe not," said Chanu. "Perhaps I should not get him involved. God knows what he will accuse me of next. A bald man does not walk under the bellfruit tree twice." He laughed. "Although I am not bald quite yet." He struggled into his pajama pants without leaving the bed, then rolled onto his stomach and picked up a book from the floor. "This is a very good book. *Sense and Sensibility*." He said it in English. "It's difficult to translate. Let me think about it."

"Razia is going to college to study English."

"Ah, good."

"Perhaps I could go with her."

"Well. Perhaps." He didn't look up from his book.

"I can go, then?"

"You know, I should be reading about politics. Nineteenth-century elections. But they make it so dry. You can learn a lot from novels as well. All sorts of things you can pick up, about society, politics, land reform, social division. And it's not so dry."

"Will it be all right for me to go?"

"Where?" He rolled onto his back to look at her. His belly showed.

"To the college. With Razia."

"What for?"

"For the English lessons."

"You're going to be a mother."

Nazneen picked up a glass from the windowsill. Yes, she was going to be a mother.

"Will that not keep you busy enough? And you can't take a baby to college. Babies have to be fed; they have to have their bottoms cleaned. It's not so simple as that. Just to go to college, like that."

"Yes," said Nazneen. "I see that it is not."

"Good. Now let me read. All this talking, talking, talking." And he rolled over again.

The fridge hummed like a giant mosquito. In the distance, traffic growled. Nazneen did not turn on the light. Half a moon, gritty tonight, clung to the dark sky. The linoleum shocked her warm feet. She took a tub of yogurt from the fridge and sprinkled it with sugar. She leaned against the countertop and ate. "Eat! Eat!" her husband told her at mealtimes. But for him she would not. She showed her self-restraint like this. Her self-denial. She wanted to make it visible. It became a habit, then a pleasure, taking solace in these midnight meals.

Amma used to make yogurt: thick and sweet and warm. Nothing like these plastic pots from the plastic English cows. But still. With the sugar, it went down. And it was very convenient. When she thought about Gouripur now, she thought about inconvenience. To live without a flushing toilet, to abandon her two sinks (kitchen and bathroom), to make a fire for the oven instead of turning a knob—would these be trades worth making? She tried to imagine Chanu, marching off to the latrine with a heavy book in his hand. He liked to read, sometimes for half an hour or more, while sitting on the toilet. The flies would see him off the latrine.

Chanu had fallen asleep with his face in the book, the page marked with dribble. All that reading was not good for him. It made his mind boil. He could end up like Makku Pagla.

It was a long time since Makku had come to her mind. But when she was small, she used to follow him around. Hasina and Nazneen walked behind him, holding hands and swinging their free arms. Hasina shouted, "Yee yaw, Makku Pagla! Lend us your umbrella. Be quick, because it's raining."

People said he was soft in his head because he was always reading. Books had cracked him, and the more cracked he became the more books he read. That was how he earned his name, Makku Pagla, or Lunatic Makku.

It was Hasina who spotted his umbrella in the well. Numerous repairs over the years and patches of different colors had made it famous, and Makku never set foot without it. "He's killed himself," screamed Hasina, running back to the house. "Makku Pagla has killed himself in the well." Amma began at once to say her prayers, while Abba picked up a rope and sprinted. Nazneen and Hasina walked over on wobbly legs.

Although a stench had been coming from the old well for a few days nobody thought it remarkable—people had begun to tip rubbish down. But now that Makku's umbrella was in there it was only reasonable to assume that he was with it. A crowd quickly gathered. Everyone had an opinion but no one was willing to be lowered into the soup of rubbish and flesh to retrieve the body.

At last, the village council retreated to Nazneen's house. Abba took charge of the meeting. Nazneen and Hasina, waiting outside, heard him say, "He had an undignified death. Let us give him, at least, a dignified burial." They repeated the words to each other, whispering behind hands, into ears. Later, they found a cricket, on its back, turning into a husk. And they said the words again and dug a shallow grave. It was a game they played over and over, Nazneen solemn as a raven and Hasina faking.

When the council emerged, the offer was made: sixty rupees plus expenses, a large bar of Sunlight soap, and a bottle of perfume to the first man to volunteer. A laborer stepped forward and was cheered. He stripped to his nengti and shouted to his wife to bring mustard oil, which he rubbed over his body. The equipment was assembled: a large bamboo basket, thick ropes, and two iron balties for clearing the rubbish.

As he was lowered down below the ground the laborer shouted up a running commentary on his activities, his voice distorted and echoing. "I've secured Makku," he reported, and another cheer went up from the spectators. The assistants began to winch the body up. "Slowly, slowly," said the voice in the well. "Do you want to knock his head off?" Makku's naked body was carefully laid on the ground. It was completely white and there were holes where the flesh had dropped off. When the laborer was lifted from the well, he carried with him an arm which he set gently on Makku's chest. Nazneen and Hasina held each other.

"They've forgotten his umbrella," said Hasina.

"We shouldn't have teased him," said Nazneen.

In the evening, Amma was still crying. Her nose was red, her eyes raw. Sometimes she made a sharp call, like a frightened monkey. She put her hand up to cover her mouth because she was ashamed of her teeth, which were shaped like melon seeds. Abba smoked his pipe and sat on his haunches.

"Don't cry, Amma," said Hasina, and kissed her with pomegranate lips.

"Your mother is a saint," said Abba. "Don't forget that she comes from a family of saints." He got up and walked away, and he held himself straighter than any man. He did not come back for three days.

"Where does Abba go?" asked Nazneen.

Amma looked towards the heavens. "Look! Now my child is asking where he goes."

Nazneen looked up too. The sky was thick with beating brown wings. The ducks were coming, it was the season. They came in hordes, casting great shadows across the rivers and threatening the sun. Amma hugged her fiercely. She took Nazneen's wide face between her two palms and spoke to her: "If God wanted us to ask questions, he would have made us men."

Chapter Four

The baby was astonishing. He had little cloth ears, floppy as cats. The warmth of his round stomach could heat the world. His head smelled like a sacred flower. And his fists held mysterious, tiny balls of fluff from which he could not bear to be parted.

Nazneen curled around him on the bed. He raised an arm, which reached only halfway up his head. He put it back down. The futility of this exercise appeared to anger him. His face squashed into a purple mess, and he made a noise like a thousand whipped puppies.

"You see," said Chanu. He sat on a chair, tucked in between the bed and the wall, knees against the bedspread. "My grandmother's cousin was fair-skinned. She was a beauty. So much so that it caused fights. One man was killed, even. That's how far he was prepared to go to win her hand in marriage. And another man, a laborer with no chance, took his own life. Anyway, that's what I heard. I never saw her myself, except when she was very old and looked like a beetle."

Nazneen sat up against some pillows and lifted the baby onto her chest. She rubbed his back. Her hands were full of magic. The baby sucked softly on her neck.

"That's where Ruku gets his fair skin." The baby's name was Mohammad Raqib. Chanu called him Ruku. Raqib's skin was like his aunt's. Hasina was pale as a water lily. Raqib was like shondesh, creamy and sweet, and perfectly edible.

"Mrs. Islam is coming again today. If I'm napping, don't wake me." Mrs. Islam was sure to have more advice about the baby.

Chanu shifted in his seat. The chair was his latest acquisition. It was made of metal tubing and canvas. The metal was rusting and the canvas ripped. It was, Chanu had revealed, a modern classic, worthy of restoration. Nazneen refused to sit in it, even when her husband told her not to be a damn fool of a woman and try it. She just refused and that was that.

"She comes from a good family," said Chanu. "Good background. Educated. Very respectable. Her husband owned a big business: import-export. I went to him once with a proposal." His jaw worked silently for a while, as if he were biting an invisible thread. "Jute products—door-mats, bookmarks, baskets. That kind of thing. He was very interested. Very interested. But then he fell sick. It was simply bad timing. I have the proposal somewhere in my papers. It's probably worth digging out. All the figures are there. Costs, revenues, and profits, down in black and white. But of course he died, and I never had the capital. What can you do without capital?"

Raqib tried to lift his head from Nazneen's shoulder as if he knew the answer to this difficult question. Overcome with his burden of knowledge, he collapsed instantly into sleep. Squinting down, Nazneen looked at his month-old nose, the sumptuous curve of his cheek, his tight-shut, age-old eyes. She closed her own eyes and hoped that Chanu would let them both alone.

"He's sleeping. Why don't you put him down? They can sleep fourteen or sixteen hours a day. Ruku doesn't sleep that long. Personally, I think it's a question of intelligence. The more intelligent the baby is, the more awake it is. And then the more time it is awake, the more stimulation it has and the more intelligent it becomes. It's a virtuous circle."

Nazneen kept quiet. Her guts prickled. Her forehead tightened. All he could do was talk. The baby was just another thing to talk about. For Nazneen, the baby's life was more real to her than her own. His life was full of needs: actual and urgent needs, which she could supply. What was her own life, by contrast, but a series of gnawings, ill-defined and impossible to satisfy?

And Chanu just talked. For him the baby was a set of questions, an array of possibilities, a spark for debate and for reflection. He pondered on Raqib. He examined, from a distance, his progress and made plans for Raqib's future. The baby opened up new horizons and closed others; he provided a telescope and a looking glass. What did Chanu see when he looked at his son? An empty vessel to be filled with ideas. An avenger: forming, growing. A future business partner. A professor: homegrown. A Chanu: this time with chances seized, not missed.

Nazneen let her lips part and breathed more deeply.

"OK," said Chanu. "Sleep now. If Mrs. Islam comes, I'll wake you."

She listened for the sound of him leaving. The little creak he made (his lungs, not his bones) when he stood. Even with her lids closed she could see him, hands on knees, eyes scanning and scanning, the hair on the top of his head standing in short, shocked tufts. A man whom Life took unawares. He had not moved. "Mrs. Islam is what you call a respectable type." Nazneen tried a snore. "Razia, on the other hand . . ." He cleared his throat and raised his voice, "Razia, on the other hand, I would not call a respectable type. I'm not saying anything against her. But what is her background? Her husband does some menial sort of job. He is uneducated. He is probably illiterate. Perhaps he can write his name. If he can't write his name, he will put a cross. Razia cuts her hair like a tramp. Perhaps she calls it fashion. I don't know. Her son is roaming around the estate like a vagabond, throwing stones and what have you. When I spoke to him he put his fingers in his nose, like this, and made a face like this." Nazneen resisted the temptation to look. "It's OK. He's a little boy. What does it matter?" Here Chanu coughed in a way which suggested to Nazneen that his speech would reach a climax. "I'll tell you what matters. The little boy is not little for very long. And when he grows, he grows with that very same lack of respect. The boy grows, the lack of respect grows. Then they are disobedient, they start vandalizing, fighting, drinking, chasing women, gambling. You can see where it ends, and how it starts." He got up, finally. "Just keep it in mind. I don't forbid you to see Razia, but I ask you to keep it in mind."

Mrs. Islam stretched the baby's legs up so that his feet touched his ears. She pulled his arms down, out to each side, and across his body. She took hold of the left leg and pumped it, so that it tucked against his chest and then kicked at the air. Mrs. Islam counted to ten. She started again with the right. Nazneen hovered to the side like a scavenger. A smile flickered around her mouth. Twice she darted, and twice she pulled back.

"You must massage the child every day," said Mrs. Islam. "Or the limbs will seize up. What are you wobbling around there for? Sit down. Or go and make some tea."

"Let me massage him," said Nazneen. "I can do it."

"You don't do it hard enough. Look! He likes it. It's also essential for their circulation."

The baby smiled. His entire face was gum. He flapped his arms like a baby bird. Mrs. Islam, big as a crow, bent over him and tickled an armpit. The baby spluttered and squealed. Bubbles formed on his lips. Mrs. Islam said, "Chit. Chit." She poked at him some more and the baby rolled his head from side to side and made such a noise that Nazneen feared he would have a seizure.

She snatched her baby from the carpet and he gasped hard, as if he had been drowning. "I'll make the tea," she said, not looking at her visitor.

Nazneen had begun to dread these visits. Raqib was five months old, and still Mrs. Islam had not expended all her advice. How much more advice could she give? How much more could Nazneen take? Mrs. Islam had started with the obvious things. The baby had to have his head shaved; the hair he was born with was unclean. He must have a thick black smear of kohl around his eyes, because the Devil takes only beautiful babies. (But he was beautiful, even so.) And he was to be rubbed regularly with oil and put in the sun to absorb its goodness. As if Nazneen did not know these things!

Then there were the special things that Mrs. Islam's mother had handed down to her. Put a finger up the baby's bottom once a week to purge his system. Suck his nostrils to clear away the snot. Roll the nipple between your thumbs before feeding so the milk is ready for him. Leave him for one hour a day on his belly to strengthen his neck and chest. Make a little pillow of feathers and bay leaves and cloves, to help him sleep. Parrot feathers were best. Add some ghee to his bathwater to keep his skin soft. Paste turmeric and aniseed on his chest to cure a cough. Rub his feet with coconut oil to draw out a cold. Never, ever turn him upside down.

Nazneen filled the kettle. She hoisted the baby on her hip. "Gi-gi," she said. "Go-gi." The baby quivered in anticipation. "Ga!" she said. "Gi-ga, gi-ga, gi-ga!" Raqib leaned back, incredulous. His bottom lip hung. Banners of drool proclaimed his adulation. Nazneen jiggled him. Up and down. Up and down. "Dah," said the baby, and kicked his fat legs. He stared at her face as if it were a wonder, as if he beheld beauty there. His eyes, unfurled now from the ancient wisdom they brought from the womb, were wide worlds, bright as stars. She put him down on a nest of cushions brought from the sitting room. He was shattered. Betrayed. He howled like a widow.

Nazneen smiled. She poured boiling water on tea bags and made ticking noises with her tongue. Then she picked him up again. "Do you cry for me? Is it me? Do you cry for me?" And with these words made good his loss.

"I'll take him back with me this afternoon," said Mrs. Islam. "Let you catch up on some housework." She made circles in the air with a finger. Her small black eyes appraised the room. "My niece is coming. She loves to play with babies."

Eleven, said Nazneen to herself. There were eleven chairs in the room, not counting the cow-dung armchairs that went with the sofa. How was she supposed to tidy up? There was nowhere to put anything. And Chanu's books and papers grew like weeds. And the dust—it came from nowhere, like a plague, and it could not be cured.

"He's so small," said Nazneen. "Send your niece to me."

"Nonsense. I'll take him." Mrs. Islam slurped at her tea. The bristles around her wart were long today. Soon they would be plucked.

Nazneen busied herself with Raqib. She dabbed at his chin with a tissue. She examined his fingernails. She put him on her shoulder and patted his back to expel some imaginary wind. He made a noise, an experimental sort of sound, which she seized upon as distress and walked with him over to the window. "There, there," she said. "Never mind. Look, look, look." But she kept him against her shoulder so that it was she who looked out.

The sun is large and sickly. It sweats uncomfortably in a hazy sky, squeezed between slabs of concrete. There is barely enough sky to hold it. Below, the communal bins ring the courtyard like squat metal warriors, competing in foulness, contemplating the standoff. One has keeled over and spilled its guts. A rat flicks in and out of them. A boy, sixteen, seventeen, walks by. He tests his shoulders this way and that. His head moves in and out like a chicken, strutting. He holds a cigarette in one hand and a radio or a tape player in the other. His friends call out to him from the shelter, next to the entrance to Rosemead. It is their headquarters. The bins have been evicted. Bhangra. That's what they play, Razia tells her. Bhangra and Shakin' Stevens. All hours of the day, and some of the night. The parents are losing control. But some of it is quite good—her eyes slide left and narrow themselves to two shiny slivers—particularly the Shakin' Stevens.

Rosemead faces her unblinkingly. There are metal frames on the windows. For one week they had sparkled and zinged. They had promised much. They had sung about how neat they were, how new. And then they fell into line. Overnight. The next morning they were subdued. The light did not play with them. The brick, dull red, got its way. The frames are as dirty, as sullen, as their hosts.

You can spread your soul over a paddy field, you can whisper to a mango tree, you can feel the earth beneath your toes and know that this is the place, the place where it begins and ends. But what can you tell to a pile of bricks? The bricks will not be moved.

A television aerial dangles from a window like a suicide. A pile of boxes blockades another window. Razia's place is curtained, and the back of a head bobs around behind the curtain: Shefali or Tariq hiding from Tariq or Shefali. The tattoo lady leans forward, watching the yard and drinking. Her hair slides down the sides of her head like an oil slick. She has dyed it, but it remains unwashed. She is wearing a man's undershirt. Her breasts, patched with dark ink, flop against it. Her thighs run over the chair. She transfers her can from one hand to the other and back again. How can she just sit and sit? What is she waiting for? What is there to see?

"You can collect him in a couple of hours. Give him a feed now, and we'll go." Mrs. Islam's voice brought Nazneen back. Her words were as sharp as an eyeful of sand. She never raised her voice. It was the kind of voice that never needed to be raised. It cut words to a fine point and launched them decisively.

Nazneen turned around. "No," she said. "He'll feed later."

Mrs. Islam took a handkerchief from her sleeve. She shook it out and wiped along her hairline. Winter and summer she wore the same thing: a cardigan over a sari, black socks, carpet slippers. She would not change for the seasons. They did not bend to her and she would not bend to them. "You better do it now. I'm ready to go."

"He's staying here," said Nazneen. "With me."

Her guest looked at her. Mrs. Islam's features could not accommodate surprise, but her eyebrows dug themselves a little closer together. Nazneen noticed for the first time how dark they were, untouched by the white that had leached her hair. "What's that?"

Nazneen trembled, but the warmth of Raqib's body against her chest fired her resolve. "He's staying here." She could have added something to soothe. Something to show her respect. She could have said, I'll bring him later. He's not well today. Another day, I'll bring him. He'll be in good hands with you. All she said was, "He's staying here."

Mrs. Islam gathered herself. She picked up her handbag and sat with it open on her lap. For a moment, Nazneen imagined her grabbing Raqib and stuffing him in the cavernous black leather. But Mrs. Islam simply closed it, rubbed the glass clasp with her thumb, and got up. "The white people," she said, "they all do what they want. It's nobody's business.

"If a child is screaming because it is being beaten, they just close the door and the windows. They might make a complaint about noise. But the child is not their business, even if it is being beaten to death.

"They do what they want. It is a private matter. Everything is a private matter. That is how the white people live." She went towards the door and Nazneen followed, watching the uneven swing of her walk and forming questions about her hip that she did not ask. Mrs. Islam passed her papery hand over the baby's face. The baby reached out to her and leaned across, but Nazneen held him fast.

The Dr. Azad question was troubling Chanu. The question was this: Was it hostility or neglect that led the doctor not to return hospitality? Or it was this: Was it a matter of numbers, so that one more dinner would ensure an invitation? Or possibly this: Did it matter, did it make any difference at all, if the invitations continued to be one-sided? More and more frequently, it was this: What manner of snob was this Azad?

"He eats my food, he reads my books. God alone knows where else he finds any intellectual stimulation, any companion of the intellect. Shall I ask him when we will be going to his house? I can ask like this." Chanu rubbed the back of his head, tipped his chair back, and spoke with the suggestion of a yawn. "So, Azad, what are you hiding at your house? Are we going to come around and find out?" He let his chair fall flat again.

Nazneen spooned apple into the baby's mouth. He grabbed at the spoon and sent it flying. He laughed, spraying her with gunk. She was astonished that she had made this creature, spun him out of her flesh. When she remembered that Chanu had made him too she was stunned.

"Maybe he never thinks of it," Chanu continued. "He just needs a little prod. Or it could be that he doesn't consider me part of his circle. A doctor is a cut above. But what is a doctor, really, when you think about it? He memorizes everything from books: broken legs, colds and viruses, eczema and asthma, rheumatism and arthritis, boils and warts. It's learning by rote. Symptom and cure. Hardly an intellectual pursuit. No. He's just a finger blown up to the size of a banana tree. Let him guard his house, and put some barbed wire around it too. I am not interested."

Nazneen put the baby on the floor while she hunted for the spoon. Beneath the table, the files and papers had been breeding, intermarrying with balls of string, boxes of staples, rolls of labels, chains of clips. A pair of pants lay exhausted in a heap; a sock sat fossilized in dust. The spoon was nowhere to be seen. The baby crawled under the table with her and pulled her hair. His face this last month had turned from awed to quizzical. His features were not fully drawn, but they were more than sketched.

When he looked at her now, he was always on the point of asking a question. Behind the question was a very big joke, and he looked as though he would let her in on it. "Hello," she told him, "I'm looking for your spoon."

"Maybe if I get the promotion," Chanu went on, "then he will be more inclined to extend his hospitality. That's probably the kind of man he is."

Nazneen came up. She scooped the baby under one arm. She checked Chanu's face to see if he required any response from her. He was mulling over his words, scrunching them this way and that, into a wrinkled brow, a taut cheek. His eyes looked somewhere far off. She was not needed. She took the baby through to the kitchen and fetched another spoon. He spoke these days of "if." It used to be "when." When the promotion came through. And he never spoke about Wilkie, or his successor, Gerard, or Howard, who came after him. He spoke more often of resigning.

It was Sunday morning. They would go out for a walk soon, around Brick Lane, and Chanu would push the pram and she would walk a step behind. When people stopped him in the street to admire Raqib, to give him a kiss or a tickle, Chanu would grow a couple of inches. If people did not stop him, he stopped them. "See how alert he is. Notice the large size of his head. The bigger the head, the bigger the brain. You think I'm joking? Do you know how big dinosaurs' heads were? And do you wonder why they are extinct?" And the person would smile vaguely and walk away. At the shops, Chanu would buy vegetables. Pumpkin, gourd, spinach, okra, aubergine. Whatever was in season. He would buy spices and rice and lentils and sometimes sweetmeats: a tub of milky ras malai, sticky brown gulabjamun, golden whirls of jelabee. He would not haggle. He would not "abase" himself, or "act like a primitive." He broke off bits of jelabee and fed them to Raqib, and licked his fingers where the liquid sugar spilled out.

Before they went out today, she had to cut his hair. She was always cutting bits off him. The dead skin around his corns. His toenails. The fingernails of his right hand, because his left could not do the job properly. The fingernails of his left hand, because she might as well do that while she had the scissors. The wiry hair that grew from the tops of his ears. And the hair on his head, once every six weeks, when Chanu said, "Better smarten me up a bit."

She strapped the baby into his seat and gave him a piece of bread to chew. Chanu sat at the table with a book open. He underlined some passages while she trimmed around his nape. The degree course would never be finished. Nazneen wondered if he really had a degree from Dhaka. Perhaps he used to finish things in those days.

"I'm fed up with the Open University," said Chanu, as if he had read her thoughts. "They send you so much rubbish to read. I'm returning to my first love." He held up his book. "English literature at its finest. You've heard of William Shakespeare. Yes, even a girl from Gouripur has heard of Shakespeare."

"That is true," Nazneen responded. No, the degree would never be finished. The promotion would never be won. The job would never be resigned. The furniture would never be restored. The house in Dhaka would never be built. The jute business would never be started. Even the mobile library, the petition for which had taken Chanu from door to door, would be forgotten.

"Have you heard of *Richard II*?" Chanu made some preparations at the back of his throat. "It's not so easy to translate. Give me one minute. This is a wonderful passage."

"If I went to the college with Razia, you would be able to tell me in English."

"To understand Shakespeare? Just like that! Is that what Razia is learning?"

"I don't know." Nazneen brushed some hair from his shoulders and wrapped it in a piece of toilet tissue.

> "O! that I were as great
> As is my grief, or lesser than my name,
> Or that I could forget what I have been,
> Or not remember what I must be now."

No. The library would not be forgotten. It would be remembered, along with the rest. It would go on the list and it would never be forgotten.

> "Mine eyes are full of tears, I cannot see:
> And yet salt water blinds them not so much
> But they can see a sort of traitors here.
> Nay, if I turn my eyes upon myself,
> I find myself a traitor with the rest."

Chanu closed his eyes. He began to hum. He played the table like a tabla. His head swayed to the tune so that Nazneen had to stop cutting. When he opened his eyes he shook himself like a wet dog. "So," he said. "Well. Let's get on."

The baby dropped his bread and began to cry.

"See how quickly he is frustrated," said Chanu.

He can see, thought Nazneen. He can comment. But he cannot act. She went to pick up the bread. The baby chewed and was quiet. Chanu was quiet. The scissors went snit, snit. She heard the air enter and leave her nostrils. Her stomach growled because on Sundays, with Chanu close by, she didn't eat much.

She had missed morning prayers again today. Yesterday she missed both the fajr and zuhr prayers. But Raqib had needed her. The day before that he was napping and she was looking at a magazine. There was no excuse for that day. Except that her mind walked off on its own sometimes. She was looking at a magazine, an English magazine that Chanu had left. There was a picture of a couple: ice skaters. She stood on one leg. Her body was horizontal and the other leg perpendicular. Her arms reached out and held on to his hand, but she looked up and smiled directly at Nazneen. Her body was spangled, silver and blue. Her legs were as long as the Padma. She was a fairy-tale creature, a Hindu goddess. Nazneen fell, somehow, into that picture and caught hold of the man's hand. She was shocked to find she was traveling across the ice, on one foot, at terrible speed. And the man smiled and said, "Hold on tight." Little green gems twinkled in his black suit. Nazneen squeezed his hand. She felt the rush of wind on her cheeks, and the muscles in her thighs flexing. The ice smelled of limes. The cold air made her flush with warmth from deep down. Applause. She could not see the audience but she heard them. And the man let go of her hand but she was not afraid. She lowered her leg and she skated on. Until Raqib woke and looked at her skeptically. "Yes," she told him, "your mother is a foolish woman." But she went to the mirror and stared hard at her serious face, the wide cheeks and big forehead and the stubby-lashed, close-set eyes, and wondered for a while about what she saw.

Her mind would not be still. It tried to pull her off here and there. Whenever she got a letter from Hasina, for the next couple of days she imagined herself an independent woman too. The letters were long and detailed. Nazneen composed and recomposed her replies until the grammar was satisfactory, all errors expunged along with any vital signs. But

Hasina kicked aside all such constraints: her letters were full of mistakes and bursting with life. Nazneen threaded herself between the words, allowed them to spool her across seven seas to Dhaka, where she worked alongside her sister. Raqib came as well. Sometimes, at the end of the day, she was surprised when Chanu arrived home. Then she made vows to herself. Regular prayer, regular housework, no more dreaming. She sent brisk, efficient letters to Hasina. *Look,* she said to Amma (who was always watching), *look how good I am now.*

She had completed the haircut. It was, perhaps, a little jagged at one side but Chanu would not check it. "Blow on the back of my neck," he said. She blew, and dusted with her fingertips. "We're not going to fester here any longer," he said, wagging a finger. She held her breath. "We're going out for a walk. Go and unfold the pram."

She still saw Razia. Shefali liked to play with the baby. She gave him a row of dolls' heads, and he pinched at each one in turn. Tariq was more or less mute these days. An eight-year-old version of his father.

"I had to shave his head again," said Razia. Tariq scratched at his bristles. "Lice. They pick them up at school."

"Can I have some money?" said Tariq. He kicked his sister surreptitiously.

"I don't have any money. Leave your sister alone."

"I want five pounds."

"What? Go and play. Run away."

"I want five pounds."

"Why?" Razia sighed, and pointed to the baby. "They're much easier at that age."

"I want a football."

"You have a football."

"I want a proper football." It was the most Nazneen had heard him say in a long while. He always looked so on guard, so tough, that it was almost a surprise to hear his child's voice. "I want five pounds," he repeated, whining this time.

"I want five pounds," mimicked Razia. She caught his voice just right.

"I want five pounds," Shefali joined in. Tariq kicked her again and she began to squeal.

"Outside, both of you," yelled Razia. "Tariq, take your sister and go and play in the corridor. If I hear her crying, I'll whip your backside."

They went out, and began bickering behind the door. Razia sat on the floor and lifted Raqib onto her lap. He reached up and pinched her nose. He went cross-eyed looking at it.

"I'm going to strangle those kids," said Razia. "I've had enough of them."

Nazneen knew she would never speak about Raqib like that.

"And I'll do my husband as well. He spends all day at the factory, comes home to eat, sleeps for two or three hours, and then he's out again. All night."

"Why?" said Nazneen. "Where does he go?"

"He's driving trucks. He delivers meat to the halal butchers all around here. When he comes in, he stinks. Good job he doesn't hang around for long." She put her hand in her trouser pocket and pulled out a lollipop. The baby was stupefied. All he could do was drool. Razia unwrapped the sweet and put the wrapper back in her pocket. She was wearing a garment she called a tracksuit. She would never, so she said, wear a sari again. She was tired of taking little bird steps.

"It's good for a man to work. I don't mind. Let him work twenty-four hours a day." Razia waved the lollipop in front of Raqib's face. He watched it devotedly. He became its disciple. For its sake, he would sacrifice everything. "But we don't see a single extra penny. That's my objection. He sends it all back. He is the biggest miser. The biggest bastard miser. If the children need toothbrushes, I have to beg. I have to get everything secondhand. Does he expect his children to get secondhand toothbrushes? I can't give them anything." She put the lollipop to the baby's lips. He cooed gently over it. "All the money goes back home. I don't know who looks after it. His brother, most likely. And most likely his brother is a thieving bastard. I don't think we will ever see that money again."

Nazneen looked around. The room was crammed with things. Furniture, Tariq's bed, bikes, clothes, stepladders, plastic crates, toys, shoes, tins of paint, stacks of wooden planks, gas heaters, electric heaters, carpets, carrier bags of stuff, a stockpile of rice, a pyramid of tinned food. There was more here than the average villager would acquire in a lifetime. A village child was lucky to have a football. To have both a football and a bike was a luxury. To have a football, a bike, and a heap of toys besides was unheard of. Yet Nazneen did not remember the children complaining, could not remember complaining herself.

"I told him straight," Razia continued. "Open up your purse, you son-of-a-whore, or else."

The swearing was new. Or Razia was relaxed enough with her now not to hold back. The grown-ups had grumbled, of course, from time to time. The carpenter needed a new saw. The shoemaker needed more customers. (All those children running around barefoot!) The sweet-maker complained of the price of pistachios. But if they had a chair and a table and food to eat every day, then God be praised!

"I'll get a job myself. I told him straight." Razia looked at Nazneen, not sideways and skeptically but straight on.

"What kind of job?" said Nazneen. In Gouripur a sweetmaker was a sweetmaker, a shoemaker was a shoemaker, and a carpenter was a carpenter. They did not want to be teachers or librarians. They were not waiting for promotions. They did not make themselves unhappy.

"I talked to Jorina. There are jobs going in the factory."

"Oh," said Nazneen. "Mrs. Islam says Jorina has been shamed. Her husband goes with other women. She started work, and everyone said, 'He cannot feed her.' Even though he was working himself, he was shamed. And because of this he became reckless and started going with other women. So Jorina has brought shame on them all."

Razia snorted. "Is that what Mrs. Islam says? Let her say what she likes, it will not stop me."

"What about the community? She will not be the only one."

"Will the community feed me? Will it buy footballs for my son? Let the community say what it will. I say *this* to the community." And she flicked her fingers.

"What does your husband say?"

Razia narrowed her eyes. She looked down her long, straight nose at the baby. "Mrs. Islam is one to talk. She's a fine one to talk."

"Mrs. Islam?"

"She of the thousand hankies." Razia smiled for the first time.

Nazneen laughed. "What is it all about? All those handkerchiefs."

"You've never heard? You've never had the mystery of the handkerchiefs unraveled?" Razia's laugh vibrated on its high, metallic note. "Sister, did you just jump off the boat? Let's see. Some people say that she is self-conscious about her nose. You know she has a wart. They say she began by using the hankies to cover it up whenever she thought someone was staring. But who would dare to stare at the old witch's wart? I bet she was an old witch even when she was a girl. Another theory is that she had a lover once who made her a gift of lace handkerchiefs, and she keeps his memory alive now through her collection. What rubbish! Some other people say it is superstition. A fakir told her mother to catch her breath in a cloth and shake it away at arm's length because it would bring bad luck. Some people are this foolish." Razia handed Raqib back to Nazneen. He sucked his lolly dementedly. Razia got up and stretched. The knees of her tracksuit bulged.

"So what is it then?" Nazneen asked. "What's the real reason?"

"It's a system. That's how it started, anyway. Her husband, he was a Big Man. Ran a business, made plenty of money. They have houses all over the place, rented out. In Dhaka they have two flats. A big house in the village with concrete pillars. The husband was only the front man, though. The brains belonged to Mrs. Islam. She never kept purdah. She says she's 'adapted' now, that she has to walk outside because she's a widow. All rubbish. Even if she stayed indoors she never kept purdah. Her husband would bring his associates home, and they would do their deals there. Mrs. Islam was always present. She kept in the back, serving and tidying. But she knew what they had come to talk about, and she pulled the strings. The handkerchiefs were how she did it. She signaled with them. Spotty one meant no. White one for yes. Lace edging for one-year contract. Plain muslin for two years. That's the sort of thing, anyway."

Nazneen bounced Raqib on her knee. He looked around as if to say, Do you mind? "Now it's just a habit she picked up."

"Yes," said Razia. "And no. There's still business to attend to. With her sons, this time."

"Import-export?" said Nazneen.

Razia shook her head. Nazneen waited. Her friend looked away. "What, then?" asked Nazneen.

"I'm not one hundred percent sure."

"What do you think?"

"I don't want to gossip."

This was news. "About what?"

"I don't know. I'd heard something before, but I didn't believe it. I talked to her the other week, and I think I believe it now. But I don't want to say anything."

Why had she, then? "All right," said Nazneen. "It's better left unsaid."

They caught the bus on the Mile End Road. The conductor was an African. "Look how fit he is," whispered Chanu. "So big. So strong. You see . . ." He paused awhile. Nazneen shrank in her seat. The baby looked around without comment. "They were bred for it. Slavery." He hissed the word, and the couple in the seats in front turned around. "That's their ancestry," said Chanu, abandoning the whisper. The bus began to move, and the noise of the engine stopped him from addressing all the passengers. "Only the strong survived that. Only the strong ones were wanted; they fetched the highest price. Commerce and natural selection working hand in hand."

Nazneen did not know what he was talking about. "If you say so, husband." She had begun to answer him like this. She meant to say something else by it: sometimes that she disagreed, sometimes that she didn't understand or that he was talking rubbish, sometimes that he was mad. But he heard it only as, "If you say so."

Chanu settled down in his seat. His elbow dug into her side but he did not notice. "Aah," he said, "it's the day." A puzzled look came over his face. "What shall I say when he opens the door?"

It was Nazneen's turn to be puzzled. Even her husband should be able to manage that. "Salaam aleikhum?" she ventured. She giggled and the baby pursed his lips.

Chanu looked like a man who had been startled from sleep. "Ha? Oh, ha! Yes, salaam and all that. What shall I say?" He chewed his lip.

Nazneen shrugged inwardly. She looked in her bag and checked that she had everything she needed for the evening: wipes, nappies, rattle, muslin cloth, banana, spoon, blankets, Raqib's pajamas. She would change him at Dr. Azad's house and let him sleep on her shoulder on the way home.

She stood the baby up on her knee so he could look out of the window with her. It was dark, and cozy with lampposts. The people were tucked into big coats, and steamed as they walked. Headlights and red rear lights turned the road into a crawling carnival. The bus bumped along. The shops were lit up still. Leather shops, dress shops, sari shops, shops that sold fish and chips and samosas and pizzas and a little bit of everything from around the world. Newsagents, hardware shops, grocers, shops that sold alcohol, shops whose windows were stacked with stools and slippers and cassette tapes and seemed to sell nothing but were always full of men in panjabi pajama, smoking and stroking their beards. Between the lights were black patches where the windows were boarded, or the For Sale signs were hung. A woman in a massive orange coat, zipped up to her white eyeballs, was darting in and out of traffic. She bunched her sari in one hand and held the other hand to her chest. The car horns worked together, goading her to run.

"I just don't know," said Chanu. "I think I will tell him straight off that I have brought a box of kalojam."

"If you say so, husband," said Nazneen. She had given up her domestic guerrilla actions. They annoyed only her. Besides which, the flat was becoming so cluttered, and the baby took up so much time, that it was as much as she could manage to keep her head above water. She had no time to mess about.

"It will be good. I'm looking forward to it." He smiled uncertainly, as if he were practicing a smile for the first time. He had on his green anorak. The one with the snorkel hood. His trousers were shiny at the knee, and the sole of one shoe (she noticed on the way to the bus stop) was coming unstitched. When they were first married he was, if not handsome, at least smart. He preened himself before he went to work. He kept two pens and one pencil in his breast pocket. He polished his shoes. He polished his briefcase. Those were the days when he talked of "when." When the promotion would come.

"I could say that we were just passing."

Raqib twisted around and made a lunge for his father's nose. Chanu surrendered. He allowed his nose to be pinched and his hair to be pulled. The baby wore a blue jacket with so many layers beneath that his arms were lifted, as if the air was thick enough for them to rest on. He showed his teeth, all four ivory chippings, and grunted. Nazneen slowly absorbed the information. Just passing. After all of Chanu's efforts they were not even invited. Why did her father marry her off to this man?

He just wanted to be rid of me, she thought. *He wanted me to go far away, so that I would not be any trouble to him. He did not care who took me off his hands. If I had known what this marriage would be, what this man would be . . . !*

What? What, then? I would have run away, like Hasina? I would have eloped with the sweeper? Hah. I would have wept on my wedding day. I did! I did weep. What good did it do?

She held Raqib in her lap and rocked him back and forth, although he was not sleepy. A sharp, hot smell came from behind as a new passenger sat down with a meal wrapped in paper. The light inside the bus was furred up. It buzzed and crackled and leaked a yellow pollution. Even Raqib's face looked sickly in this light. The bell rang twice, quickly and smartly, and it sounded impatient to get on. The bus ground along and the seats vibrated grimly, as if a tornado had passed just barely out of range.

It was her place to sit and wait. Even if the tornado was heading directly towards her. For her, there was nothing else to be done. Nothing else that God wanted her to do. Sometimes she wanted to get up and run. Most of the time she did not want to run, but neither did she want to sit still. How difficult it was, this business of sitting still. But there was nothing really to complain of. There was Chanu, who was kind and never beat her. There was Raqib. And there was this shapeless, nameless thing that crawled across her shoulders and nested in her hair and poisoned her lungs, that made her both restless and listless. What do you want with me? she asked it. What do you want? it hissed back. She asked it to leave her alone but it would not. She pretended not to hear, but it got louder. She made bargains with it. No more eating in the middle of the night. No more dreaming of ice, and blades, and spangles. No more missed prayers. No more gossip. No more disrespect to my husband. She offered all these things for it to leave her. It listened quietly, and then burrowed deeper into her internal organs.

Perhaps, she came to think, everyone has one. The trick was to ignore it. Turn your back on it. Like Amma. "I don't want anything from this life," she said. "I ask for nothing. I expect nothing." Hasina jumped up and down at that. "If you ask for nothing, you might get nothing!" But she had proved her mother's point. "How can I be disappointed?" It made sense to Nazneen. Only one thing was not clear. The cause of Amma's suffering.

"We will suffer in silence." Amma's sister paid a long visit in the summer of Nazneen's tenth year. The air was hot and wet, as if it had absorbed the sweat of countless bodies. It dripped also with scandal. Mustafa, the cowman, had become possessed. This little man, with his matchstick arms and legs, a walking splinter, had kidnapped a girl from a neighboring village and taken her into the jungle for three days and nights.

"In silence," said Amma. Her sister spat thoughtfully and inspected the proceeds. The two women sat inside away from the sun. Nazneen stood in the doorway in a lozenge of light.

What were they suffering? Nazneen wanted to ask. Her father was not the richest man in the village, but he was the second richest.

"That is all that is left to us in this life," said Auntie. She had clung to Amma when she arrived and the two of them wept so long and so hard that Nazneen feared that someone had died. Nazneen preferred Mumtaz, Abba's sister, who was not one for crying and who made herself scarce during these long visits.

"We are just women. What can we do?"

"They know it. That's why they act as they do."

"God has made the world this way."

"I told him I will not go back."

"That's what you said."

"If he carries on this way, that's it."

"You said it last time as well."

"What else can I do?"

The conversation went on, circling around and around, and Nazneen listened, breathing quietly and hoping that if they forgot about her they might reveal the source of their woes. It was something to do with being a woman, of that much she was sure. When she was a woman she would find out. She looked forward to that day. She longed to be enriched by this hardship, to cast off her childish baggy pants and long shirt and begin to wear this suffering that was as rich and layered and deeply colored as the saris that enfolded Amma's troubled bones.

Hasina tugged her away and they raided the store for tamarind sauce and henna. They stuck their fingers in the tamarind and sucked it off, like sweet-and-sour toffee. They drew circles and stars on their palms with the henna, and then smudged them doing handstands in the dust. Hasina plaited Nazneen's hair and Nazneen made two thick braids of Hasina's hair and wound them on top of her head. Hasina looked like a princess. Her face was flawless, symmetrical, mythical. She hardly belonged to this world. A lotus on a dung heap. She was not made to suffer.

That afternoon, when the rest of the village was drugged by the sun and stretched out on chokis, bedrolls, or the ground to sleep it off, Nazneen was not tired. She walked around the pond and stepped over the silvered back of a snake, which slid into the water and itself became a glittering ripple. She climbed a little way up an amra tree and wedged herself into a forked branch to look out across the flat fields. The closer ones were lavish green, dense and deep, but the far fields filled with gold jute were slick as mirrors. The sun polished them until they shone. She wondered if, when she married, she would have to go as far away as those fields. She thought she would not like to go that far. Then she got down and walked a little way along the track that led to the school that took students from the three nearest villages. Her sandals made clouds of dust and a haze of mosquitoes blackened the air over a gully. The shirt stuck to her back and her face was wet, as if she walked in an invisible shower.

Only the mosquitoes moved. The birds slept. Even a mighty dragonfly that had tumbled onto the track lay stunned in the heat, wings aglow.

"Psssh!"

Nazneen turned around. She turned back again.

"Psssh!"

There was a dead man tied to a tree. His wrists were lashed to a branch and his feet dangled a few inches above the ground. His head fell forward, as if his neck were snapped. "Come closer," he croaked. Nazneen heard herself swallow. She felt the saliva trickle down the back of her throat. The man wore a tattered white loincloth. His legs were hinged with joints that were much too large. His ribs looked like a chicken carcass. It was Mustafa the cowman, and he was not quite dead.

She stepped closer to the tree. Silence. She walked forward again. Still nothing. Only when she was close enough to smell him did he speak again. He raised his head this time. His eyes stood out of his face and the corners of his lips were caked with something white. "Untie me. Good girl." He spoke as if he had enjoyed their game but it was time for the prank to end. Nazneen put her hand against the tree trunk. She could not see any way to climb the tree to reach his wrists. She did not know if she would climb it anyway. Mustafa was being punished. "Roll a rock over here then. Or a log, that will be lighter. Put it beneath my feet." His voice cracked and broke, but he sounded angry with her now. His head dangled again, and she heard him rasp out his breaths. She walked around the tree and sat down on a stump. From the back, Mustafa looked like a wooden puppet with some broken strings. She wondered if he would die as she watched and whether she would know when he died. She did not want him to die, but it did not seem possible to intervene in such a momentous event. It occurred to her that people might be angry if she freed this man who was being punished, but that was not what stayed her hand. Matters of life and death were simply beyond her scope.

After a while, when her backside was numb from sitting and she was beginning to get thirsty, she thought of something she could do for him. She would go and fetch some water. Mustafa appeared to have fallen asleep. She shook him by the ankle and he moaned. "I'm going for water," she said. "I can bring you some coconut ice as well," she added.

She set off at a run and decided that if Mustafa was still alive when she got back, she would find a way to climb the tree and let him down. If he is still alive, she reasoned, then he has survived anyway and I won't be spoiling anything. She would let Hasina in on the secret if she could find her, but she would not tell Amma. If Abba was there she would not look at him in case he read something in her face. He might have ordered the punishment. She did not want to be punished as well.

Three men passed her on the track, carrying lathis. One was the brother of the man from the next village whose daughter had been kidnapped. They laughed and joked as they went by and swung their big sticks cheerfully, as if they were off to play cricket. When Nazneen turned around she saw them gather by Mustafa's tree, three small blank figures in the distance doing a slow dance with one spinning partner.

They had come to a small front garden paved with multicolored flagstones in random shapes and sizes, as if a huge vase had been dropped from a great height and the shattered fragments had landed directly in front of the house. Beneath the window a plaster goose in a red spotted bonnet peered into the darkness. Just to the side of the door a three-foot-high policeman bowed his jolly legs and faked a smile. Other figures crouched in the gloom, outsize animals and stunted humans. The house itself gave nothing away. The lights were lit and the curtains were drawn.

"A substantial property," said Chanu. He spoke in a whisper. "This area is very respectable. None of your Sylhetis here. If you see a brown face, you can guarantee it's not from Sylhet."

Nazneen held Raqib on her hip. She wondered if Chanu would ring the doorbell, or whether they would just leave again and get on the bus.

"We won't stay for very long," said Chanu. "We'll say a few words and then go." He pressed the doorbell and it played a startling tune. "Of course, if they ask us to stay for dinner, I don't mind."

The door swung out. A woman in a short purple skirt leaned against the doorpost. Her thighs tested the fabric, and beneath the hemline was a pair of dimpled knees. Her arms folded beneath her breasts. A cigarette burned between purple lacquered nails. She had a fat nose and eyes that were looking for a fight. Her hair was cropped close like a man's, and it was streaked with some kind of rust-colored paint.

"Yes?" she said, in English.

"I think we have the wrong house," Chanu muttered to Nazneen.

"Who you looking for?" said the woman, in Bengali this time.

"I beg your pardon. We were looking for Dr. Azad. Would you be able to point out his house?"

"I can point it out all right," said the woman. "I'm standing right in it."

Chapter Five

She showed them into the sitting room, where a pair of snarling tigers guarded a gas fire. Nazneen sank inside a large gold sofa. Chanu placed his box of kalojam on a gilded, claw-footed table and stood with his arms behind his back, as if afraid he might break something. Raqib clapped his fat hands to summon the servants who were surely lurking in the kitchen.

Mrs. Azad stubbed out her cigarette in an ivory dish. She adjusted her underwear with a thumb and a wiggle of her opulent backside. "One minute," she said, and strode to the hallway. "Azad!" she screeched. "You've got visitors."

Nazneen exchanged a glance with her husband. He raised his eyebrows and smiled. She smothered a giggle on Raqib's cheek.

Mrs. Azad climbed inside an armchair. She tucked her feet up and her skirt rode up her large brown thighs. Chanu swayed a little. Nazneen eyed the curtains: miles of velvet swagged with gold braid, enough material to wrap up a tower block. Chanu cleared his throat. Mrs. Azad sighed. She tucked her fingers in her armpits and squeezed her breasts. The baby wriggled and Nazneen put him down on the thick cream carpet, where he coughed up some of his supper. Nazneen put her foot over the spot.

Gradually, Nazneen became aware that Chanu was staring at something over her shoulder. When she turned her head she saw that Dr. Azad was standing in the doorway. The two men appeared to be frozen. The doctor was as neat as a tailor's dummy. He held his arms smartly to his sides. White cuffs peeped out of his dark suit. His collar and tie held up his precise chin and his hair was brushed to an ebony sheen. He looked as if he had seen a ghost. Nazneen looked at Chanu. He made a poor ghost, in his broken-down shoes and oversize green anorak.

"For the love of God!" said Mrs. Azad. "Get your friends some drinks. I'm the one who's been on my feet all day." She pushed her breasts higher up her chest. "I'll have a beer."

That stirred them. "We were just passing," Chanu explained, in a rush, as if he had just remembered his line.

Dr. Azad rubbed his hands. "I'm delighted to welcome you. I'm, ah, afraid we have already had our meal, otherwise—"

"You'll stay for dinner," his wife cut in. She challenged Nazneen with her battle-hard eyes. "We've not eaten yet."

Dr. Azad rocked on his toes. "Not eaten as such. We've had some snacks and so forth."

They ate dinner on trays balanced on their laps. An unidentified meat in tepid gravy, with boiled potatoes. It was like eating cardboard soaked in water. Mrs. Azad switched on the television and turned the volume up high. She scowled at Chanu and her husband when they talked and held up her hand when she wished to silence them altogether. She drank a second glass of beer and belched with quiet satisfaction. Her husband had brought orange juice at first, and she jumped up in her chair as if she would strike him. Dr. Azad drank two glasses of water in his exact manner. He used his knife and fork like surgical instruments. Nazneen chased the soggy mess around her plate and clenched her stomach to try to stop it growling.

"I'll join you," said Chanu to Mrs. Azad, "in a beer." He made the offer as if he were proposing to lend her a kidney. She shrugged and kept her eyes fixed on the screen.

My husband does not say his prayers, thought Nazneen, and now he is drinking alcohol. Tomorrow he may be eating pigs.

"Of course, all the Saudis drink," said Chanu. "Even the royal family. All hypocrites. Myself, I believe that a glass every now and then is not a bad thing."

"As a medical man, I do not recommend it. As for the religious aspect, I hold no opinion."

"You see," said Chanu, in the voice of a man who has deliberated long and hard, "it's part of the culture here. It's so ingrained in the fabric of society. Back home, if you drink you risk being an outcast. In London, if you don't drink you risk the same thing. That's when it becomes dangerous, and when they start so young they can easily end up alcoholic. For myself, and for your wife, there's no harm done." He looked over at his hostess but she was engrossed in a scene of frantic and violent kissing. Chanu still had his coat on. He perched on a chair with his knees wide and his ankles crossed. He looked like the gardener who had come in to collect his wages.

Not for the first time, Nazneen wondered what it was that kept bringing Dr. Azad to see Chanu. They were an ill-matched pair. Perhaps he came for the food.

"We will be in Dhaka before Ruku is in any danger. I've drawn up plans for the house, did I tell you? Very simple, very classical in design. I intend to be the architect myself."

"Yes," said the doctor, "why not be an architect?"

"Exactly. What is the point of paying out to someone else?"

"Be an architect. Be a designer. Be a rocket scientist."

Chanu looked puzzled. "Design I could consider, but in science I confess I have very little background." He spread his hands modestly, "Anyway, I don't quite have sufficient funds for the house yet."

"Ah, but when the promotion comes . . ." Dr. Azad sat rigid on a stiff-backed chair. He held on to the arms as if he were trying to squeeze blood from them. Since the business with the drinks he had not looked at his wife one single time.

"I have been at the council too long. Long service counts for nothing. The local yogi doesn't get alms. But I have some things in the pipeline. One or two ventures I'm developing. The furniture trade, antiques, some ideas for import-export. They're cooking away slowly. The problem is capital. If you don't have money, what can you do?"

The doctor smiled in his peculiar way, eyebrows up, mouth down. "Make some?"

"I don't need very much. Just enough for the Dhaka house and some left over for Ruku's education. I don't want him to rot here with all the skinheads and drunks. I don't want him to grow up in this racist society. I don't want him to talk back to his mother. I want him to respect his father." Chanu's voice had grown impassioned. Mrs. Azad tutted and held up her purple-taloned hand. Chanu assumed a loud whisper. "The only way is to take him back home."

A girl walked in and stood with her hands on her hips in the middle of the room. She had inherited her mother's sturdy legs, but her skirt was shorter by a good few inches. She spoke in English. Nazneen caught the words *pub* and *money.* Her mother grunted and waved towards Dr. Azad. The doctor quivered. He spoke a few sharp words. His shoulders were up around his ears. Chanu shifted in his chair and coughed. The girl chewed gum. She twiddled the stud on her nostril, like a spot she was about to squeeze. Her hair was discolored by the same rusty substance that streaked her mother's head. She repeated her request. Chanu started to hum. The back of Nazneen's neck grew warm. The doctor began to speak but his wife threw up her hands. She struggled out of her armchair and fetched a handbag.

The girl took the money. She looked at Nazneen and the baby. She looked at Chanu. The doctor gripped his seat. His feet and knees pressed together. His helmet hair held a circle of light. He would never let go of that chair. It was the only thing holding him up. The girl tucked the money into her blouse pocket. "Salaam aleikhum," she said, and went out to the pub.

Mrs. Azad switched off the television. Let's go, thought Nazneen. She tried to signal with her eyes to Chanu, but he smiled vaguely back at her. "This is the tragedy of our lives. To be an immigrant is to live out a tragedy."

The hostess cocked her head. She rubbed her bulbous nose. "What are you talking about?"

"The clash of cultures."

"I beg your pardon?"

"And of generations," added Chanu.

"What is the tragedy?"

"It's not only immigrants. Shakespeare wrote about it." He cleared his throat and prepared to cite his quotation.

"Take your coat off. It's getting on my nerves. What are you? A professor?"

Chanu spread his hands. "I have a degree in English literature from Dhaka University. I have studied at a British university—philosophy, sociology, history, economics. I do not claim to be a learned gentleman. But I can tell you truthfully, madam, that I am always learning."

"So what are you then? A student?" She did not sound impressed. Her small, deep-plugged eyes looked as hard and dirty as coal.

"Your husband and I are both students, in a sense. That's how we came to know each other, through a shared love of books, a love of learning."

Mrs. Azad yawned. "Oh yes, my husband is a very refined man. He puts his nose inside a book because the smell of real life offends him. But he has come a long way. Haven't you, my sweet?"

He comes to our flat to get away from her, thought Nazneen.

"Yes," said the doctor. His shirt collar had swallowed his neck.

"When we first came—tell them, you tell them—we lived in a one-room hovel. We dined on rice and dal, rice and dal. For breakfast we had rice and dal. For lunch we drank water to bloat out our stomachs. This is how he finished medical school. And now—look! Of course, the doctor is very refined. Sometimes he forgets that without my family's help he would not have all those letters after his name."

"It's a success story," said Chanu, exercising his shoulders. "But behind every story of immigrant success there lies a deeper tragedy."

"Kindly explain this tragedy."

"I'm talking about the clash between Western values and our own. I'm talking about the struggle to assimilate and the need to preserve one's identity and heritage. I'm talking about children who don't know what their identity is. I'm talking about the feelings of alienation engendered by a society where racism is prevalent. I'm talking about the terrific struggle to preserve one's sanity while striving to achieve the best for one's family. I'm talking—"

"Crap!"

Chanu looked at Dr. Azad, but his friend studied the backs of his hands.

"Why do you make it so complicated?" said the doctor's wife. "Assimilation this, alienation that! Let me tell you a few simple facts. Fact: we live in a Western society. Fact: our children will act more and more like Westerners. Fact: that's no bad thing. My daughter is free to come and go. Do I wish I had enjoyed myself like her when I was young? Yes!"

Mrs. Azad struggled out of her chair. Nazneen thought—and it made her feel a little giddy—*She's going to the pub as well.* But their hostess walked over to the gas fire and bent, from the waist, to light it. Nazneen averted her eyes.

Mrs. Azad continued. "Listen, when I'm in Bangladesh I put on a sari and cover my head and all that. But here I go out to work. I work with white girls and I'm just one of them. If I want to come home and eat curry, that's my business. Some women spend ten, twenty years here and they sit in the kitchen grinding spices all day and learn only two words of English." She looked at Nazneen, who focused on Raqib. "They go around covered from head to toe, in their little walking prisons, and when someone calls to them in the street they are upset. The society is racist. The society is all wrong. Everything should change for them. They don't have to change one thing. That," she said, stabbing the air, "is the tragedy."

The room was quiet. The air was too bright, and the hard light hid nothing. The moments came and went, with nothing to ease their passing.

"Each one has his own tragedy," said Chanu at last. His lips and brow worked feverishly on some private business. Raqib thought this conclusion unsatisfactory. He gazed at his father with cobralike intensity, and then he began to cry.

"Come with me," said Mrs. Azad to Nazneen. "I've got something for the baby." In the bedroom, she looked at the back of a cupboard and pulled out a chewed teddy bear. She tried to interest the baby but Raqib just rubbed his eyes and rolled off to sleep. Nazneen changed his nappy and put his pajamas on. He did not wake. Mrs. Azad smoked a cigarette. She stroked Raqib's head with one hand and smoked with the other. Watching her now, Nazneen felt something like affection for this woman, this fat-nosed street fighter. And she knew why the doctor came. Not for the food, not to get away from this purple-clawed woman (although maybe for these things as well), not to share a love of learning, not to borrow books or discuss mobile libraries or literature or politics or art. He came as a man of science, to observe a rare specimen: unhappiness greater than his own.

She woke from a dream. Hasina, in the garment factory, ironing collars in place, laughing with the girls. Hasina laughing with the girls, ironing her own hand. Hasina, laughing on her own, ironing her face.

The baby was hot. His head was burning. Even in the dark, she could make out the flushed patches of his cheeks. For a while she lay with his curled hand in hers. Moonlight shredded the curtains and streaked the wall. Chanu breathed through his mouth and sent a stale breeze across his family. The wardrobe squatted like a large and ugly sin beside the bed. Two more chairs, in pieces, were stored within its belly. The alarm clock winked its red eye. Nazneen sat up and put Raqib against her chest. She kissed the place of infinite softness at the back of his neck. She felt his boneless body mold to hers. This was all. This took the place of everything and drove out questions.

The realization itself stole the moment from her. She lifted the baby and held him out, expecting him to wake so that she could then settle him back to sleep, reassured.

Raqib's head hung forward. Nazneen scrambled out of bed and took him into the hallway. She flicked on the light. "Baby," she said. "Wake up." She tickled him on the cheeks, under the chin, beneath the arms. "Raqib," she said sternly. "Wake up now."

Chanu appeared, scratching in between his legs. His hair stood on end and his stomach fought free of his pajama shirt. The baby opened his eyes and looked ready to make some urgent inquiries into the situation.

But he was kidnapped suddenly by sleep and seemed to make a willing hostage. A smile twitched his cheeks.

"What is it?" said Chanu.

"He's sick. I can't wake him."

"Let me try. Here, Ruku, time to get up. Open your eyes. Ruku! Ruku! What's wrong with him? Raqib! What's happened? Why does he not wake? Why doesn't he wake?"

Chapter Six

The city shattered. Everything was in pieces. She knew it straightaway, glimpsed it from the painful-white insides of the ambulance. Frantic neon signs. Headlights chasing the dark. An office block, cracked with light. These shards of the broken city.

At the hospital she felt the panic. Lobby doors crashing, white coats surging, bright trolleys clanging, coffee machine snarling. She ran with her son, carried him down long corridors while the walls fled before them. And then they took him out of her hands.

Raqib lay in the glass-walled cot like a flower that had been held inside a fist and released, not crushed but crumpled. His arms were wrongly arranged, the skin around his mouth puckered, and the area beneath his ribs hollowed out.

Nazneen pressed her fingers against the incubator. He was the center. The world had rearranged itself around this new core. It had to. Without him, life would not be possible. He was on the inside and all else looked in. The nurses and doctors who rustled and sighed, and bunched around. The hospital building with its smothering smells, its deathly hush and alarming clangs. The crystal towers and redbrick tombs. The bare-legged girls shivering at the bus stop. The hunched men and gesticulating women. The well-fed dogs and bloated pigeons. The cars that had screamed alongside the ambulance, urging it on, parting in waves.

And the city itself was just a glow on the dark earth, beneath the heaven that bent down to touch the troubled oceans, and he was beside her but no longer of her and the noise that filled her head and heart and lungs was so great that if she but opened her mouth the windows, the walls, could not withstand it.

For three days Chanu ate only cheese sandwiches from the canteen. On the fourth day he went home and cooked rice, and potato and cauliflower curry. He brought the food in flat round tins to the hospital and they ate in the room set aside for the refugee families of the gravely ill. The warm, heady smell of spices blanketed the air, twitched noses and lifted heads.

A gaunt old couple, who held hands and whispered together all day as if making an infinitely complex suicide pact, halted their plans for a while and stared openly. A teenage boy, who came to be with his mother and hand her paper tissue after paper tissue, sat up straight to get a good look. The whiskered man with the flat, blank eyes of a bandicoot rat, who came alone and slept beneath the chairs, slowly licked his lips.

Nazneen ate and ate. She scraped the tins clean and put them on the floor. "I should have brought more," said Chanu. He closed a hand around her wrist.

"Yes. Next time, bring more."

"Do you want to go home for a while?"

"No. I won't go yet."

"I brought some things for you. Socks, soap, whatever I could find."

"His blanket?"

"I've got it."

"He needs his special blanket."

Nazneen thought about getting up. She would wait until Chanu released her, so that she did not pull away from him. She did not want to pull away from him.

"A letter came from home," said Chanu. His chin was gray with stubble and his hair—without coconut oil—lay like clumps of molted fur. He spoke only a little and his voice was as soft as clay.

"Hasina!"

"No, no. A letter from one of my relatives. A begging letter."

"Another."

"I have not heard from this man in nearly twenty years. When I left he was a young policeman with enormous mustaches, and he was feared far and wide."

A doctor opened the door and spoke to the teenager's mother. She blew her nose and handed the sodden tissue to the boy. As she left with the doctor she glanced back at the room as if it had betrayed her. The boy sniffed. He slipped so low in his chair, he threatened to fall off. Chanu tightened his grip on Nazneen's wrist.

"I've heard about him from time to time. He built himself a big house with all the bribe money, and he rose through the ranks. He had four or five servants and his wife gave the best parties. Not only that. He imported an American car. Chrysler or Chevrolet, something like that. It was talked about all over town."

Nazneen smiled at her husband. For now, he was speaking only to her. There was no one over her shoulder. The audience had finally gone home. She put her free hand briefly across his round cheek. To touch like this was permitted here, among these stateless people, where the rules were unknown and in any case suspended.

"Now it looks like the bribe money has dried up. He's too old to wield the stick. Or he's been kicked out altogether. It's not clear what has happened. But now he only has one servant, and he is in need." Chanu let her go. He rubbed his thighs. "He asks me, in the name of God, not to let his family suffer. He asks only for them, not for himself."

"Don't answer it," said Nazneen. He read these letters over and over. He spent longer on the replies than he ever spent on his studies, and most often left them in the drawer. "Just throw it away."

"He just has the one servant now."

Nazneen felt a bubble of laughter rise from her belly. She let it out behind her hand. "Don't let his family suffer," she said, choking.

Chanu pressed his woolly eyebrows together and looked at her. She could not stop. He smiled. She felt the others looking at them, the strange brown couple who laughed and smiled. With the end of her sari, she wiped at her eyes.

There was a mask across Raqib's face. It brought him oxygen because, Chanu explained, he needed something purer than air. Needles stuck into his arms like great javelins, and wires and tubes sprung around him, thick as coiled rope. Raqib spread his tiny limbs wide. The rash that had nearly killed him, those little red seeds, was not so livid now. The marks had changed their shape and color, and spread beneath his creamy skin like crushed berries. His arms reached across the cot. His face was screwed into a determined ball. Nazneen thought of a game she played with Hasina, leaning into the wind that whipped off the lake and held them in a ragged embrace, flapping at their baggy trousers and holding up their arms.

Raqib was still asleep. Sometimes he opened his eyes but they were not seeing eyes. Nazneen put his special blanket inside the cot. She settled in the hard molded plastic of the chair. Chanu sat on the other side, arms folded across his chest. Whenever a nurse walked by he half unfolded them and looked up.

Abba did not choose so badly. This was not a bad man. There were many bad men in the world, but this was not one of them. She could love him.

Perhaps she did already. She thought she did. And if she didn't, she soon would because now she understood what he was, and why. Love would follow understanding.

Some things had become clear in the long, halogen-lit nights and the slowly dissolving days. The din that had crashed around inside her, like a giant bee in a bottle, had gone. And the quiet that came in its wake was profound. Nazneen sat and watched her son, and watched her husband rattling around the place: fetching things and returning them, bumping into carts and nurses, questioning the doctors, accosting the cleaners, poring over charts and articles, dragging chairs out of place and back again, going for coffee, going for tea, collecting the undrunk cups and spilling them on the way to the sink.

Her irritation with her husband, instead of growing steadily as it had for three years, began to subside. For the first time she felt that he was not so different. At his core, he was the same as her.

All the while, when Nazneen turned to her prayers and tried to empty her mind and accept each new thing with grace or indifference, Chanu worked his own method. He was looking for the same essential thing. But he thought he could grab it from outside and hold it against his chest like a shield. The degrees, the promotion, the Dhaka house, the library, the chair-restoring business, the import-export plans, the interminable reading. They were his self-fashioned tools. With them he tried to chisel out a special place, where he could have peace of mind.

Where Nazneen turned in, he turned out; where she strove to accept, he was determined to struggle; where she attempted to dull her mind and numb her thoughts, he argued aloud; while she wanted to look neither to the past nor to the future, he lived exclusively in both. They took different paths but they had journeyed, so she realized, together.

"He's going to be all right now," said Chanu.

"I know."

"We'll take him home soon."

"As soon as he's ready."

"I thought it was all finished."

"I know," she said, and knew that she would never have allowed that.

Though she spent hours sitting at the cotside she was not just sitting. Her hands lay folded in the pleated lap of her sari, hard brown knuckles against the soft pink. She was as still as a mongoose entranced by a snake. Stiller than a storm-cleared sky. But more animated than ever before. She willed him to live and he did. In the quiet she realized many things, most of all that she was immensely, inexplicably, happy.

Nazma and Sorupa came and rested ten fingers each on the sides of the cot.

"It has pleased God to make all my children strong and healthy," said Nazma. "The fourth one also. I feel his legs. So strong!" She rubbed her round belly.

Nazneen looked at her. Another child was coming, but with Nazma it was not easy to tell. The pregnancies came and went but the roundness always stayed.

Sorupa said, "Also it pleases Him to make my children in fittest and healthiest of disposition."

Nazma touched her fingers to Raqib's forehead. She glared at Sorupa. "What is wrong with you? Have you come to gloat and boast at the sickbed?"

Sorupa nibbled her lip and looked away.

Jorina came on her way to work and could stay only a few moments. She said, "I can sit with him at night, let you rest. These days I don't sleep so well. It would be no bother."

In the family room, Razia clasped Nazneen against her hard chest. "You are in an agony, I know. My sister's third child, peace upon his soul, died after a long illness. The illness was the worst part. When they are gone they are gone, but when they are ill you suffer with them."

"I am sorry for your sister. But I am OK."

Razia looked sideways at the old couple who faced each other and held hands. "This woman is the bravest one you will ever see. In her youth, she wrestled crocodiles." She looked at Nazneen. "Shall I tell them in English now?"

"I'm glad you came."

"Listen, I've got something for him. For when he's a bit older." She jiggled a man doll from a plastic bag. "He can pull the head off this one all by himself."

"I won't let him. I'll keep it until he knows better. Give my respects to your husband."

Razia pulled down her headscarf. She rubbed at her strong jaw. Now that she wore trousers she sat like a man, right ankle resting across left knee and the big black shoe nodding up and down. "I can't. We are not speaking. We are arguing. We are having, in fact, an unspoken argument."

"Then how will you know who has won?"

"That son-of-a-bitch!"

"Razia—"

"He works all day and night. He keeps me locked up inside."

"You go out. You came here, to the hospital."

"If I get a job, he will kill me. He will kill me kindly, just one slit across here. That's the sort of man he is. For hours, for days, he says nothing at all, and when he speaks that's the kind of talk I get." She held on to her foot, restraining it from further bouncing.

"But you go out. You go to the college."

"The children are at school. What am I supposed to do all day? Gossip and more gossip. The children ask for things. Everything they see, they want. And I don't have money. Jorina can get me a sewing job, but my husband will come to the factory and slaughter me like a lamb."

"Talk to him." Nazneen watched the door open. She hoped it would be Chanu with more food from home. A nurse came in and touched the old couple lightly on their shoulders. They looked up at her with guilty faces. Enclosed in their sorrows, they had forgotten why they were here.

Razia pointed to the doll. "I might as well talk to him. My husband is so miserly he will not waste even words on me. Now he has the night job, driving around with animal carcasses. If he has anything to say, he says it to them." Razia blew hard out of her long nose, exhaling her anger. She uncrossed her legs and laced her fingers together. "Anyway, you don't want to hear my troubles. You have enough of your own."

"Raqib is getting stronger. I can feel it." It was possible now to leave him alone for a while. She had tamed the machines that stood guard by talking to them softly, like a mahout calms an angry elephant. *This is my son. This is my son. Take good care of him.* The machines no longer frightened her. In the night they purred like civets and their bellies lit up like fireflies. By day they droned with efficiency and the flat screens made lines and curves in modest shades of green.

"The next time I come I will be allowed to pick him up," said Razia. She smiled but she could not recover her temper. "I found out where the money goes. Shall I tell you? It goes to the imam. He is going to build a new mosque in the village."

"God will bless you."

"If he was God-conscious, I would not mind. But my husband is not God-conscious. Listen, is this how a God-conscious man acts?" Her husband was mean. It was getting worse. After much brooding in the kitchen, sorting through the shelves and cupboards, he denounced his wife as a wanton housekeeper. Too many jars, too many packets, too many tins. All shouting abundance, luxury, waste. There would be no more money until every last thing on the shelves was eaten. Now they were down to Sun Maid raisins and Sainsbury's Wheat Bisks. For three days the children had eaten only Wheat Bisks in water and handfuls of raisins. This will teach you, said the husband. Will teach you to buy Sun Maid, fancy packets, penny-waste here, penny-waste there. Tariq came home from school. Ma, Shefali going to the toilet nine times every day. She is getting ashamed to put her hand up.

Razia tackled him. Building mosques and killing your own children. Holy man.

He did not flinch. What you want me to do? Kill my own self, working and working, for you to spend it all on penny-thing here, penny-thing there and nothing to show at the end? I am working for bricks. When I am gone to dust, they will be standing.

Ha, she said, and whenever they crossed paths, the brick man!

Ask your father, she had told Shefali, ask him how many bricks he earn today. Shefali, twisting her hair, said, Abba, how many bricks you earn today? And landed on her back, and cried quietly into her mother's lap.

"Make it up with him," said Nazneen. "For the children's sake."

Razia paced the width of the room. A little bit of shin showed above her sock where her tracksuit leg had ridden up. Chanu would have no chance in a fight with Razia. But Razia's husband was big: broad with short, thick butcher's arms and his temples indented with fury. Nazneen had seen him only a few times. He was as silent as Razia said, but it was a silence charged with thunder that made the children creep away and muffled even Razia.

Razia did not answer. She swiveled and paced the long side of the wall, knocking down some leaflets from a shelf.

"Would you really work with Jorina? She has had problems. Everyone talked. Her children got into difficulties." Hasina was working, but Hasina had no choice. If she had a husband, or a father . . .

"We gossiped, of course," said Razia. She stood still, and for a moment the old glint reappeared in her narrow eyes. "We love to gossip. This is the Bangla sport." She came and sat next to Nazneen. "Listen, Jorina's children are no better or worse than the rest. Whatever trouble they're in, they're not the only ones. When I walked across the estate today, I saw a gang of boys—fifteen, sixteen years old—fighting. I called to them but they shouted abuse at me. Only a few years ago they would never speak like that to their elders. It's the way things are going."

"And they play their music so loud."

Razia began to smile. "You know, my husband has sent radios to all of his nephews and nieces. When he goes back home, he might get stones instead of praise."

"So he's not always a miser, then?" said Nazneen, anxious to draw some good out of the man.

"We only get what others don't want. There's a man at the doll factory—every few months he comes around with more junk and I faint with joy. When he comes, really, I'm just falling on my knees."

"You're saving him a trip to the dump," said Nazneen. "It's your good deed."

"Maybe I start charging him for each load, see how he likes that."

"Think what you're saving him on petrol."

"Another stepladder, tins of paint, two planks of wood. I should start a house-painting business."

"Keep you busy." Nazneen fought with a spasm of laughter. This was not the place for belly laughs.

"Keep my husband stubbing his toe when he gets up in the dark." She held her knees and inhaled loudly. "Honestly, sister, for myself I don't need anything. Have you heard me complain before? But the children suffer."

"What will you do?"

Razia looked serious. She spread her hands and examined them as if they might spontaneously volunteer what they intended to do. "I tell you—"

Chanu came in carrying bags and the complicated smell of a high feast. He paused when he saw Razia, then offered a salaam that appeared to include her only by accident.

"Next time," said Razia, gathering her things.

"Eat with me," said Nazneen. She took the bags from Chanu and willed him to go away.

He cleared his throat and with great formality inquired about Mrs. Islam, her health in general, her hip in particular, and the continuing good fortune of her sons. Razia made brief, polite replies but sprawled over her chair in a manner unbecoming to a Bengali wife. His inquiries exhausted, Chanu stood ill at ease as if waiting for an invitation to be seated.

"Raqib," said Nazneen.

Chanu startled. He seemed about to run. "What?"

"Go and check on him," said Nazneen gently.

"Why don't I check on him?" He spoke with relief, and hurried away. One heel flapped loose where it had become unstuck. His trousers were so deeply creased at the knee-backs that the concertina effect was almost a style. She followed him to the door and whispered in his ear.

The rice was perfect. Fluffy white grains, each one separate from its neighbor. In the rainy season, back home, when the land had given way to water and the buffaloes grew webbed feet, when the hens took to the roofs, when marooned goats teetered on minuscule islands, when the women splashed across on the raised walkway to the cooking hut and found they could no longer kindle a dung-and-husk fire and looked to their reserves, when the rain rang louder than cowbells, rice was the means, the giver of life. Precooked, it congealed and made itself glue. Or fashioned itself into hard lumps that only worked loose inside the stomach, the better to bloat the innards and make even the children lie down and groan with satisfaction. Even then it was good. This rice was superb. Just the rice would be enough for her. But fresh coriander made her swoon for the chicken. The deeply oily aubergine beckoned lasciviously. She wanted to stick her tongue in the velvety dal. Chanu could cook. It had not occurred to her that, in all those years before he married, he must have cooked. And since, he had only leaned on the cupboards and rested his belly on the kitchen surfaces while she chopped and fried and wiped around him. It did not irritate her that he had not helped. She felt, instead, a touch of guilt for finding him useless, for not crediting him with this surprising ability.

"It's good," said Razia. "Save some for your husband." Nazneen was eating like a zealot. Razia put down her plate and spoon. "Something I didn't mention to your husband about Mrs. Islam."

"She hasn't called. I offended her. Chanu doesn't know."

"Something else he does not know."

"You didn't want to gossip about her."

"No." Razia lowered her heavy eyelids. She leaned in. The lashes curled up like insect legs and the lids squared off the tops of the irises, which were, Nazneen noticed now, spattered with gold lights deep down in the black. "It's not gossip. It is the truth." She paused awhile, the better to hook her audience. "The woman is a usurer."

"Tcha!"

"I check my facts. It is the truth. In the eyes of God, I say it again. The woman practises usury and she will be the companion of fire."

"How can you say it?" Nazneen was forced to put down her plate.

"Listen to me. I had my suspicions. I said something to her about money difficulties and she offered a loan. Nothing specific. Then I was not sure. I thought, maybe she offers loans from the goodness of her heart. Maybe she carries bundles of five-pound notes in that big black bag, just for handing out to poor people."

"Stop."

"I'm not joking. You know me, always willing to see the good side." She smiled like a jackal. "If you don't believe me, ask Amina. Ask her what interest she is paying. Thirty-three percent."

"Razia!"

"You look a little scandalized. I don't make scandal. I just report what I see. It's not me who is going to hell on the day we are judged."

"If she repents, God will forgive her."

"Repent? Mrs. Islam?" Razia dived in her bag and came up with a handkerchief. She pinched it between thumb and forefinger and waved it with her little finger cocked in the air. "When I was a girl, no one dared to offer such insults! The best family in all of Tangail, do you not know that everyone bows before us?"

Nazneen could not speak. She stared at her friend.

Razia's gaze slid around the room. Then she became brisk. "Amina could not make the last payment. If she doesn't come up with it next time, plus extra interest as punishment, the sons will break her arm. What kind of penance will God accept for this?"

"Who knows about it?"

Razia shrugged her large shoulders. "Some people. Perhaps many people. They are all hypocrites. That is the thing about our community. All *sinking, sinking, drinking water.*"

At the English words, the teenager—as flaccid in his chair as a virgin balloon—raised himself up a little and wasted a half-glance on Razia.

"You hear all sorts of things about the sons," Razia said. "But for all I know, those things are just rumor."

The boy rolled his head on the pimpled stalk of his neck and settled back. His mother looked at him as though this were the final straw and began to cry into the back of her hand.

"Time for me to go," said Razia. "Some things to do before I collect the children."

"Kiss them for me. Give my salaam to the estate."

"OK. I do it."

"Your English is getting good. Say hello to the tattoo lady from me."

"*Thank you.* But the tattoo lady is gone."

This was barely credible, even following the hard-to-swallow news of Mrs. Islam, which should have made anything seem possible.

"Gone to an institution," said Razia. She tapped at her temple. "At the end she was sitting in her own . . . you know."

"Oh," said Nazneen.

"Someone should have got to her sooner. Always sitting there in the window, like a painted statue. Did no one see?"

Chanu had brought her tasbee. She held the beads and passed them. *Subhanallah,* she said under her breath. *Subhanallah. Subhanallah. Subhanallah.* When she passed the thirty-third, her fingers loitered on the big dividing bead. She breathed deeply and plowed on. *Alhamdu lillah.* Thanks be to God. *Yes,* she thought. *But would He not wish me to return to my son now?* Her fingers raced through to the ninety-ninth.

There had been no chance to make her prayers in the usual way. She had offered up her personal, private pleas. Now she was giving thanks. It was God alone who saved the baby. It was His work, His power, not her own. Her own will, though it swelled like the Jamuna and flowed like a burst dam, was nothing as to His. She began the cycle again, pressing the mild wooden balls fiercely. *Subhanallah.* Glory to God. *Alhamdu lillah.* Thanks be to God. *Allahu Akbar.* God is great. She dropped the beads and they rolled beneath a radiator, out of reach.

With a long-handled dish cleaner, borrowed from the kitchen area, she poked the tasbee out and dusted it off. Perhaps it would be better if Chanu took it home, where it would be safe. Anyway, all the repetition made her feel drugged when she needed to be alert. It would be better if he took the beads home again.

From now on when she prayed it would be in a different, better way. She realized with some amazement that, while she had knelt, while she had prostrated herself and recited the words, she had never fully engaged in them. In prayer she sought to stupefy herself like a drunk with a bottle, like a fly against a lantern. This was not the correct way to pray. It was not the correct way to read the suras. It was not the correct way to live.

She had wanted to make a barren space inside. To stop the discontents, the bellyaches, the intemperate demands from breeding. To stop them setting up home. It was like curing a case of tapeworm by starvation. Entirely possible, and unavoidably lethal.

On the eighth day, out in the corridor, she made her silent classifications. Patient. Parent. Distant relative. Friend. Doctor. Nurse. Orderly. The adult patients were easy. They were the ones in slippers and slip-on, ill-fitting smiles. They smiled to show there was nothing to worry about, that they themselves were not worried, and that they were enjoying this healthful, restorative circuit walk of the sick lanes. Passing down the corridors of the children's wards, they smiled especially hard to signal their knowledge of just how lucky they were. The parents were easy too. Every dark imagining had come upon them, and their eyes and lips were pinched by shock. The worst of it—how shallow their imaginations had run. The other relatives and the friends were sometimes difficult to tell apart, except that the relatives trod more lightly while the friends took the burden of clowning, of bringing cheer and huge teddies, small chattering toys. Doctors wore their authority on their white coats and in their urgent, forbidding strides. Stop me now, and you put a life at risk. The nurses doled out nods and brief, encouraging smiles that ignited in the parents a look of expectancy, as if they had remembered something to say; on the tip of their tongue and gone again. Orderlies were a variegated bunch. They scowled and slouched along, they bustled like the doctors, they sang a fantastic kind of antimusic, howling out fragments and lapsing abruptly into silence.

Raqib's room was being cleaned. She waited outside and watched out for Chanu. Chanu had been to work this morning. The first time in over a week. Here he was. Scuttling along, turning at a right angle to pass a trolley and moving sideways like a big, soft-shelled crab. He came up next to her and leaned on the radiator. If there was a solid surface in sight, Chanu would rest against it. Mental toil, he said. That is the real exercise. No harder work than mental toil.

"They're just cleaning," she told him. "Won't be long."

"Ah," he said. He chewed on his lower lip, ejected it, and began to tug with his bottom teeth on the top lip.

She waited for him to speak again and grew uncomfortable when he did not. She had become used to his chatter filling up the space between them.

"Mrs. Islam," she began, and drew a breath.

"Sinking, sinking, drinking water."

So he knew.

"Some things have to stop."

"If she truly repents . . ."

"Enough is enough." Chanu wound himself forward and faced her, straight as a plane tree. "I will have to tell them."

"Who?"

"My relatives. They will have to know. Come clean. Stop the hypocrisy."

"Your relatives? Why should they know?"

Chanu smiled, his fat cheeks dimpled. His eyes darted here and there, looking for an escape route from this inappropriate face. He explained as if to a child. "All this time they thought I was rich. Why should I stay here in this foreign land, if it did not make me rich? I let them think it. It suited them and it suited me. Actually, I told them some things that are not true, have never been true. Made myself a big man. Here I am only a small man, but there . . ." The smile vanished. "I could be big. Big Man. That's how it happened." He sighed and placed his hands atop his stomach. "So when the begging letters come and I blame left and I blame right, what I should be blaming is this, right here." He moved his hands up over his chest, to show how his heart, his pride, had betrayed him.

Sinking, sinking, drinking water. When everyone in the village was fasting a long month, when not a grain, not a drop of water passed between the parched lips of any able-bodied man, woman, or child over ten, when the sun was hotter than the cooking pot and dusk was just a febrile wish, the hypocrite went down to the pond to duck his head, to dive and sink, to drink and sink a little lower.

"No," she said. "It is not a matter for blame."

"Action, then. It is a matter for action. All matters, in fact, are matters for action. Talking is finished. From now on, I act." He cleared his throat, a little like the old, talking Chanu. "Something else to tell you. I resigned today."

"What do you mean, resigned?"

"What do I mean? Are you against it? Have I not warned you repeatedly of my intention? I warned Dalloway and I warned you also."

"So. You did it then."

"There were some surprised faces, I can tell you." His own face looked ambushed, raided by dacoits. All this action was taking its toll. He chewed again on his lip and a split appeared, stained with a little red. "I'm clearing my desk in the morning."

"They can spare you so soon?"

He coughed and hawked, and Nazneen feared he would spit on the floor. He swallowed. "Of course not. But when I decide to do something, it is done. That's the way I am. From now on." He waggled his head and blinked slowly to show there was no turning back. "If who repents?"

"What are you saying?"

"You said, 'If she truly repents.'"

"I don't think so." An orderly came by, pushing a bucket along with a mop. He whistled loudly, but not loudly enough to cover his dejection. "I think they've finished his room. Let's go." The cleaner raised one corner of his mouth as she passed and made a noise that said that he really didn't know what the world was coming to, when he was the one to be standing there with a bucket and mop while everyone else enjoyed themselves. She turned to see Chanu marching after her, his head swiveling, eyes uselessly scanning, feet knocking over the bucket, and the cleaner—propped up by his mop—shaking his head in the dignified manner of a man deeply wronged.

Raqib was awake. "Bah," he said. Enough of this nonsense. He lifted his hands in front of his face and regarded them sternly. He made pincers, tested them for strength and flexibility and was satisfied. They were released. He rolled his head to the side. Nazneen cooed as he looked at her. She stroked the back of his head where the hair matted together, soft as cashmere. With a little finger she rubbed at his swollen gums, was pleased to be bitten by his little pearl teeth. Soon they would be home and he would stagger around the sitting room as if it were a ship's deck, clinging on, undaunted by the invisible storm that buffeted him from sofa to chair to table and back again.

"Going to buy an encyclopedia for you." Chanu leaned over his son and touched his leg. "Going to buy it for myself before you start asking too many difficult questions."

"I'll go home tomorrow. Make everything ready."

"Damn clever, this boy. See it in the size of the head."

"Encyclopedias are expensive."

"Not too expensive for this boy. Let's call it an investment. All books are investments. Can't you see what a good student he's going to be?" He began to hum, then broke into song.

"We are the strength, we are the force
The Band of Students that we are!
Under the pitch dark night, we stir out
Barefooted across the road
With obstacles strewn. The soil stiff
We render red with our crimson blood . . ."

He broke off. "All right. All right. No need for faces. We used to sing that at Dhaka University. It's a respectable song." He continued the tune, humming this time.

The baby slept. Nazneen directed her energy towards him and sat perfectly still. Chanu sat with his book. Nazneen thought of asking what they would do for money. What job he would get now. She watched him take off his shoe and his sock. He bent down to examine his corns, squeezed each one in turn, and said *ish* under his breath. For a few moments, the book caught his attention again, then he hummed for a while, drummed his fingers, sat looking at the air, the shoe and sock abandoned and forgotten.

She put her hand on Raqib's forehead. Just for the feel of him. To give him strength. Although, of course, only God gave strength. Whatever she did, only God decided. God knows everything. He knows the number of hairs on your head, don't forget. Amma said that when they went off to school. She called after them, shouting in her strangled voice. "He sees you, don't forget. He knows the number of hairs on your head." She thought about it. No, all that she had done for Raqib was nothing. God decided. She thought about How You Were Left to Your Fate. See! It made no difference. Amma did nothing to save her. And she lived. It was in God's hands. Raqib's chest rose and fell. He stirred and passed wind, which moved her deeply.

At once she was enraged. A mother who did nothing to save her own child! If Nazneen (her husband's part she did not consider) had not brought the baby to the hospital at once, he would have died. The doctors said it. It was no lie. Did she kick about at home wailing and wringing her hands? Did she draw attention to her plight with long sighs and ostentatiously hidden weeping? Did she call piously for God to take what he would and leave her with nothing? Did she act, in short, like her mother? A saint?

And something else Amma was wrong about. Childbirth is like indigestion! Yes, if a snake bites like an ant. Exactly the same. Nothing different.

No wonder, she thought and shocked herself by it, no wonder Abba went off for days. The tears flooded him out. They made him angry. Even at the burial he was angry. When he lowered her, legs first, the white winding sheet already spattered with mud, while the rain raced to fill the hole, he let her go too soon. Uncle held on and stopped her rolling on her back. Abba smacked his hands together. Blue lightning ripped open the stone sky as the prayer began, thunder took the words from the imam's lips, and the rain filled all their ears and eyes and mouths.

"Go and play," Mumtaz had said. "I'll bring you in to see her when I've finished." Hasina ran off, but Nazneen stayed. "All right then," said Mumtaz. "Make yourself useful. You are a woman now, after all." She gave Nazneen the brass dish to hold, while she dipped in a cloth and squeezed it damp. She lowered the sheet and washed Amma's face. Forehead, temples, cheeks, chin, over the eyelids, inside the ears, inside the nostrils. Her hand knocked against the top lip and the lip stayed curled and raised, revealing forever two of the melon-seed teeth that Amma, all her life, was so keen to hide. Sheet raised, she turned to her niece. "I don't know what your mother would say about it."

"Fate!" said Nazneen, and pinched the back of her neck.

Mumtaz looked at her. "About you being here."

The back of her neck was on fire. "Oh."

"Anyway. You are a woman now." Beneath the sheet she began to wash the right side of the upper body. She pulled out the arm and ran the cloth along it. "You mustn't think she died alone."

"Angels." She wished she had a way with tears. It seemed wrong. No one was crying. The village had lost its best mourner.

"They were with her, and God. The sari is ruined, of course. Her best one. The rest you can share out with Hasina." She washed the torso. As the sheet lifted, Nazneen saw her mother's breast lolling against her armpit. A rag, brown with blood, plugged the hole just to the left.

When Mumtaz dipped the cloth in the bowl, little blood crusts floated free and congregated around the edges.

Nazneen went to change the water. When she tipped out the bowl she couldn't help thinking it was a shame to be pouring a bit of her mother away.

"She always said," Mumtaz reflected, "that everything can be changed, like this." She snapped her fingers. "God has made His plans. I told her, 'Sister, but until He reveals them we have to get on by ourselves.' Well . . ." She sucked her teeth. "Now the plan is clear. It's come and gone. Puff!"

She was displeased with something. Nazneen stood up straight, hoping she looked as solemn as she was trying to feel. In truth, she felt bored by now and squeamish at seeing the body.

Mumtaz finished with the left foot (how yellow the toenails!) and began on the winding. She uncovered Amma's lower half, and Nazneen in spite of herself stared at this unprecedented nakedness. A loincloth went around her upper thighs and hips. Another cloth tied the first at the waist. A third sheet made a kind of short, straight dress and the next became a veil. "Oh," said Mumtaz. "The hair." She removed the veil and began to plait the hair, squatting behind the choki and sticking out her tongue in concentration. It was then that the rain started. Heralded the past few weeks by electric skies and air so hot it shimmered just out of reach and scorched the nostrils of those foolhardy enough to breathe, the rain was greeted with joy. It beat down on the tin roof, it hit the ground and bounced jubilantly up, it hurled great fat globs through the doorway. Nazneen, holding her bowl, watched as children ran outside for a shower. Squeaking, they flapped each other's wet shirts, rubbed at their hair. The adults came more slowly, feigning lack of interest, as if the allotted hour of their regular walk around the compound had arrived. Abba walked across the yard and the children scattered, holding each other back before this mighty and unpredictable presence. He reached out and patted a sodden-headed small boy. He smiled and the children began to move once more. Nazneen at last found her tears, and spilled them over the final, all-encasing winding sheet that it was Amma's fate to wear.

She woke with a stiff neck. The hospital was quiet. The room was dark except for the glow of the machines. Chanu was not in his chair and Razia was standing on the other side of the cot. Hair disarrayed, eyes the narrowest slits. Bony hands to her face, chewing on the knuckles.

"What is it?" cried Nazneen.

Razia put a finger over her lips. "Shush. Don't wake him."

"What is it?" This time in a whisper.

"Very beautiful," said Razia, leaning into the cot. "Much better at that age, when they don't answer back. My two, they need a good whipping." Her voice was breaking, but her eyes, as far as could be seen, stayed dry.

"Do you want tea?"

"Tea? No. I'm not having any more tea. All day there has been tea drinking." She shook herself to get rid of the thought.

"Come and sit with me."

Razia came around and sat. Her shoulders heaved. She pressed on her chest and pulled at her long nose. Her shoes knocked together. Finally, she said, "He is dead."

"What do you mean?" said Nazneen senselessly.

"My husband is dead. The work has killed him."

The rage, thought Nazneen. It killed him.

"At the slaughterhouse. They were going to load up, but there was an accident."

Nazneen tried to find words.

"Killed by falling cows. He was only alone a few moments and when they went back in he was underneath the cows. Seventeen frozen cows. All on top of him." She looked at Nazneen. Her mouth twitched. "This is how it ended," she added. "And the mosque not even built."

"The children . . ."

"At Mrs. Islam's." She shrugged slightly. "People came. Made tea, made wailing, and that sort of thing. I told them I wanted to be on my own. But when they had gone, I didn't want to be on my own with . . . you know. I kept thinking about those cows. So I came here."

Nazneen took hold of her hand and massaged it inch by inch, to rub away a little of the pain, to absorb some for herself. The machines purred with satisfaction and the screens played out their endless dance. Somewhere, behind walls, a woman shouted in indistinct anguish. The disinfected floor shone dully beneath their feet, and gave off its smell of neutered grief.

Razia groaned. "I can get that job now. No slaughter man to slaughter me now."

She walked into a lunatic's room. Signs of madness everywhere. The crushing furniture stacked high, spread out, jumbled up. Papers and books strewn liberally—lewdly!—over windowsills, tables, floor. Alarming rugs of every color, deviously designed to confuse the eye and arrest the heart. Corner cabinet and glass showcase panting with knickknacks. Yellow wallpaper lined up and down with squares and circles. The clutter of frames that fought for space on the walls. Someone, delirious, had wired plates to those same walls so that it appeared that the crockery was trying to escape.

How quickly she had grown used to the hospital. With a sigh, she realized how quickly she would grow used to this room again. She examined the nearest chair. She did not remember it. To get to the far end of the room she had to climb over the glass-topped, orange-legged coffee table. The cane-backed chair had had its bottom removed. Two lone hairy strings were rigged loosely across the hole. To the side lay a ball of twine and a pair of pliers. So the chair-restoring business had begun. She picked up the pliers, thinking they were dangerous to leave around with Raqib coming home so soon. She picked up three pens, a notebook, and a mug, then put them all down again to gather up a stray nappy, half a biscuit, and an empty cocoa tin that Raqib had used as a drum. *Let's be systematic,* she thought, and set everything on the floor. Have a bath first, then make space in the kitchen drawers, then tidy things away. If she was quick, there would be time to call on Razia. (*This is the tragedy,* Chanu had said. *Man works like a donkey. Working like a donkey here, but never made a go. In his heart, he never left the village.* Here, Chanu began to project his voice. *What can you do? An uneducated man like that. This is the immigrant tragedy.*)

Hanufa came to the door before Nazneen got to the bathroom. "I've been watching for you," she said. "I've brought some food."

Nazneen took the containers. "My husband has been cooking."

"I know," said Hanufa. "But I didn't know what else to bring."

Nazneen soaped herself with a bar of Pears, washed her hair with Fairy Liquid, and when she had finished, dusted between her toes with baby talc. In the bedroom, she stood in her underskirt and choli and looked through her saris. The wardrobe doors touched the side of the bed, making another black-walled room inside a room. A pair of Chanu's trousers lay on the floor of the wardrobe. Another pair draped over a chair that was wedged beneath the hanging clothes. She picked them up, stepped out of her underskirt, and put them on. To see herself she had to stand on the bed and look in the curly-edged dressing-table mirror. Then she could see only her legs, and ducked and twisted to try to gain an impression of the whole. She took the trousers off, put her underskirt back on, and hitched it up so that it stopped at the knees. Walking over the bedspread, she imagined herself swinging a handbag like the white girls. She pulled the skirt higher, and examined her legs in the mirror. She walked towards the headboard, turning her trunk to catch the rear view, a flash of pants. Close to the wall, eyes to the mirror, she raised one leg as high as she could. She closed her eyes and skated off. Ridiculous. Her leg wobbled. She opened her eyes and was thrilled by her slim brown legs. Slowly, she drew the left leg up and rested the heel on the inside of her right thigh. She tried to spin and got caught up in the bedspread, then fell on the mattress, giggling.

Now, she thought, where's the harm? She rolled over to wrap herself up in the bedcovers and decided to float free for a while. Nothing came to her mind. She stared at the ceiling. Remember to pack his hat, she thought. He'll need that for the journey home. Then nothing. The fridge needs cleaning. More toilet roll. She slapped the bed. Write to Hasina. That was better. Wash a few clothes out, before too much piles up. No, no, no. She pulled the covers over her head. "Ice e-skating," she said aloud. "Torvill and Dean." Still nothing. She got out of bed and dressed quickly. Then she found pen and paper and a book to rest on and sat down on the edge of the mattress.

My dearest sister, she began, and chewed on the end of the pen. *I am well and my husband also. Raqib was ill but now he is better*. She chewed some more. The thought of writing was always pleasant, but the process was painful. However much she thought of to tell, however the words flowed in her head as she performed her chores, despite the emotion that swelled and throbbed while the storylines formed, the telling was inevitably brief and blunt, a poor thing, stunted as a failed crop. *We took him to the hospital,* she wrote. *I was very sad, and then suddenly I was very happy, even before he was better. Soon I will bring him home*. She read it over. Then crumpled the page. On a fresh sheet she wrote: *My dearest sister, I hope you are well. Thank you for your letter. Raqib was very ill but better now. We took him to the hospital. A strange thing happened. I sat beside him and felt happy. Not happy for him to be ill, but happy about something inside myself. Chanu has given up his job. He is well. I hope you are well.*

She reviewed the composition, then crossed out the last sentence where she had repeated herself. She changed *but better now* to *but now he is better*. Then crossed out the part about being happy. She chewed on the end of the pen.

She would have to explain more carefully. She tried to think it through. What had made her so happy? She drew a face and made it smile. I fought for him. She added a matchstick body. Not accepting. Fighting. She drew a flower and gave it a long stem. Fate! Fate business. A bird, she attempted a bird, but it looked more like a coat hanger. I move my pen. This way. That way. Began an elephant and turned the back legs to a horse. Nobody else here. Nobody else moving this pen.

Now she wrote again. *My dearest sister, I hope everything is well with you.*

The baby has been sick in hospital, but we expect to bring him home soon. Chanu has given up his job. I do not worry, and you must not worry. When the baby is home, I will write again. A long letter next time. Pray God keep you safe.

She tidied the flat and tried to make some space in the sitting room by piling furniture. Once she had finished piling, she prodded the stacks and watched them wobble. Then she began unpiling. She worked quickly and rehearsed out loud asking the bus conductor for a ticket. Suddenly the thought came to her that she had killed Razia's husband. Raqib was meant to die, but she had forced Death away. Death was forced to choose again. "Be gone from me!" she shouted. "Be gone! Back to hell, where you belong." And with these words, banished the jinni that had danced, briefly, spitefully, through the room and into her head.

By the time she reached the courtyard she had forgotten the jinni. The sun was out and the now familiar, but still nameless, tree on the corner showed pale green buds. The grass, brave despite the odds, was attempting new growth. A fresh dog turd steamed gently on black tarmac. The concrete had been covered over, and the tarmac smelled of rubber and essence of car fume. It undermined the smell of shit, even when Nazneen stepped over the mess. Sun on her face felt good; she would have liked to feel it on her legs. When she passed a group of young Bangla men on the path, they parted and bowed with mock formality. One remained straight and still and she caught his look, challenging or denying. Another lad fell to his knees. Oh, oh. I'm dying. She's breaking my heart! Nazneen pulled her headscarf over her face to hide her lips, which flickered up at the corners and parted and twitched again.

Hospital, hospital, hospital. She had another English word. She caressed it all the way down the corridor. Chanu did not hear her come in, or he heard and did not turn around. She put her hand on his shoulder, and was surprised as always at how thin it was. There was a little spot on the top of his head, an angry little spot among the thin weeds of hair. He did not look up. Then she saw the empty cot. Raqib had been taken for more tests. "Gone?" said Nazneen.

"He's gone," said Chanu and looked up at her. His stomach pressed forward beneath his shirt.

"Don't worry. They won't take long. They'll give him back to us soon."

Chanu blinked. His eyes seemed more beleaguered than ever. "Will you wash him? I don't think I can wash him."

"I always give him his bath." Nazneen went to sit.

The room was quieter than usual, a quietness that rose somehow above the muted din of the hospital. The machines were off, that's what it was.

"Sponge bath," said Nazneen. "That's how I've been doing it."

Chanu's head hung forward. He did not talk. The action man was not talking. Neither was he doing. Nazneen regarded the plastic cups by the sink, the towels and clothes playing havoc on the pull-down bed where she and Chanu took turns sleeping. She sprang up. "Got to get this straight."

"God. God," Chanu moaned. "Leave it."

"Action man," she said, and remembered with a shiver Razia's words: brick man.

"He's not even cold yet! Your son is not even cold. Don't bloody tidy up."

"My son?" Now, even now, she refused.

Chanu squeezed at his eyes, and some water trickled down his cheeks so that he looked to be wringing out the tears. "We have to go and get him. They don't bring him back here."

They don't bring him back here. She was still holding the plastic cups. She picked up another and slotted it into her stack.

"They said they will release the body quickly. They said they know we are Muslim. They know, they said they know, about how quickly we like to bury our dead."

How quickly we like to bury our dead. She began folding clothes. She picked a stray thread from an undershirt, pulled fluff off a sweater. Chanu came to her and held her arms. He pried her fingers from Raqib's jacket. To get her to sit he had to push her onto the bed. She let him take her hand in his.

Yes, she would wash him. She brought him in and she would take him out. She had seen babies buried. In the village, babies were buried often. She could remember the funerals, one or two, of cousins who came into the world and left again promptly, as if they had wandered into a room by mistake, apologized, and turned back. Little white parcels popped inside a hole and covered with leaves or canes, so that the soil would not stain them, so they left as pristine as they entered. She remembered the burying; of the buried she retained nothing.

Chapter Seven

DHAKA, BANGLADESH

May 1988

God give comfort sister in your dark hour. I say Prayer of Light for you.

O God, place light in my heart, light in my tongue, light in my hearing, light on my right hand and on my left, light before me, light behind me, light above me and light below me. O God, who knows the secrets of our hearts, lead me out of the darkness and give me light.

His soul is in Heaven. I pray for you and for your loving husband.

Hasina

September 1988

Sister I have many thing to tell. New address in Narayanganj. Job in new factory I am machinist real woman job now.

Mr. Chowdhury tell to pack and not worry. "Pukka building" he say. "Bigger room." He bring in Toyota Land Cruiser. Air conditioning radio ashtray for cigarette and everything. He is father to me. Always he tells "Anything you need. Any time you in trouble. Come to me." This is kind of man. Everyone giving him respect.

When we come it is little bit trouble here. Old tenants they have not move. The woman give some abuse. In front of childrens she say foul words. Mr. Chowdhurys men help for them to go. Then I clean the room. These people bad tenants never single penny they have pay. Rent is more takas but is big room and it respectable district. Building look like this is long and low a veranda at front and another also at back. My room is at back. Behind is family two sons and three daughter. They have two room. Dawn prayer second I take the mat I hear them begin the happy arguments. Father passing me most days on road on way to work. Tiffin tin tied on his back and the young son sit in handlebars look smart like anything in school uniforms and ringing all the way the bell. Father is clerk at District Court. That is kind of neighborhood. We have concrete floor very smooth and walls will be plaster inside soon. My room have one wall is already half plaster.

All other room along back full from jute mill mens. Three four in one room. They cooking together at far end the veranda and I keep own area. Mr. Chowdhury say if they bother you come to me. I will break hands and legs. No one bothering me. Four five men each room but no mess at all. Half veranda has fence. Other half is stolen. Mr. Chowdhury tell to me secretly he thinking the old tenants burn for fuel. Jute men put washings over the top. All is so neat. Lungis undershirts pajama one end trousers and shirt keep together.

Railway line pass the building. How easy for the travel! Jute men they hear trains coming jump down from veranda run past coconut trees go down bank sliding and throwing their body onto train. Always stick on somewhere ledge ladder door handle something. This is how they getting to mill.

Today is hartal again. Some mens here sway in hammocks chew pan and spitting. Most gone for rally. Mr. Chowdhury say all these strikers lazy like hell and only making holidays. But all and every thing shut down on hartal day so I write everything coming to mind.

He have lot to say about strikers Mr. Chowdhury. But he is fair man. He say leaders are same all bad. Managers Judges Politicians Army Trade Unions all gone to bad. When he gets Government contract Mr. Chowdhury must do adding twenty-five percent for cover cost of pay the Minister and Civil Servant. He has supply electric parts for Power Grid. Also he make ceramic toilets and sink. Just think! If he putting the electricity and sink in this building! Maybe when walls finished plastering.

No end of corruption. It make him quite sad in an actual fact. You know he have birthmark over right eye and temple. It go red like fresh cut when he talk of these things. And also as well it itch. Then he begin twirling the cane he only doing when he upset. He has new cane. Ivory on tip and handle look like bird claw and what is made from? Handle if you can believe or if you cannot is gold. He look the gentleman with this cane.

The stories he have tell. One friend has bribe tax collector for receive tax form. Without bribe he will be jail. How to pay the tax without first the form? Mr. Chowdhury himself bribing to telephone company for get receipt. Is not enough only pay for telephones this paperwork is cost extra. Even President it seem fall in bad ways. His picture it was on wall in my room. I thinking to keep as picture do pretty up a wall so nice. But Mr. Chowdhury shouting like anything. "Ershad! You goonda!" Then he put on floor and stamp on it break glass. I keep frame maybe I can use later.

University is also close down. All students hold protest. They rallying for right to cheat. In my heart I support. Some who afford pay the professor for tutoring buy exam paper. To be fair all must have mean for equal cheating.

I waiting for your letter. I fill with joy of your husband new job. Already he speak of promotion. Many men this take long time years. I send such love it reach around whole world for you. God take care and give you more sons.

November 1988

My own sister what a beautiful room you live! At last I have see it after all many years asking. I putting photo on top of crate next to Raqib picture. When I have glass I think to put both inside frame. You never say about showcase corner cabinet wallpaper. It all ordinary like anything to you now. Every day I looking and think my own sister just there with showcase and corner cabinet and everything. Little bit worry comes only your arms too thin and face as well. But Zainab say it is fashion in London get thin.

Zainab is mother who live behind. She say "This building it get pull down. Look how close to railway track." She say Mr. Chowdhury is skinning alive with rent and soon they move. I tell her about plastering man is on the way but she suck teeth make sound like whistle. Not so friendly woman. Only words come out are complaint. Husband works at District Court she thinks she the Judge and Jury now. I have friends at work. Zainab say as she please.

I tell you about garment factory. Only half hour walk from here and it fine place. Eight o'clock is the start time. All must come few minute before and eight o'clock exact they unlock gate. If you come late it is trouble because they lock the gates after to keep safe. It have three room around courtyard all new solid concrete. One place is for machine. I go there. Another for cutting and finishing. Men go there. Small room for Manager and Paperwork and such like.

My machine so new and beautiful I hardly daring to touch and put my finger mark on. When I sitting down and start it know me for beginner and prick the thumbs. It purr like a cat now but only for me. Someone else use it then it show a temper and catch up all the cloths break threads. Aleya say if trees have spirit why not machine. Shahnaz say Aleya is country bumpkin and no ancestor of her worshipping trees and rock and thing. She do not say in front of Aleya. So kind and gentle this Shahnaz.

I am machine woman and things are different now. When I was helper run around with thread and cloth I was just girl. Even in spite I think I am woman long before. We all talk together in lunch break. Four in my row stick like sister. Aleya Shahnaz Renu and me. I tell you about them my other sisters. Aleya have five children she comes from Noakhali. All our lives we think Noakhalis never wash they smelly like jackfruits but I give my vow as a true fact Aleya do not smell. Money she make she send her boys to school. Husband make problem for her but Aleya thinking of children only and not the husband. The husband say "Why should you work? If you work it looks bad. People will say he cannot feed her." But Aleya keep dropping wishes into the rice. Pinch of salt pinch of what she want and at the end he giving in. He buy burkha for her and every day walking with her to factory. Evening there he is wait at gate.

Shahnaz is only bit older one two year than me and she gone very far along in school. Most day she talking about match. Parents have pick seven eight boys but Shahnaz refuse all. And she disagree to dowry. "Why should we give dowry? I am not a burden. I make money. I *am the dowry." We have grow close. She show me how she apply her cosmetics and she teach how to make eyebrows less ugly by pull out the hairs. She try some rouge on my cheek but wipe it off. My coloring is not good for rouge. It make look cheap.*

Oldest of us is Renu a widow. She was marry at fifteen to old man who die within three month. She go back to father short time he throw out. All the life she has work but she the one who do not wish for this. Despite she have only two teeth she eat anything at all. Hard gums she say. "I can break bricks on these gums." Every lunch hour she is chew betel nut. It ban but Renu have no care about it. I asking if she marry again. "Who will marry these bones?" She wave her arms but no bones showing is bracelets from wrists to elbow. "My life! My life! Over at fifteen. Might as well be Hindu. His grave was big enough for two. Why I did not jump in?" She spit too as well never mind spitting is ban. She say there is no one to protect me. I must go here and there always alone. Anyone say anything they like because I am woman alone. I put here on earth to suffer. I am waiting and suffering. This is all.

I really feeling for her. In her life she had no love. This is great wrong.

But sometime she remind of Amma and then I must find reason to go away from her.

So shame your husband job is not good like he expecting. Skill man like him he find another quick no time at all.

January 1989

Sister so often I read your letters the paper wear out. How short these letter I have most by heart. Last one hardly is start and end come. You are cast down. I feel it. Thinking and thinking what to do. You say the friend has sewing job. Why you not also get this sewing? Wait for good time for asking husband. After he find job for his own self then he can be happy for wife to work also.

Working is like cure. Some find it curse I meaning Renu. But I do not. Sewing pass the day and I sit with friends. As actual fact it bring true friendship and true love. Love marriage maybe is better call something else than love. In real marriage it grow slow slow. Habit. Sit together. Give bit here take bit there. That is how it come at work.

Some people making trouble outside factory. They shout to us. "Here come the garment girls. Choose the one you like." A mullah organize whole entire thing. Day and night they playing religious message with loudspeaker. They say it sinful for men and women working together. But they the ones sinning take Gods name give insult to us and tell lie. Aleya husband getting anxious like anything. He want Aleya to wear burkha inside of factory. Shahnaz say why worry nobody want to look at that monkey face. She only tease and she so careful not to let Aleya hear.

Men and women keep separate here. No men doing machining. Men they cannot sit quiet so long. They have to fidget and talk and walk around smoking. They make pattern and cut cloth these are difficult job. Also they iron. That job too dangerous for woman we do not understand the electricity. So you see how it is and when we must speak it is as brother and sister. Abdul he is a pattern cutter always call me sister. Every day he have fresh shirt.

Shahnaz say I am wear wrong color of sari. I too pale for wearing red or blue or pink. Pink is most worst. Brown or green suit better. It all depend on tone of skin because on Shahnaz pink is very pretty. I spend a little on cloth. Shahnaz say you know how people talk. If you wear bright color they say you asking them to look.

Judges wife keeping it up. Yesterday she say "Better be careful. Let the jute men find out a garment girl here and then it is trouble." I ask her why what kind of trouble? "Well they see a girl go around like that. And then they find out she a garment girl. Do you want that I take a stick and draw it here on the dirt for you?" So I tell her. Pure is in the mind. Keep yourself pure in mind and God will protect. I close my fingers and make fist. I keep my fingers shut like this you cannot open my hands can you? I say like this to her. Even you try it take such long time it not worth it for you. Same thing my modesty. I keep purdah in the mind no one can take it. Then trial is over and only the Judges wife looking little guilty.

Overtime at factory next week. Big order come from Japan. Renu is miss out the overtime. She have make mistakes this week she mess up some shirts putting collars on wrong way. Someone report for chewing betel as well. Aleya say it Shahnaz but she deny. Shahnaz say Renu end up breaking bricks. "She better tough those gums up and get ready." Shahnaz is such tease. How close we getting.

Breaking bricks you see this thing it no joke. Sometime I walk a way down by railway line to work. Few minutes is peaceful good house coconut trees wild rose magnolia. Then the brick breakers. All day squatting over red bricks with little stone hammer. So huge pile wait for this little hammers. Like you take teaspoon to empty lake. Most is woman and they look hungry. Children help. Swell belly children and still laughing hitting breaking laughing. Most days I walk on back roads it is longer and there are no flowers but I like better.

Send respects to your husband. I keep you in the prayers.

March 1989

God has hear the prayers! What is date of confinement? Now husband will put all effort for finding job and God willing continue study also.

It hot like anything the leaves falling. Even coconut tree look hot. I think of Gouripur never so hot in village. Only few tree here no shade roads melting.

In London do roads ever melting? Aleya have cousin is Londoni. She tell me in London the people have no God. I keep quiet when she say. She is nice woman but from Noakhali.

Mr. Chowdhury come for collect the rent take only what I have not bother at all for rest. He bring chair in back of Toyota Land Cruiser. Another tenant leave behind. I make tea and he go inside the room for inspecting the wall. Such busy man still he take the time. He sit on chair little pain come in his face and birthmark getting bright bright. What is it uncle I asking him. "Am I not father to you?" I agree to it. "Then why you do not call me father?" This is how he wants me to call. Then he speak of sons. They gone for study in America it make him proud like Hell. "But if I had a daughter lovely daughter like you to rub my feet I will be happy man."

Father I will rub feet. I tell to him. I take off sandals and pleased to do this small thing for him. It did look like it make happy. He ask if jute men bothering me. "These boys around pretty girl like wax to flame. They cannot help it." But no one dare bothering me. Someone is staring so what? It only their eyes they hurting. One man is coming close by my pot when I cooking. Yellow skin and big wobble arms. Only he looks never daring do anything.

Judges wife come around. She talks the hands fly around all around. They do look like little brown flock seven-brothers birds. "This place was respectable Establishment" she say. "Now this man filling with all lowlifes and skinning with rent. I know his game. He is after Eviction Notice for us for reason we are respectable tenant. He wanting more space for his lowlifes." She really getting excited. "My husband working for District Court. Let him try his Eviction Notice. Let him try. We going to serve Notice on him."

All this after she say they moving and also as well the building get pull down. Take care she say. I giving you a mothers warning. Today I am everybodys daughter.

Beside she not really Judges wife. Mr. Chowdhury know really Top Brass people. I tell you something. Last week President Ershad at Golf Club lying down by swimming pool with girlfriend. The girlfriend is wife of Minister! They lying like this and President wife come and throw self on girlfriend start catty fight. President try to part these two but he take knock to head. At present time President in hospital girlfriend in foreign land having face stitch together and wife still rage and mad due to girlfriend get given business contract. All these things in actual true fact. No one calling them in street. How easy to call the garment girls. Zainab say one hundred and fifty girls in one factory getting pregnant. This is kind of thing people say. Who going to stop them?

July 1989

Sister I hope you well and resting. We all floating like ducks only time I get dry is in factory. Water coming through roof at home. Even it come through brick wall. When the plaster is finish then rain cannot come to the inside. I buy small table make set with chair. Now it all splinter and thing everywhere top cracking up. I put on veranda to sun but only make worse. Hussain one of jute mill men say he fix in no time. He yellow like ladoo and arms wobbling whole time but is nice man.

Overtime at factory is finish. I think this month I have enough for rent. Some new design for making next week. Abdul show the patterns. Shahnaz is worry he look at me wrong way. It seem he use to look at Shahnaz but quick smart she put him down. I think he not meaning anything bad. It look a bit funny only due to glasses slide down nose and he look over top. Shahnaz say any man wears so much scent is loving self too much. But the

Prophet (peace be upon him) instruct us to keep clean and care the bodies we have. Shahnaz worry for me. That is all.

Only other day she advising again on cosmetics. She is skill in cosmetics. She have notice my lips too pink too big can look impure. Religious protest people outside gates seek out all impures like this. Putting powder on the lips makes hide them little bit.

Big bonfire you husband make in courtyard sound nice all village children gather around. Why he is burning chairs? There is no other wood?

August 1989

I think of Amma too sometime as well. She is not come in dreams as she come to you. Why you think she angry? Sometime I feel angry to her. She have no reason be angry with me or with you sister. You remember what Abba use to call? "A saint she come from family of saints." He go to other women. He want to take other wife but she give threat to kill own self. My husband tell me. Everyone know it but us. Tears will come but I tell the truth.

Aleyas husband give beating. Last month gone she best worker in factory and get bonus. They give a sari and for this sari she take beating. Foot come all big like marrow and little finger broken. Bending over her stomach give trouble. Renu say at least you have husband to give good beating at least you not alone. The husband say he will beat twice each day until she tell name of the man.

I thread Aleyas machine and I spend lunch time help to catch up. Renu getting all in trouble talking at bench. She wind thread around tooth and pull to break it but yesterday she pull out tooth. No one ever curse so loud inside building.

We giving Aleya our love is best thing we can give. Shahnaz say husband is get jealous hearing all gossip about garment girls. Renu say few bad ones spoiling for all. It is awful for Shahnaz it might ruin marriage prospect. She say "It look bad on you too." She do not know I am married woman. I tell them I am widow I am orphan. I too ashamed to say truth. Then I did not know like sisters. How I can say anything now?

September 1989

Sister it wrong thing I write about Amma. Only apostate speak of killing own self. No loving mother no God conscious woman speak like this. Burn letter take it out of mind.

Today another hartal. I sit inside hear mens on veranda. They put money together and buy chess set. But no one can agree the rules. Six seven play at one time it make few fight. Nothing serious. Trains not running today without these games it too quiet outside. Judges family gone for wedding. That family do make more noise than all lowlifes together. Morning time the arguing begin. Evening time they stop arguing and go to war. Every pot and plate broken. I collecting banana leaves for them.

Mr. Chowdhury come again for rent. Again he take few less taka no fuss. He is fakir as well also businessman. I find out he letting me have the room cheap. This is how he look out for me. So concern for me. "These boys like wax around a flame. They come close and they melt. How they can help this thing? It is you who must take care." He scratching at birthmark. It really look like bleeding. He say the boy can think bad thought and then they dream of girl and in dream they commit sin and the sin make them unclean. He holding stick and swing it back at wall. Little bits ivory come off tip. Look I will break ten thousand stick on those boys. Say one word I do it. His hand shaking and he put on my cheek touch me like father.

I wash his feet and rub and he come calm only groan time to time due to he have two son far away. I thinking of you sister and I think of you now. Oil is run low and I must save for tomorrow. I kiss you and I turn out the light.

January 1990

May daughter be so sweet as the mother. God give strength and grace and courage. Auntie sends all love. My salaam to your husband. God bless his study and make them give fruit.

I out from favor at factory. One week past they shunning me. I go to sit with the others for lunch time they make silence. I sitting apart and only look at chapati. They put hands up and whisper. I am not looking still I see. I sit near the tap. Everyone use after eating and is always puddle it never run off to drain. I close to puddle and it shake with insect eggs. Eggs hatching I do not like to eat so close but everyone have own space in the yard. No one is speak to me only Abdul. I say to Aleya when she come for handwashing "Sister how I can defend myself? I do not know the charge." For reply she putting hands too close under spout water spraying on my shoulder.

I sad but it will pass. Just a mix up going around. Only small bad patch. Days going slow slow making feel a little tired.

April 1990

I speak with Shahnaz. Some gossip going around about me. "Everyone know about the landlord" she say. "You getting cheap rent or what?"

I tell her Mr. Chowdhury is father to me. Shahnaz will put right quick sharp. The women listen to her. Only last month she saying nose ring do show up country bumpkin. No woman wearing nose ring now only stud.

June 1990

Abdul my brother walk with me to home. Protest people gone no danger but he say it is better he walk with me. Outside gate he puts his glasses in shirt pocket. Without them you see is just boy. He is neat and clean and kind. Shirt never flapping outside the trouser.

Little thing happen today. I ask Khaleda for scissor and she pass with sharp end open and pricks on my hand. When I make a cry sound is only surprise all holding up hands and hiding smile. I go outside and really cry. Renu come to me and say never mind these girls they just think they ripe fruit. Dont want to go near a bad one because they know how quick quick they going rotten their own selves. She meaning me to be the bad one. I explain everything but she just pulling on tooth. "We waiting and suffering. That is why we here."

I am not waiting around suffering around. Let her suffer if she like it.

August 1990

No need to trouble for me sister. I celebrate you husband success in Bookkeeping certificate. You say one time he wanting to build house in Dhaka. My sister I wait for this day. How the plans coming?

Nothing bad happening in factory. Only little quiet around me. That is all. I never mind it. I work in lunch break and at end of month I will get bonus. Abdul taking care for me. He is a great study man like your husband. One day whole entire factory come in his charge. He have the brain for it and he jump on detail. I give you example. Every day sock and belt are match. Brown sock for brown belt black sock for black belt. If you wanting to rise up in Management you must jump on detail like this. This is how he tell me. Clean shirt every day too as well.

He walk me home and we talk of many thing. He looking out for me. Mr. Chowdhury also taking care.

Abdul in actual fact love me. If it possible we marry. But his family looking for girl and I have husband in Khulna. I dont know. Maybe my husband divorce me after some time. Is it possible get divorce and no one tell you about it?

There is more quarrel at home. Hussain have got two goats and they eating washing. Only Zainabs washing they like. Anything she put out they eat it. Judges wife in high old temper. She come and scream at him yesterday. She is serving Notice but Hussain only laughing and copying hands flying around the place. "These goats got good taste" he say. "Why you complain? It all of us they insulting nobody elses washing good enough." I think about getting some chickens myself.

January 1991

Something has happen. It happen one month past but sometime I think not to tell you.

Shahnaz did try and warn. We waiting for gates to get unlock and she say "Do you remember what I tell you about Abdul?" Yes I say but he is like brother to me now. She look sad and she tell me "I am disappointed. All the help I give you. But you throw it back in my face." I try to talk to her but she turn away. Sister I say I dont want to throw anything. I am your friend. These my last words to her. I did not see after that.

Straight away I called to Managers office. Only two reasons to go there. Sacking and death-in-family. Last week Khaleda was call. There was fire at her home. Three sons one daughter dead. All children and mother-in-law also. They have to carry Khaleda out from building.

I see few times the Manager walk around. Three four Baby Manager always walk behind write on boards. Skin on cheeks is dry like anything. Fish scales Shahnaz call it. "Whole body rotting under that suit. Quick quick hold your nose." He smell like fish head curry. He never surprise us and catch out talking at bench. Someone always sniff him first.

I go inside the office and he reading. I standing there wait and wait it seem like hour and hour. Then Abdul come in he stand there clean the glasses I think he come for saving my job. Manager putting down his papers and say "You know why you are here." Yes say Abdul. I say yes as well. I know I there for the sack.

"You have behave in lewd manner. You have show no regard for reputation of the factory. I am not running a brothel. Do I look like brothel keeper to you?" He is looking at me. No I say. Not a brothel keeper. Then he stand up. Get out. You are finished in garment business.

I just standing there and smelling him and smelling pomade on Abduls hair and perfume he puts on his cheek and thinking I going to faint. Go on he say. Get out. But I have to ask. What it is I did?

"The boy admit to all" he say. "Dont tell me your shameless lie. Go before I beat shame into you." I look at Abdul but he not look at me. His shirt sticking to his chest I remember I never see him sweat before. He say nothing and I go out. I wait outside door for him also getting sack and walking home with me. Manager I hear him. "Pretty girl eh? You boys! Have to get a little practice in before marriage eh?" He laughing. Only him laughing not Abdul.

You have this letter by this time I have other job. Mr. Chowdhury looking out for me. He have many business. I send you love as always.

March 1991

Oh baby is walking! How I like to see it send photo if you have.

Your husband is right Mr. Chowdhury looking out for me. I under his protection do not send money. If husband allow to do shopping it is good. You can go out. But do not hide accounts and send money to me. You have good husband. This make me more happy than anything and I have no need.

Two days past Mr. Chowdhury come here. He ask to comb hair. I did it and I massage feet. Much tension in feet but with me he say he can relax. He tell me all day long people climbing around him waiting outside office running to catch him walk backward in front of him and wave papers. He can never be alone because of all day people want something. Even in spite he feel alone. He in actual fact lonely like hell. He trust no one. Everyone cheating. Wife is dead for long time. Sons have gone. Half money going in bribe. New Government coming new people lining up for bribe.

He tell me "You are my daughter. I like to bring you to my house. But what people will say? We are not related. I have no wife." Then he sigh and I rub his feet and when I look up there is water in the eyes. "If a girl comes to a mans house as servant there is no trouble. She must come as servant. Or as wife. Then all is well."

Sister can Mr. Chowdhury mean to take for wife? It keep going around in my mind but it is a foolish thing. Is it foolish thing? He is rich and powerful man he know Top Brass people. And I am like daughter to him. I tell you? He growing mustache. It look well with his cane. He look like gentleman. And very fit also as well for man this age. He believe in exercise.

Sometime he leave Toyota Land Cruiser at home and walks never mind it not done in Top Brass circle. Not such old man maybe like your husband age.

You see how it is. Mr. Chowdhury not even ask for rent and I get a little money cook for jute men. I make breakfast and dinner and they give portion for my meal and little money also.

I buy chickens and they have begin to lay. Ten twelve eggs under veranda every morning. Day it is quiet and I talk to the goats. They tied up now and washing is safe. I watch trains go by and think of the train that bring me from Khulna. I think of people on those trains where they going and where they from. Sometime I hear the bauls in the street and I run around to the front listen to them sing about love. Or I talk to Zainab she is friendly with me now.

Her boy youngest one have failed in exam. Father did not flog properly or he would have learn. She say "What kind of father is that? How many times I told to flog properly. I do my best but I am only a woman." Then she say "I told him to pay more for tutoring. He did not listen. Now the boy has failed." Then she has idea. She come to me hands with flutter. Looks like cat jump in the bird nest. "The teacher is at fault not only the father. These teachers must be responsible. Only way to make them responsible is take the whole damn lot to Court. Tomorrow I serving Notice." That Court getting crowded like anything.

Evening time I cook the meal and I serve. I sit a little way apart and eat. I listen to men make talk and joke and I watch the sky. I look at the moon and I think of you sister look at same moon. We cannot see each other but we see it and we are join.

Jute men all saving up money. Most night is money counting. Many sending back to village. They save for wife and children and parents. Few saving only for own selves. For starting business or build a house or take a wife. These ones save hardest. Others buying hair oil or sweets or ticket to cinema. They smoke more and take more pan. However much they saving it not enough so they spend a little to forget a little. Young ones have not learned and they saving hardest counting most often.

They still playing chess but some of piece are lost there not so many fight now. Also they tell story and everyone try to tell the best. Some are jute farmer before they lose the land. Do you remember Abba take us one time in boat to watch jute harvest? Mens stay down so long we cannot hold breaths until they come again to surface.

These ones tell biggest story. One say I have dive twelve feet down to cut the jute. The next diving fifteen feet. Third must be diving always twenty-five feet and fourth going down thirty and fighting with crocodiles. I stay apart and listen.

Sometime Hussain come and talk with me. He so yellow like he turning into jute himself. I tell him what happen at factory. I tell everything. I only tell Mr. Chowdhury I get laid off due to how easy he get upset.

Hussain say "Sometime when people see a beautiful thing they want to destroy it. The thing make them feel ugly so they act ugly." He meaning me for the beautiful thing. Then he say "Me I too ugly anyway. Any beautiful thing coming my way just make me laugh. Ha! You think that making me feel bad? I already too ugly."

May 1991

How to write? What to tell. Sister I have bring shame on self. Hide this letter from your husband.

I tell you what happen. If you write to me even in spite you know what I have done it not because I trick you to think I am good person.

Thursday evening Mr. Chowdhury come here. I not expecting he have come last week. I sleeping on my mat in underclothes and a knock coming on the door. I call out and he reply then bang with his stick. Just a minute I tell him I getting dressed. But he kick the door and break catch.

"Light the bloody lamp." He yelling like hell. I get up from bed I still undress. "Let me see her. Let me see the whore." And I cannot light it my hand is frighten. He take the lamp and do it. Then I see how his face look.

He marching up and down room with the lamp. I moving out of way. I trying to climb inside the dark. His cane find me. My legs afraid. He shout again. "What you have done to me? You screwing every motherfucker in the factory! Did they put roof over your head? Did they treat like daughter? What did they give you? What did I get?"

All I thinking that everyone can hear. He still going on. "I am a fool." He screaming it really. He put lamp down and he starting to take off shirt. He quiet and I glad for it. Then he take off trousers. I say nothing I do nothing and then it done and he sit in the chair. He ask me to rub feet and I do it. He tell me not to cry and I stop. He ask if it he who taking care of me and I say yes it him.

This is what happen and afterward I cry. All the time I thinking my life cursed. God have given me life but he has curse it. He put rocks in my path thorns under feet snakes over head. Which way I turn any way it is dark. He never light it. If I drink water it turn to mud eat food it poison me. I stretch out my hand it burn and by my side it wither. This is what He plan for me. This is how I thinking. I telling you everything so you know the sort of person I am.

Little and little I getting stronger. I pray God forgive me. I sick then inside my mind. Everything has happen is because of me. I take my own husband. I leave him. I go to the factory. I let Abdul walk with me. I the one living here without paying.

This is all I have to tell and I have tell everything.

August 1991

Where I can go sister? I run away for my husband. And I run away from him also. Now I afraid to run again.

You want to bring me to London. I like to come. But again this time your husband right and you must listen. Save money for new baby coming. Husband starting new business. He need money for that also. Tutoring is very good idea. Here no one can pass exam without tutoring.

Zainab in trouble. I talk to her and forget own trouble. One day her husband was cycling to District Court and he knocking into man on Suzuki scooter. You think it Zainabs husband get bashed up but that is not how it happen. Suzuki man fall on neck and now arms and legs not working. Police put Zainabs husband in police station and she take savings there for releasing husband. And now Suzuki man wife serving Notice on Zainabs husband. They want money but now Zainab do not have money. She done everything but it useless. She tell me "I went to the house. Look. This is how I getting down on my knees and this is how I pulling my hair and this is how I tearing my clothes and screaming. Wife looking at me like dirty rag. Why she think this dirty rag got money?" Then she start wailing and beating on chest. "Oh why my husband cant break his *neck. Then* we *the ones serving Notice."*

The son have been taken out of school. He wear his uniform but it not looking so smart anymore. He like to take a stick and tease the goats. I think he taking eggs but I waiting to catch him. The house quieter now. Zainabs family too sad for arguing.

He comes every week. Sometime he comes twice.

February 1992

God blesses me. Another niece! I think of her. I think of Shahana. Send photo of both.

He still come to me. Only quick visit. He did used to say "Next week I take you to my house. I need another maid." Now he say nothing. He come only once a week and sometime not at all. If he stop visit how long before he puts me out?

I go to every garment factory in Dhaka. Nobody have machining job. This is all training I have. I think of making some things at home and trying to sell. I make whistles out from bamboo and I take outside and sit with them. Nobody wanting to buy. Hussain see and he laugh. "Put a little sunshine in bag and sell that too." This is how he say. I go to bazaar for cloth scraps and I make dolls. Then I go to Motijheel and sit on pavement. Police kick the box and they make threat. Hussain tell me "Dont you know the pavement for rent? The pavement it do not belong to you. Everything for rent."

He give me some goat milk. And he make little cabinet for me. I keep soap and comb and pen in it. His arms so flab and flop. Little wind makes them swing. But he is kind. He make me laugh. He can turn eyelids inside out and he move his ears without disturb single muscle on face. "God blesses each one" he say. "How He love me to give such talents." And he say "To you He give the gift of beauty. How He show His love in you!" For long time then I cry. In night he come to my room. I do not send away.

October 1992

Zainab have gone. Whole family gone. No word to me just disappear like that.

Everything going on same way. Hussain give me sari some ribbons and pretty box with pearl lid. His friend Ali also giving presents.

You ask to write but I cannot think what to tell. Nothing much to tell. Only God see what is in my heart.

Pray for me, sister.

September 1993

I not mean to make you frighten. Few time this last year I take my pen and sit down. Once twice I begin the letter but words do not come. Even I do not write I think of you.

After long time I start to think of factory again. I go there and I wait outside across road. I think to speak to them my friends. I see Shahnaz she come out and I pull my headscarf around face. She expect a child. It make me feel my shame. God will not give child to me. I thinking I see Aleya but one burkha looking like another. No husband come for her. Renu I have not see.

Three time I go there and watch and all time I asking self if ever there love between us and what kind of love it so easily broken. Shahnaz wearing too much cosmetics. I never did see with so much cosmetics before.

I walk around factory gates around the walls. If it possible to hate bricks I hating them. This factory have ruin me. Many families living around there now. Before the security guards come and clear up like leaves but now is all sort of tent and cardboard shack. One family living in big pipe is mean for taking water. I walk around.

I thinking this one thing all day. They put me out from factory for untrue reason and due to they put me out the reason have come now as actual truth. This is how I was thinking.

Hussain still looking out for me. He the one making sure I get the money. If he not look out anyone take what they like and not pay. Landlord no longer come. I pay rent now.

Eight ten months past Hussain stop the jute mill job. He have other girl over near Borobazaar and two other who go around for work. These he call floating girl. Government office are good for floating girl. Big hotel also good but girl must be younger. Hussain not yellow now. Now he orange like marigolds. He tell me work hard only few year left to work. Best price for girls eleven twelve. He take good care. Someone not want to pay Hussain deal with them. Arms are flab and flop but they strong.

July 1994

I have the photo of girls and I put with others. I have frame. Three photos will fill up nice and I will buy glass and put on wall. Picture do pretty up the wall.

Your husband is very good in finding jobs. What is Leisure Center? Is it Government job?

I give you word as you ask to send more letter. Even I have nothing to tell that is what I writing and sending to you. Only thing here is rain. Seems like wetter in my room than pond. Hussain building bed for me high up on legs. Easy for working with high bed. Sometime I feel bad I sit with him. All time he joking. He say "You got to look for good side. Everything got good side. How about we throw some rice in there get selves paddy field?" Is another talent besides ear waggling and eyelid turning.

I wake up time to time and think I back home. But is only smell of goat come bleating outside door. City smell different smell of men and cars. I like to smell the village again.

Oh there only one goat now. Other got on railway track and we eat it up. Chickens also make a feast. They stop laying.

Renu come into mind. If she still suffering still waiting. Then I think of Mumtaz and of Amma. I not daring enough to think of Abba. One time I think of his second wife how quick she come after mourning. How quick she go again. If only Amma know how quick she go. That is way with men. Why she did not know it?

March 1995

Do not be angry I have not kept word but I writing now and you must forgive.

Something too strange has happen. You cannot guess it. I have receive proposal of marriage.

He come for first time only two weeks past. Next day he return. It not so strange. But third day he come and drink tea with me and we talking only. In spite this he paying in full.

Every day he have come and just for talk. His name is Ahmed. He is tall. At least five feet and eight nine inches. And he is Albino. Because of this his skin like lassi and end of nose is toast like seed. When sun touch him it like acid in the face. Even the evenings he wearing dark glasses. From me he go to shoe factory. He is supervisor for night shift.

He is quiet man. When we talking most time he keep mouth closed. Most time we are sitting. I try to draw out. I dont want him pay in full for nothing. He turn my hand over and over like as if he never seen another hand. Jute men slap on back and call out. "Eh babu are you making eyes at our sister?"

But Ahmed do not bother. He is serious man. His hair the color of silt. He have supervisor job for six year. Fifth day he take off glasses and give me fright like anything. Look like cats eyes inside head. Blue and waxy. You never see eyes like that. But is only because of the Albino. Nothing in actual fact wrong with the eye.

He bring bakul for me and hibiscus. Pretty though only one day lasting. What pity it is I cannot marry.

Give kisses to my nieces and best wish for your husband. I hoping he get better quick quick. Dhoie and also ghole is good for stomach ulcer.

March 1995

I do not know what to do. Ahmed pressing for marriage. He do not listen to anything. Hussain come and he talk to me. He say "This man is odd like five-leg donkey. Nature reject these things. What chance he has? You are damaged past repair. What chance you has also?" This is how he explain. And he tell me "My liver is gone I cannot last much longer. Who will protect you if not him? I let you go. This life is finish. Begin another."

I speak to Ahmed again. Again he is pressing. I tell him this. I am a low woman. I am nothing. I have nothing. I am all that I have. I can give you nothing.

Still he insist. I do not know what to do.

April 1995

I give thanks to God. As it is written in the suras "Do not despair of the mercy of God for Allah forgives all sins. He is the Compassionate the Merciful."

I am here with my husband. Not so far from Ghulshan which is best district in all of Dhaka. Three weeks now without I leave the flat. My husband go out in evening and return from shoe factory in morning. Then we have big meal and go to sleep. In afternoon we are together. Always he watching me with love. If I move he move. If I go to wash he follow. And he keeps hand on me. Like he thinking I going to vanish if he stop touching. This is kind of devotion.

When he go out in evening I begin housework. Everything have to be in good order. That only thing my husband asking. Good order. All jars and tins must keep the place. Tallest one first then next tallest next one bit shorter and so on to the smallest which is for saffron. All to be wiped each day so none is sticky. It do make everything easy to find. My husband roll his cigarettes each evening and leave on shelf and you never see such straight line. Good order of house meaning good order of mind. And he have three pairs of proper shoe and twenty-one pairs of lace. Each laces set match with only one of pair of shoes. They need keeping careful like anything.

I begin housework at night but even taking all care it done before morning and sometime I do fall asleep. Then it difficult to sleep when husband comes and it is my turn to do the watching.

Sister I know how you enjoy to leave your flat. But I have come inside now. How I love the walls keep me here.

April 1995

My husband have gone to bazaar. I go up on roof with other wives. I growing mustard in a pot chili plants in another. I speak with wives and they grumble about husbands. I must grumble also or they looking strangely at me.

I stare down in street yesterday watching the road it getting dug up. The women have big spade and long handle axe. Some carrying basket of stones on shoulder. All thin like sticks. When men work in field at least they have mathlas. These women go bare head. And sun is red like a hell and big like anything.

Then they finish the work and lining up for pay. They getting pay in wheat. The wheat coming all way from America. This is what wives telling me. This is how they getting paid. How to live on wheat?

All day I thinking about these women who are not housewives like me and like you sister. I thinking what I do if I one of them. Which way I turn? How I think to get out from under the stones?

My husband soon he return and getting ready for job. Storm is coming. But it too early for rain. Now we long for rain. Storm stays in the sky. Red and white lights. How hot it is today. Grisma going on for longer in city it seem. Before the rains come my husband taking me to his village. Mother no longer alive but he have father and two brother not yet marry. I going to meet my new family. Sometime I worry they find out about me. I cant tell to husband. If I speak that way I remind of what is behind me.

He rub my head for me. He is quiet man. Sometime I think he fallen asleep but is just peaceful. He is a serious man. If someone say only few words every word takes more weight.

How Shahana liking school? Is natural for mother to cry when the child begin to grow away but if your friend give advice to see doctor then go. See the doctor and he will tell you how well your sister reads your heart.

May 1995

All his life people been stare at my husband. I think that how he getting so serious. Also how he understand things for woman like me. Not many men getting stare at in their life. He have few blister on cheeks and nose is fry like pakora. Also in spite of these thing he handsome in an actual fact. Now I am use to blue eyes and blue eyes very nice as well.

It night now and I try to stay awake. This evening I go up on the roof. Talking with wives. They smoking secret cigarette cleaning children feeding babies. All are great Authority on this thing or that. One know all about wind. If someone burp in certain way it meaning they eat too quick. Another kind of burping mean too much spices. Deep belch is sign of twisted stomach tube. And wind from other end can be read in many way. Some lucky ones is sign of money coming. I call her the Windy Wife. Then there is Great Disaster. If someone stub a toe she say "You lucky. Only the other day I mash two toes in the door." Someone else has sick daughter. "You can count blessings. Only the other week my daughter rushed to hospital." Another wife have take beating. "Thank God for one rib only broken. When my husband beat he make sure to break all bones." And biggest Authority of all is Woman Who Know Men. "Aaahh she says if you want your husband faithful you must hide his toothbrush in the morning." She do always say Aaahh before everything. "A man not going to another woman with smelly breath. I know men!" Aaahh another thing. "To stop him snoring you must burn incense in the room and always turn him on right side. I know men!" "Aaahh I can tell you something. Give your mother-in-law the best pieces of meat and next day he bringing jewelery for you." She know men!

One of young wife cannot have child. She have cut hair short and she praying. Not even short hair can bring child for me now. I have tell my husband and he accept it.

Before the rain come we going to his village. It must be soon.

Sometime I look out from roof and think I see my first husband. I see him with shirt unbutton to the chest. I see riding a motor bike. I see talking on mobile phone. I see man walk with hand on hip just like he use to do. And this when my fear is escaping. Other time I see man who come to me very often in Narayanganj. These time I feel the fear on my back.

May 1995

I pass these nights write to you sister. Flat is clean everything in good order. What I can say?

My husband is please with me. I am good housekeeper. I never mix up laces and laces are important to shoe man.

You know my husband tell me this. First moment he see me it the perfect moment in his whole and entire life. This is how he say. In his whole and entire life. He like to live it again and he planning to make it come again as an actual fact. He have me sit in bed and put my hair in certain way over one shoulder. Sheet is smooth at one end and crumple at other. I must tilt my face so or so. But light is never right. I hold head too tight or too loose. It hard for him not to get angry he trying to make something perfect. Sometime he say my face have change and he tell me to change it back but I soothe and he is quiet again.

The rains come now and we will not go to the village for a while.

If doctor gives pills you must take even in spite I do not know what kind of pill can cure disease of sadness. When you get use to Shahana being out from house you feeling like your old self again.

June 1995

Hussains funeral it pass today. Someone bring word for me and I go to say goodbye. I stand apart away from rest. Few of jute mens nobody else. I cover myself but they know who stand behind. They do not speak with me and I take for respect.

Sides of grave falling down with rain and I cry for our mother.

My husband working long long hour. He saying I have change my face but I do not know what he mean. I put more cosmetics less cosmetics but he cannot see what he saw before. I thinking he need more rest but he cannot be still and he go out. Is what is call bad patch for the marriage.

June 1995

He say things not in good order anymore even I do always try to keep it good ordered like anything. He say I put curse on him and that is why we marry. He say how his family going to take daughter-in-law like me?

I saying to him this is bad patch for the marriage. Every marriage has bad patch. Even my sister sometime having bad patch and she respectable like hell living in London and everything.

July 1996

My own loving sister I always dreaming of you sending your letter and waiting. I do not have address for you to reach me. When I am settling somewhere you hear from me.

Do not worry. When I have work I send news.

January 2001

I hope this reach you. I hope you are in same address. Some time past I living here and there. Some time past only food for one day and the next. Everything I putting out of mind now. They have taken me in and I am maid in good house. All are kind. Children are beautiful. My room is solid wall room. Clean place. Nothing here for making scared of. Mistress is kind. Mister is kind. They give plenty of food. If you are in same address now you write to me again.

Chapter Eight

Tower Hamlets, London, February 2001

The girls stood before their father and twisted their toes into the carpet. Chanu sat cross-legged on the floor. Leaning forward, his belly filled the thigh-and-calf cradle. Chairs were out of favor. He was a floor man now.

"Come," he said. "Begin." He clapped his hands together.

Shahana pushed Bibi with her elbow. Bibi drew circles with her big toe. Her plaits hung around her face; rope ladders to the roof of her head. Nazneen pulled laundry from the wooden clothes rack and began a campaign of vigorous folding and sorting. Activity, ordinary and domestic and cheerful, was needed. The clothes were still damp.

"She knows it," said Nazneen. "Only yesterday I listened to her practice."

Chanu held up an open hand. It was a gesture for peace, or a threat to Bibi.

At last she began:

> "*O Amar Shonar Bangla, ami tomay bhailobashi*
> Forever your skies, your air set my heart in tune . . ."

Chanu sighed and rubbed his stomach. He plumped it like a cushion, fists working in a circular motion. For five days he had been teaching his daughters to recite "My Golden Bengal." This evening they were to perform the entire poem. Chanu was taking his family back home and Tagore was the first step of the journey. Bibi continued:

> ". . . As if it were a flute.
> In spring, oh mother mine, the fragrance from
> Your mango groves makes me wild with joy—
> Ah what thrill."

Her voice gave no hint of joy or of thrill. It plodded nervously along, afraid that a sudden burst of intonation would derail the train of recall.

Chanu ceased his kneading. "Ah," he said loudly, and looked around the room. "What thrill!"

Bibi twisted her head to look behind, and then looked at her father. His invisible audience was, for her, a perplexing yet palpable reality. She felt the presence though she could not see it as he did.

"Try it again," he urged. He moved his attention to his left foot, probing a new bunion with tender fingers.

"Ah. What. Thrill." Bibi joined her plaits beneath her chin as if to stop her mouth from opening again. She waited for clearance.

Chanu inclined his head to the side and remained philosophical. "Can't expect the amra tree to bear mangoes."

Now she raced:

"In autumn, oh mother mine
In the full-blossomed paddy fields,
I have seen spread all over—sweet smiles!
Ah, what a beauty, what shades, what an affection
And what a tenderness."

There she halted, before a sudden precipice of uncertainty. Chanu looked at Shahana. She had her arms folded across her chest and her top lip tucked into the bottom lip. Nazneen moved about the room, inventing chores and making brisk, everyday noises. From the dangerous set of her daughter's mouth, Nazneen divined a flogging ahead.

Terrible in the incantation and stunningly inept in the delivery, these beatings were becoming a frequent ritual. They took their toll on each member of the family but most of all on Chanu. It was inevitably Shahana who incited his anger and it was Shahana who appeared to suffer least.

"Tell the little memsahib that I am going to break every bone in her body." Chanu never addressed his threats directly to his elder daughter. Nazneen was the preferred intermediary or, if a new and particularly lurid threat had been invented, Bibi would be chosen. "I'll dip her head in boiling fat and throw her out of that window. Go and tell the memsahib. Go and tell your sister." Bibi could be relied upon to convey the message word for ringing word, even though Shahana was rarely more than a couple of feet away. In this way she proved to be a more reliable stooge than her mother, who only murmured low soothings and tried to move the girls out of range.

Shahana did not want to listen to Bengali classical music. Her written Bengali was shocking. She wanted to wear jeans. She hated her kameez and spoiled her entire wardrobe by pouring paint on them. If she could choose between baked beans and dal it was no contest. When Bangladesh was mentioned she pulled a face. She did not know and would not learn that Tagore was more than poet and Nobel laureate, and no less than the true father of her nation. Shahana did not care. Shahana did not want to go back home.

Chanu called her the little memsahib and wore himself out with threats before launching a flogging with anything to hand. Newspaper, a ruler, a notebook, a threadbare slipper, and once, disastrously, a banana skin. He never learned to select his instrument and he never thought to use his hand. An instrumentless flogging was a lapse of fatherly duty. He flogged enthusiastically but without talent. His energy went into the niyyah—the making of his intention—and here he was advanced and skillful, but the delivery let him down. Busy still with his epithets of torture, he flailed about as Shahana ran and dodged and dived beneath furniture or behind her mother's legs. And Bibi hugged herself and was covered in pain, and a hand reached inside Nazneen's stomach and began to pull entrails up her throat, and Chanu stopped shouting and stopped flailing and began a twitching that ran from his eyebrows to his fingers, and Shahana took on his temper and yelled the ending, which everyone already knew.

"I didn't ask to be born here."

"Your sister will continue," said Chanu, addressing himself to Bibi. Bibi opened her mouth, as if to show that she was on standby.

Shahana disentangled her lips, rolled her eyes up to the ceiling, and recited in an even tone:

> "What a quilt you have spread at the feet of
> Banyan trees and along the banks of rivers!
> Oh mother mine, words from your lips are like
> Nectar to my ears!
> If sadness, oh mother mine, cast a gloom on your face,
> My eyes well up with tears . . ."

Chanu closed his eyes as they spilled over. His stomach rolled a little farther forward into its nest of thigh. He began to hum and took up the verse in song. The children looked at Nazneen, and she agreed by a slow blink that it was finished. She spread wide her arms and herded them away to their room.

In the late evening, to the sound of the walls that buzzed their eternal prayer of pipes and water and electricity, Nazneen clipped hair from her husband's nose. The quiet made Nazneen alert. All day and into the evening she was aware of the life around, like a dim light left on in the corner of the room. They used to disturb her, these activities, sealed and boxed and unnerving. When she had come she had learned first about loneliness, then about privacy, and finally she learned a new kind of community. The wife upstairs who used the lavatory in the night. She and Nazneen had exchanged only pleasantries but Nazneen knew her by her bladder. The milkman's alarm clock that told Nazneen the grueling hours her neighbor must keep. The woman on the other side whose bed thumped the wall when her boyfriends called. These were her unknown intimates.

Somewhere above, a man's muffled laugh slid into coughing and the coughing became muted by footsteps. From behind the wardrobe, a television hooted and applauded. Nazneen relaxed. She snipped a fat hair from the left nostril and watched it land on the sprigs of Chanu's chest.

"Finished," she said. She knelt on the floor at the end of the bed and began on his corns.

"You see," said Chanu, "she is only a child." His voice was grave. It was the voice a doctor might use to deliver bad news.

Nazneen sliced the waxy skin. Shahana was only half child now. Or rather she was sometimes all child, and sometimes something else. The most startling thing possible: another person.

"She is only a child, and already the rot is beginning. That is why we must go."

Nazneen worked around the corn. There was a time when it disgusted her, this flaking and scraping, but now it was nothing. Time was all it took. She looked up and saw the photograph of Raqib on the bedside table. The glass needed dusting.

"Planning and preparation," said Chanu. "The girls must be made ready. Fortunate for them that I am at home." His mouth, pulling in different directions, looked skeptical. He picked up his book and lay back on the bed.

Nazneen gathered her parings. If they went to Dhaka she could be with Hasina. Every nerve ending strained towards it as if the sheer physical desire could transport her. But the children would be unhappy. Bibi, perhaps, would recover quickly. Shahana would never forgive her.

In the picture Raqib looked a bit like Chanu. Or maybe all babies, fat-cheeked, looked a bit like Chanu.

They would go. Or they would stay. Only God would keep them or send them. Nazneen knew her part, had learned it long ago, and rolled the dead skin around in her palm and sat quietly, waiting for the feelings to pass.

When Hasina had been lost and found and lost again and returned to her once more, Nazneen went to her husband.

"My sister. I would like to bring her here."

Chanu waved his thin arms. "Bring her. Bring them all. Make a little village here." He shook his delicate shoulders in a show of laughter. "Get a box and sow rice. Make a paddy on the windowsill. Everyone will feel at home."

Nazneen felt the letter inside her choli. "There has been some difficulty for her. I only have one sister."

He slapped the side of his head and he appealed to the walls. "Some difficulty! There has been some difficulty! How can it be allowed? Has anyone here experienced any *difficulty*? Of course not! Anything we can do to stop the *difficulty* must be done. At once." His voice, though it had become a squeak, lost no measure of volume.

She could not explain. Hasina was still working at the factory. This was all Chanu knew. She hovered for the postman, hid letters, invented bland statements of well-being and minor mishaps. All she could do for her sister was deliver her from further shame and this was all she had done. Nazneen turned away and walked to the door.

"My wife," he called after her. "Are you not forgetting something?"

She stopped.

"*We* are going *there*. I have decided. And when I decide something, it is done."

But they did not have money. And money was needed. For tickets, for suitcases, to ship the furniture, to buy a place in Dhaka.

"Some of the women are doing sewing at home," said Nazneen. "Razia can get work for me."

"Raz-i-a," said Chanu. "Always this Razia. How many times do I tell you to mix with respectable-type people?" He lay on the sofa in lungi and undershirt. He no longer wore pajama, a sign of imminent return to home, and he often spent the day prostrate on the sofa without dressing, or pinned to the floor beneath his books.

For a while he ruminated and explored the folds of his stomach. "Some of these uneducated ones, they say that if the wife is working it is only because the husband cannot feed them. Lucky for you I am an educated man." She waited for more, but he fell into a deep reverie and said nothing further.

These days, with the children at school and Chanu littering the sitting room, Nazneen often retreated to the kitchen, or sat in the bedroom until the wardrobe drove her out to wander around the flat with a damp cloth, wiping and straightening. He showed no sign of getting a job. The small edifice of their savings was reduced to dust. In a final bout of activity he had put on a suit and gone out to lobby the council for a transfer. The new flat was in Rosemead block, one floor from the top, two floors above Razia, and it had a second bedroom. "Playing the old contacts game," said Chanu. "Yes, they jumped up pretty sharpish when they saw me. Old Dalloway shook my hand. Sorry he lost a good man. That's what he said." The toilet blocked persistently and the plaster had come off in the hallway. "Got to get on to my contacts," said Chanu, but he made no move.

Nazneen sat down and looked at her hands. Chanu read his book. He no longer took courses. The number of certificates had stabilized, and they were waiting in the bottom of the wardrobe until someone had the energy to hang them. Now he was more teaching than taught and the chief beneficiaries were the girls. Nazneen also benefited.

"You see," said Chanu, still supine, holding his book above his face, "all these people here who look down on us as peasants know nothing of history." He sat up a little and cleared his throat. "In the sixteenth century, Bengal was called the Paradise of Nations. These are our roots. Do they teach these things in the school here? Does Shahana know about the Paradise of Nations? All she knows about is flood and famine. Whole bloody country is just a bloody basket case to her." He examined his text further and made little approving, purring noises.

"If you have a history, you see, you have a pride. The whole world was going to Bengal to do trade. Sixteenth century and seventeenth century. Dhaka was the home of textiles. Who invented all this muslin and damask and every damn thing? It was us. All the Dutch and Portuguese and French and British queuing up to buy."

He got up now and retied his lungi. Nazneen watched him stride around the sofa and knew he was rehearsing for this evening's lesson with the girls. Bibi would sit on his lap and attempt through her stillness to reassure him that the lesson was being learned. Shahana would alternately hop about and lounge sullenly across an armchair. As soon as he stopped speaking she would rush to the television and switch it on, and he would either smile an indulgence or pump out a stream of invective that sent both girls to the safe shoreline of their beds.

"A sense of history," he said. "That is what they are missing. And do not forget—the Bangladeshis they are mixing with are Sylhetis, no more, no less. They do not see the best face of our nation."

"Colonel Osmany," said Nazneen quietly. "Shah Jalal."

"What?" said Chanu. "What?"

"Our great national hero and—"

"I know who they are!"

Nazneen apologized with a smile, and then added, "And that they both come from Sylhet."

"But that is the point I am making. These people here simply do not show our nation in its true light." He pounced on the book and began riffling pages. "Do you know what Warren Hastings said about our people?" He purred and exercised his face as he prepared the quotation. "'They are gentle, benevolent . . .' So many good qualities he finds. In short, he finds us 'as exempt from the worst properties of human passion as any people on the face of the earth.'" He waved the book in triumph. "Do you think they teach this in the English schools?"

"I don't know," said Nazneen. "Is that an English book?" She wondered who this Warren Hastings might be.

Chanu ignored her and played to the gallery. "No. This is not what they teach. All flood here and famine there and taking up collection tins." He used the book to scratch inside his ear.

Nazneen thought about Shahana, how her long thin face would group all its small features as if trying to make them vanish, closing down its operations. She had a way of glazing over that seemed accomplished, mature beyond her years. I'm going inside now, it said, and I may not come out again. But when it was over it was only a sulk, and the sulk was made clear in the tantrum that followed. Then her mouth became a round angry hole and she began to kick. She kicked the furniture, she kicked her sister, and most of all she kicked her mother.

"Four European countries fought over the place. And when the

British took control, this is what gave them strength to take all India." There was sweat on his brow although the room was not too warm. He wiped it with a forearm. "During the eighteenth century"—he looked down from behind the sofa into the soft well that his backside had left on the cushion—"this part of the country was wealthy. It was stable. It was educated. It provided—we provided—one third of the revenues of Britain's Indian Empire." The book slid from his hand and he bent for it. He rubbed the edge of the cushions and he looked at the far wall, at the place where his certificates had hung in the old flat. He smiled and his cheeks pushed up into his eyes.

"A loss of pride," he said, talking to the wall, "is a terrible thing."

Nazneen got up in the night and went to the kitchen. She took a Tupperware container from the fridge and ate the curry cold, standing up against the sink. If she had a job, she would be able to save. And if she saved then they would have enough money to go to Dhaka. Or if they didn't go to Dhaka, she would save enough to send money to Hasina. Chanu would not know how many linings she had sewn or how many jackets she had buttonholed. He would not know how much money there should be, and she would be able to put some aside.

The moon was uncertain tonight. Pockmarked, it lurked behind a purple ink cloud and tried to drown itself in a too-shallow sky. Hasina wrote once that she watched the moon and thought of her, watching the same moon. But the sky here was so low, so thin, that it was hard to believe it was the same high heaven that soared over Hasina; and the moon would not be out in Dhaka, and maybe it was a different moon after all.

She put her face beneath the tap and turned on the cold water.

"Amma."

Bibi stood in the doorway. She watched as Nazneen dried her face with a tea towel. Her brow was made broad to carry all her worries.

"Hungry?" said Nazneen.

Bibi nodded. She came and leaned up against the sink and shivered. Nazneen reached for the biscuit tin but Bibi pointed to the Tupperware. She ate with Nazneen's spoon, but only managed a mouthful. They spent this time together and they did not waste it by talking. They watched each other and Nazneen pretended to look out of the window while Bibi, who was too short to see out, pretended to look at the cracked tiles behind the taps.

* * *

Razia pressed her palms into the small of her back. "You know what they say in the village—a woman is elderly at twenty—well, you are looking at an old, old woman now."

Her hair was thick with gray. She wore glasses with wide black rims that shortened her nose but amplified the deep lines around her eyes. Since gaining her British passport she had acquired a sweatshirt with a large Union Jack printed on the front, and in a favorite combination paired it with brown elastic-waisted trousers. The trousers had a thick seam down the front, designed to look like a sharp crease. She held out her hands to Nazneen. "See the joints? Arthritis." She returned the hands to press against the ache. "And my back is killing. Sewing all day and all day. Children take the money, I get the arthritis."

"Everyone gets a little creak in their bones," said Nazneen. She circled her shoulders to show she was not exempt. "You are not so old."

"Eh-hrerm," said Razia, pretending to clear her throat. "Eh-eh-*hrerm*." She waggled her head and rolled her lips up and around. "Azraeel is at the door. How can you deny it? This woman is old. This is an old woman."

Nazneen laughed. "My husband, you are always right."

Razia laughed her metallic laugh. No matter how often she heard it, the sudden clang always startled Nazneen. She looked around now to see if the door was closed. The girls were in their bedroom attending to homework, and she did not want them to hear Razia poking fun at their father.

"A serious thing, though, the business with the machine work. Ruins the hands, the back, the eyes." Razia shrugged. The Union Jack rippled. "I don't care. What else is this body for? I'm just using it up now for my children. Only thing I care about is they don't have to do this same thing as me. Making a nice home as well. New chairs, new sofa, no more secondhand toothbrush for my kids. This is what I'm working for."

"Tariq is enjoying his IT?"

"It's OK-Ma," said Razia, in English. "Everything, all the time 'OK-Ma.' Boy thinks I'm called OK-Ma."

"How long must he study?"

"Another two, three years. What do I know? Ask your husband how long the boy must study. Depends how long is the wall and how big is the certificate."

Nazneen giggled. She wondered briefly, through her giggles, if she should really allow Razia to be so free about her husband. And then the giggles got up her nose and she snorted and kicked her legs and fell sideways on the sofa against her friend.

"Yes," said Razia. "If the certificates don't fill the wall, his backside is going to be whipped."

"Enough," said Nazneen, wiping her eyes. She got herself straight.

"I just hope he fills it up damn quick because all of it is costing arms and legs. However much money I give, he always needs more. 'Can I have twenty pounds for textbooks, Ma?' I just gave twenty pounds only the day before. I told him, in the village—one textbook between five children. 'OK-Ma. Can I have twenty pounds?'"

"They need the books for studying. What can you do?"

"Not just books. This thing and that thing for computer. Disk and drive and pad and all sorts." Razia crossed an ankle over her knee and held on to the lumpy shoe. She was quiet, and for a moment Nazneen stopped seeing her friend and looked at the crumpled woman with the arthritic hands and the uncared-for face.

"He is a good boy," said Nazneen.

"Oh, yes. Good boy. Loves his OK-Ma. But sometimes I worry that he studies too hard. So quiet. Always in his room. I tell him to go out and see friends. And he tells me OK-Ma and goes back in his room."

"Shefali has her exams soon?"

Razia leaned back hard and dug around in her trouser pockets. She pulled out a packet of Silk Cut and a disposable lighter. It was a new thing, and final confirmation to Chanu that Razia was of irredeemably low stock. Nazneen began to think of air freshener and whether Chanu would be back before her friend left. Razia lit up and light gray trails from her nose mingled with the fibrous gray of her hair.

"Yes. Then she wants a Year Off." She spoke the words as if they were two turds dangling from the end of a stick.

"What is it?" asked Nazneen. "Year Off?"

"Before going to university. She wants to spend one year doing nothing."

But Year Off had an official ring to it and Nazneen knew that she had not yet understood. "What sort of nothing?"

Razia put her cigarette on the orange-legged, glass-topped table and held out flat palms. "See this left hand—nothing on it. See this right hand—nothing on it. Now, tell me how is one nothing different from one other nothing?"

"Oh," said Nazneen. "The cigarette." It had rolled from the table and was burning on the green-and-purple rug.

"Shit. Your rug is spoiled."

"I don't know," said Nazneen. "If a rug is already green and purple, it is very hard to say it is spoiled."

The girls were brushing their teeth when Chanu got home. He staggered down the hallway and dropped a large cardboard box at his feet. He wriggled out of the straps of a canvas bag that was slung across his shoulders and swung it down. It dislodged another large chunk of plaster from the wall. The dust settled on Chanu's hair.

He slapped his hands together a few times, the way a man might if he has finished his tasks and is waiting for praise. "Here," he said, still trying to catch his breath. "Don't I always do as you ask? I got it." He beamed at Nazneen. The girls stuck their heads out from the bathroom. "Come on," he called to them. "See what I have got for your mother."

The girls came out in their nightdresses and stood close to Nazneen. They smelled of toothpaste and soap powder and the unvarnished scent of small, clean bodies. Nazneen could think of no excuse to grab them now and kiss their shining heads.

"You know, when I married your mother I thought I was getting a simple girl from the village and she would give me no trouble." He was playing the fool for them. Rolling his eyes and puffing his cheeks. "But she is the boss woman now. Anything she says, your father goes running off and does it. Look. Look inside the box."

The girls moved forward together. Bibi began pulling at the brown tape. Shahana pushed her aside and took charge. Suddenly both girls were ripping at the cardboard, plunging arms inside and squealing.

"Ah, wait. Let your mother see."

Nazneen came close and squatted beside the box. Inside there was a sewing machine and a tangle of wire.

"Birthday present," said Chanu.

It was not her birthday.

"Early birthday present."

"It is what I wanted."

They never celebrated their own birthdays, only the girls'.

"Let's try it," said Bibi.

Chanu bent down and unzipped the large canvas bag. It contained a computer.

"Is it your birthday present?" asked Bibi.

"That's it." He was delighted. "That's what it is."

They put the computer on the dining table and the sewing machine next to it. Thread was found and pieces of cloth. Nazneen broke one needle, Chanu fitted another, and she sewed a dish towel to a cloth that she used to wipe the floor. "It is lucky for your mother," Chanu told the girls, "that I am an educated man."

Shahana sewed a hem on a pillowcase. Bibi had a turn, but could not manage the foot tread and the needle at the same time. She held the cloth steady while Shahana took another turn. Then Chanu found the setting for zigzag stitches and made patterns on a pair of old underpants. Nazneen wiped the pale green casing although the only marks on it were tiny worn-in scratches that could not be removed. The machine had become a little warm from its exertions and she felt it should rest.

"The computer," cried Bibi.

"Let me do it," said Chanu as the girls pressed up to the screen. There was much plugging and replugging and poking of buttons before the screen began to burr and turn slowly from black to gray to blue. All the time Chanu kept up an informative commentary. *You see. This is what is called. This wire goes in the. Must never touch any. I'll show you how the.* Shahana twisted her arms up in the loose fabric of her nightdress. She wanted to tell her father to take off his coat. Nazneen stopped her with a pleading look. These gay moods came rarely enough.

Bibi listened intently to her father as if she would be tested later. The unfinished sentences were quizzes and she might be called upon to supply the missing words.

Chanu sat down and began to type. He examined the keyboard closely before each stroke, putting his face right down by the letters as though something valuable had slipped between the cracks. Minutes later he had completed a sentence. The girls pushed up to take a look. It was long past bedtime.

Bibi read it out. "'Dear Sir, I am writing to inform you.'"

"It all comes back so quickly," said Chanu, in English. His cheeks were red with pleasure.

Nazneen began to wonder about the money. Where did he get the money? She decided not to think about it.

Shahana walked away and Nazneen followed her into the girls' room. Shahana was sitting at her desk. Chanu had built them a desk each from a length of kitchen countertop he found dumped in the street. He had put shelves over their beds to hold schoolbooks, but no amount of nails or glue or swearing could keep them on the walls and finally the girls, a little wiser and a little more bruised, had refused to sleep beneath them. The wood sat on the floor under the desks and the books were piled on top.

Nazneen stood behind her daughter and stroked her hair.

"*We* are not allowed to speak English in this house," said Shahana, transgressing at top volume.

There was always this tension between them. They could never get over their disappointments. If Shahana had been a boy, would it be different? Bibi he barely noticed. He talked to her, but how surprised he would be if answers started coming back.

"And *we* are always keeping to the rule?" said Nazneen.

"But it's his stupid rule in the first place!"

"I know," said Nazneen.

When Chanu went out the girls frequently switched languages. Nazneen let it pass. Perhaps even encouraged it.

Years ago, before even Raqib was born, Razia had attempted to transfer the fruits of her community education classes to Nazneen. But they were delicate items, easily bruised. "I need a help with filling form." She had practiced it about one hundred times a day. So far, she had found no use for it.

Over the last decade and a half she had gleaned vocabulary here and there. The television, the brief exchanges at the few non-Bengali shops she entered, the dentist, the doctor, teachers at the girls' schools. But it was the girls who taught her. Without lessons, textbooks, or Razia's "key phrases." Their method was simple: they demanded to be understood.

Nazneen went back to Bengali. "When I was first married, I wanted to go to college to learn English. But your father said there was no need."

Shahana flicked her mother's hand away from her hair. When she sighed and her chest rose up against the white brushed cotton of her nightdress, Nazneen saw that breasts were beginning to come.

"And he was right. I know enough." Her hand hovered above her daughter's shoulder. "But when I was younger I was always worrying about everything."

Shahana turned around. Her eyes, mouth, nose pinched up. "So what? What are you talking about? What do I care? I hate him. I *hate* him." She jumped up and clenched her arms and teeth. And she kicked her mother's shins with her little soft feet.

* * *

Two weeks was enough to learn all the features. She mastered basting stitch, hemming, buttonholing, and gathering. Razia came to supervise and set homework. Nazneen put in zips, flew through seams. She stay-stitched the flabby end of Chanu's undershirt and chain-stitched patterns on a doll's dress. No more broken needles. No more snarled-up tea towels. Every spare piece of cloth in the house had been stitched together and taken apart and married to another. To practice on a long length she took down the curtains and sewed them into tubes. They lay across the dining table like deflated sails. Spools of colored thread sat on Chanu's books, bright flags signaling the way to knowledge. Nazneen bent to her task while Chanu read and tapped the keyboard, sang and muttered, remembered his dislike of chairs and got to the ground, remembered his stiff knees and got up, hummed and read, tapped and talked.

Today he had gone to buy food. Shahana, leaving for school, requested Birds Eye burgers. Chanu was planning fish-head curry, dried hilsha if there was no fresh. Nazneen, with cloth reserves depleted, was unpicking the lace edge of an underskirt and thinking she would get a finer needle when a knock came at the door.

Mrs. Islam was propped up in the communal hallway, Ralgex Heat Spray in hand. Nazneen carried the cavernous black bag for her and put an arm beneath Mrs. Islam's elbow as they walked inside. Mrs. Islam had surprisingly sharp elbows. Nazneen cleared the sofa and the visitor lay down. She tugged her sari at the hip, applied the Ralgex, and moaned. She sprayed her stomach, inserted the tin into the sleeve of her cardigan, and sprayed again. Then she sprayed a handkerchief and placed it over her face. It was understood that these exertions must be made in silence and a proper recuperative period be allowed. Nazneen stood by.

Although she appeared in no way older than when Nazneen was a young bride, Mrs. Islam had declared herself to be in her dotage. The black bag, which had itself aged severely, was a pharmaceutical cornucopia—as if, late in life, the bag had found its true calling. It carried a stockpile of tablets, lozenges, powders, and bottles. There were jars of ointment and packets of mysterious granules. And there were canisters of medicinal spices and a few loose sheaves of herbs. But all these were merely held in reserve, for emergency procedures, perhaps. Whenever Nazneen was ordered to delve for a medication it was invariably Benylin Chesty Coughs.

Mrs. Islam waved weakly towards the bag and Nazneen leaped forward and undid the destoned clasp. She handed over the bottle and Mrs.

Islam drank deeply beneath her handkerchief. During the past ten years, Nazneen could not recall a single occasion on which she had heard Mrs. Islam coughing. Benylin Chesty Coughs was very effective. Sometimes, in an afternoon visit, she would drink an entire bottle and fall asleep for an hour or so. Chanu would creep around and speak in exaggerated whispers to Nazneen. "Isn't it an honor? See how relaxed she is here. I knew her husband."

The Ralgex Heat Spray she also carried around. The smell, mixed with the mints she kept under her tongue and the sweet syrup cough preparation, produced about her an aura of the sickbed. But her eyes were hard and bright and her voice came like darts.

"Gold mine," she said, removing the handkerchief from her face and casting a glance in the direction of the sewing machine.

"I have been practicing," said Nazneen. She sat in the cow-dung-colored armchair and held up a gather-stitched duster as evidence.

"When I was a girl we learned to stitch by hand. We did not have things so easy."

Nazneen, who had a bit of cramp in her right hand and was toying with the idea of borrowing the Ralgex, could only agree. "Yes. It is very fast. Good machine."

Mrs. Islam wiggled her carpet slippers. "Are you going to start sending the girls? Your husband said you would send them but they have not been seen."

"Oh," said Nazneen. "Yes."

Through a fug of Ralgex Heat Spray, applied to the collarbone, Mrs. Islam said, "I am a sick woman now. Very, very sick. Anyone can say anything to me. They know how weak I have become. You tell me 'Yes, they will go,' but you do not send them. But to sick old women it is possible to say anything."

She was talking about the madrasah, the new mosque school. It had been established with a generous endowment from Mrs. Islam. Shahana and Bibi were supposed to go after ordinary school had finished for the day but Chanu forbade it. He raged. "Do they call it education? Rocking around like little parrots on a perch, reciting words they do not understand." He would teach them. The Qur'an, but also Hindu philosophy, Buddhist thought, Christian parables. "Don't forget," he told Nazneen, "Bengal was Hindu long before it was Muslim, and before that Buddhist, and that was after the first Hindu period. We are only Muslims because of the Moguls. Don't forget." And to Mrs.

Islam, he said, "Yes, my wife will send them. I remember your husband. He was the most respectable-type man. One time we thought of doing some business. Jute industry. Import-export sort of affair."

Nazneen opened her mouth to protest but Mrs. Islam cut her off. "You do as you please. I tell my sons—Mrs. Ahmed always does as she pleases, I don't interfere. I tried to look after her son, loved that child like my own, but she slapped me down and I don't interfere." She took a swig of Benylin and a little red ooze appeared down the side of her chin. "Only I can tell you this. A sick woman still has ears. If you think I have gone deaf, let me tell you my ears are good. I hear what goes on." In her excitement she had half sat up but she remembered now her invalid status and rested with her forearms across her forehead. The bottle and the spray can framed her face.

"I will speak to my husband," said Nazneen. She looked for a way out. "How is your hip? Is it giving much trouble?"

Mrs. Islam hitched down the side of her sari to expose a large, perfectly smooth brown hip. She grunted as if to say, Satisfied now? "My sons tell me to go for a hip replacement, but I say no. Do not waste a good new hip. I do not want to be buried with a new hip. God does not love a wasteful woman. Save the good hips for those who can use them. Give the money to the mosque and give me only a little for the Heat Spray. That's all I ask." She paused a while and then said it again, more gently. "That's all I ask." Then she tried once more, attempting softness, the suggestion of fading, a hint that now—even now—she might be slipping from life. "That's all I ask."

Nazneen sat on the edge of her chair, within reach of the black bag.

"Open the bag for me, child," said Mrs. Islam, her voice still feeble.

Nazneen knelt and opened it.

"Place the money in the side pocket. I don't count it."

"You don't count it?" Nazneen ran her fingers over the tarnished, twisted clasp. She looked inside among the packets and tubes to see where the money might be. It would clearly be more convenient to keep the money in the side compartment where it would be easy to find, rather than hiding somewhere in the depths of this pharmacy. She fished around. Something sticky on the lining. Some powder bursting through from a thin cardboard pack. The whole contents needed sorting out. She was just about to offer when Mrs. Islam said, "Ah, to be young and strong again."

A packet of throat sweets was lying crushed at the bottom of the bag. Nazneen pulled it out and held it up. "Look. Leaking honey."

Mrs. Islam twisted herself around and propped herself up on an elbow. "Did you put the money in?" Her voice came sharply, and immediately she added in a weaker tone, "Did you, child?"

"I can't find it."

"Look again, child. Fifty pounds. As arranged."

Nazneen looked closer, her head practically in the bag. The smell was overpowering, an essence of ill health.

"What are you doing?" screeched Mrs. Islam. "Get out of my bag."

Nazneen sat up and the back of her neck had been branded. Heat spread around her skull and into her cheeks. "You asked me . . ." she said slowly.

"Do I look like a dead woman to you?" said Mrs. Islam, suddenly very alive.

Nazneen could only open her mouth and close it again.

"Are you trying to rob my grave? Get. Me. My. Money."

She knew now. Everything was clear. Chanu took a loan. Mrs. Islam had come to collect. But still Nazneen did not move. She had no money to give. As arranged. Gesturing towards the sewing machine, she gave her only defense. "Still practicing. No work yet."

Mrs. Islam considered for a moment. Her small black bird eyes fixed on Nazneen's burning face. "I understand. Forgive a sick and anxious old woman. This arrangement is between friends. Pay when you can." She made a show of struggling to her feet and Nazneen helped her so that when she was up they stood in a sort of embrace. Mrs. Islam kissed her, hard mouth to soft cheek. "We understand each other. I will come again. My salaam to your husband."

They went to the door. Mrs. Islam tucked a fresh mint beneath her tongue, applied a general mist of Ralgex, a prescription of perfume, and took her bag from Nazneen.

"You will find a way," she said. "God always gives a way. You just have to find it. And I will bring my sons next time. They would like to see your husband again."

Chapter Nine

On his computer, Chanu could access the entire world. "Anything," he said. "Anything you want to see. Just tell me and I'll find it. This little wire that goes into the telephone socket—do you see it?—it all comes down the wire."

"We go on the internet at school," said Shahana, in English.

Chanu pretended not to hear.

Bibi held on to her plaits. She tried so hard that she could not think of anything.

"I'd like to see kadam again," said Nazneen.

He held up a finger. "So you shall." He jabbed away. "I am typing it in. Key words: Flowers of Bangladesh." The computer thought for a while. Bibi looked over her shoulder at Nazneen. Shahana blew up at her fringe, a new development that Chanu read as insolence. The screen flickered into life. "One hundred and sixteen entries," marveled Chanu. He fiddled with the mouse and a picture wove itself, strand by thick strand. Clustered over the screen was an array of pink prickly balls.

"Kadam," said Nazneen.

"Bor-*ing,*" sang Shahana, in English.

Chanu remained calm. "Bangla2000 website. Who wants to take a look?"

Bibi stepped closer to her father. But he was waiting for Shahana.

Nazneen put her hand on Shahana's arm. "Go on, girl," she whispered. Shahana did not budge. "Take a little look."

"*No*. It's bor-*ing.*"

Chanu jumped up and turned round in one movement so that the dining chair toppled. His cheeks quivered. "Too boring for the memsahib?"

"She's going to look now," said Nazneen. Bibi backed away from her father, a barely perceptible shuffling that gave the impression that she was responding to the tug of her mother's force field.

"What is the wrong with you?" shouted Chanu, speaking in English.

"Do you mean," said Shahana, "'What is wrong with you?'" She blew at her fringe. "Not 'the wrong.'"

He gasped hard as if she had punched him in the stomach. For a few seconds his jaw worked frantically. "Tell your sister," he screamed, reverting to Bengali, "that I am going to tie her up and cut out her tongue. Tell the memsahib that when I have skinned her alive she will not be looking so pleased with herself."

Bibi began to repeat, "He is going to tie you up and cut out . . ." She squinted up at Nazneen. "I don't want to tell her. You can tell her for me, can't you?" Anxiety pressed on her forehead and lowered it against her eyes.

Inside Chanu, a tornado was at work. It shook his body and twisted his face. "I'll kill you now," he shrieked. He ripped the mouse from the computer and launched himself at Shahana. The wire caught Shahana across the cheek and she ran for cover behind the sofa. Chanu approached but stood indecisively in front of it. He moved to the right and Shahana feinted left. He took a step to the left and she dodged the other way. He lunged across the top and grabbed hold of a skinny wrist. He began to flail with the mouse while Shahana wriggled and lashed out with her free arm.

If only she would cry, thought Nazneen. She should cry now and save his tears.

"Don't touch my computer," yelled Chanu. "You are forbidden." He slowed down. Shahana risked putting her head above the sofa back. He stopped. "Your sister is forbidden as well. Do you hear me?"

"Yes, Abba," said Bibi smartly.

"Yes, Abba," said Shahana. "I won't touch it."

Nazneen took the girls to their room. A redness circled Shahana's wrist. She pulled her arm away from her mother and sucked her lips inside her mouth.

"Time for bed," said Nazneen. She kissed Bibi and she tried to kiss Shahana. Leaving the room, she turned around in time to see Shahana land a kick on her sister's behind. Bibi rubbed her bottom and sat down on her bed. Shahana flung herself facedown and began to kick the mattress.

Chanu rubbed his hand hard over his face and shook his head. He wobbled his fleshy nose with the center of his palm. "Gone to bed?" he asked.

"Yes," said Nazneen.

The computer was turned off.

A chair scraped overhead.

"These girls," said Chanu, baffled by their very existence.

"Mrs. Islam came today."

"These girls."

"Mrs. Islam."

He was annoyed. "Don't keep telling me 'Mrs. Islam'!"

"She came today."

"Yes. You told me that." He put his hands beneath his stomach and lifted it up and down.

"For the money."

With his undershirt riding up over his chest, Chanu pressed his stomach up as high as it would go. The effect was startling. It became taut as a water-filled balloon and exposed a band of purplish flesh, eager to greet the air. He let go and the flesh cascaded onto his lap. "Money? Oh, yes. I'll take it next week." He smiled unevenly and rubbed his hands together. "You look a bit hungry. Why don't you make some shimai? Let's have a little sweet something before bed."

Later, when the shimai had been made and Chanu had eaten while Nazneen washed the dishes, they went together to watch them sleep, to hear them breathe, to rearrange limbs beneath blankets and administer secret doses of love. Chanu smoothed Shahana's hair away from her face. He sat on the edge of the bed and put an arm across her insensible form. His small eyes were lost in creases. Then they swapped places and Chanu went to Bibi. He kissed her cheek and he held her hand and Nazneen saw him and saw that he was not just baffled but afraid. They went out together and she turned from closing the door and leaned into him so that her head rested on his shoulder and his chin brushed against her hair.

There had been a period, weeks or perhaps months but to Nazneen it seemed an infinity, when he had gone to bed and stayed there. He stopped making plans. His plans, to which he gave his all and from which he expected so much, had deserted him. Before that, each collapse of ambition, though it dented his surface, had goaded him to new determination, a more urgent reaching. He started every new job with a freshly spruced suit and a growing collection of pens. His face shone with hope. And then grayed with frustration, with resentment. He began businesses with a visit to the shoe repairer and made outlays on hard-sided, brisk briefcases. Energetic numbers on his furiously written and rewritten business plans showed the way to fortunes. And he worked hard; worked late on his plans; joked with Nazneen; became indulgent with the children.

But he was slighted. By customers, by suppliers, by superiors and inferiors. He worked hard for respect but he could not find it. There was in the world a great shortage of respect and Chanu was among the famished.

Finally, he lay down on the bed and began a monotonous grumbling. Then he took his certificates and spread them around and looked at them day after day. He stopped the grumbling. He stopped eating and his stomach became alarmingly small, puckered and loose, a depleted rice sack. When he stopped reading, Nazneen was overpowered with worry.

The Jobcentre called him for an interview. He was offered a job washing dishes in a restaurant. He went back to bed, but he was in some way galvanized. Some vestige of fight was reignited within him and he began setting tasks for his daughters.

"Shahana," he would call. "Quick, girl. Look. Be quick." When she arrived in the bedroom, scratching intensely at her arm, he ordered her to fetch his slippers. She picked them up from the foot of the bed and dangled them by the heels.

"OK?" she said.

"Put them on. Quick." He lifted his feet.

On her way out she was recalled to arrange his pillows, pass the water jug, find his pen, pull the curtains or draw them back.

Or he would call out for Bibi. "Bibi, everything in this bedroom is in a muddle. How many times do I tell you to help your mother?" And Bibi would scurry around, banging between bed and dressing table and standing on the mattress, which was the only way for her to reach into the wardrobe, to rearrange trousers and shirts and saris.

But the execution of these tasks was unsatisfying. The girls hurried through them and when he could think of nothing more, they left. Eventually he hit on something. He took up his books again and employed the girls as page turners. It was perfect. Lying against a bank of pillows, Chanu had one of the girls hold up a volume while sitting on the edge of the bed. They had to watch his face for signs that he was nearing the end of the page and then turn to the next. He was fair with them. He gave signs, little anticipatory raises of his tangled eyebrows. Only an inattentive daughter could fail to see. A disrespectful daughter. Who fully deserved the lashing, verbal or otherwise, that followed such dereliction of duty.

* * *

Nazneen thought about it now, as she undressed. The eternal three-way torture of daughter-father-daughter. How they locked themselves apart at this very close distance. Bibi, silently seeking approval, always hungry. Chanu, quivering with his own needs, always offended. Shahana, simmering in—worst of all things—perpetual embarrassment, implacably angry. It was like walking through a field of snakes. Nazneen was worried at every step.

She had to concentrate hard to get through each day. Sometimes she felt as if she held her breath the entire evening. It was up to her to balance the competing needs, to soothe here and urge there, and push the day along to its close. When she failed, and there was an eruption, a flogging or a tantrum or a tear-stained flat cheek, she felt dizzy with responsibility. When she succeeded, she made it a mantra not to forget, not to let it go to her head. *Be careful, be careful, be careful.* It took all her energy. It took away longing. Her wants were close at hand, real and within her control. If only she focused sufficiently. When she drifted she thought of Hasina, but she made her thoughts as efficient as possible. How much could she save? How much could she send? How would she hide it from Chanu?

Sometimes, when she put her head on the pillow and began to drift into sleep, she jerked herself awake in panic. How could she afford to relax? Then she would go into the kitchen and eat without knowing what she put into her mouth. On bad nights when her thoughts could not be submerged by rice or bread or crackers she began to wonder if she loved her daughters properly. Did she love them as she had loved her son? When she thought of them like this—when they grew distant—her stomach fell down through her legs and her lungs shot up against her heart. Which was exactly the feeling she had when, on a cool winter night, she went down to the pond with Hasina. It was the feeling she had when she was about to jump, knowing that the water was cold enough to make her scream.

And she squeezed Raqib from her mind. That way lay the abyss. So she swallowed hard and prayed hard, and she used prayer, in defiance of her vows, to dull her senses and dull her pain.

Back from collecting the girls, Nazneen made a cup of tea and mulled over the school-gate gossip. She picked up only Bibi now that Shahana went to the big school and preferred to walk back with her friends, but she still thought of it as "collecting the girls." Jorina said that police had been to the mosque and questioned the imam for two hours. No one had any idea why, although many predicted trouble and everyone doubted that a church had ever been treated with such flagrant disrespect. Nazma was talking about Razia with Sorupa and broke off mid-sentence when Nazneen approached. Most intriguing was an overheard conversation between two white women discussing how to slim down their dogs. One favored a home-enforced diet while the other took her animal to a weight-loss clinic. Although English words did not come easily from her mouth, Nazneen had long been able to follow conversation. Not much surprised her anymore. But some things still did.

She was making a second cup of tea and thinking about the emaciated piebald curs of Gouripur when Chanu came home with a plastic-wrapped bundle.

"No time for tea drinking," he said. "Come on. Come." He hurried through to the sitting room and Nazneen followed.

He ripped the thin sheath of plastic and unfurled the legs of a dozen or so pairs of men's trousers. "Hemming," he announced to the world at large. "Test batch." He tugged at the other end of the bundle. "Zips," he said. "All will be inspected."

Nazneen wanted to begin at once, but Chanu insisted on calling the girls.

"When I married her, I said: She is a good worker. Girl from the village. Unspoilt. All the clever-clever girls—" He broke off and looked at Shahana. "All the clever-clever girls are not worth one hair on her head."

Bibi opened and closed her mouth. Her white lacy socks had fallen around her ankles and her shins looked dry and dusty. Shahana had begun to use moisturizer. Yesterday she had refused to wash her hair with Fairy Liquid. She wanted shampoo now.

Nazneen held on to the casing of the sewing machine. Chanu waggled his head and beamed at her. She fixed the thread and began. One trouser leg, then the other. When she had finished, they clapped, and Bibi became sufficiently carried away to venture a small cheer, and Chanu's applause was emphatic, and Shahana smiled fleetingly and marched back to the bedroom.

Chanu brought home holdalls of buttonless shirts, carrier bags of unlined dresses, a washing-up tub full of catchless bras. He counted them out and he counted them back in. Every couple of days he went for new loads. He performed a kind of rudimentary quality control, tugging at zips and twiddling collars while probing his cheeks with his tongue.

Chanu totted up the earnings and collected them. He was the middleman, a role which he viewed as Official and in which he exerted himself. For a couple of weeks he puzzled feverishly over calculations, trying to work out the most profitable type of garment assignment, the highest-margin operation. But he had to take what was available and the calculations were themselves a low-margin endeavor. Then he had time to supervise in earnest and he made himself available at her elbow, handing thread, passing scissors, dispensing advice, making tea, folding garments.

"All you have to do," he said, "is sit there."

She got up to stretch her legs. She picked up one of his books and blew off some lint, hoping something in him would respond to the call of neglected type.

"We're making good money this week." He pulled at his lower lip, working it out. "Don't worry. I'll take care of everything."

For two whole months she did not even know how much she had earned. It was a relief when, for the first time since the piecework began, Chanu retired to the bedroom one evening and called for a page turner. The next day, a Saturday, he made a kind of fortress of books around him on the sitting-room floor and delivered a pungent oration on the ancient history of Bengal. On Sunday he shaved with extra care and limbered up in front of the mirror in a suit, but did not go out. The next day he went out all day and came back singing fragments of Tagore. It was a good sign.

Tuesday and Wednesday passed in the same pattern and Nazneen completed the linings of thirty-seven miniskirts. She had no more sewing to do.

Chanu gathered his family together and exorcised some troublesome blockages in his throat. "As you are all aware." He noticed Shahana's dress. She had hitched up her uniform at school so that it bloused over the belt and rode up towards her thigh. Without changing her expression she began to inch it slowly downwards.

"As you are all aware, we have decided—as a family—to return home. Your mother is doing everything possible to facilitate our dream through the old and honorable craft of tailoring. And don't forget it was we who invented all these weaves of cloths—muslin and damask and every damn thing." He seemed uncertain. He looked at his daughters as if he had forgotten who they were. Only when his darting gaze fixed on Nazneen did he remember himself.

"Ahem. So. We are going home. I have today become an employee at

Kempton Kars, driver number one-six-one-nine, and the Home Fund will prosper. That is all I have to say."

Nazneen and Bibi clapped their hands. It came as a surprise that Chanu could drive a car.

As if to dispel their silent doubts he took a tattered piece of paper from his pocket. "Driving license," he said, in English. He inspected the document. "Nineteen seventy-six. Never had it framed."

So Chanu became a taximan and ceased to be a middleman. And on the first hot day of the year, when the windows were closed against the ripening of waste bins and the flat hummed to the tune of its pipes, and Nazneen had mopped up the overflow from the blocked toilet and washed her hands and sighed into the mirror, a new middleman appeared. Karim, with a bale of jeans over his broad shoulder.

This was how he came into her life.

Chapter Ten

It was a strange thing, and it took her some time to realize it. When he spoke in Bengali he stammered. In English, he found his voice and it gave him no trouble. Having made the discovery, she went back to the beginning and made it afresh. She considered him. The way he stood with his legs wide and his arms folded. His hair. Cut so close to the skull. The way it came to a triangle at the front, and the little bit that stood up straight at the center of his forehead. He wore his jeans tight and his shirtsleeves rolled up to the elbow. No. There was nothing there. No clue to the glitches in his Bengali voice.

And he was sure of himself. He took a strong stance. Sometimes his right leg worked to a random beat. He wore white trainers and a thin gold chain around his neck. He said, "My uncle owns the factory." He said, "The sweatshop. My uncle owns it." And he bounced his leg and fiddled with his mobile phone, waiting for her to count up the linings.

He wore the phone at his hip, in a little black leather holster. He felt the length and breadth of it and tested the surface with his thumb, as if he had discovered a growth, this tumorous phone on his side. Then he refolded his arms. They looked strong, those arms. His hair. Razored short against the skull. It was odd, that the shape of a skull could be pleasing.

When his phone rang, he took it out to the hallway. She caught only fragments. A word, a phrase, a word repeated, a word struggling for release. The caller would not let him speak. So it seemed. It took some time to work out that it was his voice, not his listener, that had failed him.

"My husband had a mobile phone," she told him. "But he gave it up. Said it was too expensive."

"Y-y-your husband is right."

She switched to English. "Very useful thing."

"Y-y-yes, but t-t-too expensive."

She saw at once that she had made a mistake. She had drawn attention to the very thing she had thought to hide. He would not speak English now. He would not disown himself. She thought of what to say and how to say it. But by then he had put money on the table and left.

She still had five more hems to do when he came the next time. Opening the door, she knew that something was wrong. The look on his face. He rushed past and into the sitting room. He held the window frame. "Gone," he said. "They've gone." His head and shoulders slumped forward, and he began to pant just then though the action was over.

"What it was?"

He turned around. Sweat across the top of his lip. Sunshine in his hair made it sparkle. Some kind of oil. Or more sweat. He told her about the two men pushing leaflets through front doors. Pushing their filthy leaflets through letterboxes. He picked up the box—right under their noses—and he ran with it.

He got into position now. Legs wide, right leg working, and she saw the thigh strain inside the denim and she looked down at her sewing, which she had not finished. They had chased him but he was faster. He put the box, the filthy leaflets, in the bin where they belonged. He looped the estate, they didn't see where he went, he looped back again to check, and nobody saw him come up to the flat. It was safe. Quite safe.

"They'll get what's coming to them, man. That ain't the end of it."

"What they say? The leaflets." She had forgotten to cover her hair.

He sat down, across the table from her, and now the sun was directly behind him so that from the corner of her eye she saw him in silhouette. It was the first time he had sat down in her home. She thought about tea but she was unsure what it would mean, to have tea with this boy. He was not a relative.

"I know who they are."

"These men."

"I know them, man. I know them."

"Yes."

"Lion Hearts. They are behind it. We are going to make them pay, man."

"Who they are?"

"Just a front. They are only a front. We know everything about them. Everything." He had his hands palms up on the table, slightly cupped, vibrating. Weighing it all up, or asking for trouble.

He put his hands under the table. She watched him obliquely.

"In our country," she said, "everyone would stop. Come and help you."

He rocked back in his chair. "This is my country."

She told him she still had five hems to do and he said that he would wait. Though she kept her eyes to her work, she felt his gaze. Sun on the needle surround flashed iridescent prisms over her fingernails. She machined in bursts and thought of drawing the curtain but the thought was, somehow, confusing to her and she did not do it. The last hem snagged and she had to get up for the scissors.

She saw then that he had been reading all this time and a heat came into her face. He looked up and she looked away.

"That sari," he said. "My mother had one. Same material I mean."

It was soft blue with a deep green band around it. Chanu had picked it out. He called it subtle and he said it was like her, subtle beauty, which she liked though she knew it was the words that pleased him.

She said nothing.

"She's dead now. Man." He looked at his magazine, as though his dead mother were nothing to him.

"I sorry."

"Yeah," he said. "Man." And he turned the page. "'Are you a good Muslim? Twenty ways to tell.'" He held up the magazine, and Nazneen saw that it was no more than a few flimsy pages in black and white, stapled at the side.

Driver one-six-one-nine was frequently on duty in the evenings. Evenings in the flat became more relaxed. The girls did their homework in front of the television. Shahana said it helped her to concentrate. Bibi chewed the end of her pen. The laughter on the soundtrack never made her smile, although Shahana developed a sophisticated giggle. Nazneen continued with her piecework. If she worked fast, if she didn't make mistakes, she could earn as much as three pounds and fifty pence in one hour. Maybe a little bit more. She heard the television and she caught glimpses of Shahana on her tummy, legs in the air, crossing and uncrossing. She thought about the five-pound notes inside the jar, wrapped in a cloth, inside a plastic bag, snapped into a see-through container that sat in the cupboard beneath the kitchen sink. She reminded herself of the money in an envelope on the high shelf, near the Qur'an, and decided it was haram and would have to be removed. She counted the money pushed into the foot of a pair of tights, wound up in a ball at the back of her underwear drawer. Another five pounds put away today. Fifteen more pounds wrapped in Clingfilm, inside a sandwich bag, pushed into the hole in the wall next to the boiler. She would take it to the Sonali

Bank in the morning. Hasina would have it before the end of the month. Some she would give to Shahana for the things she coveted, shampoo and lotion and clips for her hair.

Sometimes Chanu was out for the whole night. Then she would rise early and have the food heated, rice cooked fresh, ready for him on the table. "I'll eat now." He said it as he came through the door and he sat down with his coat still on and ate, jumping up when he remembered he had not washed his hand, preparing another mouthful before he had even taken up his place again, calling for pickle and chutney and a slice of lemon, some chopped onion on a side plate, a glass of water. "Oh, well, put it here," he said when she told him it was already on the table. "Put it just here so I can reach it."

"These people," he would say. "Ignorant types. What can you do?"

She never learned anything about Kempton Kars. She did not hear about any Mr. Dalloways, any Wilkies. The customers retained their mystery. All she knew was what he told her, that they were ignorant types.

But he was philosophical. "You see, all my life I have struggled. And for what? What good has it done? I have finished with all that. Now, I just take the money. I say thank you. I count it." He put a ball of rice and dal in his mouth and held it inside his cheek. "You see, when the English went to our country, they did not go to stay. They went to make money, and the money they made, they took it out of the country. They never left home. Mentally. Just taking money out. And that is what I am doing now. What else can you do?"

These speeches he made in the simple language of a simple—though not ignorant-type—man. But when he took out his books in the evenings he spent at home, he began to speak differently.

He had Shahana turn pages as he lay on the sofa. Bibi was in the bedroom, twisting her ankles together beneath the desk and worrying a bit of paper. Shahana's face was pulling in on itself, setting into a mask of utter disregard. She knelt by the sofa and held the book at an angle to her father's face. He raised his eyebrows. Then he raised them again, farther this time so that they untangled from each other at the center. Shahana turned the page.

"Ah," said Chanu. "The search for knowledge. Is there any journey more satisfying? Call your sister." But he called her himself. "Bibi. Come quick." She came running and stood behind Shahana. Chanu took the book in his own hands, sat up, and chewed over some knowledge that he planned to share with them.

"I will tell you something. All these people who look down on us do not know what I am going to tell you. I have it here in black and white." He waved the book. "Who was it who saved the work of Plato and Aristotle for the West during the Dark Ages? Us. It was us. Muslims. We saved the work so that your so-called Saint Thomas could claim it for his own discovery? That is the standard of our scholarship and that is the standard of their gratitude." He held up a finger and it trembled with emotion.

Bibi took the end of one plait and tucked it into her mouth.

"Dark Ages," said Chanu, and his face flinched from the insult. "This is what they are calling it in these damn Christian books. Is this what they teach you in school?" He threw the book on the floor. "It was the Golden Age of Islam, the height of civilization. Don't forget it. Take pride, or all is lost." He lay down again, exhausted by the slander, and the girls began to back away.

He called after them. "Do you know what Gandhi said when asked what he thought about Western civilization?"

The girls hovered at the end of the sofa.

"He said he thought it would be a good idea." Chanu laughed and Bibi smiled. "I'll teach you," he said, "more about our religion. And we will study Hindu philosophy. After that, Buddhist thought." And he put a cushion beneath his head and began to hum.

Nazneen was helping the girls to tidy their room. A piece of wallpaper had begun to peel away from the wall above Bibi's bed and was turning itself into a scroll. She picked up a doll from the floor and put it on the end of the bed. There was a man doll under the chair, eyeless now and one-armed, naked and imprinted with dirt. Nazneen looked at it but did not pick it up.

"I'm not going," said Shahana. "I'll run away." She opened a cupboard and pulled out a bag. Inside she had put a nightdress, a pair of shoes, jeans, and a T-shirt. "I'm ready to run."

Bibi rubbed her fists into her cheeks. Her eyes went red. "I want to stay with her."

"Shush," said Nazneen. "No silly talk."

"It's not silly," shouted Shahana. "I'm not going."

Nazneen straightened up the desk. She picked up a small pile of dirty clothes and held it to her chest. Bibi tested the thin carpet with her toes and Shahana was busy scratching her arms.

"We just have to wait and see." Nazneen sat down on Bibi's bed with the dirty clothes on her lap. "We do not know what God has in His mind."

It was not enough and Nazneen looked for something else. For one dizzying moment she was flushed with power: she would make it right for the girls. It strained her insides, as if she would vomit. And then, just as quickly, it left her.

Bibi came and sat next to her so that she felt the heat from her body. There was an ink stain on her school blouse and a white sheen of dry skin across her shins.

"Do you want to go?" Bibi turned her broad face to look up at her mother, as if she would catch the reply between her own lips.

Nazneen told the girls a story. The story of How You Were Left to Your Fate. It was not the first time they had heard it, but they both listened well. She began with the words "I was a stillborn child," and she ended with "that was God's will." It was the way she always told it.

Bibi discovered a scab on her knee and played with it. Nazneen began to fold the clothes on her lap, remembered they were dirty, balled them, and stood up. As she reached the door, Shahana called to her.

"You didn't answer. It wasn't an answer."

"It was my answer," said Nazneen.

The village was leaving her. Sometimes a picture would come. Vivid; so strong she could smell it. More often, she tried to see and could not. It was as if the village was caught up in a giant fisherman's net and she was pulling at the fine mesh with bleeding fingers, squinting into the sun, vision mottled with netting and eyelashes. As the years passed the layers of netting multiplied and she began to rely on a different kind of memory. The memory of things she knew but no longer saw.

It was only in her sleep that the village came whole again. She dreamed of Mumtaz that night, and her mynah bird. The bird lying on its back in Mumtaz's palm while she stroked its shining black chest. The clatter of its feet across the top of an oil can and the collar of white around its throat. "You make me laugh. Ha, ha, ha." It put back its head and ducked it, ducked again. "You make me laugh."

Mumtaz fed it with her own hand. It slept on the roof of her hut and she swept up its droppings each morning. For a couple of years they were inseparable.

Amma sucked on her large curved teeth. "Treat it like a baby, but it will fly away. Waste your love on a bird, but it cannot love you back. It will fly away."

"You're bad," Mumtaz told the bird. "Go away." But she smiled at Amma. "If it is God's will, he will fly."

"It's a terrible thing," Amma told Nazneen. "A widow and childless and she had to return to her brother. Giving her love to a bird. Depending on a man like that."

"Terrible thing," said Nazneen.

But Mumtaz did not seem to know how terrible it was. She sang to the bird and the bird made her laugh. "You make me laugh," she told it, and the bird laughed back. They played a game with a small rubber ball. Mumtaz threw it and the bird caught it in its beak.

"It will fly away," said Amma, grinding the spices and testing her teeth against her lip. Her toes curled into the soft mud floor of the yard. From the shade of the pomegranate tree she withstood a few minutes more of her luckless life. She shouted at the servant boy because the yard was not properly swept and she shouted at the new widow (a relative taken in but a lesser relative who was suffered as long as she served) because the fire was not properly set. Groaning, she continued to grind.

"You're bad," the bird told Nazneen one day. "Go away." Obedient, she went.

Everyone laughed and Nazneen made up her mind to return and join the laughter but her legs still carried her forward. She went to the edge of the village and looked across the fields, the river; watched a sampan with its ragged sail lazy in the still air, the boatman unconcerned on his haunches. When the smoke began to rise from the mound of the farthest village, the thought of dinner pulled her home. Mumtaz said, "Well, my serious friend. Still glad you came back to life?"

The bird did not fly away. Someone taught it a bad word. Amma was furious. Abba laughed and said, "Naturally she is upset. She comes from a family of saints." He went away for a few days and when he returned there was a bounce in his step. The bird learned another bad word. It called out to everyone that passed and it had a new laugh, a chuckle at the back of its throat, and when Abba laughed as well they sounded like brothers.

A table had been brought out into the big yard. Stools set around. The women kept to their quarters and the men chewed their pipes.

Nazneen and Hasina watched the elders arrive and take their seats. Hasina pulled on her imaginary beard and coughed and spat. Nazneen thumped her on the arm. Abba began to speak and the men sucked with all their strength on the hookahs and sipped the cups of steaming tea. Abba finished and another man began to speak, another joined in and another until soon they all struggled to be heard. A scream from the women's quarters scattered their words like a handful of seed; they fell and were lost and if anything grew from them it would be later. For now it was quiet, and Abba rose and walked quickly across the yard and Nazneen and Hasina darted around the back so that from different directions they reached Mumtaz at the same time. She held the bird, on its back, in the palm of her hand and she stroked its black chest. They went closer and they saw the way the head hung down. It was certain now. It would not fly away.

She woke from the dream and looked at her husband's face, squashed against the pillow. Her legs were involved with his and she reclaimed them. Then she went to the sitting room and began to sew. After a short time the machine was idle and she only sat.

A heap of sequined vests lay to the side. She had put zips in three of them. She picked one up and held it out. The little plastic disks caught the light, wavering between pink and white. She took it to the bathroom and locked the door, unbuttoned her nightdress and removed her arms from the sleeves, tied the sleeves around her waist. The zip went at the back and it was difficult to do it up, but she managed. She looked in the mirror and looked away quickly. In the cabinet she found a band for her hair and piled it on top of her head. Facing her reflection once again, she saw that her breasts looked flat. She put her hand inside the top and pulled her left breast up and then the right one so that they sat together at the sequined neckline and made a deep valley between them. She looked in the mirror but she did not see herself, only the flare of the sequins, and then she closed her eyes and the ice smelled of limes and she moved without weight and there was someone at her side, her hand in another, and they turned together, arms around waists, and through her half-closed lashes she saw him. The fine gold chain about his neck. And then she opened her eyes and took off the top. She held it out again and she saw that the sequins were cheap. She turned it over in her hands. The sequins looked like fish scales.

DHANMONDI, DHAKA

January 2001

Bismillahir rahmanir rahim.

How much I have to praise for Him! How much He have given me! All times I making mistakes, all times I going off from straight Path and He is giving chance again and then again. Here is for me another chance.

They took me from House of Falling Women is destitute hostel in Hazaribagh under wing of Brother Andrew who has come here from Canada for saving us. Friend of Lovely have take another woman out from there and Lovely say "She is not only charitable lady in whole of Dhaka. Let us take one too." That is how she say to husband James.

In actual fact husband name is Jamshed Rashid but everyone calling James. Lovely have name Anwara Begum but nobody call her like this. Everyone call Lovely even own children.

House in Dhanmondi. Good good place and house too good also. Downstair big room with plenty wood furniture television video machine. Special wood the furniture you never see like this how much it glow. This room know as reception room. Little room full toys and books is playroom. Is one whole entire room for children for play. Bathroom downstair and kitchen beside. My room is next kitchen. It have electric light.

Upstair is room for Lovely and James. Is call master bedroom. The boy name Jimmy. He have next big room. The baby name Daisy. She have own room all for she. Other bedroom have name guest room. Every day I go inside and turn down sheet for the bed is airing. Lovely say "In good household the guest bed is always properly air." Every evening I must keep to my mind to pull sheet again up.

Oh sister He has not turned His face from me. All the mistakes I make. Here I am in spite even so.

Street is wide and nice. But plastic bag blowing everywhere. Walk in street for five ten minute and by finish you cover in bag on legs and arms and stomach. Everyone hate the bag but also all accepting what can you do? Like as if Allah making mosquito and plastic bag equal-equal for being in this world.

End of street it go narrow and here one or two shop and also rickshaw workshop. You see them painting back panels and also on baby taxi. I like to watch. Most often is painting Taj Mahal or mosque but also is peacock tiger elephant and film star. One is painting picture for face of woman and I stop and ask. It face belong to singer in USA country she call Britainy Spear.

Very beautiful she too. But when I find self there go slow and stop then I bring to mind that I must hurry and do errand for Lovely. How many time He bring me luck again? No I must hurry always.

My duty in house is for care the children cleaning wash plate wash clothes shopping and errand and thing. That is all. There is man for cooking and he also take heavy work in garden and I only do is bit watering weeding and grow some special few vegetable behind house. You see how is. Very good position.

Sister I waiting for your letter and praying. But maybe since long time you have move and these words stay words as they do not go into you and it my love only that reach somehow to you. Wherever you are still it come and it find you always.

Hasina

February

I have your letter. All others are lost. Gone in that time I hold on to nothing. I have your letter. So much I want from it that I feel to eat it and make part of me. But then too it gone to look at.

The girls are pride to you. Tell them auntie send love and never forget. You say you husband teach to them poetry. How it cause trouble? Good man for him to do this task. We never have teaching and learning this things but somehow it always there tangling up with us. It stay in the bone. You say nothing have change. Something saying you sad about it. But sister count your blessing. This unchanging of thing it is number one blessing. And the doctor still come to eat at your home. How I like to think of it. My sister giving food to doctor! Husband have big job now after this time I think. Entertaining with doctor. This is Lovely word for it.

She is very much love to entertaining. It in her own nature to give dinner and party no matter what how tired it make. Only few short years gone Lovely is Miss Comilla in Regional Beauty Pageant. She for certain sure have been Miss Bangladesh but marriage come in the way and stopping it all. She say "I go around the world but for my James. So much he love me he cannot wait. It sweet really. He so sweet."

Sometime she come in playroom and lie on couch. Children jumping on top and putting little arm round the neck. Darlings (is how she call them) thats very sweet but look at all your lovely toys. It true. If you try to count how many you running out of numbers before you running out of toys.

Jimmy is three and one half year old and he goes like bluebottle in jar.

Most time he playing army game and like to give blow on arm and leg. Only toy he pick up is gun and sword. Very full energy this boy. When he tire out he drop down anywhere and I carry to bed. Baby Daisy is just start walk. Now she follow around me like baby duck and she never let out from sight or else begin the squawking. One time Lovely pick up and take outside but she bring back and say I dont know what is wrong with this girl. At first Daisy missing old maid who go away due to cheating of shopping money. But now she is all right with me. When Lovely take the children to go for visit she put sweet in baby mouth and that keep sound from coming.

I doing well in duty. Lovely say Oh you have saved my life you are an angel. She is nice kind lady. "I will speak to James for building extension. Proper servant quarter. This house is so small." I not sleep in my room at present time. Baby Daisy is start to wake in night and from my room is too hard for hear. Few nights sleeping on landing but husband is tripping over and stubbing toe on head. So I take bedroll and sleep on baby room floor. Is better in actual fact than own room. Now if I turn over in night I not hitting against door. And there is window for air too. Is nice room. Zaid (the cook) have put rice sacks and flour sacks in my room all on top of my things and I did must speak to him. "Room?" he say. "What room? I see cupboard. I see shelf. I dont see any bloody room." Zaid sleep in kitchen on table. That if he here at night. Many night he go away and not come back until morning late. "Do you think he has woman?" say Lovely. "Do you think he is going to leave us? He could get job anywhere. His kitchari is famous whole length of the Buriganga. Somebody have poached him. I know it. I know it."

It not simple thing to run household. Sometime I feel Lovely got too many things weigh down on her.

April

Both children is now sleep afternoon time is how I sit down with pen for you. Many days children is sleep different time and then it keep me busy busy for all day. Baby Daisy get up early maybe five and half past five. Brother is later get up and very late in evening go to the bed. When I lie down at night my head touching to ground and two three seconds sleep come. Yesterday Lovely have party for twelve people guest. Zaid spin around kitchen so fast it look like Sufi in there dancing spinning. Children too more excited with all guest and present and sweet. It take long time to calm. Then after is washing and clearing. Zaid watch me for some time. Then he say "My time is coming." And he go out.

Lovely just now come here look for childrens. She see me with pen and I jump up but she tell me be calm. I tell her about you sister. Lovely is say how sweet. That is kind of lady. No word of anger pass through the lip. She sit with me and discuss. She wear robe color like ripe peach not yet dress because of late entertaining. Hair all way hang down back too beautiful. You have see this Britainy Spear? That more less how Lovely look. Rickshaw workshop make more carriage paint with this singer picture. It too surprising to me sometime how much like Bangla girl she look have long black hair and black eye.

Lovely do face exercise. One time judge in Regional Beauty Pageant tell chin is weak. Every day she do face exercise for strengthen though it look plenty strong for eat talk everything. When she finish she say "You know we live in capital city but really is so provincial." Then she tell me about big fashion show is call BATEXPO. This is meaning Bangladesh apparel and textile show. She sighing like she seen a piece of heaven. Show at Pan Pacific Sonargaon Hotel. Is very smart place and almost is not provincial. How she made it sound! She show me how the models walk and say this walk come natural to her in spite some model have struggle with it. Very wonderful way she move with hand on hip like she melting and you can tip over and pour out. Some famous model there. Miss India there. She famous for world over. Lovely describe me all clothes food drink dance music. Have you hear song Barbie Girl? Is everyone favorite song.

Lovely sit down with me for all this discuss. She ask "Will you tell me something and swear to tell truth?" I say I will never tell lie to you who is giving this roof for head. "Do you think Betty is more beautiful than me?" Her face come all serious. Betty is friend of her and she was Miss Chittagong 1997. I tell her no and it true for Lovely is more beautiful in my eye. She look a little pleased. "I hear it said many time that Betty is more beautiful than Miss Beautiful Smile." Then she explain about Miss Beautiful Smile who is daughter of Government Minister. Oh it is too too shame when that girl say she will become lawyer and help destitute women and all the photographer and reporter gather round to her and hang on to words when what she ever done at all for destitute woman and doesnt Lovely have destitute living right here in home with her. I say too it shame. Lovely think that girl only so high up in Beauty Pageant because of father name. I agree to her. Then she tell me television camera came for take film of BATEXPO. Indian fashion designer there speak into camera and it her opinion recorded in film that people of Bangladesh should be more fashion aware. Lovely sigh and say how you expect it in place where even capital city provincial like hell.

She speak to me many often and explain me her problems. If I sweeping floor then Baby Daisy hanging onto leg Jimmy running around diving in dirt pile and Lovely time to time sit on chair and tell to me. Betty is best friend and she have everything it seem all come to her no effort at all. This is instance—husband James have driver and sometimes driver come for Lovely and take around. But driver is come with job and not always time available for Lovely. Betty ask to her husband for car and driver and get it straight away no question is asking. Lovely is still wait for own driver. Also this house is not so big house in this street many house too much bigger. Betty house bigger than this house. Beside Lovely must manage house and children with one maid only and one cook. Husband James say no need of ayah as well maid. But in actual fact Lovely need ayah too also. And she is expect spend much time for Charity working and for party which is important for husband position and job.

James have job with company is call Bangla National Plastics. Sound like big big company but in an actual fact is only medium size of company. Lovely say "It sounds so much like big company." A few times she say this. Very much she loving husband James and this also cause for sad in her as he must work many hour away from home. This man I know him by knee alone. When he at home he push chair away from table and sit with leg cross with face inside papers. Even he eat a meal many time and face inside paper. Always I see his knee. If he passing me I washing floor or playing with baby and keep the eye low at the knee height. Every crease of trouser I have learn.

Lovely say there is difficult thing come in job. Two years now waiting on court case to clear Bangla National Plastic name. Also there is talk of ban the plastic bags. Lovely say "When they see us on the street then they will be happy." She really have care on her head.

In spite and even so most times she is good high spirit especially at party when you hear her laugh so nice to everyone. One day she tell me "I missed my chances in life Hasina." No dont talk like that is what I say to my mistress. Allah always will give another chance. He give to me and He give to you. She just smile at me and say how sweet you are.

She worry the cook up and leave for other job in house with real servant quarter. He is very expert cook and always his food admire by guest and friend. But I think Zaid will stay. He come and go in any case as he please. Miss the breakfast the lunch sometime he even miss cook the dinner. Lovely just say Oh you here and will you trouble to make some of your wonderful niramish for evening meal?

He is strange man. Always practice his kung fu move kick leg shoot arm chop hand even while he cooking. He small hard man like made of wire with little skin on top. No soft anywhere can crack nut in between the toe. When Lovely go out he watch the kung fu movie on video machine. Jimmy watching with him only time the boy come still. At night often Zaid going out. He say for few next month he must go out because election coming and his time is coming. Which is party you support I ask but he does not say. Maybe BNP maybe AL maybe Jamaat-e-Islami is how he tells. In morning time he has fresh cut or bruise but he do not say anything and I do not ask. Jimmy run at him with little arms going around like fans and shout KILL DIE KILL KILL KILL. They doing kung fu together. Bedtime now the boy give to me kiss and hug. Baby Daisy always want her face to me and she sit on my hip all day if only no work to do. When she smile she put her head back and show all her teeth. All my life I look for one thing only for love for giving and getting and it seem such a thing full of danger can eat you alive and now I stop the looking it come right up to me and show all it tiny little teeth.

Razia came when she was reading Hasina's letters. She had read them many times already so that now the words were in her mind even before her eyes moved over them.

Nazneen hid the letters under the cotton spools.

Razia fanned herself with a book. She wore the Union Jack top over shalwaar pants. The loose folds of material in the trousers made her backside appear enormous. The trousers were designed to be worn with a long top and it was too hot to be wearing a sweatshirt.

"These bloody health inspectors," said Razia. "Closed the bloody factory down. Came with an interpreter and went around asking stupid questions. 'Is it always hot in here?' I told them, 'No. In winter you have to take a chisel and knock off the ice between your toes.' And they wrote it all down in their stupid book."

"How long will it be closed?"

Razia took off her glasses. "At least it gives my eyes a rest." She blinked hard. She picked up one of the glittery vests.

"Shefali tried to go out of the house wearing some little thing like this. I told her no way." She replaced her glasses and rolled her eyes. "Daughters! They are trouble."

"How is Tariq?"

"Sons!" said Razia. She put the vest down and lit up a Silk Cut. "They say they are closing the factory for health and safety, but everyone thinks it is something else. The people who came are from immigration. But I have my passport. I said I would bring my passport but they didn't want to know." She pulled at her top. "British citizen. Nothing to hide."

She fanned herself again and waved her cigarette at Nazneen. "This top is too hot. Too hot."

"Yes. It looks hot."

Razia sighed. "But I must wear it, from time to time. I hear what they are saying. Razia is a little touched. Crazy, crazy." She clucked a little and made some crooning noises. "'Razia is so English. She is getting like the queen herself.'"

"They always talk." Yesterday, Nazma—whose brother-in-law had turned up unexpectedly—had popped around to borrow a pinch of saffron. She rolled into the sitting room holding up her hands. "Can't stay, she said, can't stay," ready to fend off any onslaught of hospitality. But she stayed long enough to drop a few hints about Razia. "Do you know? The woman *smokes*!"

"Let them talk," said Razia. "If I stop wearing this now, they are going to think I listen to them."

"If they have the time, let them gossip."

"Come on," said Razia. "Let me help you. Or I *will* go crazy, crazy with all this sitting around. I'll do five zips for one cup of tea."

Nazneen drank her tea and watched her friend. Through the open window drifted wafts of music and snatches of curry. It was the shift work. Main meals were cooked at all times of day or night. There was nothing to anchor them. Voices were raised in the courtyard, and she looked out at a group of Bengali lads. One was kneeling next to a large pile of leaflets, which he was dividing into smaller piles. As she turned back she thought that one might be Karim, but she forced herself not to look again.

"They don't have jobs," said Razia. "They don't study and they don't have jobs."

"You are lucky with your son."

"OK-Ma, I am lucky. But I wish he would go out sometimes and make a few friends. I told him to go to mosque and make friends but he wouldn't go."

"What about college? He has friends there?"

Razia considered. "Yes, that must be true."

They both listened to the sewing machine. Nazneen thought of

Hasina. She thought of Hasina in the garment factory, how happy she had been. Her stepmother came into her mind, a young woman with a large nose ring, thick gold bands on her ankles. She came to the compound and she slept in Abba's sleeping quarters. She came suddenly and she went, and no more was ever said of her. She left no impression other than a young woman with a jeweled nose ring and gold ankle bracelets. Where did she go? Where was she sent? How long before the bracelets were melted down and spent? How long before she came to be where Hasina had also been?

Nazneen pushed her thumbs into her temples. Her mind was becoming too loose again, tramping this way and that without discipline. Under her breath she began to recite the Opening:

Praise be to God, Lord of the Universe, the Compassionate, the Merciful, Sovereign of the Day of Judgment! You alone we worship, and to You alone we turn for help. Guide us to the straight path . . .

"And show us where it leads," she said to herself.

"What?" said Razia.

Nazneen fiddled with her teacup. She wondered if they would take teacups with them to Dhaka, or whether they would be left behind.

Razia finished the last zip and drank her tea though it was nearly cold. "I have to go back to work. The children need money. Tariq is going hysterical. This morning he did not even get out of bed. He needs money for books or he will fail the exam."

"When did the factory close?"

"Three days ago. Not long, but Tariq is so anxious. I will have to break in myself if they don't open it. Or go to see Mrs. Islam."

Nazneen put the cup to her lips and tipped it to cover her face. It was empty. She repeated the action. But Razia, she saw now, was not hinting at anything. She did not know about Chanu's "little arrangement" with Mrs. Islam. And Nazneen, complicit in the sin, would not tell. Razia rubbed at her hip and adopted a feeble voice. "Just bury me now. I am as good as dead."

Nazneen laughed. "Don't worry. Benylin Chesty Coughs can cure anything."

Razia barked. "When I was a girl, we gave respect to our elders." She became feeble again. "But I am practically dead. Take your fun. Take anything you want. Take my hip. I leave you my Ralgex."

Nazneen snorted, but Razia became thoughtful. "We are always thinking: How does this woman come so high? Do you think that those who come so high think about us: how do they stay so low?" She worked her big shoulders. "But we already know about her. It is just hard to believe."

Mrs. Islam had been the day before. She came with her sons, and Chanu jumped around the room as though it were scattered with nails. He counted out the money loudly, and had got to seventy-five when Mrs. Islam raised a spotted handkerchief and let it float onto the mighty ruin of her chest. One son undid the bag. The other said, "Put it in." Chanu put the rest of the notes back inside the showcase. The sons helped her to the door. One of them was trusted sufficiently to carry the Ralgex.

"How much are we paying?" said Nazneen.

"It's between friends," said Chanu. "She is doing me a favor. I knew her husband."

Karim came the next morning to collect the vests. Before they had exchanged two words his telephone started up. He parked himself in the hallway. Nazneen saw him lean against the wall with one trainer pressed flat against the skirting board. She returned to the sitting room but did not know whether to stand or to sit. When he came in she made herself busy with folding.

"My father," he said. He snapped the phone shut and holstered it.

She glanced at him. His hair stood up at the front, tiny short black feathers.

"He's always calling the mobile. I tell him not to waste money like that. He doesn't listen." He flexed his leg, testing that it still worked. "And what's he ringing up for anyway? Hasn't got anything to say to me, man."

"He is worrying. Perhaps."

"Yeah, man. Worrying and nerves. Out of his mind with worrying and nerves."

Nazneen sat. She folded her hands in her lap. She smoothed the soft blue fabric of her sari and folded her hands again. She had once more forgotten to cover her hair.

Karim sat on the arm of the sofa. She did not know what she could say, so she said nothing. Karim sat on the place where Chanu rested his head. The plastic sheaths had long gone and hair oil made the fabric shiny. She had thought the phone calls were about work, or other things—that she could not imagine—that belonged to the world out there and which she would never understand. They were from his father and that brought him a little step nearer her world. Still, she could think of nothing to say.

"He had to retire because of the nerves. Couldn't hang on any longer. Twenty-five years as a bus conductor, and now he can't even leave the flat. That's what you get, man. That's what you get."

"Yes. Is what you get."

He nodded with great vigor as if he had heard a new idea, one that would change his life forever.

"I know what you're saying. That's what you get. All those years on the bus, getting called all the names, taking all the cheek. Kids giving him cheek. Men giving aggro. Got a tooth knocked out. Someone was sick on his shoes, man." He looked at his trainers. They were clean.

"I make tea."

She went to the kitchen and he followed. He leaned with his back to the cupboards. When Chanu was in the kitchen he leaned as well, but facing the other way, with his stomach resting on the worktop.

"He had to take early retirement and now he's just sitting at home biting his nails and calling the mobile. 'Don't make trouble.' He never made any trouble for anyone. Only trouble he made is for himself."

Nazneen moved past him to get the milk. He smelled of detergent. A crisp, citrus smell of clean clothes.

He shook his head. "'Don't make trouble.'"

The tea was ready. But he showed no sign of moving. Would they drink standing up in the kitchen? Would she invite him to sit down with her in the other room? How would that seem? Would it be better to have him sit, while she continued to work? She decided that was the best plan.

"He thinks he is Mahatma Gandhi. He thinks he is Jesus Christ. Turn the cheek, man. Turn the cheek."

She picked up the cups.

"What about Muhammad? Peace be upon him, he was a warrior."

"Yes," said Nazneen.

He looked at her as if he needed more time to absorb the impact of what she had said. He squeezed the back of his neck.

She was still holding both cups when his phone began to beep. He flipped it open.

"Salaat alert," he said.

"What do you mean?" She was so surprised she slipped into Bengali.

"On th-th-the phone. It's a service you can get. To warn you of prayer time."

"Will you do namaz here?" She said it without thinking, in the same way that another time she had switched instinctively to English.

He rolled his shoulders. He stopped leaning. "Yes. I will."

He went to the bathroom to wash. In the sitting room, in the small space behind the sofa and in front of the door, she rolled out her prayer mat. "I'll pray a little later," she said. There was nothing wrong with it. No reason why he should not pray here; it only delayed her a short while.

"Allahu Akbar."

He stood at attention, with hands raised to shoulder level.

He put his right hand over his left on his chest. She tried to stop the prayer words forming on her lips. To pray with an unrelated man, it was not permitted. She would pray later.

"Glory and praise be to You, O God; blessed is Your name and exalted is Your majesty. There is no God other than You. I come, seeking shelter from Satan, the rejected one."

She heard the blood pound in her heart and she trembled because he would surely hear it. She closed her eyes. At once Amma came to her, shedding her famous tears, wailing with her hand over her mouth.

"He is God the One; He is the Eternal Absolute," said Karim. His voice did not falter.

In prayer he does not falter, thought Nazneen. And she pleaded with herself to keep fast to the words.

"None is born of Him and neither is He born. There is none like unto Him."

He bowed, hands on knees, straight back. She saw how well he moved. Twice more. It was he who moved, but she who felt dizzy.

Nazneen rolled up the mat and put it in the wardrobe. She would need it again soon but this setting straight was necessary. Later, when she changed the sheets after he had been, she remembered this action. She remembered it perfectly. In the only way that pain can be truly remembered, through a new pain.

He had packed the vests himself and he was waiting to go. He fiddled with the strap across his shoulder and he fingered the mobile. He began to leave and then he adjusted his bag again and he said, "I want to ask you to come to something. A meeting." He ran a hand over his hair. "Please ask your husband. It's for all Muslims. We want everyone to be represented. And we don't have any older women."

It was only after he had gone that she realized. He meant her as an older woman.

Chapter Eleven

Of course she would not go. It was out of the question. She did not mention it to Chanu because there was no question of her going. There was no point in raising it.

On the day, she had little to do. She had finished her sewing in the night, moving between the kitchen to eat and the sitting room to work. She had gone into the bedroom and taken Chanu's book from the pillow. She had gone again and pulled up the bedclothes to hide his shoulders. A third time, she watched him from the door, and stepped out of the way when he stirred.

She was tired today but she was restless. The fridge was stacked with Tupperware and there was no real excuse to cook. She washed a few socks in the kitchen sink, and then she went out.

The meeting was in a low building at the edge of the estate. It had been built without concession to beauty and with the expectation of defilement. The windows were fixed with thick metal grilles that had never been opened and notices were screwed to the brickwork that read, in English and Bengali: Vandals Will Be Prosecuted. This was pure rhetoric. The notices were scrawled over in red and black ink. One dangled by a single remaining screw. Someone had written in careful flowing silver spray over the wall, *Pakis.* And someone else, in less beautiful, but confident, black letters, had added, *Rule.* The doors were open and two girls in hijab went inside.

Nazneen, seeking cover, rushed to follow. Sunlight lit up the entrance but inside the hall was gloomy. The girls had gone straight to the front and were arranging themselves on chairs. Nazneen hesitated; she considered turning around. Nobody had seen her.

"Get on the train of repentance, sister, before it passes your station."

Her mouth was full of saliva and she could not swallow.

A small young man with a scabrous-looking beard grinned at her. He was drowning in white panjabi pajama and he had a skullcap in his hands. He waved the skullcap at her. "Welcome. You are welcome, sister. Go and sit down."

She walked uncertainly past empty folding chairs. Four rows at the front were at best half full. Where to sit? Next to someone. Not a man. Not next to someone. Leave a seat between. It will look rude. No, it will look as though I am expecting someone to join me. My husband. But he won't come, and then they will wonder about me. Talk. Even before I have left they will talk. She held on to the edge of a chair. She saw people indistinctly and she heard voices without hearing words.

He put his face in front of hers. He was saying something. Now he was pointing. "Sit there," Karim said. She sat down hard.

He walked to the front and jumped up on the small stage. He clapped his hands.

"Right," he said. "Thank you all for coming."

She heard the door open. Now the same voice that had greeted her at the entrance. "Get on the train of repentance, brother, before it passes your station."

She allowed herself to look around. Mostly young men, jeans and trainers, a few kurtas, a handful of girls in hijab. Maybe twenty people.

"Right," Karim said again. "I shall ask our secretary to read out the business for today. Anyone wants to add anything, please raise your hand."

The small man with the ineffectual beard ran up from the back. "Business of the day. Number one, name selection. Number two, mission statement. Number three, election of board."

Immediately a hand went up. The secretary pointed to it. "Yes?"

"Why don't we do this all in our own language?"

The secretary grinned. He looked at Karim. "Question from the floor. Do I allow it?"

Karim stood with his arms folded. "I will answer. This meeting is open to all Muslims. I'm talking about the ummah here. Every brother and every sister, wherever they come from."

The Questioner stood up and looked elaborately around the hall, even at the empty chairs. "*Ekhane amra shobai Bangali?* Anyone here not speak Bengali?"

There was a moment's silence before a chair scraped back and a black man in a wide-sleeved swirly-print shirt stood up. "Do I look like a Bengali to you, brother?"

The Questioner showed his palms as if the game was up, and they both sat back down.

"OK," said the secretary. "Name selection. Item one. I open it to the floor."

"Muslim League!"

"United Muslim Action."

"Muslim Front."

The two girls whom Nazneen had seen coming in whispered behind their hands. Eventually one called out, "Society of Muslim Youth, Tower Hamlets."

The secretary waved his arms. He dropped his skullcap, picked it up, and thrust it in his pocket. "Enough suggestions. We'll take a vote. What was the first one? Who made the first suggestion? Speak up."

The Questioner jumped to his feet. "This man is secretary, but he takes no notes. It is totally un-Islamic."

The secretary drew himself up to his full height. His small face bulged with indignation. "Where does it say in the Qur'an anything about taking notes?"

"It is clear in the hadith and the sunnah that a man must take his responsibilities seriously."

The secretary wound himself up to reply. His beard quivered. The turn-up of one pajama leg had come down and covered one foot entirely. Nazneen worked it out. His beard was too young to grow full.

Karim put a hand on the boy's shoulder. "Get a pen and a pad. You will be in charge of keeping the record."

There was some discussion then about whether the name of the group could be chosen without the purpose of the group being voted on first. The secretary grew excited. As his excitement grew, so his pajama seemed also to grow until he became a thin voice squeaking inside a tent. "It's the agenda, man. We got to stick to the agenda."

Karim settled it. "We'll take the name first. We all know what we are here for."

There was a general, murmured agreement. Nazneen found herself joining in although she was only there because there was no sewing and no housework to be done.

Karim walked about the stage, and she saw that it was a show of command. He stood at the edge of the stage and said, "The secretary has noted all your suggestions. I have another to add. The Bengal Tigers."

There was a collective gasp, and the hijab girls raised their hands to their mouths for some more intensive whispering.

"Ben-gal Ti-gers," shouted a young man in the front row. He punched the air with his fist in time to the syllables. "Can I have that name for my band?"

The Questioner was on his feet again. "Are we forgetting our non-Bengali brother here?"

Karim walked across the stage to stand in front of the swirly-shirt man. The secretary followed, pad at the ready. "I ain't meaning," said Karim, "to alienate you, man."

The black man stood up and bowed deeply. "Man, I think it is a *powerful* name. I gonna be proud to be a Bengal Tiger."

The vote was taken and the motion carried (unanimously, said the secretary, with one ununanimous vote against), and the meeting moved on to item two: mission statement.

Suggestions were shouted up from the floor while the secretary scribbled on his pad. He sat on the edge of the stage now with his legs dangling and he chewed the end of his pen, just like Bibi. Karim remained standing, though every so often he moved about so that when he became still again he could plant his legs and fold his arms and show his strength anew. The girls in hijab had grown more relaxed. They no longer whispered but talked to each other without raising their hands. And they shouted out suggestions freely. "Women's rights," called one. "Sex education for girls," called the other. "Got to put that in." But she lowered her head immediately she had spoken, ducking out of it.

Karim called for a break and from somewhere a trolley was found, decked with white plastic cups. The girls placed themselves behind it and served. The young men took out their packets of Marlboros.

Directly in front of Nazneen, some lads had broken the line of chairs to form a subcommittee.

"They take down one of ours, right, we'll take down ten of theirs. Simple as that."

"Burn their office. What we waiting for?"

"We don't know where it is."

"They shouldn't come round here. What they doin' round here if they don't like it?"

"We don't want no trouble. But if they come asking, yeah, we'll give them what they want."

"Few years ago—think about it—they'd never dare."

"We was better organized."

"Now we's too busy fighting each other."

"Brick Lane Massive 'gainst the Stepney Green Posse."

"The racists—they cleared out of here *ages* ago."

"What about Shiblu Rahman?"

Nazneen recognized the name. The man had been stabbed to death.

"It could happen again."

"Thing is, see, they is getting more sophisticated. They don't say *race,* they say *culture, religion*."

"They put their filthy leaflets through my front door."

"We all know what we're here for. Why don't we get on with it?"

Karim called the meeting to order. "Right. We're taking a vote. What are we for? We are for Muslim rights and culture. We're into protecting our local ummah and supporting the global ummah."

The secretary scrambled onto the stage. "Voting. Everyone raise your hand. I mean, those in support—raise the hand."

All hands were raised.

"Unanimous." He made a mark on the page.

"What are we against?" said Karim. "We are against—"

"Lion Hearts," someone shouted from the floor.

"We are against," said Karim, "any group that opposes us."

It was carried.

The musician made a request for his band to become the official musical group of the Bengal Tigers. "Spread the message, like. Are you cool with it, man?"

The Questioner was on his feet once again. "What will we do?" He had changed his seat during the break and was close enough now for Nazneen to see that he had the dangerous face of an enthusiast. "We are 'for' this and 'against' that. Are we a debating club?"

There was some laughter and the Questioner's face grew keener still. He was spare and hungry, this boy. His clothes hung from his bones as if flesh was an unnecessary expense, as if his passion consumed him. The only extravagance was his nose, which was large, though being hard and bony-looking it managed yet to add to the impression of austerity.

"What do we want?" said the Questioner. "Action, or debating?"

Karim cut off the laughter. "Item three. Election of the board." He looked at the Questioner. "If I am elected, the action will begin straight away."

The secretary was elected to be secretary. Though no one else stood for the position, he looked down into his crotch as the vote was taken as if the suspense were unbearable. Afterwards, he hitched his pajama in the manner of one girding his loins.

Karim and the Questioner stood for chairman. It was close. Nine votes for the Questioner and ten for Karim. I have given him victory, thought Nazneen. She felt it a momentous thing. By raising her hand, or not raising it, she could alter the course of events, of affairs in the world of which she knew nothing.

The Questioner went to the front and got up on the stage. He shook Karim's hand with great energy, and they slapped each other on the back. Nazneen understood that they hated each other. Then he proposed himself as treasurer and the position was quickly secured.

In the hall, the air vibrated to the tune of a meeting about to break up. Dozens of tiny adjustments, and the anticipation of a greater movement. The secretary waved his pad. "Wait. Wait. One more election. Spiritual leader." He jumped off the stage, dragged an old man from his seat, and pushed him onto the platform. Nazneen saw that the old man was wearing flat, open-toed sandals with a white plastic flower on the heel strap: women's shoes. And she knew that the imam had only recently been imported. He kept wetting his lips and smiling. He had not the slightest idea what was going on. He was duly elected.

Karim came with his bundles of jeans and unlined dresses slung over his shoulder. He sat on the arm of the sofa and talked. When his phone rang he no longer took it out into the hallway. Sometimes he spoke into the phone about leaflets and print runs, meetings and donations. Sometimes his voice was soft and slid away from him, and he closed the phone and said briskly, "Worry and nerves. That's what you get."

He began to talk to her about the world. She encouraged him. "Is it?" she said.

His knowledge shamed her. She learned about her Muslim brothers and sisters. She learned how many they were, how scattered, and how tortured. She discovered Bosnia. "When that was?" she said. He could not have been more than fourteen or fifteen at the time. He shamed her. And he excited her.

In a place called Chechnya, there was at this time jihad. He read from his magazine. "'Allah willing—the Mujahideen will see you in the heart of your Mother Russia—not just Chechnya. Allah willing—we will inherit your land.'" He held up the flimsy pages, offering her proof. "It's a worldwide struggle, man. Everywhere they are trying to do us down. We have to fight back. It's time to fight back."

Holding up the magazine with English words on the front, he said, "Can you read this?"

She inclined her head, side to side. "*Amar ingreji poda oti shamanyo.'* In English, I can read only a little bit."

He left Bengali newsletters for her. One was called *The Light*; another was simply titled *Ummah.* Chanu had never given her anything to read. And what good were his books anyway? All that ancient history.

She put the newsletters on the table for her husband to see. *You are not the only one who knows things.* But when she heard him coming she hid them. Those next few days, reading became a sweet and melancholy secret, caressing the phrases with her eyes, feeling Karim floating there, just beyond the words.

One thing she could not grasp: the martyrs.

"But Allah does not allow it."

"It's not *suicide,* yeah? It's war."

She knew about Palestine. He told her, "They go to the streets protesting a child has been killed. They go home carrying the body of another."

It gave her pain. Now when she walked the anxious tightrope between the children and their father, when she was disquieted by her undisciplined mind or worried about her sister—now she felt the smallness of it all. So she mistook the sad weight of longing in her stomach for sorrow, and she read in the night of occupiers and orphans, of Intifada and Hamas.

And he prayed in her home several more times. As he took the mat from her, the tips of their fingers found each other and she smelled the crisp smell of his shirt.

The smell of limes.

Chapter Twelve

Dr. Azad had the misfortune of youthful hair. It was hard not to smile at his thick and shiny pelt, especially as the years had not bypassed his face. They had, in fact, trampled it. His cheeks hung slack as ancient breasts. His nose, once so neatly upturned, appeared to crumble at the end. And the puffy skin around his eyes was fit to burst.

He sat up straight, as if his entire body was in splints, and he drank two glasses of water.

"Next time," said Chanu, "you must bring your wife."

"Of course," said the doctor.

"She is well? I hope she is very well. Such a superb hostess—to produce a meal like that, even without a moment's notice. We must have her to dinner. I tell my wife, let us return hospitality to Mrs. Azad."

They had never, in all these years, been invited back. And we were never invited in the first place, Nazneen reminded herself.

Chanu hunched towards his food to abbreviate the journey between plate and mouth. There was a fleck of dal in his eyebrows. Dr. Azad barely inclined his head to eat. His elbows never strayed far from his ribcage.

"It is good of you to remember," said the doctor. "After more than a decade many people would begin to forget."

"Daughter, too. She is well?"

Dr. Azad pronounced his daughter healthy. He took advantage of Chanu's overstuffed mouth to launch his own line of inquiry, his own method of point scoring. It was the usual. "I've been meaning to ask, how many signatures have you succeeded in amassing now? Are we far from the new dawn of a mobile library?"

Chanu leaned his wrists on the edge of the table. He pressed down the tip of one finger after another, all on the left hand and two on the right. "Only seven this week." He squeezed a bit of lemon and appeared saddened by his calculation.

The doctor's wife and daughter were steadfastly healthy. There was nothing to report except the inevitable absence of the wife on visits to the daughter (married now, with children of her own) or to other relatives. Chanu's petition gathered new names without ever leaving the drawer. It no longer amazed Nazneen that these fictions should be so elaborately maintained. What worried her now was the possibility of their collapse. The fence that they formed, though rotten, was better than nothing.

The girls came in to say goodnight. Chanu held his arm out. "Come on. Come, I'll feed you from my plate."

Shahana flinched, sucking in her cheeks. Chanu glanced at Dr. Azad. He smiled and his arm became more expansive still. "Come, don't be shy."

Bibi went to him and he pulled her onto his lap. "Prawn and marrow. Delicious." He fed her, as promised, from his plate and patted her gingerly on the back, as if she were an unknown dog and might bite his fingers.

Bibi got down and stood next to Shahana.

"Very good girls," said Chanu. He looked around the room, seeking proof. It came to him. "Shahana, what is the name of our national poet?"

She felt the carpet with her toes. The smile died on Chanu's face although the corners of his mouth held their position. "Tagore," she said.

"Not your favorite poet, Shahana. National poet. Quick."

She swayed slightly. Her face was blank, as if she had entered a trance.

Nazneen chewed her tongue. She watched Chanu. His face began to twitch.

"Kazi Nazrul Islam," said Bibi. Her face popped with tension, as though a weight had been placed across her windpipe.

"Shahana, would you like to recite something by your favorite poet for our guest?"

Nazneen stood up. She would say it was too late. She would go with the girls and help them get ready for bed.

"Another time, perhaps," said Dr. Azad. "The girls are tired after their homework."

"Yes, yes." Chanu waggled his head. "Studying, studying all the time. Very good girls. Come now and kiss Abba before you go to bed."

Bibi went first and Shahana followed. She squashed her lips inside her mouth before brushing it briefly against her father's cheek. But Chanu was satisfied. When the girls had gone he appeared exhausted but relieved, as if a tornado had spun him once or twice around the city and deposited him by some miracle in his chair.

Chanu and the doctor began their main business of the evening. They did what friends do, talked. From time to time their conversational paths intersected. More frequently, they walked around each other.

"It's really quite alarming," said the doctor, "that the rate of increase of heroin abuse in our community should have exploded, and yet the elders are giving no leadership. And the funding for counselors and outreach workers and so forth is totally inadequate."

"This is the tragedy. When you expect to be so-called integrated. But you will never get the same treatment. Never."

"I am making quite a study of the situation, preparing a paper for publication. You could call it an epidemic. Even a few girls are getting hooked."

Chanu's left hand was busy beneath his shirt, massaging his meal into place. "You see, I myself have struggled for a long time. But now I am simply taking money out. 'Every rupee of profit made by an Englishman is lost forever to India.' That is how I am playing them at their own game now."

"If we get funding we will set up a specialist clinic. But the main thing is education. The parents are so ashamed they don't know what to do. Sometimes they send the child back home, where the heroin is really cheap." The doctor's neck had grown thin. It failed to fill his spotless collar. His lustrous black hair, cut still in the same sharp flat fringe, refused to accord him the dignity of age. It looked like a mockery, like a wig. Nazneen felt for him. It would, she thought, be troublesome to be set upon all day by this reminder of a youth long gone.

Chanu sighed. He cleared his throat. "Educate the parents and they must educate the children. I myself am teaching the children, many things about history and politics and art."

"It is absolutely and fundamentally the key," said the doctor, and Nazneen marveled at the way this all worked so smoothly: how these two men could find themselves in vehement agreement over their separate topics. "Teach them to spot the signs in their own children. Tiny pupils, shallow breathing, constipation, constant need for money, becoming withdrawn, secretive. Sometimes I wonder how the parents fail to see it."

Nazneen opened her mouth and sucked breath. She thought of Razia's son. Every time Razia mentioned Tariq, she talked about money. The men looked at her. She began to clear some plates.

"The parents can become preoccupied," said Chanu, who had known no other state. "But we must think of our children first. God knows what they are teaching them in these English schools."

"Do you know, some of my patients have never so much as smoked a cigarette, and heroin is the first drug they touch."

"In all my life, I feel this is the best decision I have made—to take my daughters back home. I am preparing them. You see, to go forward you must first look back. We are taking some stock of the glorious British Empire. When I was in school, do you know what we learned? The English gave us the railways. As if we should get down on our knees for this." He appealed now to his public. "Do you think they would have brought the railway if they did not want to sell their steel or their locomotives? Do you think that they brought us railways from the goodness of their hearts? We needed irrigation systems, not trains."

"Good, good," said Dr. Azad. Chanu had strayed too far from the point of their intersection. The rules of the conversation, to the doctor's mind, had been breached. He fingered the sacs beneath his eyes.

Chanu was oblivious. Nazneen reached across him for a dish but he picked it up before she could get it. They rose: Chanu, the bowl, his voice. "They bequeathed us law and democracy. That's what they think. And never a word of the truth—that they beggared us, that they brought Bengal to its knees, that . . ." The speech left him at a dead end. "Here," he said to Nazneen, and held out the dish. "Do you want this?"

"It was bad enough when it was alcohol," said the doctor. "Now I wish it was only alcohol. We need two things. More drugs counselors and more jobs for the young people."

"They will never make jobs for us," said Chanu, sitting down again. "Look to history. When the English went into Bengal . . ."

"I have read the literature." Dr. Azad checked his watch and stood up. "How is your . . . job? I forget which one."

Chanu blew hard. "Driving job. Doesn't matter how it is. I just take the money, that's all. How is your son-in-law? All this time, and we still have not met him. You must bring him around here. Next time you come."

"Of course," said Dr. Azad, and though he gave his peculiar smile and took care to walk with energy and not let his shoulders hang, Nazneen could see that it was her husband who had made the final score.

Shahana heard the letterbox and went to the hallway. She sat on the edge of the coffee table and read the leaflet.

"How many times do I tell you not to sit on there?" said Chanu. He sat in front of the showcase on the red-and-orange rug. His stomach appeared to be balanced on a mound of books.

Shahana slid off the table. She turned the leaflet over.

"What is that?"

Shahana held it up. "It's a leaflet."

Chanu stirred. His stomach toppled the books. "Don't be clever," he shouted. "Give it to me."

She made an issue out of getting up, but eventually she took it to her father.

"*'Multicultural Murder,'*" he read in English. "Where did you get this?"

"The hallway."

"You are not too clever to be thrashed," said Chanu, but his heart was not in it. He was busy with the leaflet. He read both sides then turned it over and read it again. Shahana practiced lowering her eyelids in the manner best calculated to invoke fury. He did not notice. He turned the piece of paper around and around.

"These bloody bastards. Next time they come, I'll cut off their testicles."

At the word *testicles,* Shahana smiled.

"You think it's funny?" He got quickly to his feet and his lungi slipped. He paused to retie it and Shahana went to stand behind Nazneen at her sewing machine.

"Come on," said Chanu, and his voice shook. He gave himself a few moments of throat clearing. "Come on, let's all have some fun. Bibi!" She ran in and stumbled over some files. "Give this to your sister. She is going to read it for us."

The leaflet was returned to Shahana.

"*'Multicultural Murder,'*" she read.

"Notice," said Chanu, holding up a hand, "notice how the thought of violence is introduced right away. In the very first words." He lowered his hand.

"*'In our schools,'*" continued Shahana, "*'it's multicultural murder. Do you know what they are teaching your children today? In domestic science your daughter will learn how to make a kebab, or fry a bhaji. For his history lesson your son will be studying Africa or India or some other dark and distant land. English people, he will learn, are Wicked Colonialists.'*"

"See how they do that?" Chanu tried to pace, but he was trapped by his books. He stood still and waved his arms instead. "Putting Africa with India, all dark together. Read the other side."

Shahana turned it over. "*And in Religious Instruction, what will your child be taught? Matthew, Mark, Luke, and John? No. Krishna, Abraham, and Muhammad.*

"*'Christianity is being gently slaughtered. It is "only one" of the world's "great religions." Indeed, in our local schools you could be forgiven for thinking that Islam is the official religion.'*"

Chanu rushed over and grabbed the leaflet. "This is where they get down to it. This is what it's all about." Nazneen noticed the hole in his undershirt, the curling gray hairs at the hollow of his throat. Chanu read, "*'Should we be forced to put up with this? When the truth is that it is a religion of hate and intolerance. When Muslim extremists are planning to turn Britain into an Islamic Republic, using a combination of immigration, high birth rates, and conversion.'* On and on, this rubbish." He crushed the leaflet in his fist.

Bibi leaned on Nazneen's shoulder and chewed on the ends of her plaits. Nazneen looked at Shahana, who was adjusting the straps of her first bra. She willed Shahana to speak to her father, to say the right thing. Shahana put out her bottom lip and blew up at her fringe.

Chanu sat down in the armchair. "Shahana, go and put on some decent clothes."

She looked down at her uniform.

"Go and put some trousers on."

Nazneen said, "Bibi, you go as well."

Chanu smoothed the leaflet out. "*'We urge you to write to your Head Teacher and withdraw your child from Religious Instruction. This is your right as a parent under Section 25 of the 1944 Education Act.'*"

He breathed hard. His tongue probed his cheeks, like a small rodent snouting blindly beneath a thick blanket. "From now on," he said, "all the money goes to the Home Fund. All of it."

That night, for the first time since they were married, Nazneen watched him take down the Qur'an. He sat on the floor and he stayed with the Book for the rest of the evening.

Nazneen walked a step behind her husband down Brick Lane. The bright green-and-red pendants that fluttered from the lampposts advertised the Bangla colors and basmati rice. In the restaurant windows were clippings from newspapers and magazines with the name of the restaurant highlighted in yellow or pink. There were smart places with starched white tablecloths and multitudes of shining silver cutlery. In these places the newspaper clippings were framed. The tables were far apart and there was an absence of decoration that Nazneen knew to be a style. In the other restaurants the greeters and waiters wore white, oil-marked shirts. But in the smart ones they wore black. A very large potted fern or a blue-and-white mosaic at the entrance indicated ultrasmart.

"You see," said Chanu. "All this money, money everywhere. Ten years ago there was no money here."

In between the Bangladeshi restaurants were little shops that sold clothes and bags and trinkets. Their customers were young men in sawn-off trousers and sandals and girls in T-shirts that strained across their chests and exposed their belly buttons. Chanu stopped and looked in a shop window. "Seventy-five pounds for that little bag. You couldn't fit even one book in it."

Outside a café he paused again. "Two pounds ninety for large coffee with whipped cream."

A girl at a wooden table on the pavement bent the screen of a laptop computer back and forth to angle it away from the sun. Nazneen thought of Chanu's computer, gathering dust. A spiderweb shivered between keyboard and monitor.

They walked to a grocer's shop at the corner of one of the side streets. Nazneen waited outside. She walked a little way down the side street. Three-story houses, old houses, but the bricks had been newly cleaned and the woodwork painted. There were wooden shutters in dark creams, pale grays, and dusty blues. The doors were large and important. The window boxes matched the shutters. Inside there were gleaming kitchens, rich dark walls, shelves lined with books, but never any people.

Nazneen walked up and down the street. Some young Bangla men passed on Brick Lane. She recognized the Questioner. His voice carried well and his walk was urgent. Karim did not like him. He had not said anything yet, but she knew.

When Karim came he talked of the world or of his father. He told her about the pills that he left out for his father each morning, blue and yellow for the heart, white tranquilizers, pink for indigestion. The sleeping tablets each evening. He told her about his father's job, twenty or more years on the buses. The uniform, belt, and badge. The peaked cap. The ticket machine that he kept in a brown leather case, and the satisfying noise it made as the handle turned. What a proud little boy he had been.

Chanu came out of the grocer's with white plastic bags. She fell into step behind him. He walked a few yards and then stopped. She waited for him to comment. She looked in the shop window, but he said nothing and she saw that he did not know that he had stopped. After a while he said, "You see, they feel so threatened." Nazneen turned her head, and then she smiled to herself because she had been caught out like Bibi.

"Because our own culture is so strong. And what is their culture? Television, pub, throwing darts, kicking a ball. That is the white working-class culture."

He began to move again. Nazneen followed. For a moment she saw herself clearly, following her husband, head bowed, hair covered, and she was pleased. In the next instant her feet became heavy and her shoulders ached.

"From a sociological standpoint, it is very interesting."

A young woman with hair cropped like a man's pointed an impressive camera at a waiter in a restaurant doorway. She wore trousers, and had she been wearing a shirt her sex would have been obscured. To alleviate this difficulty she had dispensed with a shirt and come out in underwear. She turned around now and pointed the camera at Nazneen.

"You see," said Chanu to the street, "in their minds they have become an oppressed minority."

Nazneen adjusted her headscarf. She was conscious of being watched. Everything she did, everything she had done since the day of her birth, was recorded. Sometimes, from the corner of her eye, she thought she saw them. Her two angels, who recorded every action and thought, good and evil, for the Day of Judgment. It struck her then—and the force of it made her gasp—that this street was filled with angels. For every one person there were two more angels; the air was thick with them. She walked with her face turned down to her feet and she felt her head pushing through a density of wings. She was seized with a fear of inhaling a spirit, and pulled cloth over her mouth and nose. For the first time then, she heard the beating of a thousand angel wings and her legs would take her no farther.

"Are you resting?" Chanu put his shopping bags down.

She looked up and saw the waiter shaking out a tablecloth.

"No."

"OK, then. Rest," said Chanu.

They stood for a while. Chanu hummed. He had one hand on his hip and nursed his stomach with the other.

"Where are all my notes from Open University?"

"You kept them?"

"Yes, yes. Somewhere."

They walked again, past the sweetshop. A pyramid of golden ladoos and a white brick tower of shondesh.

All the time, Nazneen felt the angels at her back. She jerked her shoulders. Karim came into her mind. The angels noted it. She felt irritated. *I did not ask him to come into my mind like that.* It was recorded.

On Tuesday, when she had counted out twenty-five skirts for him and he leaned in to gather them up, their shoulders missed each other by the slimmest, smallest whisker.

It was not for her to decide.

"In a way," said Chanu, "you can't really blame them."

Sitar and tabla music, mixed with incense, drifted from Ishaq's Emporium. Outside, three old men discussed the state of their knees at a volume that suggested—or possibly induced—deafness.

His neck, thought Nazneen, was just right. Not too thick, and not too thin. And he was taqwa. More God-conscious than her own husband.

"It's their country," said Chanu. His heels hung off the back of his sandals.

It was, Nazneen realized, more complicated than that. Even if Karim was her future, and could not be avoided, there were problems. Happiness, for instance. That would count against her. Because fate must be met with indifference. For the benefit of her angels, she said, "Whichever way, it does not matter."

Chanu considered. His eyebrows evaluated. "No, I would not say that it does not matter." He smiled at her and his cheeks were full of kindness. "But you must not worry about it. Soon, we will be home again."

Some tears came to her eyes. Her neck and cheeks were so hot that she thought she had a taste of hell. It was less than she deserved.

"Ah," said Chanu, "I can see how much you long for it."

How had she been so foolish? She put her fingernails against the balls of her eyes. What evil jinni had come to her to play such tricks with her mind? To make her think that this young boy would be part of her life, that he would not retch and tear his hair at the very thought.

Chanu grew animated. "Yes, it is an emotional thing. Do you know what I have been thinking? I could get a job at Dhaka University. Teaching—sociology or philosophy or English literature."

To cover her distress she spoke with unusual conviction. "That is a very good idea."

"It is," he confirmed. "And I will send an e-mail this evening."

At once she was concerned and wished she had not spoken so.

"At first, of course, I will have to take any opening that is available. I will not be too proud to take anything."

She smelled disaster, and for the first time it occurred to her that it was not only Shahana she would have to worry about if they ever went to Dhaka.

"Eventually, I should like to return to my first love—English literature."

In the distance, a white-haired woman defied the sun with a thick cardigan over her sari. At her side a younger man walked with a swagger and a medicine bag.

Chanu spoke in English:

> "O rejoice
> Beyond a common joy, and set it down
> With gold on lasting pillars."

Nazneen stared ahead.

"Shakespeare," said Chanu. He followed her stare, and when they were both sure that it was Mrs. Islam, by a mutual and unspoken plan they turned away into a side street.

On the estate there was war. The war was conducted by leaflets. They were crudely constructed, printed on the thickness of toilet tissue, and smudged by overeager hands. The type size of the headlines became an important battlefield. After much heated inflation and experimentation with tall but thin type and fat but squat titles, the Bengal Tigers emerged victorious by simply using up an entire page for the headline and relegating the text to the other side.

The Lion Hearts made the opening salvo:

HANDS OFF OUR BREASTS!

> The Islamification of our neighborhood has gone too far. A Page 3 calendar and poster have been removed from the walls of our community hall.
>
> How long before the extremists are putting veils on our women and insulting our daughters for wearing short skirts?
>
> Do not tolerate it! Write to the council! This is England!

Chanu was sanguine. "You see," he explained, "they feel threatened. And this is their only culture—playing darts and football and putting up pictures of naked women."

The Bengal Tigers replied the next day:

> We refer to a leaflet put recently into circulation by those who claim to uphold the "native" culture. We have a message for them:
>
> KEEP YOUR BREASTS TO YOURSELF.
>
> And we say this. It is not us who like to degrade women by showing their body parts in public places.

"We always kept quiet," said Chanu. "The young ones don't want to keep quiet anymore."

The return of fire took a few days. Nazneen watched the leafleters at work on the estate. A young boy and an older man, distant enough by age and clothes to be father and son. The father dressed like one of Chanu's "respectable types." He looked like one of the teachers at Shahana's school. The son was the kind that Nazneen would cross the road to avoid. This time they called for the community hall to be turned into a disco at the weekends and a bingo parlor on other evenings. They proposed the sale of alcohol on the premises.

SAVE OUR HALL!!!

The addition of three exclamation marks filled up the space nicely and set the tone for the Tigers' riposte.

> Undesirable elements are seeking to turn our community center into a den for gambling and boozing.
>
> Do not tolerate it! Write to the council!

Chanu laughed. He was having a good war. "So they think the council is going to read all these letters? I was once a council man myself," he informed his wife. "What is the council going to do? They were not able to keep hold of their best people."

> **MARCH AGAINST THE MULLAHS**
>
> Most of our Muslim neighbors are peaceful men and women. We have nothing against them. But a handful of Mullahs and Militants are throwing their weight around.
>
> March with us against the Mullahs. All interested parties, send details to the P.O. Box number below.

Chanu frowned. He called for the girls. "Stay away from marches," he advised. He studied the leaflet for a long while, and then he brightened. "They have not even set a date. By then we could be in Dhaka."

Four red letters filled the front page of the counterattack. *DEMO.* On the back, in green ink, it said:

> Stand up and be counted when the infidels march against us. Very elderly and infirm only are excused from this duty. The organizers will lead you, in a peaceful rally. Spiritual guidance to be given by our Spiritual Leader. All interested parties, send their details.

"They have given no address," said Chanu. "And the punctuation is poor. It gives a wrong impression of Muslims."

The leafleting campaigns geared up a notch. Small crowds began to gather around the leafleters. Insults were exchanged. From her window, Nazneen watched the Questioner jab the air, as if all opposing thoughts were mere bubbles he could burst with the tips of his fingers. She began collecting Shahana as well as Bibi from school. They walked back in a long line with the other mothers. It would only be a few more weeks until school ended for the summer. Although, for many reasons, Nazneen could not allow herself to think of it, she knew that Karim's visits would be curtailed. This made them all the more painfully sweet.

Karim came and worked on draft texts at the dining table while she sewed. He read them out and provided his own comments. Twice he came while Chanu was still at home after a long shift that had stretched through the evening and into the night. And though on these occasions he only made the necessary exchanges and left quickly, this proved somehow to Nazneen that there was nothing wrong in his visits, nothing that could not happen in the presence of her husband. A few times he said to her, *You've got to stand your ground,* and it was marvelous to her that he should be so sure of where he was standing and why. If the salaat alert came on his phone, she took out her mat and listened to him pray. His father, he told her, had no religion now. He had nothing but his pills. Her husband's religion, she told him, was education.

"What we need," he said, "is action. What's the point of all these leaflets? We must stop talking and start doing."

But he continued to work at his texts.

"All I get is moaning," he said. "How can they expect me to run everything and still be out in the street the whole time? It all takes a lot of organizing, man. That lot ain't smart enough to work that out."

He bemoaned the lack of interest shown by the dissolute youth, most of whom had resisted the charms of the Bengal Tigers. "We set it all up for them. When I was at school, we used to be chased home every day. People getting beaten up the whole time. Then we got together, turned the tables. One of us got touched, they all paid for it. We went everywhere together, we started to fight, and we got a reputation." He smiled at the memory. "But now, these kids—they don't remember how it used to be. They're in their gangs, and they fight the posse from Camden or King's Cross. Or from the next estate. Or they stay away from all that, earn good money in the restaurants, and that's all they care about. They don't think they can be touched."

But the Questioner was the main thorn. "It's a strategy question," Karim said. "He just don't get it." He was a man and he spoke as a man. Unlike Chanu, he was not mired in words. He did not talk and talk until he was no longer certain of anything.

Sometimes he became angry, and his anger was direct and to the point. "It's my group. I'm the chairman." It was a strong statement, though Nazneen could not help thinking of Shahana and Bibi fighting over their toys.

"I say what is radical and what is not."

Radical was a new word for Nazneen. She heard it often enough from Karim that she came to understand it and know that it was simply another word for "right."

She observed him more openly now, and when he saw her looking at him she did not look away immediately.

"You're always working," he said.

"Buttons will not sew themselves."

"Talk to me. Leave it."

"I will listen. You talk."

He picked up a handful of brass buttons from the cardboard box. He put them in the front pocket of his jeans. He tipped out the remaining buttons onto his palm and pocketed those as well. Nazneen felt an electric current run from her nipples to her big toes. She sat very still.

"Do you know about our brothers in Egypt?" He found his magazine on the table and searched for the right page.

Nazneen tried not to think of the buttons. She could think of nothing else. Why did he take them? Why put them in his pockets? Her skin was attached to thousands of fine silk threads, all of them pulling, pricking at the point of tension.

He told her something of Egypt, the oppression, the jailings, the cowardly American-loving government, and they both pretended that he was not just reading from the magazine. Nazneen thought of Chanu with all his books. He read too much and it did him no good.

"It is sad," she said.

"Tumi ashol kotha koiso." Yeah, man, you're so right.

This was something he did: made her feel as if she had said a weighty piece, as if she had stated a new truth.

Chanu and all his books. How much he knew and how baffled he seemed.

Karim pulled the buttons out of his pocket and put them back in the box. When his phone began to ring he flipped it open, checked the number, and turned it off. This meant it was his father calling. Now that he had a smaller, sleeker phone he seemed unable to take calls from his father. The gold chain around his neck had grown fatter.

Nazneen began her work, but Karim could not settle. He walked—with some difficulty, for the way was strewn with obstacles—around the table. He watched from the window but found nothing to comment on. The showcase attracted his attention and he bent down to slide the doors back. He pulled out the pottery tiger and lion, and a porcelain figure of a girl on a swing. He lost interest and put them back without remembering to close the doors. The corner cabinet was stacked with books and he took down a couple and turned them over as if he would judge them by their weight alone. Next he moved across to the far corner of the room and stood by the trolley. It was loaded with files and papers and the computer keyboard which Nazneen had removed in order to make more space on the table. He pushed it right up against the wall. Then he went to the sofa, kicked off his trainers, and lay down.

Her fingers trembled and she could not work. Karim squeezed the back of his neck. He closed his eyes. His right leg vibrated up and down. When Chanu fidgeted he showed his unease. When Karim could not be still, he showed his energy. For a few moments she drifted helplessly on a tide of longing. Her mouth became loose and her eyes unfocused.

"When I was a little kid . . ." He sat up and put his feet on the coffee table. It was as if he were taking possession of the room, marking each item as his own. "If you wanted to be cool you had to be something else—a bit white, a bit black, a bit something. Even when it all took off, bhangra and all that, it was Punjabi, Pakistani, giving it all the attitude. It weren't us, was it? If you wanted to be cool, you couldn't just be yourself. Bangladeshi. Know what I'm saying?"

"Yes," said Nazneen. She did not know what he was saying. She was waiting to be claimed as well.

"There was no one to look up to."

"Your father."

"Exactly."

He looked straight at her and she held the look. She wished her eyes were not so close together.

"Exactly," he repeated. "It's different now. For the little ones. We're the ones who had to stand our ground."

In the bath, while the incontinent cold tap dribbled and the extractor fan rasped, she examined the hairs on her legs. They were fine and sparse but clearly visible. She ran a hand along a calf. On the ceiling was a little flower of damp. She imagined the plaster breaking and falling into the bath, coating her in white dust. She heard footsteps and the flush of a lavatory. The woman upstairs would be up three or four times in the night. It was getting to be quite a condition.

She thought of her shopping list (tinfoil, mustard oil, and fennel seeds to add). She thought of plastering the hallway herself: how difficult could it be? She thought of the homework planner that Shahana had pinned on the bedroom wall and how quickly she ticked off the items. Nazneen looked in her exercise books. "This doesn't look finished," she said. Or, "Have you written enough here?" Shahana showed her red ticks that the teacher had marked. There was a red Biro on Shahana's desk. Nazneen thought about Bibi, who had begun to chew her nails. She rehearsed a letter that she would write to Hasina. She counted in her head the money in the hidey-holes. And when she could keep him out no longer she thought of Karim. She thought about his forearms and she rejoiced that they were not thin. She thought about the small flat mole on the left ridge of his jaw and how stunned she had been to discover it only this week. She thought about his certainty, how he walked a straight line while others turned and stumbled. And most of all she thought of what he had that she and Hasina and Chanu sought but could not find. The thing that he had and inhabited so easily. A place in the world.

She sat until the water was cold and then she took Chanu's razor, soaped her legs, and began to shave.

The next day, when she was walking back from school with the children, there was a police van parked in the courtyard where no cars were allowed. The door was open and inside was a policeman petting a large dog that quivered to be released. Four police stood with their backs to two Lion Hearts. The police wore short-sleeved shirts and their helmets all seemed too big, as if they were just dressing up. A group of young Bangladeshi men stood shoulder to shoulder facing the police. The Questioner was at their center.

The younger of the two leafleters stepped out from his police barricade, stuck a finger in the air, and stepped back again. The Questioner moved forward but the boys at his side held on to his arms and he seemed willing to be held. The policemen shared a joke. Their radios crackled and their helmets hid their eyes.

Shahana walked on in front. As she passed the Bengali group a couple of the boys turned around. She looked at them and cocked her head. Nazneen wished that Shahana had her trousers on. But today Chanu had ordered skirt and no trousers. Yesterday, both the girls had to put trousers beneath their uniforms. It depended where Chanu directed his outrage.

If he had a Lion Hearts leaflet in his hand, he wanted his daughters covered. He would not be cowed by these Muslim-hating peasants.

If he saw some girls go by in hijab he became agitated at this display of peasant ignorance. Then the girls went out in their skirts.

Sometimes he saw both sides of it. "The poor whites, you see, are the ones that feel most threatened. And our young ones are rebelling. Young ones will always rebel. If the parents are liberal then how can they rebel except by becoming illiberal themselves?" On these days it was left to Nazneen or the girls to decide what they should wear.

They went up to the flat and the girls settled with their books in front of the television. Nazneen sat with pen and paper. What could she tell Hasina? She wished she could tell her what was happening on the estate. But how to make sense of it? She did not know where to start, and besides, it might sound alarming. She made a beginning.

Sister, I hope you are well. The children are doing well at school. I am still doing the sewing at home. I am sending a little money. I wish it could be more.

Something is happening here in the flats.

She smoothed out of the paper some imaginary wrinkles. Bibi had a book open on her lap; Shahana made no pretense of reading.

Something is happening here in the flats. Men are writing leaflets and pushing them through the doors.

She smiled. That was all that was happening. She began to giggle. Shahana flicked channels. Bibi looked up.

Nazneen went into the bedroom and, from the modest seclusion of the underwear drawer, unveiled her sister.

April 2001

It good news you send about sewing machine and work you have now. You say you send money soon but sister I am not in need. Allah provides. Write me longer letter that is what I need.

Everything here is same. It is good. Sometime I feel so tired I think to lie down when children take nap but it is chance for washing clothes and I must do my duties. I take clothes outside for washing and time to time I see maid from next door. Her name is Syeeda and she is from Jessore. In all your life you did not see face so untrouble as Syeeda. She never say much but she come and squat along beside me and it soothe to be with her. It funny I thinking about Lovely and Syeeda. Lovely is very often time with smile on face and it beautiful smile on beautiful face but underneath something not happy. Like she smile to please you or to cover something or make face pretty without it ever make you think she really happy. Syeeda have lumpy round face plain as potato and I never see her smile. But she look like she happy all the time you feel it like she yogi squat there with hand between knee other hand shade the eye. I ask how it is work in that house look like palace with little fountain all about on lawn. She say very fine and you believe she mean it. In house on other left side is maid around eight to ten year old. I call out to her few time but she look frighten and run inside. Little and little I will make her come to me.

Husband James have worry about election. If Begum Khaleda Zia come to power it is bad for him. Zaid say strange thing. They pay the dogs to bite and mind it come a time when the dogs turn on them. Then he say but my time is coming. He chopping around in the air like he slicing up great big onion. He is very dark skin man and also not so bad looking for man without flesh. Lovely say "My husband James tell me everything. He shares all his thought with me. Thats why I know he is so worried about money and share price and election. Many husbands dont tell wife anything at all. It so sweet of James really."

She gone now for Charity Affair at Betty house. This new Charity for HIV Innocents is for women infected in innocence by straying husband and also child victim. Betty is always top in fashion in clothes and also in Charity Affair. This is how Lovely tells. Driver come to pick her up and she has kiss the children and tell them darlings you are too too tiring. Daisy say "Lovey! Lovey!" We all laughing. She wearing tight white jean and lacy blouse with underwear see through it like film star and more jewelery than bride. She call it "Bombay Look."

May

Something horrible has happen. I went yesterday in Motijheel and saw this thing and picture all time stay in front of eyes. Closing eyes even still picture there paint on back of lid. I see whole what happen. Two men come out from Islami Bank and when they walk few step on pavement there is five six bang and both fall down. I stand still. Two men dress with dark glasses and good shirt come for robbing the body and jump straight away on motorbike. Only few yards they got and crowd blocking the way. Motorbike is try to get between old Biman building and Hotel Purbani is where fast road begin. Hundreds people come. All is shouting and swear. I run across road. Crowd get big and noise deaf the ear. Mens pull robbers from bike and they beat with fist and foot and lathi also. After few second robber have vanish inside crowd. Somewhere they are on ground and many people push to middle for also applying the blows. Then motorbike petrol tank is open and they set light. Fire come too fast. I watch it. Crowd must move back away. Then I see robbers a time again lie there burn on ground not know if already death or live burning watching I am watching. This is picture I cannot clear from eyes.

Sister what is happen to police and court and thing? In England could such thing happen like this? People justice is quick and is terrible. Everyone talk about this thing. Lovely say how dreadful but she say is good example for showing robbers street is not belong to them and other people money also.

This evening husband James eat at home and has keep Jimmy up for meal together with. I sweeping up food Jimmy throw and wiping table leg and underneath table. Husband James talking with face inside a paper. Heavens he say just goes to prove. What this country need is more stability. How it going to help if government is change? The opposition parties is cause much trouble and go to people house for scare them and even rape of wife. Sometimes they pay police for arrest-and-scare. Also student these day should not have name of student but name instead thug. The opposition party give gun and money and student have not one second for looking at book. Is big problem for business. All boils down is instability. Then he talk-

ing this and that about business Jimmy making rice ball and sticking to underneath table. Husband say all big national industry is corrupt and rotten. It seem a Certain Person who have high up influence have stolen one crore fifty lakh taka from steel company everybody do know it. Husband James say it goes to prove. Prove what darling say Lovely. He put head out from paper and explain all around is crook and thief steal from company and all this judges do is chase little private company around for bribe money. Lovely look like she hiding yawn. Very sweet for husband James to tell all things to her but it do make her tired. She try to keep eye open. "Medium size company" she say.

Zaid stand behind door and listen. When we go to kitchen he say to me listen this people is all the time shitting and say stink is not come from own behind. He speak like this never tell you what he mean. Also he say all sides is hiring muscle for street politic and only sometime the muscle has brain belong to itself. He tap on the head. Is small head and forehead come low like not much space for brain but is not stupid look in an actual fact he look pretty smart.

May

Sister I pray Allah keep you safe. I pray this letter find you unchanged. I have more news again to tell. I had word it came from mouth to mouth that friend to me Monju is lie in Dhaka Medical College Hospital very near to death. I went to Lovely and explain her what has happen and she tell to me "Go and see her. A mother can care her children for one hour." In spite she paint toenails at that time she push me to go straight and not linger around.

Sister how can I tell what I saw? I do not know how.

I go to hospital ward and I look around for friend Monju. No one there looking like her. I ask nurse and she point in corner. Bed is push right to wall and space left around. When I walk close is bad odor emitting from thing lie on mattress. I must put hand over nose and mouth and stomach make threat on me. I kneel down by bed and put face very close. I see is Monju. I know by right eye alone. Left eye is narrow and stuff come out. Cheek and mouth is melt and ear have gone like dog chew off. I whisper to her but nurse pass by and tell to shout. Hearing is very small now. "Monju" I shout. "Monju." Is all I can think to say. She say God give them the pain I suffering now. Mouth cavity shrinking from which she cannot shout cry or talk loud. I stay for ten fifteen minutes. She must whisper and I must shout. It is her husband who have done this with his brother and sister. Brother and sister hold tight and husband pour acid over head face and body. All over is infection on body and smell make it difficult for people to go near.

She say to me see that dirt mark on ceiling like thumb print. I see it. She say I dont want that the last thing I see. I tell her it going to be all right and last thing she see is grandson but I dont look at her.

I come back to house and sit some time with Syeeda. She right to be happy. I feel to stay always beside her. But I must look after children and Baby Daisy poke me in cheek and rub nose on my nose and I give thanks to Allah for this love which come at last.

Nazneen went back to the table and looked at what she had written. Now she could not see what was funny.

Men are writing leaflets and pushing them through the doors.

Her head felt full to bursting. The children and Chanu, her sister, the cleaning, the cooking, the sewing, the worrying. It all took up space and her thoughts circled as busily and broke up as easily as a cloud of flies on a dung heap.

She decided to begin the letter again. This page could be used for a shopping list. She turned it over. Without thinking, she began to write. She scribbled out the words, screwed up the paper, and then ripped it into shreds. It was not true. She had not fallen in love. She had not done anything.

She took a fresh sheet and held her pen ready. She thought she heard footsteps outside the front door. Over the television she could not be certain. If the knock came she would have to answer it. The television could be heard from outside. In the morning she had been able to hide when Mrs. Islam called. Her words pierced the door and Nazneen crept to the bed and got under the covers. If the sons broke down the door she would pretend to be sleeping. They went away.

Nazneen wrote down some numbers on her clean page. The last payment was one hundred pounds, the one before was eighty-five, there were six at seventy-five and four or five at fifty. How much money did Chanu borrow? How long would it take to pay it back? At one hundred pounds a week Nazneen would be able to save nothing, even if she worked half the night.

Bibi came up and looked at the page. "Amma, what are you doing?" She kept her voice light and she kept a frown away from her face. She was worried about worrying.

"Nothing," said Nazneen. "Housekeeping. Let me feel your throat."

She pressed her fingers along each side of her daughter's throat, feeling for swelling and at the same time soothing.

"I've been better for a week."

"Yes, you're better."

She had been off school with tonsillitis. Nazneen took her to see Dr. Azad. His chair had grown larger since the last time she went to the surgery. She almost expected him to swing his legs, but he held himself with his usual correctness.

"Say, 'Aaah,'" he told Bibi, who complied. He gave his diagnosis and from his computer produced a prescription. Bibi was looking at the snowstorms on his desk. There was a line of them along the back in every shade of colored glass. They were arranged by color, running from clear glass at the far end to a small black dome over a frozen winter garden. He picked out one and offered it. Bibi held it on the flat of her palm and peered at the little lattice-worked tower inside.

"No, no. You shake it." Dr. Azad explained that he had got it in Paris. They watched the snow swirl around inside the glass and come to a peaceful arrangement at the bottom. "That's it." He took it back. "That is like life," he told Bibi. "Remember that is just like life."

"Why?" said Bibi, surprised into speaking. She swallowed with difficulty.

Dr. Azad picked up another snowstorm and shook. "If you are strong you withstand the storm. Can you see? The storm comes and everything is blurred. But all that is built on a solid foundation has only to stand fast and wait for the storm to pass. Do you see?"

Bibi nodded, so slowly that she might as well have shaken her head.

"And do you know how to make a solid foundation?"

Again, Bibi gave her slow, negative nod.

"Then would you mind," said Dr. Azad, "telling me just how to do it?"

As they went out Nazneen saw Tariq in the waiting room. He leaned up against a noticeboard with his hands in his pockets though there were plenty of chairs to choose from. His lids looked heavy and his hair was flat with grease. The bones had been removed from his body. She stopped for a moment and she thought of speaking to him. His head rolled across his shoulder then hung down, and Nazneen began to move again because she knew she would not be able to look in his eyes.

It was the same every morning. When she opened her eyes beneath the large black wardrobe she had the sensation—a relief in her bones—that the day had finally arrived. Then she strained to remember what the day was, its significance, and she realized that it was a day like any other. This particular morning, without moving from the bed, she ran her hand along the smooth lacquer of the wardrobe door. There was barely a scratch on it. She had hated it for fifteen years but this had made no impression.

Chanu stirred and put an arm across her belly. She regarded his malnourished limb, the two bright pimples above the elbow. She put her hand inside his and in his sleep he gripped it.

Again, the feeling came to her that this would be the day. She closed her eyes and enjoyed the warmth that spread across her stomach.

Chanu snored. Two long hard grunts like the death of an engine.

She got rid of his arm and turned on her side with her knees drawn up and her fists between her knees. It was no longer the day, and the tension inside her chest, which had been there for weeks, returned. She had taken a deep, deep breath because she had to shout—something urgent, some matter of life or death—but the breath and the shout got stuck. They would never come out. That was how it felt.

It was because of the leaflet war.

It was because of Mrs. Islam.

It was because she had not told Razia yet.

It was because of Hasina.

It was because of the Home Fund, which was not growing quickly enough.

It was because of the girls, who did not want to go home.

She sat up now and looked at the clock.

"It's because of me," said Karim.

"What?"

He held a finger to his lips. His hair, the tuft at the front, moved playfully though there was no breeze in the room. "It's because of me," he whispered.

She closed her eyes and he was still there. His fingers brushed her cheeks. To get rid of him she had to get out of bed and begin this day.

The leafleters had changed tactics and begun leafleting in the night. By day, the estate was quiet. So when Chanu finished brushing his teeth, came out of the bathroom, and picked up a Bengal Tigers leaflet, his anger was the loudest thing in all the three hundred and thirteen flats.

"What peasant," he roared, "what peasant has written this?"

He waved the paper in the air and directed his glare in every corner.

Bibi, with very small incremental movements of her head, checked behind her. Shahana ate her cornflakes. She fiddled with the dial on the radio.

"Turn it off," yelled Chanu. His dimpled chin vibrated in the aftershock.

He began to read.

"'A reminder to give thanks to Allah for our brothers who gave up their lives shaheed to defend the brothers.'"

Chanu wobbled with indignation. "Brothers! These peasants claim to be my brothers. They cannot compose even one proper sentence. Shahana, do you know what *shaheed* means? It means 'martyr.' Do you know what that means?" He continued without waiting for her reply.

"'We give thanks for Farook Zaman who died in the Duba Yurt operations in Chechnya, February 2000. He lived most of his life an unbeliever until he repented and devoted himself to jihad. He was killed by a bullet to his heart. After three months his body was returned by the Russians. By an eyewitness account, his body was smelling of musk and it was the most beautiful of all the shaheed bodies he had seen in Chechnya. *Verily, Allah has purchased of the believers their lives and their properties; for the price that theirs shall be Paradise.*'"

Chanu flapped his mouth; only spittle emerged from the corners, no more words. His hair, insulted to the roots, was tumultuous. His eyebrows wild with consternation. After a while, he turned the leaflet over and read the other side.

"'Insh'Allah our brother Farook has reached Paradise. He leaves a wife and a baby daughter.

"'Insh'Allah may his story give us courage to use our lives for the cause of Allah. We are taking up collections for those who are left behind.'"

Chanu was disabled with anger. Shahana had finished her breakfast and was hovering dangerously close to the television.

Eventually, words came. "Smelling of musk. After three months! What is all this mumbo-jumbos? Are they mad? Poking these mad letters through white people's doors. Do they want to set flame to the whole place? Do they want us all to die shaheed?"

Nazneen tried to signal to Shahana. *Don't turn it on.*

"Shall we send money at once? They must have more guns. Quick, get some money to send." He began patting his lungi as though it could contain some coins.

Nazneen felt the back of her neck grow warm, as if the sun had just come on it. When Karim came last time he'd read from a magazine about the orphan children in refugee camps in Gaza. He was moved, and Nazneen watched as the cycle of emotion started turning. It was possible —this she knew—to be deeply touched by one's own grief on another's behalf. That he was moved, moved him. As he explained the situation his eyes became watery. She had gone to the kitchen and looked beneath the sink for her Tupperware box. She wanted to do something for the orphans. And she wanted to do something for him. When she gave him the money, he spoke in her own language and, though it took him a long while and he suffered through his stammer, he told her it was a beautiful thing to do. But if Chanu found out, what would he think? What would he say?

Nobody said anything. The air hummed with the sound of distant water pipes, filling or disgorging. Bibi's jaw clicked as she worked it from side to side. Nazneen looked at her elder daughter. For the first time she saw that Shahana had Hasina's mouth, the same impossibly pink lips, full at the top and straight and wide along the bottom. But Shahana's lips were so often pinched together that it was not easy to notice. The girl reached across the television screen and pressed the button.

"How many heads on your shoulder?" Chanu screamed it, but then he was telling her to get out of the way and he stood close to the television and the leaflet fell unnoticed from his hand.

There were pictures of hooded young men, scarves wrapped Intifada-style around their faces, hurling stones, furious with the cars that they set alight. Between the scarves and the hoods it was possible to catch glimpses of brown skin. There were pictures of police, too, but they were hiding behind sheets of clear plastic, sometimes shuffling forwards and sometimes shuffling back. Nazneen wondered why they did not simply take their lathis and charge. They would not have to beat all. Just a few would set the example.

"You see," said Chanu. "You see." He appeared satisfied.

The riot was in a place called Oldham. The pictures changed to daylight and the camera swept across tedious deserted streets, enlivened now and then by the presence of the blackened carcass of a car. In Oldham the roads were pocked with holes and the houses packed together, tight as teeth.

Chapter Thirteen

There was no reason to wear it, but she wore her red-and-gold silk sari. All morning, the little gold leaves distracted her from work. They demanded to be looked at. She moved her legs beneath the table to make them dance in her lap. She pulled the free end of the sari over her face and moved her neck from side to side like a jatra girl. The next instant she was seized by panic and clawed the silk away as if it were strangling her. She could not breathe. The table trapped her legs. The sari, which seconds ago had felt light as air, became heavy chains. Gasping, she struggled from the chair and went to the kitchen. She drank water straight from the tap. It hurt her chest and the last mouthful made her cough.

When the coughing subsided she went to the bedroom and climbed on the bed. If she stood at the back, next to the pillows, she could see herself in the dressing-table mirror. Suddenly, she was gripped by the idea that if she changed her clothes her entire life would change as well. If she wore a skirt and a jacket and a pair of high heels, then what else would she do but walk around the glass palaces on Bishopsgate and talk into a slim phone and eat lunch out of a paper bag? If she wore trousers and underwear, like the girl with the big camera on Brick Lane, then she would roam the streets fearless and proud. And if she had a tiny, tiny skirt with knickers to match and a tight bright top, then she would—how could she not?—skate through life with a sparkling smile and a handsome man who took her hand and made her spin, spin, spin.

For a glorious moment it was clear that clothes, not fate, made her life. And if the moment had lasted she would have ripped the sari off and torn it to shreds. When it had passed she got down and sat on the end of the bed with her knees against the dresser drawer. She picked up her brush, pulled two pins from her hair so that it fell around her waist, and brushed it so hard that it hurt.

In the afternoon she needed more thread. She walked around the back of the estate, past the cycle racks which no one was foolhardy enough to use, past the car park, the Nissans and Datsuns lightly frying in the noon sun, each with a yellow steering-wheel lock braced against the dashboard, past the stunned clumps of rosemary and lavender that the council had put in a raised bed and left, defenseless against the onslaught of dogs and takeaway wrappers and small children. She crossed the rasp of land that had once sprouted a playground, a swing and a slide and a roundabout. Now the tarmac was rotten and split, it seemed, by the blades of grass which sucked huge strength from this black grot but wilted on the lawns. Only the roundabout remained. It was fenced around with two layers of gray metal barriers, blocking its chance of escape.

To come to the street she had to pass the hall, the low brick shed with the metal shutters, set in a concrete valley at the edge of Dogwood. Skateboarders used the smooth planes, for exercise and for spraying their messages to the world. As she descended the steps into the low basin, Nazneen saw that the graffiti on the shed walls had kaleidoscoped to a dense pattern of silver and green and peacock blue, wounded here and there with vermilion, the color of mehindi on a bride's feet. She took the last step and adjusted the end of her sari across her shoulder.

The secretary jumped out in front of her. His skullcap was on his head this time, a whitish lacy thing that looked as though it had much handling. He beamed at her and showed his small teeth. "Get on the train of repentance, sister, before it leaves your station. Have you come for the meeting?"

Before she had time to react he ushered her inside. When she paused, he shooed her down the aisle as if she were a baby goat. She let her hand trail over the backs of the folding metal chairs, all the time thinking she would turn around and push past him. Instead, she sat down in the front row where he pointed. One seat away from her was the Questioner. He was busy with a bundle of papers which he shuffled and straightened, shuffled and straightened. Across the aisle, Nazneen saw the musician. Next to him were two small black tents. She recognized the voices. The girls who attended the last meeting, who wore hijab, had upgraded to burkhas.

From behind she recognized another voice, and half turned. The black man was standing at the center of a group. He wore a gray felt cap and baggy white robe. "I tried Pentecostal, Baptist, Churcha Englan', Cat'olic, Seventh Day, Churcha Christ, Healin' Churcha Christ, Jehovah Witness, Evangelical, Angelical, and the Miracle Church of our Savior." He sucked his teeth and shook his head. "All loose 'n' lax like anything. Loose *and* lax."

The hall was beginning to fill. Dozens of voices peppered the air with Bengali and English. In spite of everything, Nazneen began to catch their excitement.

She imagined Karim walking in and seeing her there, right beneath him, by the stage. She thought of him standing with his arms folded and his legs wide, and everything he said (though only she would know it) would be for her benefit. In the gloom of the hall, with its bare bulbs and eczema-ridden walls, she became dizzy with relief that she had worn her red-and-gold sari.

The doors were closed and the Questioner and the secretary on stage. Karim had not come.

"We can't wait any longer," said the Questioner, assuming a tone of command.

The secretary stood on tiptoes. "I open the meetings," he squeaked. "I open the meetings."

"Open this one, then."

The secretary consulted his clipboard. His pen slipped from his hand and slid down the sleeve of his kurta. There was snickering in the row behind Nazneen.

"While you are fiddling with your stationery, Oldham is burning. Let's take a vote—all those in favor of opening the meeting . . ."

"Stop, stop." The secretary waved his arms about and the pen flew out of its mooring and landed somewhere in the audience. "No votes to be taken before the meeting is open."

Nazneen put her hand over her mouth to hide a smile. She wiped it away.

Just then the room grew lighter as the door opened and Karim strode to the front of the hall. He wore a white shirt with the sleeves rolled neatly up to the elbows. His jeans were new and dark and the belt superfluous. In one seamless movement he mounted the stage and turned around.

"OK," he said, "let's get started." He pulled a piece of paper from the back pocket of his jeans. It was printed in green and red. "First item"—he gave it to the secretary, who pretended to study it—"first item is this leaflet about Chechnya. Who wrote it? Who authorized it? Who distributed it?"

He made a show of looking around the hall, being careful not to look at the Questioner.

"I shall ask the secretary. Is this a Bengal Tigers leaflet?"

The secretary assented, and he held it out as an exhibit for the audience.

"And was it authorized by the Publications Committee?"

The secretary held the leaflet very close to his face, as if searching for some secret stamp or watermark of authority.

"And was it passed for distribution by the Publications Committee?"

At this the Questioner, who had been pressing his knuckles together, could no longer contain himself. "Committee? This ain't no time for committee. This is time for jihad." His nose swelled with enthusiasm and his eyes were slits of intensity.

"Don't teach me, brother, about jihad. I'm talking about discipline."

"Discipline," spat the Questioner. "By committee? Only you is the committee and the committee is you."

Karim fingered his telephone, which he had strapped on his belt. He looked down from the stage and saw Nazneen for the first time. He folded his arms and pulsated his right leg.

"Don't push me, brother."

"If you're still standing, I ain't pushing."

For long seconds they engaged in a combat of killer looks and deadly self-belief.

"Shall I put it to the vote?" asked the secretary, stepping in between them. He showed his little milky teeth. "Erm, what is the motion?"

"No motion, no vote," said Karim. "Anyone who wants to form their own group can get out now. And take their leaflets with them."

The Questioner glided to the very edge of the stage. The tips of his trainers stuck over the end. He wanted to get close to his crowd. He wanted to walk on air. "All around the world we are being destroyed. Let's not fight about leaflets."

He sidled a little farther forward and Nazneen could see the deep tread of his undersoles. There was a general rearrangement of backsides on seats. "I will show you something." He reached inside his jacket and took out his bundle of papers. After some shuffling he held up a photograph, the size of one of Chanu's writing tablets. It curled at the edges and it glazed over where the light hit it, but Nazneen could see that it showed a child.

"This is Nassar, aged one year. Weight, nine pounds and four ounces. Ideal weight, twenty-two pounds. The photograph was taken in Basra, December 1996." He stooped and handed the photograph to Nazneen. "Pass it around."

The child lay on her back in a short white dress with red sleeves. Nazneen put her fingers over the baby's wasted legs. She knew that the baby had never walked, never crawled. She looked at the shrunken face and the large dark eyes that demanded much of her. Only the hair belonged on a baby, fine and wispy and softly curled.

The Questioner held up another photograph. "Some more Iraqi children. Mashgal, Adras, and Misal. All under one year. This was taken in 1998."

Nazneen relinquished Nassar and she held Mashgal, Adras, and Misal. The photograph was in black and white. Three babies on a blanket, and between them they had nothing but their small bones and a thin covering of skin. They all reached for something that had moved beyond them, and the urgency in their eyes told Nazneen that they did not know that they should give up hope.

"Since the sanctions against Iraq began, over half a million Iraqi children have died as a direct result. This is a conservative estimate."

The Questioner riffled through his sheaf of papers. He squatted for a moment and pulled out a few sheets. "This is Noor. Six years old. This is what you can see of Noor after an American AGM-130 missile hit the Al Jumhuriya neighborhood of Basra on 25 January, 1999."

It appeared at first to be a black-and-white shot. From the gray halftones of ash and rubble, a girl's face in profile, a beautiful stone carving. It took time to decipher a shoulder and a sleeve sunk in the dust. The girl's hair was scraped back and a scratch of little pebbles pinned it flat against the debris. It was a beautiful picture, not of life ended but a study in lifelessness. It was only when she noticed the hands at the corner, a father's hands that would cradle the small head, that Nazneen realized the shot was in color and understood what it meant.

"She was only a Muslim girl. One more, one less, who cares? We should keep quiet about these things," said the Questioner. "We should print nothing and do nothing. If a few Muslim children die, who cares? If it's a few hundred, a few thousand, half a million, a million, who cares? We should not write about our brothers in Iraq, or in Chechnya or anywhere else, because we do not care about them. To us, they ain't nothing."

The hall, which had been mute, found its voice. Chairs scraped as people got to their feet, the walls echoed in two languages, the tiled floor rang out. Everyone talked at once and no one would stand for any more.

Nazneen watched Karim. He was pulling on the back of his neck, as if attempting to remove his head. Though the photographs had brought her close to tears, she found herself wondering what he would do.

The Questioner pulled back from the edge of the stage. He stood in the center because now the stage was his. Holding up his hands for calm, he waited until the noise had subsided. "Listen, I am only the treasurer. I'm not allowed to talk. Some people say, 'Throw him out. He's too radical for us.'"

At this there was a little upsurge of dissent.

Karim spoke up. "No one's talking about throwing out. We came together to get radical, man. But what are you going to do about all these things? I say, let's get our own neighborhood straight first."

This raised a little popular support among the audience, signaled by way of a couple of hoots and one raised fist that Nazneen discerned from the corner of her eye.

"Bingo and beer?" said the Questioner. "Will we be killed by bingo and beer? Or half-naked women?"

This occasioned some laughter. The Questioner moved to capitalize on his advantage. He tossed down a final photograph to Nazneen. His small, heavy-lidded eyes appeared almost triangular. "This is what the sanctions do. This is the price that the sick and the old and the children are paying with their lives."

With the end of her sari, Nazneen wiped away the tears that finally came.

But the crowd was becoming restless. The photograph was passed around very quickly and returned to the edge of the stage.

"Why do you think they call themselves Lion Hearts?" Karim had moved to the left of the stage. He leaned against the wall. "Do you know what it means?"

The Questioner had not sensed the change of mood in the hall. "I'm going to read you something now." He fished around inside his jacket. Though it was warm he had not removed it. It served, evidently, as a traveling office. The lining, Nazneen noticed, was of the same material as the gusset of Chanu's underpants. It was patched with a network of pockets.

He quoted now. "'There is one crime against humanity in this last decade of the millennium that exceeds all others in magnitude, cruelty, and portent. It is the US-forced sanctions against the twenty million people of Iraq.'"

"But what can we do?" called someone from behind Nazneen. "How are we going to fight the Americans?"

Karim's wall looked comfortable. He tested his jawline with his fingertips. With a shiver, Nazneen remembered the mole.

"Let's fight the ones on our doorsteps first." This was shouted from the back.

"We know what Lion Hearts means."

The girls in burkha stood as one creature and spoke as one voice. "We get called names. We want to make them stop."

"Let me finish, let me finish," said the Questioner. "'If the UN participates in such genocidal sanctions backed by the threat of military violence—and if the people of the world fail to prevent such conduct—the violence, terror, and human misery of the new millennium will exceed anything we have known.' This is what the former US attorney general says. It is the new millennium now."

"If it's violence you're advocatin', I shall have to renounce me vows to Allah."

Nazneen turned around to see the black man on his feet. He had removed his skullcap and was holding it against his expansively robed chest.

Someone shouted, "Apostate!"

"Who you callin' a postate?" He had a finely sculpted head, black as Nazneen's cast-iron frying pan, and in his white garb he looked like a king. "I ain't no postate," he grumbled.

"Brothers," said the Questioner, "let's keep our heads."

The two girls in burkha rose. "And sisters," they said.

The Questioner glared at them. "The Qur'an bids us to keep separate. Sisters. What are you doing here anyway?"

In defiance, they remained standing.

"There is always the Quakers," said the black man. He resumed his seat.

For a time, Nazneen lost hold of the conversation. She stared down into her lap at the backs of her hands, at the green-blue veins that raised the skin, the freckles scattered between the tendons. Words brushed against her now and again, like moths at dusk, there and gone, barely noticed but troubling. She twisted her hands together. And she longed to be in the flat, Karim with his magazine, she with her sewing. He would walk around and fill up the space. He would walk around as if he were learning to fill the space. Each time he came now he inhabited the flat a little more.

Suddenly, she knew that what he was building up there in the flat could be pulled down here, in the hall. And she began to pay attention.

The issue under discussion was Oldham, whether to charter a coach for a trip to the north. The secretary squatted on the stage with his clipboard balanced on his knee. He took notes and chewed on the end of his pen. Karim and the Questioner stood on either side of him, and each attempted to control the meeting.

The musician was on his feet. He wore a tight black T-shirt with silver lettering on the front, and a pair of black leather gloves with the fingers cut off. Nazneen wondered what they were protecting, whether his hands were burned.

"If we take a sound system, we'll get more support. I went to this gig, right, with DJ Kushi and MC Manak, and it was rammed. Most of the crowd were white. It was, like, amazing."

The Questioner was dismissive. "It's a demo, not a disco."

"Yeah, but, like, we want to get people there."

Karim nodded his head. "Yeah. Man. That's what we want." He kept on nodding, as if it were impossible to show the full extent of his agreement.

"Brothers," said the Questioner, "do we want—"

"And sisters," said the girls in burkha.

"Brothers," repeated the Questioner. "Do we want to turn it into a carnival? Do we want all the white kids showing up for a disco?"

The black man spoke. "When I was 'bout your age, the black kids went to the black clubs and the white kids went to the white clubs. I like to see it all mix up." He addressed the musician. "Bhangra music, is it?"

"No, man. No. Bhangra?" He looked amused. "We're like, bhangramuffin, know what I mean? Bitta raga infusion. We're like, bhangle, sometimes. Jungle roots. Know what I'm saying?"

"Are we talking about clubs? Discos?" said the Questioner. He had the air of a man who could be pushed only so far.

The musician popped up again. "Maybe we should, like, talk about it."

There was a mixed reaction from the audience. Those who agreed began immediately to debate it with their neighbors. Those who disagreed began immediately to talk to their neighbors about how this should not be discussed.

"Brothers," began the Questioner, but no one paid him any attention.

"Brothers and sisters," began Karim, and the girls in burkha started a campaign of shushing on his behalf. "Brothers and sisters, let's hear all your ideas. Raise your hand, and everyone can take a turn."

Karim called on people to speak and he made each one feel as if he or she had said something of great importance. The Questioner attacked his paperwork and shook his head. He rearranged his portable office and picked his fingernails. While Karim caressed his audience with blunt syllables of wonder, his rival began to squeeze a spot at the side of his mouth. By the time Karim had finished, the crowd was sated and calm and the spot hugely inflamed.

Then Karim made a brief speech to sum up. Think global but act local, he said. Official messages of support would be dispatched to the appropriate ummahs around the world—Oldham, Iraq, and elsewhere. The Publications Committee would see to it. And all leaflets would, from now on, be vetted by the committee. He asked anyone who opposed this to raise a hand. No one stirred. The Questioner had his arms crossed and his hands tucked into his armpits. The meeting, Karim declared, was now closed.

Nazneen stood up and walked quickly down the aisle, looking neither left nor right. All the way home she fought the desire to run, and once inside she waited just by the door so that she opened it before Karim even knocked.

He kissed her on the mouth and he led her into the bedroom. "Get undressed," he said, "and get into bed." He left the room. She got changed into her nightdress and lay beneath the sheets. Through the window she looked at a patch of blue sky and a scrap of white cloud. She pulled the covers up to her neck and closed her eyes. What she wanted to do was sleep. It would be impossible to stay awake. She was sick and she needed to sleep. She had a fever and her body was shaking. She turned her face into the pillow and moaned and when he kissed the back of her neck she moaned again.

Chapter Fourteen

Thirty or so years after he arrived in London, Chanu decided that it was time to see the sights. "All I saw was the Houses of Parliament. And that was in 1979." It was a project. Much equipment was needed. Preparations were made. Chanu bought a pair of shorts which hung just below his knees. He tried them on and filled the numerous pockets with a compass, guidebook, binoculars, bottled water, maps, and two types of disposable camera. Thus loaded, the shorts hung at mid-calf. He bought a baseball cap and wore it around the flat with the visor variously angled up and down and turned around to the back of his head. A money belt secured the shorts around his waist and prevented them from reaching his ankles. He made a list of tourist attractions and devised a star rating system that encompassed historical significance, something he termed "entertainment factor," and value for money. The girls would enjoy themselves. They were forewarned of this requirement.

On a hot Saturday morning towards the end of July the planning came to fruition. "I've spent more than half my life here," said Chanu, "but I hardly left these few streets." He stared out of the bus window at the grimy colors of Bethnal Green Road. "All this time I have been struggling and struggling, and I barely had time to lift my head and look around."

They sat at the front of the bus, on the top deck. Chanu shared a seat with Nazneen and Shahana, and Bibi sat across the aisle. Nazneen crossed her ankles and tucked her feet beneath the seat to make way for the two plastic carrier bags that contained their picnic. "You'll stink the bus out," Shahana had said. "I'm not sitting with you." But she had not moved away.

"It's like this," said Chanu. "When you have all the time in the world to see something, you don't bother to see it. Now that we are going home, I have become a tourist." He pulled his sunglasses from his forehead onto his nose. They were part of the new equipment.

Nazneen looked down at his sandals, which were also new. She regarded the thick yellow nails of his big toes. The spongy head of a corn poked from beneath the strap. She had neglected them, these feet. She brushed an imaginary hair from her husband's shoulder.

He turned to the girls. "How do you like your holiday so far?" Bibi said that she liked it very well, and Shahana squinted and shuffled and leaned her head against the window.

Chanu began to hum. He danced with his head, which wobbled from side to side, and drummed out a rhythm on his thigh. The humming appeared to come from low down in his chest and melded with the general tune of the bus, vibrating on the bass notes.

Nazneen decided she would make this day unlike any other. She would not allow this day to disappoint him.

The conductor came to collect fares. He had a slack-jawed expression: nothing could interest him. "Two at one pound, and two children please," said Chanu. He received his tickets. "Sightseeing," he announced, and flourished his guidebook. "Family holiday."

"Right," said the conductor. He jingled his bag, looking for change. He was squashed by his job. The ceiling forced him to stoop.

"Can you tell me something? To your mind, does the British Museum rate more highly than the National Gallery? Or would you recommend gallery over museum?"

The conductor pushed his lower lip out with his tongue. He stared hard at Chanu, as if considering whether to eject him from the bus.

"In my rating system," explained Chanu, "they are neck and neck. It would be good to take an opinion from a local."

"Where've you come from, mate?"

"Oh, just two blocks behind," said Chanu. "But this is the first holiday for twenty or thirty years."

The conductor swayed. It was still early but the bus was hot and Nazneen could smell his sweat. He looked at Chanu's guidebook. He twisted around and looked at the girls. At a half-glance he knew everything about Nazneen, and then he shook his head and walked away.

The avenue that swept down to Buckingham Palace was as wide as forty bullock carts and it was the grandest of roads. It was not black or gray. Nor was it brown or dusty yellow. It was red. It was fit for a queen. The tall black railings that guarded the palace were crowned with spikes of gold. Nazneen held on to a rail and surveyed the building. After a couple of seconds she looked behind her. The pavement was rife with tourists. Young couples, joined at the hip; families, each with a disconsolate member of its own; tour groups, homogenized by race and tourist equipment; small bands of teenagers, who smoked or chewed gum or otherwise engaged their mouths in ferocious displays of kissing. Many people looked at the palace, as if they were waiting for it to do something. Nazneen looked back at the building. It was big and white and, as far as she could see, extraordinary only in its size. The railings she found impressive but the house was only big. Its face was very plain. Two pillars (in themselves plain) sat at the main doorway, but there was little else in the way of decoration. If she were the queen she would tear it down and build a new house, not this flat-roofed block but something elegant and spirited, with minarets and spires, domes and mosaics, a beautiful garden instead of this bare forecourt. Something like the Taj Mahal.

Chanu had found his page in the guidebook. "Buckingham Palace has been the official residency of British sovereigns since 1837. The palace evolved from a town house owned from the beginning of the eighteenth century by dukes of Buckingham."

He stood with his hands on his hips and appreciated the view. Shahana and Bibi stood next to Nazneen, Shahana with her back to the palace. She wanted to have her lip pierced. This was the latest thing. Last week she wanted to get a tattoo. She did not bring these demands to her father. She presented them to her mother as proof that she could not be "taken home." When she asked for the lip ring, she said, "It's my body," as if this solved anything, and Nazneen smiled and was kicked for her failings.

"Queen Victoria added a fourth wing to the building because of an absence of nurseries and too few bedrooms for visitors. Marble Arch had to be relocated to the northeast corner of Hyde Park." Chanu took off his cap and wiped his forehead. He noticed his daughter leaning against the rails. "Have a look, Shahana. Look at this beautiful building."

Nazneen regarded the palace. "Oh yes," she said, "it is very clever of your father to bring us here. It is a good choice." Some of the windows were hung with net curtains, like the windows on the estate. She wanted to ask questions so that Chanu could answer them. What came to her mind was unsuitable. How many cleaners do they have? How long does it take to change all the beds? How does one family find each other in all that space? Eventually she asked, "Which is the biggest room, and what is it used for?"

Chanu was pleased. "The ballroom is one hundred and twenty-two feet long, sixty feet wide, and forty-five feet high. When it was built it was the largest room in London. It is used for all sorts of big functions. The queen, you see, must entertain many people. It is part of her duty to the country. Most British people know someone who has, at one time or another, been a guest at a palace tea party. This is how she maintains the affection and loyalty of her subjects."

Nazneen asked more questions. With the help of his book, Chanu gave detailed information and elaborate conjectures. Bibi kept gazing at the palace as if she were trying to memorize it. She held on to one or other of her plaits and, when Chanu mentioned a particularly astonishing fact or figure, raised herself on tiptoe to grasp it. Shahana fidgeted and looked around. She did not like to stand in the sun. "I'll go black," she moaned to Nazneen. "At least you should have bought me sun protection cream."

"Your father is talking," said Nazneen.

"If he ever stops," said Shahana, "let me know."

Chanu was listing the treasures and artworks of the palace. A tour guide, speaking in a language that Nazneen did not recognize, had taken up a station close to Chanu. They both raised their voices.

Nazneen clapped her hands together. "What a wonderful holiday. Girls, aren't you enjoying yourselves?"

"Yes."

"Yes."

"Come on," said Chanu, "let's walk a little way off and see it from another perspective. It will be better for photographs also." He located the bottle of water in his shorts and took a swig. He offered it to Shahana, who pretended not to notice.

Two hundred yards down the Mall was a cart with a big tin drum of hot caramelized peanuts. Nazneen, pursuing her campaign for enjoyment, became animated. "Mmm," she said, and clasped a hand to her chest. "That smells delicious. Will you buy some for me?" Chanu patted his money belt. "I have made provision for treats."

They sat on some steps opposite the entrance to the park and ate the nuts from paper twists with the smell of burnt sugar in their nostrils. Nazneen ate and talked and laughed and asked as many questions as she could. After a while, when Chanu began an answer and she laughed again, he stopped and looked at her with his head to one side. "Are you feeling well? Too much sun, perhaps?" She flushed, and she laughed again. She was laughing too much, but now that she had started this laughing business it was difficult to keep it under control. "No, no. I am very well." She hiccupped and this triggered another quake of laughs.

She held her stomach, which was beginning to hurt. Shahana smiled, and then giggled. As a kind of caress, she applied the toe of her trainer to her mother's shin. "Stop it, Amma." She began to laugh as well. Bibi joined in, at first without any sign of mirth, and then with serious symptoms. Her eyes watered and her small body shook. Shahana held her hand and they shrieked at each other as they had on their one and only ride at a funfair.

"Well, now," said Chanu. He swelled with pride at how marvelously he had managed the day. "It is a lot of fun."

They walked on the other side of the road, following St. James's Park, back towards Buckingham Palace. The girls went in front, with a carrier bag each, still holding hands. "That is the best of all the sights," Chanu told Nazneen, and she stumbled and grabbed his arm.

They had to return to the palace because Chanu wanted to try out the panoramic-view camera. It should be possible, he explained, to come close to the building and still fit the whole thing in one shot. He fiddled around with the little cardboard box for several minutes. "It's a disposable camera," said Shahana. "What's he got to fiddle around for?" But when he had finished with that camera, the situation grew worse. He searched for the other camera and announced that he had been robbed. He proposed to tell the Guards who stood in little black boxes inside the palace forecourt. "They have guns, they could shoot the bastard." Nazneen suggested he empty all his pockets. "God," he said. "I'm not a child." He emptied all his pockets and found the camera, and then the girls had to pose.

They began by smiling dutifully, but by the time people had been cleared out of the way, their limbs had been arranged and rearranged, they had turned their heads this way and that, and Chanu had found a satisfactory angle, even Bibi was unable to keep her mouth upturned. "Smile," said Chanu, and someone would walk into the frame. "For God's sake. Look happy."

Nazneen had to take a turn with the girls. She whispered to Shahana, "If you smile nicely, I'll buy you those earrings."

"The dangly ones?"

"Yes."

"The really long ones?"

"Down to your knees. Now, smile."

Chanu stood with his arms around his daughters. Nazneen held her finger over the button. She took the shot that would live in the kitchen, propped up against the tiles at the back of the work surface, accumulating a fine spray of turmeric-stained grease from her cooking pot. It showed a middle-aged man with stringy calves poking out from long red shorts, a white T-shirt stretched over a preposterous stomach. Under each arm he had tucked a girl in salwaar kameez. On the left, holding up a hand to protect her face from the sun, was a creature whose near-brush with adolescence showed in a few spots around her chin and an impression—mystically conveyed—that she had curled up her toes with embarrassment. She wore a green suit, so dark that it was almost the black that she desired, and her hair hung loose around her face. In time, Nazneen could not recall if the black mark across her face was a piece of grit on the photograph or a strand of hair that she was chewing. On the opposite wing was a girl who stood with her arms glued to her sides. Her face tilted up to look at the man and she smiled as if there were a knife to her back. She wore a pretty pink kameez, and her scarf trailed on the floor. The man grinned straight at the camera and his capacious cheeks were jolly. His eyes were wrapped up in dark glasses.

"We must have one of us all together." Chanu looked around for a collaborator. He selected a young man who glowed with well-being, as if he had been fed all his life on dates and milk and honey.

"Sure," said the man, as though he had been expecting this call. "Stand a bit closer together."

Nazneen moved over, so that her shoulder brushed against Chanu. The photograph would show a dutiful and modest wife, in a cotton print sari. She put her hands on Bibi's arms.

"Whereabouts are y'all from?" His accent was familiar from the television.

"We are from Bangladesh," said Chanu. He spoke slowly, as if he expected the man to have trouble understanding.

"Y'don't say."

Chanu was puzzled. "Yes," he said. "Bangla-desh." Carefully, as if the man wanted to write it down.

"Y'don't say." The man returned the camera. He had an easy way about him. He was as relaxed as a child in its mother's arms.

"I do say," said Chanu.

Shahana rolled her eyes. "I'm from London."

"Is that in India?" He wore a blue checked shirt and his face glowed with health.

"No, no. India is one country. Bangladesh is another country."

"Y'don't say." He seemed simultaneously surprised but resigned to this fact. "Do you mind if I get a shot of all of you together for myself?" He toted his own camera. And by way of explanation he added, "I'm hoping to go there one day, India."

As she posed again, Nazneen realized that today was the first time they had stood together as a family for the camera. It filled her with a mixture of panic and hope, the possibility of holding things together with the unexceptional ritual of family life.

When the film was developed, a few shots were only blurs of color, like a glimpse through a doorway when the monsoon washed away the shape of things, and of the family together nothing could be made out except for the feet.

They sat on the grass in St. James's Park and Nazneen laid the picnic out on four tea towels. Chicken wings spread in a paste of yogurt and spices and baked in the oven, onions sliced to the thickness of a fingernail, mixed with chilies, dipped in gram flour and egg and fried in bubbling oil, a dry concoction of chickpeas and tomatoes stewed with cumin and ginger, misshapen chapatis wrapped while still hot in tinfoil and sprinkled now with condensation, golden hard-boiled eggs glazed in a curry seal, Dairylea triangles in their cardboard box, bright orange packets containing shamelessly orange crisps, a cake with a list of ingredients too long to be printed in legible type. She arranged them all on paper plates and stacked up the plastic tubs inside the carrier bags.

"It's ready," she cried, as though calling them to the table.

Shahana extricated a Dairylea and picked the foil apart. She rolled the cheese inside a chapati. Bibi sat on her feet and chewed at a chicken wing. Chanu took his time loading a plate with each item, including three crisps and a slice of the cake. He balanced it on his knee. "It's quite a spread," he said in English. "You know, when I married your mother, it was a stroke of luck." He gestured at the tea towels as if his luck were plainly on display. Then he ate with a fervor that ruled out conversation.

After lunch, Chanu removed his money belt and his sandals and lay down. Though his eyes were buried beneath his dark glasses, Nazneen became aware from the rise and fall of his stomach that he had fallen asleep. The girls decided to go for a walk around the lake, and Nazneen told them to follow the path and not to get lost. She would have liked to go with them to explore the seductive contours of the park, linger among the flowers, and stand close to the fountain that shot fabulous jeweled arrows against the plate-blue sky. But to leave Chanu here stranded on his back would be, she felt, to dishonor him, so she stayed.

She rubbed the grass with her toes and watched the people passing by with red cans and white ice creams. A heron landed by the lake and stretched its wings and folded them flat again. Gaily colored ducks strung themselves across the water, bobbing aimlessly, like a garland of flowers. On the far bank a tree trailed its leaves, green and braided hair, onto the lake's ever moving, ever still surface. The sun worked its warm fingers on her arms. She watched the people, all colors, all sorts, and they shared an aspect. Here they were, seeking the moment, ambling or strolling or trotting and eager to have their share of enjoyment. A brown-skinned family passed by. They looked like Pathans, tall and dignified, with sharp cheekbones and high brows. Nazneen wondered if they, too, were on holiday from a different corner of this city, but something in their way of looking told her that they had made a longer trip. A girl on roller skates, her shorts smaller than her buttocks, split the family apart, and they watched her speed along the path; if she had raised her arms and flown they would have been no more and no less surprised.

Nazneen plucked a blade of grass. She cut it along the ridge with her thumbnail and curled the ends one way and the other to form two spirals. She tossed it away. *We are no more than this,* she thought. *Each life is no more than a blade of grass on this lawn.*

The last few weeks, since the first time with Karim, since her life had become bloated with meaning and each small movement electrified, she had taken to reminding herself. *You are nothing. You are nothing.*

They had developed a routine of sorts. In the early afternoon she watched from the window. When he appeared, she raised her hand as if she were about to scratch her face. Then he would come up. If Chanu was still at home, she leaned her head against the glass, and he did not wave or smile, or do anything other than continue his walk across the yard. Then she imagined that she would do the same every day, until he stopped appearing. She would simply watch and eventually he would understand and not come back again for her. But the next day she trembled just the same as she raised her hand.

He was the first man to see her naked. It made her sick with shame. It made her sick with desire. They committed a crime. It was a crime and the sentence was death. In between the sheets, in between his arms, she took her pleasure desperately, as if the executioner waited behind the door. Beyond death was the eternal fire of hell and from every touch of flesh on flesh she wrought the strength to endure it. Though they began with a gentle embrace, tenderness could not satisfy her, nor could she stand it, and into her recklessness she drew him like a moth to a flame.

In the bedroom everything changed. Things became more real and they became less real. Like a Sufi in a trance, a whirling dervish, she lost the thread of one existence and found another. "S-slow down," he moaned. But she could not.

Out of the bedroom, she was—in starts—afraid and defiant. If ever her life was out of her hands, it was now. She had submitted to her father and married her husband; she had submitted to her husband. And now she gave herself up to a power greater than these two, and she felt herself helpless before it. When the thought crept into her mind that the power was inside her, that she was its creator, she dismissed it as conceited. How could such a weak woman unleash a force so strong? She gave in to fate and not to herself.

After she had changed the sheets (this is where the pain, without the balm of passion, became severe) they went into the sitting room. Karim sprawled on the sofa. He checked his mobile for messages. "Nerves and worrying," he said. "The man is a worrier." As if the son could not give cause for the father to worry.

"I fancy a bit of chanachur," he said. And Nazneen went to get his snack.

"A glass of water."

"I left my magazine over there."

"Could you pass my phone?"

"Leave that sewing now, for God's sake."

Nazneen danced attendance. It was a thrill, this playing house. But she knew she was playing, and she sensed for Karim it was a serious business.

He told her about his mother. "She was always the one with her feet up. It used to make me boil up to see my father bring her tea, bring her food, wipe her hands. She was always lying down if he was around. And if he wasn't there she did everything so slowly, like she didn't want to be bothered, couldn't be bothered with her children. She started staying in bed, calling for everything. It made me furious. I was furious with him as well for being so weak, for not being a man. I never thought—funny how children are—that she might be ill."

"So your father was strong," she said.

He put his fingers over his hair. It was cut so short that it could not be ruffled. "I don't know. I never thought of it that way."

Sometimes she fell into a state of bottomless anxiety. She spent the night eating leftovers in the kitchen as if layer on layer of food inside her would push out the anxiety, displace it like water from a bath. And at the end of these sessions she felt nauseated and tired, too tired to care what would happen and certain that in any case that nothing could be helped.

But much of the time she felt good. She spent more time talking to her daughters, and they surprised her with their intelligence, their wit, and their artless sensitivity. She served her husband and she found that he was a caring husband, a man of integrity, educated, and equipped with a pleasing thirst for knowledge. She did her work and she discovered that work in itself, performed with a desire for perfection, was capable of giving satisfaction. She cleaned the flat, and even wiping the floor after the toilet had flooded was not so tiresome if it was done with a song on the lips and in the heart. It was as if the conflagration of her bouts with Karim had cast a special light on everything, a dawn light after a life lived in twilight. It was as if she had been born deficient and only now been gifted the missing sense.

She did not go to any more meetings. The Bengal Tigers got along without her, but they were not getting along very well. The trouble was a lack of trouble. The Lion Hearts' press had stopped rolling. The Bengal Tigers put out a couple more leaflets (one entitled "Ten Ways to Taqwa" and the other designed as a foldout poster for Islamic Jihad with the words emblazoned across an AK-47 rifle), but without the spark of the Lion Hearts the fire had gone out.

Karim fretted about it. "They're planning something," he said. "When they go quiet, that's when you've got to worry."

In the north, there were more disturbances. "They've gone up there to agitate. But they'll be back. It will be '93 all over again." That was when the BNP councillor was elected and it was not safe to go out. "No," he said, "it will be much worse than that."

But the Bengal Tigers dwindled; they became an endangered species. At one meeting only five people turned up and Karim seethed. "The Lion Hearts have gone underground. They are gathering their forces. And what are we doing about it?" He stood in the hallway, and all Nazneen could think of was the bedroom. "When the time comes, will we be ready?" He worked his leg. He pushed his sleeves up, above the elbow. Nazneen undid a button on his shirt, and she ran a finger along the gold chain around his neck. She put a hand to his chin, where the mole was now covered—only just—by his beard.

He had begun to grow a beard soon after they became lovers. Now the hair on his face was the same length as the hair on his head. And he began to take religious instruction from the spiritual leader, the imported imam with the women's shoes.

"Do you know, in the Bukhari collection there are seven thousand five hundred and sixty-three hadith. The second most important is Hajjaj, containing seven thousand four hundred and twenty-two." He sat on the dressing table while she pulled the sheets from the bed and rolled them up. "To be an Islamic scholar . . . man, you've got to have a good memory." He moved out of the way while she took bed linen from the drawer. "Do you know, the Ka'aba was built by the first human, Adam, and is therefore the first shrine for worshipping God?" She spread the sheet and worked her way around the corners. "Do you know, when you do tawaf, how many circuits around the Ka'aba you're actually supposed to run? Three. I thought it was all of them. Basic things—I never knew." She listened and she was glad to have the words—any words but her own—in her ears while she covered the traces of their un-Islamic deed. In the evening, when he had long since gone and she moved around the kitchen preparing food, Shahana followed her with a textbook in her hand. "Do you know," she said, "that humans have forty-six chromosomes, dogs and chickens have seventy-eight, scorpions have four, and peas have fourteen?"

"No," admitted Nazneen. "I did not know. And what is 'chromosome'?"

Shahana was offended. "Well, it's something to do with biology. But aren't you interested that we have less than the chickens?"

Nazneen picked another blade of grass. She forced herself back into the moment. The girls returned from their walk and asked for ice creams. Nazneen considered whether to wake Chanu, but before she could decide he sat up. He belched lightly with his hand over his mouth and then yawned with abandon. "I'll go for the ice cream," he said. "Stretch my legs."

"I'm having a good time, Abba," said Bibi.

"Then it is worth it." He looked at Shahana. "And you?"

"Oh," she said, "nothing could be better."

He hesitated. Something dark passed across his brow. But then it was gone. He lifted his jowls in a smile. "As long as the memsahib is pleased." And he walked across the grass, down to the lakeside.

"Are you in love with him?" Shahana looked fierce. Her eyes narrowed.

Nazneen went into free fall. She bowed her head.

"I mean, have you ever been in love with him? Perhaps before he got so *fat*?"

Nazneen reached out to her daughter. She stroked her arm and she would have liked to embrace her, hug her tight against her body. "Your father is a good man. I was lucky in my marriage."

"You mean he doesn't beat you," said Shahana.

"When you are older, you will understand all these things. About a husband and wife." Nazneen did not know which one of them was wiser, the mother or the daughter. She did not know if Shahana's questions were acute or naive, but all the same she felt proud of the girl.

Shahana was not satisfied. "But do you love him?"

Bibi sat with her feet drawn up to her bottom and her arms around her knees, bracing herself for a crash. "Do you, Amma?"

Nazneen laughed. "Well, you silly girls. Don't you think I love my family? Look, here is your father now, and he has chocolate ice creams."

On Monday morning Mrs. Islam came for her money. She leaned against the wall in the hallway and another chunk of plaster was dislodged. For a few moments she massaged her hip and she let out a groan that at once suggested great pain and the capacity to bear it. She sprayed a cloud of Ralgex Heat Spray. Most of it landed on her chiffon sari but it appeared to revive her. "I've brought you something, child. Here. Carry my bag for me."

When she was recumbent on the sofa, Mrs. Islam closed her eyes.

Nazneen stood by. From the next-door flat there came a faint and rhythmic knocking. It was the bed moving. The neighbor had another new boyfriend. Nazneen blushed. She wondered if others listened to her bed and how much it had already told.

"Whenever He is ready, I am also ready."

Nazneen was used to this. She no longer bothered to protest. She waited. Listening to Mrs. Islam was like being in Gouripur, listening to the radio in a storm. She kept on cutting out.

In the flats immediately next door, there were white people. And they minded their own business—something Mrs. Islam had told her years ago—and now she knew why. For this English peculiarity, she was grateful.

"The mosque school is full. Do not send your daughters. We cannot take them."

Nazneen saw that the wart on the side of Mrs. Islam's nose had grown a secondary knobble. From this nodule grew a fourth hair. The hairs were long. Perhaps Mrs. Islam's hand had grown too unsteady to pluck them, or her eyesight too weak. Perhaps she was, at last, attaining invalidity. And the hair on her head was not tied tightly, as it usually was, in a neat spool of white held together by the invisible powers of godliness and elastics. Now it more nearly resembled the nest of a slovenly and spectacularly incontinent bird, and it glittered with the demented treasure of a dozen black metal pins.

Nazneen went to the showcase and opened the door. From beneath the wooden elephant she pulled out a yellow envelope, and counted for the third time that day the five ten-pound notes. Chanu was determined the woman should have no more. For a couple of weeks he had said, "That crook, I'll give her nothing. All money goes to the Home Fund." But after a persuasive visit from her sons, he had settled on fifty pounds per week.

"How much money do you have, child?" Mrs. Islam began to press along the length of one hand with the other, still with her eyes closed.

"Fifty pounds. As agreed."

Mrs. Islam opened her eyes. Those eyes could not miss anything. They were small and dangerous. "Arthritis. The hands of a cripple. But do not worry. I am too old, anyway." She fished in the pocket of her cardigan and held something up. "Take them, take them." Her voice faded away, and her head fell back as if she had fainted.

She recovered. "When I was a girl, my mother massaged my hands every day. I had the smallest and most supple hands in all of Tangail. But now"—she sighed—"I can't get these bracelets on. Take them, child. Take them."

The bangles were of dark green glass, motes of gold suspended inside.

Mrs. Islam took a handkerchief and wiped her brow. She smelled of mints and cough syrup; a layered smell, such as of perfume over sweat, the sweet smell of decay.

"Very pretty," said Nazneen.

"Yes, yes. Take what you want." She allowed her eyelids to droop. Her voice was barely louder than the rustle of her lilac chiffon sari.

Nazneen held the envelope. She held her tongue.

Mrs. Islam began to massage her temples with her crippled hands.

Before her elder, Nazneen waited without comment or patience. The old woman, the better to relax her face, let her mouth hang open. Nazneen imagined cramming the money inside that black hole.

"So you are going back." The geriatric voice had vanished.

Overhead, a vacuum cleaner was switched on. The bed next door had stopped moving against the wall. "I don't know." Nazneen counted the money a fourth time.

"You don't know. Of course you don't. Why should you know? If you are planning to rob an old woman of her money, then you should know nothing. Better keep your mouth closed."

"I have your money here."

"You have it all?" snapped Mrs. Islam. Her black eyes glittered. "Give it to me. How much is here? A thousand pounds still owing, and you are going to run away? Give me the rest."

"That's all I have." A taste of bile came into her mouth.

"No, child. Are you going to swim back home with your pots on your head? You have money for the plane ticket."

Nazneen could have spat, right there and then, on the lilac chiffon. She swallowed. "Not here. I don't have any money here."

A change came over her guest. Mrs. Islam began to breathe heavily. She held her chest and she shrank inside her sari, as if she were being eaten alive from the inside. She gasped and waved her hand. Nazneen rushed to the bag to find Benylin or some other, more extreme form of unction. But Mrs. Islam waved the bag away. "Come close to me," she croaked. Nazneen knelt down by the sofa and Mrs. Islam grabbed her hand. Her skin was hot and dry as sun-baked leaves, and her knuckles were sharp. From this close range it was possible to see all the thousand tiny veins on her cheeks and nose. They showed through, so it seemed, where the skin had worn away. "I have been a widow many years." Nazneen breathed in the complex smell of the sickroom, of smells hiding smells. "God knows how I have suffered. Without a husband all these years. Listen to me. Get close. God has tested me, a widow's life is no joke. I think I will take a little Benylin.

"Good girl. Put it back now. No, give me your hand again. I was telling you about my husband. He left me alone. But even before he died—God bears me witness—he was no use at all. I do not know what substance filled his head, but it was not brain. He was Dulal, the son of

Alal. Do you understand me? He was like a spoilt child. Without me, he was nothing."

She paused awhile. She inspected Nazneen's face as she would inspect a mango at market, squeezing it gently with thumb and forefinger.

"You have too much tension in your face. You should press at the temples, and the tension will disappear. If you don't do this, lines will come."

"I already have lines."

"Nonsense, you are just a child. You are barely older than my sons." She sighed and then sucked on her teeth. "They are no better than the father. God gave them only half a brain each. Worse than that, they do not know it. To know that you are not clever, you must reach some minimum standard of intelligence. Do you see? All they give to their mother is trouble. I thank God for giving me sons, but why such sons as these?" There was a wet look to her eyes and she blinked hard a few times. Nazneen pressed her hand.

Mrs. Islam's voice grew harsher. "What they lack in brain, they make up in muscle. We must look to the positive. We must make the most of the opportunities God gives. I always find a way to manage. Don't make any mistake about that."

"Can I get something for you? A glass of water?"

"When I am gone, my sons will be all right. See how weak my pulse comes? But I have provided for them. Not too little, and not too much either, because why should they squander what I have built? I would rather give it to the mosque. I would rather give it to the school and let those who have brains make use of them.

"Yes, I do all these things for my community, and I expect no thanks." She raised her hand as if to ward off gratitude. "If someone is sick, they come to me. If someone's husband runs off, they come to me. If a child needs a roof, they come to me. If someone has no penny for rice, they come to me. And I give. All the time, giving." Her head lolled to one side. She had given everything, her last ounce of strength.

Nazneen looked down at the parched, translucent hand of her elder and better. She bent her head and kissed it.

"From the goodness of my heart, I give. And when those who have received don't want to pay what they owe, they run off to foreign countries, and they say, 'Why should we pay her? She's just an old woman.' And so it is. So it is."

Nazneen went into the kitchen and opened the cupboard under the sink. She moved aside the rice pan and the frying pan, the colander and the grater. From behind the plumbing she retrieved a Tupperware box and took out three blue notes and five pale gold ridged coins. She took the twenty pounds to Mrs. Islam and put it in the zipped compartment of the portable black pharmacy. Mrs. Islam took her bag and struggled to her feet. "Don't look so sad. When you leave for Bangladesh, I will make a big party for you. All my own expense. Just finish paying the debt, and then leave it all to me." She walked across the room with a surprisingly light step.

Razia wanted to buy cloth and Nazneen accompanied her to Wentworth Street. Market stalls lined the road, selling leather goods, coats of every kind of synthetic, bright handbags on cheap chains, shoes that looked disposable, Jamaican patties, tinned food at 40 percent off. They ignored the stalls and stuck to the pavement. Past Regency Textiles and Excelsior Textiles Ltd, cloth draped on wire hangers in windows, Balinese prints, wax-block African prints (with certificate of authenticity), beyond the "exclusive" luggage of Regal Stores, past the untitled window where cellophane-wrapped blocks of fabric were suspended on end in a pattern of diamonds. They crossed the street and looked inside Narwoz Fashions. Yellow Rose Universal Fashions caught their attention briefly, and Nazneen was pulled into Padma's Children's Paradise (East End) by a keen assistant who offered "special prices" on all the stock. Nazneen fingered a little baby dress, all plum velour and silver netting.

"Something you're not telling me?" said Razia, patting her stomach.

Nazneen let go of the dress. "Of course not."

Razia perused the stock of Galaxy Textiles Ltd: Retail, Wholesale and Export at 70% Clearance Permanent. She found nothing suitable, and they moved on to Starman Fabrics.

"How is Shefali?"

"We are waiting for the exam results. If she gets good marks, she has been accepted at Guildhall University."

"Such a clever girl." Nazneen examined a roll of raw silk, the color of marigolds. She thought it would look well on Shefali. "And Tariq?"

Razia was bending over a cotton print, fine wavy lines of pink on a lemon background. "Tariq is getting out more and more. Some weeks I hardly see him." She laughed, and tucked her hair behind her ears. The cut of her hair had grown blunter and blunter over the years, as if the scissors had become worn out with use. "Now I have to start complaining that he is never at home. This is our role as mothers. Whatever the child does, we must complain."

The shop assistant, a girl of around twenty with a heavily powdered face and patches of mauve above the eyes, regarded Razia with suspicion. Razia was dressed in stretchy brown trousers that accidentally finished before her socks began, and a collarless man's shirt. The assistant hastily checked over her own clothes, smoothing down her outfit as if it might become infected with a nasty antifashion virus.

Nazneen gave the girl a stare which the girl unblinkingly returned.

"Where does he go?" said Nazneen. She had thought and thought of telling her suspicion to Razia. But how could she say such a thing to her friend? And what evidence did she have?

She had no evidence but she had a certainty that would have been overwhelming, were it not for the fact that only a grain of doubt was needed to tip the scales. Karim talked about drugs on the estate. He knew a great deal about it.

"See those kids down there?" He stood at the window but Nazneen would not go and stand with him. She did not want to stand in view with him. "Those kids, they're all users."

She did not understand.

"They're users, addicts. They're all scaggies."

"What it is? Users?"

"They're all on heroin. All of that lot."

"Drugs."

"This estate is *full* of it. You got no idea." He came away from the window. He passed close to her but they did not touch. They touched only in the bedroom. "Some of them, right, twelve years old. Know how it got this way? Ten years ago, this place was clean, yeah? There was just Tippex, or gas—you know, lighter fuel. A bit of weed. Ganja. All right. Nothing bad. But then, what happened, this area started going up. And the City started coming out towards Brick Lane. You got grant money coming in, regeneration money. Property prices going up, new people moving in, businesses and that. And we started to do well, man."

He sat down at her sewing machine. "That's the problem. *That* is the start of it. No coincidence. S'like what happened in America when the blacks got organized. Black Panthers, all that. You've got to keep them down, keep them quiet."

His phone was on the table. He spun it around. Nazneen traced the cords of his forearms in her mind.

"The FBI—the government—they got together with the Mafia, and flooded the blacks with drugs, set them up with all the guns and stuff, so they can just get high and shoot each other. Long as it stays in the ghettoes, man, they're not *bothered.*"

Nazneen wondered if her English had failed her, misled her. She said, "The government gave the drugs?"

"Know what I'm saying?" said Karim. "You got to ask the questions."

For a while he looked inside his magazine. He rubbed his beard, cupped his chin in his hand, and tested the bristles.

"Not like they *couldn't* stop it, if they wanted to. Everyone *knows* the dealers." He gave a short, bitter laugh. "It's not hard. The dealers are the ones the kids look up to. With the flash cars and all the gold. But, know what I'm thinking? I'm thinking—" He shook his head as if it could not be true. "I'm thinking as long as they're on the scag, they stay away from religion. And the government—it's more scared of Islam than heroin."

"Where does Tariq go?" Razia shrugged. She pulled on her long nose. "Who can say? Certainly not him."

"Looking for something special?" The assistant's face powder was several shades too pale. It made her neck look unwashed.

"For my daughter." Razia removed her glasses and pressed her eyes. Nazneen saw that the seat of her trousers hung low and unfilled, her bosom had strayed down towards her stomach, and her arms strained against her shirt. It was as if she had been tipped in such a way that her flesh had run into all the wrong places.

"What about this one?" said Nazneen.

Razia studied the orange silk. "I'm not sure." She turned to the girl. "We will look around."

"Right," said the girl, as if she had thought as much.

"These young ones," Razia hissed in Nazneen's ear, "they don't know about respect."

"That's what Ka—"

"What?"

That's what Karim says. He says that the young ones would do anything. If they lit a cigarette in the street and they saw an elder coming, they did not bother to hide it. They walked with their girlfriends. They even kissed, in the street, in front of an elder. There was no reason not to say it. "The man who brings the sewing for me, he says the same thing."

"The middleman? The boy who comes?"

Nazneen pulled out a roll of cherry-red cotton jersey. She took a keen interest in it. "Oh, yes. Everyone says it." She was aware of Razia watching her.

"He has been keeping you busy."

Nazneen pulled the material. The stretchiness of the fabric was of great importance to her. Razia was making small talk, and Nazneen listened with only half an ear. "Huh? Oh, plenty of work."

Eventually, she had to look up. Razia, expectant. Her lashes, enlarged by the spectacles, seemed like thick spider's legs. In the depths of her irises, gold lights played at an infinitesimal remove. It should have been possible to tell her anything.

"Well, which one do you like?" It should have been possible for her to ask anything. But Razia decided not to ask. Instead, they discussed material. They spoke of weight and color, texture and sturdiness, loveliness and ease of care. They pulled out roll after roll and failed to return the stock to its rightful position and the assistant clacked around them on her heels.

All the while Nazneen counted her secrets. How had it happened? It was as if she had woken one day to find that she had become a collector, guardian of a great archive of secrets, without the faintest knowledge of how she had gotten started or how her collection had grown. Perhaps, she considered, they just breed with each other. And then she imagined her secrets growing like a column of ants, appearing at first like a few negligible specks and turning so quickly into an unstoppable force.

She scratched her leg and her arms. Razia caught the itch and scratched also. Nazneen felt overrun with secrets. She wanted to tell everything to Razia—about Karim, what she suspected about Tariq, the truth about Hasina, the saga of Mrs. Islam's money.

When the assistant was at a safe distance, checking her makeup in a strip of mirror behind the counter, Nazneen said, "We borrowed money from Mrs. Islam."

Razia made an unfamiliar sound: she squeaked. In all the years she had known her, Nazneen had never heard her friend squeak.

"What for? Why?"

"To buy the sewing machine. You can't do anything without capital," said Nazneen, quoting her husband. "And we bought the computer."

"Certificates from here to here," said Razia, stretching out her arms, "but the man is a bloody fool."

"The thing is, however much we pay back, she always wants more."

"Of course she wants more. That is how it works."

"Yes," agreed Nazneen, "but how much more?"

"She is a witch."

"I don't know. Whenever someone needs something, they go to her. She gives. She gave us the money when we needed it. And she is old. Her hip . . ." She trailed off, but felt that she had not said enough. "Her hands are bad too."

Razia snorted and tossed her head. "Hands are bad! The only thing that's bad is her heart. Look at my hands. For the past two months I have worked only on leather. Let me see her hands! Perhaps they would benefit from a little honest work." She drew her mouth tight and made it lipless. "When I was a young girl, I had the most beautiful hands in all the country, East and West." She had Mrs. Islam's new "deathbed" voice exactly. "People came from far and wide to get a glimpse." She looked at Nazneen sidelong and a tremor of laughter crept into her voice. "If they caught a sight," the words rose on a crescendo, "my father chopped off their heads."

Nazneen laughed loudly. The assistant looked uncomfortable, as though laughter were something new and unsettling. She picked up a piece of paper, a price list or inventory, and walked around with a pencil to show that she certainly had things to be getting on with.

"But how much do you owe?" Razia grew serious again.

"Around a thousand, I think."

"And how much did you borrow?"

"Around the same. I'm not sure."

"And how much have you paid already?"

"I don't know. It's difficult to keep track, but it seems like we should nearly be finishing instead of just starting."

"Listen, you will never be rid of this debt. Whatever you pay, she will say you owe interest and fees and this and that. I know of one case where they have been paying for six, seven years."

"We have some money saved for going back to Dhaka. I don't know how much. Chanu has it in the bank."

"Keep it," said Razia quickly. "Don't let her get her twisted fingers on that money. I'll think of something. Leave it to me."

She decided on a length of ivory silk and a turquoise voile to make the scarf. "I'll make it at work. It will be a surprise for her. I know she's going to pass the exams."

The assistant wrapped the fabrics in tissue paper, her little pink tongue poking out between her lips, as she made sure to align the edges. She named the price.

Razia opened her purse and looked inside, holding it practically at eye level. Then she began removing pieces of paper, receipts, photographs, tickets, and coins. When the purse was empty she conceded, "There's only two pounds here."

The assistant stood with her hands on her narrow hips. Then she put them on the package and looked at Razia. She had seen her sort before.

"Can you make a discount?" said Razia.

The girl did not smile. She drew the package closer to her.

"I don't know," Razia told Nazneen. "I can't remember anything these days. I thought I had forty pounds in here. Must have left it somewhere."

Nazneen reached inside her bag. "I'll give you the money. I have some here. I was going to send it to Hasina."

But Razia would not take the money and they walked together to Sonali Bank at the bottom of Brick Lane, and on past the newsagent's with the window stacked with amulets and herbal remedies, the Sangeeta Centre stocked with paper flowers, garland kits, and Gloy glue. "Do you know," said Nazneen, "Dr. Azad told my husband, so many of our young men are getting hooked on drugs."

"Truly I am grateful to God." Razia looked straight ahead. "He has kept this curse away from our home."

"To pay for the drugs, they must steal. Dr. Azad says that sometimes they steal even from"—she hesitated—"their own parents."

Razia looked at her now, with an expression that Nazneen could not read. "As I just told you, I am grateful to God."

They walked on past the Bangla Superstore declaring "Dates from Madinah," the waiters who fished for customers from the restaurant doorways, and the grocer where all year round the window sign bore the sweet lie "New Season Lengra."

The curtains were closed though it was not quite yet dark. The walls by the window held oblongs of rich light, neat cutouts pasted onto the wallpaper. From the television came feathery rays both bright and weak. The tall floor lamp against the back wall cast light up and down and into the television, where it made a picture of itself. Chanu's reading lamp was positioned on top of the trolley. Its yellow beam formed a circle which took in Chanu's book, his belly, his knees, and some part of his papers. Nazneen cleared and wiped the table, working in the last warm melts of sun which soaked through the thin gray curtains. The girls, in their nightdresses, drew their feet up on the sofa, caught in the misty glow of television. And Chanu sat beneath the yellow light, his face filled with shadows.

"Do you know that the British cut the fingers off Bengali weavers?" It was unclear whom he was addressing. Shahana stared hard at the television screen. Bibi looked from the screen to her father and then her mother and then back at the screen.

"Oh, I went to buy cloth with Razia today." Nazneen could not stop thinking about Razia's empty purse.

"It was the British, of course, who destroyed our textile industry."

"Yes," said Nazneen. "How did they do that?"

Chanu expelled whatever it was that was sticking in his windpipe. He coughed as well, to be on the safe side, and then he began. "You see, it was largely a matter of tariffs. Export and import duties. Silk and cotton goods had seventy or eighty percent tax slapped on them, and we were not allowed to retaliate."

Nazneen had drifted. She straightened the dining chairs and shivered at some remembered pleasure.

"The Dhaka looms were sacrificed," said Chanu, "so that the mills of Manchester could be born."

Nazneen came around to her duties. "They were closed down by the British?"

"In effect," said Chanu, waggling his head. "Not closed down, exactly." He put his book aside and placed his hands beneath his undershirt, where they grew busy. "It's like being in a race, where one man runs without hindrance, and you must run with your arms tied behind your back, a blindfold on, hot coals beneath you, and, and . . ." He thought for a while and his cheeks moved this way and that. "And your legs cut off," he finished, and indicated with a chopping motion to the knee the exact location of the severance.

"Ah," said Nazneen, "I see how it happened." She wished that Shahana and Bibi would pay more attention. A sudden regret came to her. How much time she had wasted over the years, eating up her mind with a thousand petty worries and details that added up to nothing. She picked up one of Chanu's books and turned it over, pressed her thumbs on the cover, as if she could squeeze the knowledge from it. She waited for Chanu to continue.

Chanu bounced his knees up and down. He spoke a few words to himself, of summation or consolation, and then he got up. He went out of the room and returned with a small mat of wooden beads. "This is an automatic back massager," he said. "It's amazing what you can buy." His face grew full of wonder, as if he had received this revelation from the Angel Jibreel himself. "Let me try it now." He motioned to the girls to move aside.

"It's for the car." Chanu positioned the mat over the back of the sofa and wedged himself against it. "All sorts of gadgets and gimmicks you can get."

This was true. Chanu had invested in many items for his driving job. There were gloves for the glove compartment, an ice scraper (bought at a good price, much cheaper than buying it in the winter), an extra mirror that enabled him to conduct surveillance on the ignorant-type people in the back, an air freshener in the shape of a frog, and an eye mask made of thick black nylon that allowed Chanu to sleep in his seat between jobs. The most serious investment was a device that monitored traffic conditions and worked out alternative routes through the city. Chanu was awestruck. "It's a mystery, how man can invent such things." It had cost a great deal of money. It cost a deal more in heartache. However Chanu coaxed and cajoled it, the machine never gave up its mystery. He could never get it to work.

On top of these costs were the fines and penalties. Though Chanu was a very careful and able driver, it seemed that the Authorities conspired against him. There were fines for speeding and one for going too slow. On one occasion Chanu had to attend court over some fabricated indictment. He put on his suit and he rehearsed his speech in front of the mirror. "They don't know who they are dealing with," he told Nazneen. "They think it is some peasant-type person who will tremble at their gowns and wigs." He left in high spirits and returned in a black mood. He lay on the bed with his face turned to the wall. Nazneen brought food and left it on the dressing table. "The trial was not fair," she suggested. She touched his back. It was rigid. "Just leave me alone," he said.

The parking tickets mounted up and an outrage occurred when the car was towed away and held for ransom. By the time these various expenses were added up and the rental cost for the minicab paid to Kempton Kars, the profit margin was tender and exposed. Chanu worked hard, and the harder he worked the more he suspected he was being cheated of his reward. "Chasing wild buffaloes," he said, "and eating my own rice."

The automatic back massager seemed to be working. Chanu ground himself into his seat and let out a series of grunts. "I just don't know," he said, and interrupted himself with a moan: "A man could fall asleep at the wheel."

"Can I try it, Abba?" Bibi always took an interest in Chanu's latest gadget. She even played with the frog air freshener, tapping it on the back until Chanu said, "All right, Bibi, don't waste it all."

"It's for the *relief of tension* and the *unknotting of muscles,*" said Chanu, quoting in English from the packaging. "You don't have any tensions."

"No," said Bibi in a small voice.

"What is this rubbish you are watching, Shahana? Switch it off now."

"How do you know that it's rubbish if you don't even know what it is?"

Nazneen held her breath.

It was dark now outside. The room was sealed. There were too many things in it. Too many people. Too little light.

Chanu stood up and turned off the television. Then he returned to his seat and extended an arm to his elder daughter. "Come. Come on, sit close."

Shahana did not move. She blew at her fringe.

Nazneen went towards her. "Go on. Sit with your father. Don't you hear him?"

Chanu waved her away. "Leave her be. She is too big for all that. She is not a child anymore. You're not a child, are you, Shahana?"

Shahana moved her shoulders a fraction of an inch.

"All right, all right," said Chanu. He picked something out of a back tooth. He pushed his back against the massager and circled his ankles. "How is school? Still top of the class? Clever girl, eh?"

Shahana turned her head a little. "It's OK," she said in English.

"*OK, OK.* All this television watching and still she comes top of the class." He spoke quietly. "When I was at school, I used to get very good grades. Your mother is also clever, though she takes care to hide it. But, you see, we have not been able to make our way. We have tried . . ." He broke off and became lost in thought. "Well, we have tried."

Nazneen sat down in the armchair. Bibi sat on the arm.

"I know," said Shahana. "Don't worry about it."

"You're right. Worry does no good." Chanu smiled and touched his hand briefly to Shahana's shoulder.

"It's time for bed," said Nazneen.

But Chanu objected. "Let them stay. We are having a conversation here, father-daughter." He looked at Shahana and raised his eyebrows, as if to say, *That woman, how she always spoils our fun.* Shahana allowed him a smile and Chanu was very pleased. "I don't know, Shahana. Sometimes I look back and I am shocked. Every day of my life I have prepared for success, worked for it, waited for it, and you don't notice how the days pass until nearly a lifetime has finished. Then it hits you—the thing you have been waiting for has already gone by. And it was going in the other direction. It's like I've been waiting on the wrong side of the road for a bus that was already full."

Shahana nodded quickly. "But don't worry," she said.

"You are old enough now to talk to. That is a great comfort to me. And to have such a clever daughter . . ." His eyes grew full and he cleared his throat a little. "You see, the things I had to fight: racism, ignorance, poverty, all of that—I don't want you to go through it."

Bibi chewed her nails. Nazneen gently pulled her hand away from her mouth.

"Abba, I'm . . ."

"You know Mr. Iqbal? In the newsagents. He comes from a very good family in Chittagong. God knows how many servants. And he is an educated man. We talk of many things. Why can he not rise out of that little hole here, always buried under newspapers and his hands black with ink? In Chittagong he would live like a prince, but here he is just doing the donkey work by day and sleeping in a little rat hole at night."

"Mr. Iqbal just sold his flat," said Shahana.

"It's these things that make me sad," continued Chanu, captivated by his own oration.

"For one hundred and sixty thousand pounds."

"Living in little rat holes." Chanu waggled his head, and his cheeks were filled with sorrow.

"He did *Right to Buy,*" said Shahana. "Fifteen years ago. Paid five thousand pounds in cash."

"So that's why your mother and I have decided . . ."

"You should have bought this flat."

". . . to go back home." Chanu explored his stomach, checking the texture, the density. He appeared satisfied. "Good," he said, and he beamed at Shahana. "I'm glad we talked like this, father-daughter. Now you understand. That's the main thing—understanding. Good. Go and brush your teeth, and get ready for bed."

Nazneen could not sleep. She looked in on the girls and stroked the hair out of their eyes. She was tempted to wake them, as she had when they were babies to make sure they could be woken, and to have the comfort of comforting them to sleep again. She picked up a few stray clothes and went to the kitchen. She washed them beneath the kitchen tap, rubbing them with soap and kneading them on the draining board. Then she rinsed them until the cold water made ridges on her fingertips. Her mind boiled with indistinct thoughts, like a room full of people all shouting at once. She let the clothes fall into the sink and pressed her hands to her temples.

She massaged her face and jaw and began again at her temples. Only a short time ago it had seemed that she worried unnecessarily about everything. Now it was clear that she had not worried enough. She was back on the tightrope that stretched between her husband and her children, and this time the wind was high and tormenting.

And there was Karim.

The horror came to her now. She vomited over the clothes she had washed. She was stunned. As if she had just now gained consciousness and discovered a corpse on the floor, a bloody dagger in her hand.

She wiped her face and rinsed her mouth.

"God sees everything. He knows every hair on your head." Amma squatted on her haunches in the corner, just by the cupboard with the dustpan and brush, bleach and spare toilet rolls.

Nazneen turned the tap on full. Water splashed off the sink and over her arms.

"When you were a little girl, you used to ask me, 'Amma, why do you cry?' My baby, do you know now?" She began to weep, and blew her nose on the end of her sari. "This is what women have to bear. Once, when you were a little girl, you could hardly wait to find out." She set up a keening that tore Nazneen's ears. Nazneen cleared vomit from the plughole to allow the water to drain.

Amma shuffled closer, still on her haunches so that her bottom swept the floor. "Listen to me, baby. Don't turn away. I don't have long here." Nazneen turned and looked at her and Amma smiled, showing her curved yellow teeth. "God tests us," she said. "Don't you know this life is a test? Some He tests with riches and good fortune. Many men have failed such a test. And they will be judged. Others He tests with illness or poverty, or with jinn who come in the shape of men—or of husbands." She took hold of the hem of Nazneen's nightdress and began to tug at it. "Come down here to me and I will tell you how to pass the test."

"No, Amma," said Nazneen. She tried to pull her nightdress free. "You come up here."

"No, baby, come to me." She pulled harder, so hard that Nazneen gave way and slid down to the floor. "It's easy." Amma began to cackle, and she did not cover her teeth and her mouth became wider and wider and the teeth became longer and sharper and Nazneen put up her hands to cover her face.

"It's easy. You just have to endure."

Chapter Fifteen

Chanu woke in the night and, he told her later, missed her heartbeat. He found her on the kitchen floor, vomit dried on the corners of her mouth, eyes open and unseeing. He had turned on the light, but she did not blink. He carried her to the bedroom and laid her on the bed. It was the only time he had carried her, and she wished that she remembered it.

For several days she stayed in bed and clung to her collapse. She pushed down into it like a diver, struggling against buoyancy, fighting her way into the depths. Where the water clouded with mud, where the light could not reach, where sound died and beyond the body there was nothing: that was where she wanted to be. At times she found this dead space and rested within it. But then she was caught in a net of dreams and dragged up to the surface, and the sun hit the water and sliced her eyes and she saw everything in pieces as if in a smashed mirror, and she heard everything at once—the girls laughing, her son crying, Chanu humming, Dr. Azad talking, Karim groaning, Amma wailing—each sound as clear as a lone sitar string on a hot and drowsy afternoon.

When the dreams would not let her go, would not let her go back under, she began to come out of her delirium. For several days, awake or asleep, she had kept her eyes closed. Now she opened them. Dr. Azad stood over her in his dark suit and white shirt. She took in the disorder of the bedroom—trays and plates stacked on the dressing table, clothes hanging over the wardrobe door, tissues, books, and newspapers coating the floor and bedside table—and she looked back at the doctor. He bowed slightly, as if greeting a dignitary.

"Are you feeling a little better?"

"Yes."

"Shall I call your husband?"

Nazneen considered it. She thought she had better tidy up first. Then she closed her eyes.

"We are glad to have you back."

Nazneen wondered why the doctor was shouting. She had never

heard him shout before. She was forced to open her eyes again and look at him.

"He has been concerned." Dr. Azad smiled his special antismile, with the corners of his mouth turning down. "No. I don't think that is the correct word. It's not an adequate word." His hair was glossy, black and improbable, like a mistake made in his youth and carried with him for the rest of his life. Nazneen realized there was something she ought to be worrying about. She could not think of it.

"Your husband is an excellent cook. He made many special dishes for you." He indicated the trays stacked on the dressing table, his gesture as formal as a policeman directing traffic. "I'm afraid I have been the chief beneficiary."

Chanu came in and saw Nazneen sitting up. He became wreathed in smiles, bright and gay as the garlands that cover a groom's face.

"She is sitting up. Why did you not call me? Look, she's sitting up. Is the nervous exhaustion finished? Does she speak? Is it as before when she would go to the bathroom and barely keep her eyes open for long enough? Will she take some soup now? A little rice perhaps? Does she speak? But why did you not call me?" Chanu hovered by the bed, and though he did not move he gave the impression of perpetual motion.

"I prescribe some more bed rest," said the doctor, "and not too much excitement."

Chanu put his finger on his lips, as though to quiet the excited doctor. "Yes, yes, we must take it very gently. When will she eat?"

"Why don't you ask her?"

"Of course," said Chanu. It was the very thing he had in mind. He coughed, but very softly. "Will you take a bit of food now? Some rice? An egg?"

Nazneen drew her knees up under the covers. They protested at this unwarranted abuse and she massaged them. "Just rice."

Chanu clapped and rubbed his hands together. "Oh, rice! Did you hear her, doctor? Keep your hospital beds and fancy medicines. It is rice that will do her good."

Dr. Azad had, from somewhere, produced a yellow paper file. He began to write in it, still standing, and he spoke to the top of his pen. "I'm delighted to see that you've come around to my perspective. In cases like this, what is needed is a rest cure."

"I always respect a professional opinion," Chanu declared, as though this in itself were an achievement.

"Yes," said the doctor, so quietly now that Nazneen doubted if Chanu could hear, "unless, of course, you disagree with it."

Chanu peeped at Nazneen over his cheeks, so inflated with happiness that they almost hid his eyes. He rubbed his hands some more and then began to crack his knuckles.

"I would like some rice," said Nazneen. She bent forward, as if to get up.

Chanu at once grew busy. He stacked a few plates on the dressing table. "Doctor's orders," he said, waving an arm. "You stay there and follow the orders. I will fetch and carry." He bustled out of the room, forgetting the dirty plates.

The girls came in as Chanu left. In a loud whisper, he forbade them to disturb their mother. Bibi and Shahana climbed on the bed and hugged her without saying a word. Bibi began to brush her mother's hair, working the plastic teeth into her scalp to stimulate it and fussing over every knot. Shahana stretched out on the pink bedspread, her hair full of static from the nylon. She had, noted Nazneen, taken sufficient advantage of Chanu's distraction to be wearing her tight jeans. Dr. Azad finished writing, took Nazneen's blood pressure, and began writing again.

Chanu returned, balancing a tray across his stomach. "Make way," he cried, though nothing but the furniture blocked him. "I have rice and some potato." He put the tray on the bottom of the bed. "Very little spice with the potato," he told the doctor, as if issuing a warning. "And a small dish of shon-papri. For energy."

"Good, good," said the doctor. He collected his belongings. "You will be able to get back to work," he told Chanu. "The London transport system is breaking down without you."

Chanu waggled his head. "Let them go to hell while I look after my wife." He began to eat the crumbly sweatmeat, but with the first mouthful Nazneen could see that he had remembered it was for her. He put the bowl of shon-papri down again. "How is your wife?" he asked cheerfully.

"Couldn't be better," returned the doctor, with equally determined good cheer. "Any word from the council?"

"Council?"

"About the—"

"Library. Thank you for asking, but as you observe"—he beamed at his girls and his wife—"I am too busy with my family. Let them go to hell too—ignorant types, readers and illiterates, council as well. Let them all go together." He sighed with tremendous satisfaction.

"Stay in bed," Dr. Azad told Nazneen. "As long as you can manage. Call me if you start to feel bad again; I can prescribe something to calm you."

"Nonsense," sang Chanu. "My wife is very, very calm. No one is more calm than my wife. She has nothing to get excited about," he said, with pride.

"Good, good. I must go. I have rounds to make. For some of us, work will not wait."

"Yes, you must go," agreed Chanu. "Go and heal the sick. And give my regards to your family."

Nazneen rolled a modest ball of rice between her first two fingers and thumb. She remembered the night, many years ago, when she had first wondered what brought these two men together. Now, what kept them together was clear. The doctor had status and respect and money, the lack of which caused Chanu to suffer. But the doctor had no family; none he could speak of without suffering. Chanu had a proper wife, daughters who behaved themselves. But this clever man, for all his books, was nothing better than a rickshaw wallah. And so they entwined their lives to drink from the pools of each other's sadness. From these special watering holes, each man drew strength.

It was late afternoon when she had decided to open her eyes and participate in her life once again. By way of celebration the girls stayed up long after bedtime, and Chanu became a clown. He gave an account of his mishaps in the kitchen and, in a reenactment of a slip of the knife, hopped around holding his thumb. At night he had been sleeping on the very edge of the bed to give her "room to breathe." He demonstrated just how he had rolled onto the floor on the first night, and his acting-out of befuddlement was gifted. Shahana rolled her eyes but she smiled despite herself. Bibi, more formal, applauded. Nazneen smiled and wound her hair into a knot. Her arms felt heavy as she lifted them, and her legs ached. Resting, it seemed, had made her unbearably tired. The feeling returned to her that there was something she ought to be thinking about.

"I'll get up for a while."

Chanu shook a finger at her. "Did she not hear the doctor? Bed rest. That's the prescription."

"But I've been in bed so long. I want to get up."

"She is disobeying the doctor. What a lot of trouble she will be in." Chanu smiled so hard that his cheeks were in danger of popping.

Nazneen wondered why her husband spoke of her as "she." If she had more energy, she decided, she would find this irritating. She marshaled her resources for getting up, ignoring Chanu's continued admonishments.

The sitting room crawled with toys, clothes, books, and abandoned kitchen utensils. A pack of toilet rolls stood on the table; five tins of baked beans nested on the sofa. Attempts had been made to unpack shopping bags, but at some stage between bag and cupboard each attempt had foundered. If a bag had been emptied, it lay on the floor and gaped at the mess. Emergency rations of food marked the path from door to sofa to table. Nazneen picked her way across the room without comment. It gave her some satisfaction. For years she had felt she must not relax. If she relaxed, things would fall apart. Only the constant vigilance and planning, the low-level, unremarked and unrewarded activity of a woman, kept the household from crumbling.

Chanu picked up a shoe and a packet of felt-tip pens. He put them on the arm of the chair. "The girls are on school holiday. What can you do?" He shrugged and shook his head, helpless in the face of this natural disaster.

Nazneen went to the window and looked out at the orange glow of the lampposts. The light was sickly; poisonous. She felt a memory gather like a lump in her throat, a thing without substance but with an undeniable presence.

Shahana looked out of the window with her. A group of children, ten or twelve years old, came around the corner and lined up along the wall as if they had taken themselves prisoner.

"There's Aktar," said Shahana, "and Ali."

"What time is it?" said Nazneen.

"Almost eleven o'clock," Chanu told her. He came up to the window and worked his lips and eyebrows into expressions of disapproval. "Why do they let their little children roam around like goats?"

"They're not little children," said Shahana. "And Ali's got ten brothers and sisters. His parents don't want them all inside all the time." She tossed her head to get her fringe out of her eyes. "They'd only get on each other's nerves," she added, with feeling.

"Ah, it's *overcrowding,*" said Chanu, dropping in the word in English. "*Overcrowding* is one of the worst problems in our community. Four or five Bangladeshis to one room. That's an official council statistic."

"Anyway," said Shahana, "it's not that late. Most people are allowed to stay up later than this."

"What? Later than this? Going around in gangs, late at night, and not one book between them. What do you think these goats are studying? What are they learning?"

Shahana's face began to shut down. She turned away from the window.

Chanu recalled that this evening was special. He put his arm around his daughter.

"Calm, calm," he said. "Doctor's orders. Don't let your mother get excited."

Eventually, Bibi began to yawn. Chanu sent the girls to bed and lay down on the sofa, nursing his belly. Nazneen regarded the room and fought the impulse to tidy up. She sat very still to allow the memory to form.

"I have to go back to work," said Chanu. "Does she think she could cope without me?"

Nazneen saw her sewing machine. It was pushed to the back of the table, half hidden behind a pile of books and a cardboard box.

"Oh, work," she said and jumped up. She looked in the box. A nest of zips, still waiting to be sewn into some jackets.

"She can't work," cried Chanu, twisting his head around. "The patient can't work."

"I was supposed to finish these last week."

"They'll have to wait."

Nazneen leaned against the table. She felt dizzy and sick, the same way she felt when she once tried to smoke a cigarette with Razia.

"That's it," declared Chanu. "She's going back to bed."

But it was Chanu who, after further third-person remonstrations, removed himself to bed. Nazneen could not be budged. Memory returned to her like a tidal wave and she had to stay on her feet or else drown. She walked around the room picking up any object, without knowing what it was or where she put it. When the floor was clear she began rearranging the things she had moved, grouping them promiscuously, deranging as she arranged. Karim had been here. He had come and come again until Chanu was suspicious. And the girls. The girls knew. Or Karim had not been. Worse. He had come and *he* had been suspicious. Why would she not see him? He would not come again. This was good. No. It was bad. At least it was an end. But how could it end like that, without her there? And if it had ended, why did it ever begin? If that was all that would happen, then why did it happen at all? He would come again, and she would explain. Or perhaps, she would not explain, and that—*that*—would be the end. She would end it. But she could not. When she saw him, she would not be able. She was not strong enough. And, anyway, it was not for her to choose. When would he come? Would he come?

Exhausted, she collapsed in the cow-dung armchair and picked the stuffing out of a hole. She made herself think more slowly. For each five breaths, she said to herself, you are allowed one thought. She counted them out. Karim was supposed to come on Tuesday, when the girls were going to a friend's house for the afternoon. She blew out each breath as hard as possible. He would have come straight up, because he had another batch of sewing for her. On the in-breaths she filled up her lungs from the bottom until she felt the pressure beneath her collarbone. Or he looked for her in the window, and walked straight past. She raced through her next set, shallow intakes through her nostrils. What did it matter, anyway, what had happened? The important thing was what would happen now. The importance of it stole her breath altogether and she gasped and gulped at the air.

You are nothing. You are nothing. She rocked back and forth. The words offered some relief from the overwhelming, crushing significance of it all. She got up and took down the Qur'an. She looked for familiar passages, the words that she knew would give comfort. In her panic, she could find none and the words on the page kept her out, hid their meaning and pushed her away.

She went into the bedroom and observed her husband heaped in the middle of the bed, listened to his innocent snores. Then she found the letters, bundled together and wrapped like holy relics, inside her underwear drawer, and took them out of the room.

By the frugal yellow light of Chanu's reading lamp, she absorbed her sister's words, her exhalations. When she had finished she smoothed the pages over and over, as if by this action she could transmit to Hasina all that she felt. She sat for a while, in peace.

June 2001

I tell to Lovely about Monju everything how she end in hospital. At thirteen year age she marry and have baby. When is seven day old husband want to sell the child.

Lovely say "We must get her some help. Let me see. Maybe State Farming for Reformed Addicts. Very good Charity all the best people on committee. Is she addict? Do you think she can reform?"

Only thing Monju think of for seven years is son Khurshed. Only thing she do is beg. "Hah" say Lovely "thats what is wrong with this country. Money has to come from somewhere. Lets say she beg from me. Where do I get the money? Lets say I beg from my friend. Where she get the money? Lets say she get it from her friend. Where she get the money?"

I think to say from the husband. But I keep my mouth close.

"See what I saying? Money has to come from somewhere. That is why all the Charities now do stress the work-and-skill." She shake her pretty head. "Money is not the answer."

Monju refuse to give up child and man throw acid on baby of seven only days. Slow slow it coming out the man involve for child traffic to India and his sister is suffer four year imprison for same offense also. All money Monju beg pay for two operation for deform son.

Lovely was get ready for going out. She trying on clothes and I putting back on hanger and put away again. She stand by mirror in underwear and pinch two little handful of flesh around the sides. It look like she want to pull it off. When she hear about Khurshed she sit down. "This country" she say very sad. "I always dreamed of leaving."

Then she jump up and move very quick and her voice come sing-song and her eyes come bright. "What about Goats for Life? Special project for women only. Only last month UK Academic coming here to study results. Many per cent improvement in these womens motivation and self esteem. How is your friends self esteem? Often it is root cause of poverty. Low self esteem."

Sister she go out then for Pantene Head and Shoulder show at Sheraton Winter Garden. It is competition know as You Got the Look. Girl and boy have get prize for best hair and best Look. Lovely say it show a development in this country and also give confidence to young men and women to achieve target in life. One of winner is girl only five feet in height and not model to international standard but Lovely can make allowance. Maybe come improvement in judging standard by next time of competition. When she was away and children take nap I walk around her room and touch everything put hand on bed on embroider elephant hang on wall on table is made marble on silk clothes on all bottle jar perfume jewelery. I begin touching and think—everything beneath her hand feel different. When she touch it how different it feel to her. But now I dont know. I think I was wrong.

Zaid has start creep up behind me and shout Hiiiiaaah in ear very loud to make jump. Then he smile and say "Surprise is weapon. Remember that when you attack." What I is attacking? I ask him. He just smile and begin his kung fu leg and hand. Little Jimmy chop on back of my knees so I must either sit down or fall. Baby Daisy also shouting Hiiiiaaah but surprise is not on her side.

July

Sister the money you sent have arrive thanks be to Allah. Do not be angry I took to the hospital and pay for Monju for clean dressings on the body. It hurt the nose to smell her. It hurt the eye to see her. Most it hurt the heart to know her.

When nurse come with new dressings Monju tried to make protest. "Already all this money wasted. Keep it by for Khurshed." But she can only whisper a little and she helpless to move so it was done.

She have save nearly nine thousand taka for next operation. That is why the husband burn her. She would not give to him the money.

Now money gone to save her life and all she think is how to get more for the boy. This eat into her more painful than acid.

Baby Daisy back tooth come. All time she want I carry her. When I putting down is like sentence of death. She scream. Yesterday I walk around veranda is only place she like yesterday. She put head on shoulder and close eyes. If I stop walking she open eyes very wide and shock. It too too hot outside but I also like veranda too. Did I tell how nice the house? Is paint pink like your fingernail. On veranda is long chairs for resting whole legs and cover with green and white stripe cushion. There is kingfisher on roof. He sit on parapets and call and call. Fly away and find some water I tell him. But he do not fly just sit there never stretch the wing and call like as if all his brothers better join there on roof where he find some secret like paradise.

Garden is fade into brown only next door garden of house where Syeeda work still green. Near drive is coconut tree which long time now dead. Zaid is suppose cut down this tree but he sit inside reception room with Jimmy watch the kung fu film. I watch kingfisher and he looking down at me. Through rose arches (Lovely proud like anything of all her rose even now of course they flower have finish) I watch men mix cement for new building is know as summer house. They have two little boy for fetch water carry brick and thing. Even when they not carry anything the boy move like old men heat press down on them.

Daisy after long time fall asleep and I sit down with head still rest on shoulder. Back of head is curls. If you see these curls! How pretty the face. I kiss her with very care. I feel like hold the breath sometime when I look at Baby Daisy. Is like have soap bubble on the hand catch light with thousand beautiful color.

Zaid come out and he say "Dont make the mistake. She is not for you."

He has bruise on jaw color like brinjal and cut on left arm above elbow.

I do not like him then. I put my lip against the curls and I think how it feel when Lovely do this same thing. It different for her I think. This time I am not wrong. When she touch the marble table the Italian chair the jamdanis in her wardrobe the peacock feathers in silver vase she feel how easy they slip from out her fingers. She must get as much as possible. Make as safe as possible. But when she touch her lips to babys head then she know what she has and this she cannot lose and I can never have.

July

Something bit change in your letter. First time now I know more how the girls grow how different one daughter and another. Sound like your husband have very good job with taxi full time take him around all the place.

Lovely have had entertaining dinner for Betty and she husband. Only two people come but many days preparation you imagine is Bangabandhu return to earth and honor house with presence. Lovely wear special trouser sparkle everywhere look like make from crush diamond. Betty wear yellow sari and Lovely say after even best one can trip up in fashion.

I serve food and care children go in and out from kitchen. Men is talk all election and plastic bag.

Betty husband say "Look like if BNP come to power they push the polythene ban through."

Husband James get red in face and speak with very control voice. "That is what so wrong with this country. Nobody want progress. In New York and Paris and London you think they carry shoppings in jute bag? No! Is all polythene."

Betty and Lovely is look bored. They make show of this. Yawn and roll eyes. In an actual fact they are bored but also they must pretend they only pretending.

Betty husband say "One hundred and twenty-nine million plastic bags produced each day in Bangladesh. One hundred million used each day. I dont know. Is it progress?"

Husband James say "What the hell is problem? All this hug-a-tree types saying plastic bag block the drain cause the flood ruin the farmland—but something gone wrong in their heads. Four thousand people work to make these bags. It put food in their mouth. These hug-a-trees they prefer to see dead body block the drain." He sitting up really straight now and bang fist on table.

"Awami League is also in favor of ban." Betty husband say this and Betty put hand on his arm. Lovely smile has come a little bit stuck around the mouth. She play with hair and say my husband James know everything about plastic.

Late in evening I put children to the bed and go to kitchen. Lovely still entertaining the friends but dinner is finish. Zaid make some dhoie. The children like for breakfast. The cook say do you hear them how they talk? Politics is this. Politics is that. Turning noses up twitch arse like cat step through puddle. All strike and violence and guns and stabbing and this thing and that. Like as if had nothing to do with them. But this is system. And who has made the system? Is not the laborer. Is not the beggar.

He little man of wire. Did I tell? You can fold up and fit in pocket. But he do not look like weak man.

I ask him again which side he is support for politics? He tap the head and say "My side." Then he tell me. He support whoever give pay. So far is Awami League Bangladesh National Party and Jamaat-e-Islami. All is think they hire muscle but this muscle have brain attaching also.

He have save up much money and then he plan what to do. He have many idea. One idea is food stall for office worker. Good standard. Other is restaurant for family dining. He is also look into possibility of train for kung fu actor. Another idea is set up as fixer for sending people to foreign country for working there. Only expense is needed a mobile phone. Do you know how many taka for going to foreign country? One hundred and fifty thousand taka. And that is not for good country. For going to Singapore much more is need.

One time he think to go himself to the overseas. But he say—what do you get when you come back? Spend three four year never see one chink sunlight all work work work and come back with fridge and television and when electricity die every evening time then you take hammer and smash whole bloody things into piece. He know one woman sell her plot land for send her son to Singapore. Three years he work construction site and when he come back he do not have enough to buy back land. He know another woman who see job advertising in newspaper and go to Malaysia. She sew clothes from eight in morning to ten in evening seven days out of seven. This she do for five year. When she come home husband have spend all money she sending and all she have is debt.

If you go say Zaid you got to know what you coming back for. While you away who going to build anything here? I tell him about you husband and how he have big job and everything. He say "How long he been Londoni?"

I think it more than twenty year.

Zaid for first time I see look impressed. He slice the air a little. "Then its worth it. After twenty years he can come home build his own town where everything work like it meant to."

August

I go again to College Hospital. Lovely say Oh be a sweet girl and take the darlings with you. I tell her bit how Monju look and dont say anything how she smell. Lovely cover the ear and say sometime you feel like stop the Charity work because nothing is ever enough.

No money now for Monju drugs. Praise Allah most time she go unconscious.

Late late Syeeda came on back veranda watch rains. We hardly speak two word. Side by side we smell the earth. When she leave she say "Right. Thats it." Like we discuss all things under moon and decide every move for life.

The next day Chanu did not go to work. He stayed at home and in the way. Nazneen began, bit by bit, to restore order to the flat. The girls attacked each chore that she set them with unusual vigor. Chanu directed operations and philosophized about the nature of housework. It was a little like God, without end or beginning. It simply *was.*

"Are you not nervous anymore, Amma?" asked Bibi, chewing on a fingernail.

"Nervous?" said Nazneen.

"Nervous exhaustion," Chanu pronounced. "She had a condition known as nervous exhaustion."

"Why?" said Shahana.

Chanu, very briefly, looked unsure. Then he rallied. "Nerves. Women's thing," he said. "You'll know about it when you get older."

"But not anymore?" Bibi insisted. "She doesn't have it anymore?"

"Not anymore," said Nazneen. She looked at her daughter's wide, flat cheeks, her heavy forehead. Her soft brown eyes filled with anxiety. It was an open face, neither plain nor pretty but pleasing in its willingness to please. How like her mother she looked. Nazneen flushed, first with pride and then with worry. "Don't be anxious. Don't even think about it."

"I won't," said Bibi promptly, and looked worried when Nazneen laughed.

They worked together as a kind of unrehearsed circus team, with too many leaders and frequent missteps. Shahana complained that Bibi had pulled everything out of a kitchen cupboard. "But I'm cleaning it," said Bibi. "But I just put everything in there," moaned Shahana. Chanu chuckled and slapped his stomach. "You think your mother has an easy job? How many times do I tell you to help your mother? It's not easy. Not easy at all." He ate slices of bread spread with ghur and saw no necessity for a plate. Nazneen swept around him.

"Razia came to see you," he told her. "Do you remember? I think you spoke one or two words to her, though you would not speak to me." He smiled to show her there was no accusation involved.

She did not remember.

"Yes, she came," he continued. "Not a respectable type, you could not call her that. But she is genuine in her affection."

Nazneen went on with her cleaning. In these activities, the scraping and scouring and sweeping and washing, within their sweet-dull void she found the kind of refuge she had—the night before—sought and lost in the Qur'an. Razia looked in on her and Nazma came with Sorupa and fed her with choice morsels of gossip that passed through her undigested. A day slipped by in this way and at night she slept a dreamless sleep.

As she cleaned the bathroom the next day, Nazneen thought of Hasina. Fate, it seemed, had turned Hasina's life around and around, tossed and twisted it like a baby rat, naked and blind, in the jaws of a dog. And yet Hasina did not see it. She examined the bite marks on her body, and for each one she held herself accountable. *This is where I savaged myself, here and here and here*.

She dusted off the sewing machine and settled down to work. Chanu, who seemed to have slipped out of the work habit, fussed around.

"She must not overdo it," he said. Whenever he wanted to emphasize her fragility, he put her at this linguistic remove.

"She will not overdo it," muttered Nazneen. I've already overdone it, she thought to herself.

"She is still under doctor's orders."

Whatever I have done is done. This thought came to her, as fresh and stunning as the greatest of scientific breakthroughs or ecstatic revelations.

"She is supposed to be taking bed rest."

Now I have earned myself a place in hell for all eternity. That much is settled. At least it is settled.

"Her husband also recommends it."

A degree or two hotter, a year or two more or less. What does it matter?

"She really ought to listen to him."

Good. That's it, then. That is it.

"She doesn't seem to be listening."

"Oh, she is," said Nazneen, "she's listening. But she is not obeying."

Chanu smiled expectantly, waiting for the joke to be explained. The smile lingered awhile around his lips, while his eyes scanned her face and then the room, looking for clues, for changes. "All right then," he said, after a while. "I have some reading to do. Shahana! Bibi! Quick. Who is going to turn the pages for me?"

It was an August afternoon, warm and sunless. The estate seemed muffled by the thick gray sky, dense as a blanket. Nazneen looked out and up and watched as an aeroplane smeared the gray with white and disappeared behind a coagulation of buildings. She had come to London on an aeroplane, but she could not remember the journey. All she remembered now was being given breakfast, a bowl of cornflakes which had broken some sort of threshold and released a serving of tears. She had borne everything but this strange breakfast. Chanu, she remembered, seemed to understand. He took the bowl and hid it somewhere and promised her this and promised her that and made so many promises that she had to beg him to stop.

That was a long time ago, when she took such things too seriously. She looked over at the old flat in Seasalter House and saw that the window was filled with potted plants. She should have bought plants and tended and loved them. All those years ago she should have bought seeds. She should have sewn new covers for the sofa and the armchairs. She should have thrown away the wardrobe, or at least painted it. She should have plastered the wall and painted that too. She should have put Chanu's certificates on the wall. But she had left everything undone.

For so many years, all the permanent fixtures of her life had felt so temporary. There was no reason to change anything, no time to grow anything. And now, somehow, it felt too late.

She looked across at the brickwork, flaking beneath the windowsill, black within the cracks like dirt caught beneath fingernails. She had spent nearly half her life here and she wondered if she would die here as well.

Into her reverie broke the sound of knocking at the door. Before she even opened it she knew it would be him, knew the way that he knocked with gentle impatience. Karim had a bale of jeans over his shoulder, tied together with thick cord. He set it down on the floor and folded his arms. They did not speak but regarded each other with caution, each wondering who would offer an explanation and what would be explained.

Looking became unbearable and, as if by mutual agreement, both lowered their eyes. Nazneen breathed air that was choked with things unsaid, their suspense caught in molecules like drops of condensation. She was aware of her body, as though just now she had come to inhabit it for the first time and it was both strange and wonderful to have this new and physical expression. A pulse behind her ear. A needle of excitement down her thigh. Inside her stomach, a deep and desperate hunger.

She did not know who moved first or how but they were in the bedroom and locked together so close that even air could not come between them. She bit his ear. She bit his lip and tasted blood. He pushed her onto the bed and tore at her blouse and pushed the skirt of her sari around her waist. Still dressed, she was more than naked. The times when she had lain naked beneath the sheets belonged to another, saintly era. She helped him undress. She felt it now: there was nothing she would not do. She drew him in, not with passion but with ferocity as if it were possible to lose and win all in this one act. He held a hand across her throat and she wanted everything: to vanish inside the heat like a drop of dew, to feel his hand press down and extinguish her, to hear Chanu come in and see what she was, his wife.

Karim lay on his back with his arms behind his head. Nazneen did not move, her limbs strewn around like the result of a traffic accident. She lay and waited for disgust to stalk its way over and into her. But nothing came. Only the warmth of his body radiating into hers. She had begun to drift into sleep when Karim turned on his side and started to talk. He uttered caresses, whispered promises, moaned and mumbled his love, sweet with the stupidity of youth, humbled by his stutter. She got up and went to wash and rinsed away his words.

Later, he sat on the sofa with his feet on the coffee table while she worked. There was a hole in his sock and a big toe poked out of it. Nazneen tried not to see this. She brought him a glass of water. She brought him some dates. All the time she tried to keep her eyes away from the white socks with the gray bits at the heel and ball and the extra hole.

A couple of times he punched numbers into his mobile phone but there seemed to be no one to speak to. He stretched his arms and fidgeted. "Got to get things going," he said, to nobody in particular.

Nazneen worked on her zips. If he asked her, she would tell him everything—about her illness, about the impossibility of continuing—and then they would talk, and out of the talking would come an ending.

"You angry with me?"

She looked up, to check he was not speaking into his phone.

"Are you angry because I haven't been here for a while?"

"No."

He smiled. "OK, I can see that you're angry." He seemed amused. "I've been away, up to Bradford to see some family."

"I am not angry."

"I'll make it up to you."

Suddenly, she was furious. "Why do you not believe me when I tell you I am not angry?" She spoke in Bengali and she hissed the words.

He enjoyed the joke. "I believe you, sister. I can see that you are happy."

She did not answer and for several minutes she shoved silence at him. After a while she wanted something to say but nothing seemed suitable.

"Better go, man," said Karim, and he took his feet off the table. He spoke lightly, as if they were just fooling around. "Places to go, people to see."

"No," she said. "Don't."

"Things to do. Jeans to deliver." But he didn't get up.

"The girls will be here tomorrow. And the next day."

He paused awhile. When he spoke again he had dropped the tone. "Maybe it's, like, time I got to know them."

She had wanted to talk and now she did not want to talk. She wanted things to go back to the way they were, not the old way but the new way: just two weeks ago, or ten minutes ago.

"Who did you see in Bradford?"

He shrugged, as if it were impossible to say. "Family. Cousins and that."

"How many cousins?"

He shrugged again. "Loads."

She worked on him, and it was not difficult to make him stay. He decided to use Chanu's computer. She wiped the dust off the screen. While he fiddled around with plugs and wires he began to talk about the Bengal Tigers.

"We've got to get things going again. Nobody bothers to turn up. It's pathetic."

She ran a damp cloth over the keyboard. He was close enough to smell: limes and cloves and the lingering afterburn of sex, washed away but still there if you knew about it, like a removed stain.

"Everyone was coming, you shudda seen it," he told Nazneen, as though she had not. "Then—smack"—he clicked his fingers—"all gone again."

His beard had grown in. Even a beard could not hide how handsome he was. She remembered the meeting in the community hall at the edge of the estate, sitting below the stage, flaming inside her red sari, watching him pull the audience to his side, running home and waiting for him, knowing yet scarcely believing he would come. That was how she wanted him, like that, not with his feet on her coffee table and holes in his socks.

"When we were going to organize that march . . . different story." He bent down and unraveled some wires.

"Make another one."

"Lion Hearts were going to march against us. We were going to march against them. But they bottled it. They knew they were going to be outnumbered. We were going to hammer 'em." He banged his head on the table coming up again, and rubbed it with his fist.

"Make another march. Why you have to do it against someone?"

He looked at her and transferred his fist to his beard and rubbed that as well. "It don't work like that."

"Why not?"

"You can't march for no reason. That's, like—like just walking around, man."

She grew stubborn. "Why?"

He looked her slowly up and down, as if she might be an impostor. "Because," he said with quiet emphasis, "it is."

"You want people to come back in the group?"

"Bengal Tigers is dying out. We need new blood." He pressed a button on the keyboard and the computer made a whirring noise, like insects at nightfall. He sat down and pressed more buttons.

"Make it into a celebration," she said. "People always come out for a celebration. Some singing, some dancing."

"What, like a mela?" He looked around at her and gave her the kind of smile that substituted for a pat on the head.

"Yes," she insisted. "Like that."

He was absorbed in the screen and she could not say any more. She stood by his shoulder and demanded his attention silently. After a few minutes he spoke again without turning his head.

"You know, it could be like a mela."

"Oh, but do you think so?" said Nazneen.

"It don't have to be a *negative* thing. It can be positive."

"Well," said Nazneen, "if you say so."

Karim spent an hour or so in front of the computer screen and Nazneen blunted two needles on the zips. From time to time it occurred to her that Chanu, who had gone back to the taxi driving early in the morning, might arrive home and find them in this compromising domesticity. The thought of it left her indifferent. He comes, he doesn't come, she said to herself. By this attitude she was vaguely shocked and nearly thrilled, for it seemed at once wanton and sublime, the first real stoicism she had shown to the course of her Fate.

"What are you looking at?"

"Day in the life of a typical Bangladeshi village."

She got up and looked over his shoulder at a picture of a bullock cart and driver, both animal and man jutting bones like rude gestures.

"When was the last time you went there?"

"N-no," he said, and his stammer grew worse than ever. "Never been there."

She went out to the kitchen and made tea. Somehow, she felt sorry, as if she had asked casually after a relative, not knowing that he had died.

When she returned the picture had disappeared, and the screen was filled with English text. "What's this?" she said, and was surprised at how she sounded, almost as though she had a right to know.

"Hadith of the day, on an Islamic website."

"Go on—what does it say?"

He read in English. "'On the authority of Abu Hurairah (may Allah be pleased with him) who reported that Allah's Messenger (may the peace and blessings of Allah be upon him) had said: A man's share of adultery is destined by Allah. He will never escape such destiny. The adultery of the eye is the look, the adultery of the ears is listening to voluptuous talk, the adultery of the tongue is licentious speech; the adultery of the hand is beating others harshly, and the adultery of the feet is to walk to the place where he intends to commit sins. The heart yearns and desires for such vicious deeds. The loins may or may not put such vicious deeds into effect.'"

After the first few lines Nazneen heard only the blood in her ears. She watched Karim as a mouse watches a cat; when he turned she would be ready.

"Lot of good stuff on here, sister." Karim did not even look at her. His voice was unchanged. What form was this punishment to take? Was she to believe that he had found this hadith at random?

"An Islamic education—open to everyone." He worked the mouse and kept looking at the screen. Even if he had chanced upon it, what then?

"*The Islamic Way of Eating,* or *Sleeping the Islamic Way*." He looked at her now, and she saw that nothing had changed. "Which you want to hear first?"

"It's time for you to go," she said, and she took his tea back to the kitchen and poured it away.

All around the Dogwood Estate posters began to appear, drawn in red and green felt-tip pen and attached like some late-flowering blossom to the lampposts and litter bins. Shahana brought one home.

"Can we go?" She delivered this like an ultimatum. "Everyone's going," she added, and managed to sound as if she was already sick of explaining.

Chanu took the piece of paper from her hand. "What is this rubbish?"

Shahana blew up at her fringe. "Everyone's going."

"Bengal Tigers," said Chanu, and chewed it over.

"And Bengal Cubs."

"You see, I think I remember this name." He put his head this way and that, trying to roll a memory out of the corner of his brain.

"They're organizing a festival. Everyone who wants to help has to turn up next Monday."

Chanu remembered. "Those idiots who were putting the leaflets through my door." He cleared his throat and folded his arms on top of his stomach. "In this society—"

"Can we go or not?"

"Bibi," shouted Chanu, "tell the little memsahib that she is going to get beaten to a bloody pulp. Body parts will not be identifiable."

"It's not fair," shouted Shahana.

Bibi, who was standing near the doorway, slipped out of the room.

"Nothing will be left," screamed Chanu, "only a little bit of bone."

Nazneen stood between her husband and her daughter. "I say she can go," she said, but as they were both shouting she could not be heard. "I say she can go," she yelled. They were silent and shocked, as if she had ripped out their tongues. "And Shahana, show respect to your father."

"Yes, Amma," said Shahana.

"And you," she told Chanu, "should be careful what you say to such a small girl."

Chanu's mouth worked silently. "That is true," he managed, after a few moments. Father and daughter looked at each other, caught in a conspiracy. The conspiracy transpired to be one of amusement. They smiled and fought against laughter. Neither of them looked at Nazneen. Then Chanu winked at Shahana and said, "We must remember, she has not been well."

"Amma," said Shahana, still avoiding her eye. "Would you like to sit down?"

"I will sit down," Nazneen told her. "And shouldn't you be spending some time with your schoolbooks?"

Chanu wobbled his cheeks and made some restrained hand gestures to Shahana. *Better escape from this madwoman while there is still a chance*.

Having descended from her high wire, Nazneen spent the next few days stamping along on the ground, and the ground—to her surprise—appeared to be solid. The girls and Chanu took their turn at tiptoeing. "Now, what did we agree?" Chanu would say to the girls and they would nod their heads very slightly as though Nazneen must not see.

"We should all go to the meeting," said Chanu. "It will be fun." She said that she would go if he liked, and he touched her cheek and said, "That's it. Now that's better, isn't it?" and generally fussed around until she was forced to smile just to make him go away.

On the day before the meeting was scheduled Chanu sat cross-legged in his lungi and undershirt on the floor, reading the newspaper.

"Shahana! Bibi! Come quick."

The girls came and each tried to stand behind the other.

"Which do you think is the happiest nation on earth?" A smile puffed out his cheeks.

Shahana shrugged and Bibi put a finger in her mouth.

"Can you guess?" In his delight, he rocked a little so that his stomach slapped on his thighs. "Come on, take a guess."

"Happiest?" said Bibi, finding difficulty understanding the word.

"Bangladesh," said Shahana, in a monotone.

"You are right. It says here that Bangladesh ranks Number One in the World Happiest Survey. India is fifth, and USA is forty-sixth."

"God," said Shahana.

Chanu ignored her. "'Research led by professors at the London School of Economics into links between personal spending power and perceived quality of life has found out that Bangladeshis are the happiest people in the world.' And LSE is a very respectable establishment, comparable to Dhaka University or Open University." He handed the newspaper to Shahana so she could verify the facts. "You see, when we go there, what will you lose? Burgers and chips and"—he waved at her legs—"tight jeans. And what will you gain? Happiness."

"God," repeated Shahana. Bibi stood on one leg and grimaced in concentration.

"Where do you think this country comes in the league table? Go on, have a look. Thirty-second. So, you see how big the difference is." He began to hum an old film song and examine the corns on his left foot. The girls slid away leaving the newspaper on the floor.

"Maybe needs a bit slicing off here," said Chanu after a while. He bent as far over as his belly would allow and poked around his toes.

"I don't believe it," said Nazneen. She was sitting at the table, not working or tidying, but just sitting.

"Well," said Chanu, "I will do it myself."

"No. I don't believe this survey. What kind of professors are these?"

Chanu's eyebrows shot up high, leaving his small eyes vulnerable, unprotected, like two snails out of their shells. He reached for the newspaper. "Here—have a look. I am not making it up."

"It may be written down," said Nazneen. "But I do not believe it."

"Why?" It was scarcely possible for one face to contain such a quantity of astonishment.

Nazneen did not know how to answer. She was unsure why she had spoken. She did not know if she believed the newspaper report or not. Finally, she said, "My sister—she is not happy."

"But Hasina is very happy," insisted Chanu.

"No, she is not. Has not been . . ." said Nazneen. And she started to tell him the things she had hidden from him over the years, and at first she stumbled around as if it were lies she were telling and not the truth, and then the words began to flow and he was stiller than she had ever seen him, a slackness in his face, and she told him about her sister and left nothing out, beginning with Mr. Chowdhury, the landlord, the one who (Chanu had said) was respectable-type. When she spoke of the rape she named it in the village way: Hasina was robbed of her nakphool, her nose ring; and the selling of Hasina's body she did not name, saying only my sister had to stay alive, and she saw that Chanu understood.

When she had finished, she folded her hands in her lap and sat up very straight, defying with her neatness the chaos and disorder of the world. Chanu waggled his head and looked around the room.

"I will make a plan," he said. "Something must be done."

On the morning after the Bengal Tigers' meeting, Nazneen made the short journey across the estate to visit Hanufa.

Hanufa presented her with a stack of old margarine and ice cream tubs. "Dal, kebabs, and niramish. I made too much."

"But I'm fine now," said Nazneen.

"Take it," said Hanufa. "I made too much." She fetched a stool and suggested that Nazneen put her feet up. It was not worth the bother of protesting. Nazneen did as she was told.

Hanufa filled her in on the news. Nazma's eldest had been made manager at the Bengal Lancer, Jorina was trying to get her daughter and her son-in-law back to the UK but immigration was making trouble, Sorupa had a summer cold that refused to budge. "And everyone is talking this mela." Nazneen closed her eyes for a moment and slipped back into the meeting.

It had been a bit like a mela itself. The hall was festooned with children in best clothes and babies in arms. People milled around the hall and out of the doorway, or sampled the bhajis and samosas on sale at thirty pence apiece from a trolley in the left-hand aisle. At the far corner a man in a grimy apron sold sweet lassis and cartons of mango juice. Shahana waved discreetly at a group of young boys who wore complicated trainers and conspiratorial looks. Bibi found a schoolfriend and the two sat together, swinging their legs under their seats. Chanu had greased the clumps of his hair together with coconut oil, sharpened three pencils, and found a reporter-style notebook which he fitted, with some difficulty, into the breast pocket of his shirt.

"So many people here," said Chanu. "How can you run a meeting with all these people?"

"I'm going to buy a lassi," said Shahana.

"The milk will be sour," warned Nazneen. "He has no ice or anything."

"I'm just going to have a look," said Shahana, slipping away.

Chanu extracted his notebook. "When I was a council man we used to say that a meeting with more than four people was just a talking shop."

Nazneen thought about it now. It was more than that, surely. It was her husband who was the talker.

Someone in the row behind had begun to grumble about Karim. "He seems to have forgotten his mother tongue."

"So far it's only waffle anyway," Chanu whispered back.

There was the usual business with procedure. The secretary bouncing on his toes and trying to keep order. More elections. The black man had a title now: Multicultural Liaison Officer. The battle of wills between Karim and the Questioner.

"What's this mela supposed to be celebrating?" said the Questioner. "Are our children doing well in school? Have they come, suddenly, from the bottom of the education tables to the top? Has the drugs problem—that we like to keep our dirty secret—has it vanished? What's changed? Our brothers in Palestine and India and around the world, are they no longer being persecuted?"

Chanu stood up then. Every head in the room turned towards him. Chanu made some spectacular excavations of his voice box, throwing out all manner of irritating sounds. "I myself would like to add that Bangladeshis are the most deprived ethnic group in the whole of the UK. This is the immigrant tragedy. As a student of philosophy though . . ."

Nazneen lost the rest of it. She did not care what he was saying. She did not care if people were looking. Sitting next to her husband, in front of her lover, she gave way to a feeling of satisfaction that had been slowly growing. It began at the edges and worked its way in so that eventually it found its way to her heart and warmed it. She gave herself a little hug and smothered a smile on her shoulder. She considered how much of her life, how much time, how much energy, she had spent trying not to care, trying to *accept.* Do you see me now, she said to Amma, do you see how I accept it all? At once the warm feeling had begun to subside.

Hanufa said, "It's at the women's drop-in place on Berners Street."

"What is?" said Nazneen.

"The massage course. Do you want to come?"

"Maybe another time," said Nazneen, forcing herself to get up. "I've got so much work to do."

On her way back Nazneen recognized four Bangla lads who had turned up halfway through the meeting. They had driven a car, silver, flashy-looking, into the courtyard. The doors were open and the music hammered out. They leaned against the bonnet, waiting for a challenge. There had nearly been a fight when they walked into the meeting. Some of the other lads wanted them thrown out. *They don't own this place. What they doing here?* Karim had calmed it down, sorted everything out, as usual.

She gave the car and the lads a wide berth and went up to the flat. Razia was waiting outside the door. She wore her Union Jack top and her face was wet. Her sweatshirt was damp and her trousers stuck to her legs.

Nazneen went to her. "What is it?" she asked, but she knew.

Razia held her arms. Dark eyes, flecked with gold and laced with fear, gray hair taking flight, lips cracked at the center, long nose, nostrils flared. She held Nazneen's arms and said, "He's sold the furniture."

Chapter Sixteen

After her husband was killed by the seventeen frozen cows, Razia had cleared out the flat. Nazneen watched her shift the pyres of wood, the half-empty paint tins, the massacred dolls, even the stacks of cheap tinned food. Anything she could pick up, she removed. Nazneen felt that Razia would like to pick up the children too, bag and bin them. The children dodged out of her way. Nazneen, home from the hospital, could not clear anything, and eventually Razia had come around and taken away the baby things.

At that time, Razia's flat had lost the feel of a settler camp, a temporary pitch in hostile terrain where all resources had to be grabbed and held, and over the years she made the place a home. She saved and bought new carpets, for the sitting room the first year, the hallway the next, and so on. She hung mirrors on the walls and looked at herself sidelong and said that mirrors made a room seem larger. Twelve months ago, after several years of saving, she had bought a new three-piece suite with gold-tasseled fringes that set off the deep green cushions and tickled the backs of your ankles.

"What did I do?" said Razia. The room was almost bare. A single bed was pushed against one wall. This was Razia's bed. On the floor, at a right angle, was the mattress where Shefali slept. Tariq was favored with the bedroom. Shefali sat, as if marooned, on a solitary high-backed wooden chair.

"Did you know about it?" she said to her daughter, and Nazneen knew this was not the first time of asking but the tenth or the twentieth.

Nazneen leaned against the windowsill. Her bones felt heavy, as if her body was sleeping. She would have liked to lie down. "And the television?"

Razia moaned. She pulled at the sweatshirt where it was sticking to her chest. "He took it last month to be mended, and the video as well. All gone."

"Where is he now?"

They both looked at Shefali, who became indignant. "I am not hiding him." She had inherited Razia's long nose, and she cocked her head back now and looked down it.

Razia lit a Silk Cut and sucked it hard. "I should have whipped him first and asked questions later. Now he has run away."

"Don't worry," said Shefali. "He'll come back. He'll be back when he needs more money. He knows you'll give it."

Razia ran at her daughter but pulled herself up short and turned away. Ash fell from the end of her cigarette and she ground it into the carpet with her heel.

"Your precious son," said Shefali.

"What did *I* do?" said Razia.

Nazneen forced herself to get up. She went to Razia and held her friend. They stood together for a long time and then Nazneen released her grip slowly, bit by bit, as if Razia might fall literally to pieces.

The story came out. Shefali filled in what Razia could not bring herself to name. It had been going on for nearly two years. Razia cursed her eyes for not seeing. There was a showdown with Tariq and he confessed everything, one moment bent with shame, defiant the next. He had been selling a little bit here and there, just a little bit of selling, enough to pay for his own. He made it sound good. He was supporting himself. Her own son, selling drugs. And she was happy that he had started going out.

But then something happened. Boys came from another estate. They said, "You can't sell here, we're taking over." They wanted taxes on what he'd already sold. *Taxing him, as if they were the government.* Tariq didn't want any trouble. "After all of this, now he says he doesn't want trouble. So he took the television, and the furniture."

Razia rubbed her hands, turned them over and over, as if trying to wash something away. "I don't know what to do now. I don't know what to do."

Nazneen went with Razia to the doctor's surgery. On the way she said, "About Karim . . ."

Razia kept quiet.

"It's true," said Nazneen. "It's what you think."

Razia looked away. They walked past a car with the windows down. Three young Bengali boys listening to some vicious music, heads rocking back and forth.

"They're too young to drive," said Razia. "Why are they always sitting in cars? Why don't they just go home?"

"You are the only friend I have."

Razia looked at her. "You don't have to tell me. Just because I am in trouble, you don't have to make trouble for yourself as well."

They walked together in silence.

Dr. Azad had a way of making chairs look uncomfortable. He sat with a rigid back, in a manner that suggested an equation between physical and moral rectitude. As a result, even his padded leather swivel chair appeared to be specifically designed to mortify the flesh. He turned now and wrote something in the file on his desk, then he turned back to face them.

"Does he want to come off?" He had expressed no surprise. He seemed to be expecting it.

"Want?" said Razia. "How should he know what he wants? How can he know anything now?"

"If he wants to come off the drugs I can help him." Dr. Azad looked down at his feet. He made a small adjustment so that the ends of his shoes lined up precisely.

"I have come to you for help," said Razia. "And the other thing is, nobody can know about it."

"You have my assurance—they will not hear it from me."

Razia jumped up. She paced the office as though she had been locked inside it for days and was looking for an escape route. "But they know already. Everybody is talking. I can feel it."

"Take a seat, Mrs. Iqbal. Do take a seat."

Nazneen thought, He is tidying up. She makes the room look messy.

Razia stayed on her feet. The sweat had dried on her clothes, leaving faint white salty lines around the sleeves. "What do they say about me?" she asked Nazneen.

"Let them talk if they have the time," said Nazneen. She could imagine what Nazma would say. Sorupa, of course, would say whatever Nazma said.

Razia hooted, a strange sound that came down her nose. "Oh yes, I don't need anyone. I live like the English."

"I'll make an appointment for him. He can come on his own, or with you." Dr. Azad pressed his palms flat against the sides of his thighs. Every inch of him was tidy.

"Will you cure him, Doctor?" Razia approached and touched his feet. The doctor regarded the tips of his shoes, concerned perhaps about fingerprints.

Nazneen was surprised to see her friend bow. Plenty of children came home from school every day and touched their father's feet. Chanu said it was Hindu mumbo-jumbos. "Muslims bow to no one. Remember that, Shahana. It's only this peasant type—mostly they are illiterate—that mixes up all this Hindu mumbo-jumbos." But Razia was just not the bowing type.

"He has to want to be cured," said the doctor.

"Want?" cried Razia. "What is all this 'want'? What if he wants to take drugs until the day of his death? What if he wants to kill himself with these drugs?"

"Go and talk to him. You are wasting time here."

Razia rolled her head around to release a crick in her neck. She looked at the doctor but there was nothing more to say.

Preparations for the mela were under way. Shahana and Bibi collaborated on a giant mosaic made out of numerous dissected cereal boxes. It was to be a backdrop for the crafts stand. Bibi used a pair of blunt-ended scissors, the same shape as the tip of her tongue, which came out every time she did some cutting. Shahana worked with the glue and her artistic temperament, sighing and blowing and even screaming sometimes when the design threatened to go wrong. They didn't know what would go *on* the stand. "That does not fall within our remit," said Shahana, sounding like her father.

"Craft *things,*" said Bibi, to be obliging.

Chanu fiddled with the radio–cassette player. He managed to trap his finger. "Ish," he said. "That's the one I use for the windscreen wipers. Let us hope it does not rain."

He was on the Classical Music Committee. He listened to Ustad Alauddin Khan and Ustad Ayet Ali Khan, waggling his head and playing his stomach like a duggi.

Shahana put her fingers in her ears and screwed up her face.

"How did you come to be such a little memsahib?" said Chanu.

"I didn't ask to be born here," she said. They both spoke quickly and quietly, and glanced at Nazneen, afraid she would catch them bickering.

Chanu switched off the music. "You see, what I would really like is the Poetry Committee. What do those young boys know about it? Perhaps they will get hold of a few books, but they won't have the background. Poetry is something different. You have to drink it with your mother's milk." He embarked on a round of throat clearing.

"Clouds rumbling in the sky; teeming rain.
I sit on the riverbank, sad and alone.
The sheaves lie gathered, harvest has ended,
The river is swollen and fierce in its flow.
As we cut the paddy it started to rain.

"One small paddy field, no one but me—
Floodwaters twisting and swirling everywhere.
Trees on the far bank smear shadows like ink
On a village painted in deep morning gray.
On this side a paddy field, no one but me."

Chanu exhaled and took a deep breath, as if he could smell the wet paddy where he sat with his turrets of books. "The simple life, you see. That's what we have lost." He grew brisk. "And will gain again. After we have the Dhaka house sorted out, we will build a place in the village. Nothing like your mansions that these Sylhetis are building, just a little simple house. Something rustic."

Nazneen was sitting at the table. She often sat now, and it seemed that the less time she spent doing things, the less there was to do. Sometimes she would sit down with a thought in her mind—the fridge needs cleaning, for instance—and find that half an hour, an hour or more had passed and it was still as if that thought had just come into her head.

"Of course, I don't mind the Classical Music Committee," conceded Chanu. "But I will argue—and I have taken a short course in debating—that the Bauls are also part of our classical heritage, although of course it is folk music that they sing. I would even consider offering my own humble voice as an instrument." Here he began to tune up:

"The mirror of the sky
Reflects my soul.
O Baul of the road,
O Baul, my heart,
What keeps you tied
To the corner of a room?

"As the storm rampages
In your crumbling hut,
The water rises to your bed.

Your tattered quilt
Floats on the flood
Your shelter is down.

"O Baul of the road,
O Baul, my heart,
What keeps you tied
To the corner of a room?"

During the rendition, Chanu had closed his eyes. The girls got to their feet, stealthy as cats, but they did not go. Something in the song kept them. When he had finished, Chanu's eyes remained closed, prolonging his dream. Still they did not go. Nazneen thought, *We are all tied to our corners of the room.* This thought stayed at her breast like a sucking baby for the rest of the day.

August 2001

Betty have picture in newspaper for HIV Innocents. This has cause of grief for Lovely. Same page also have picture of Shafin Ahmed. Do you know? Is top celebrity of Rock Band name Miles. Lovely say Betty think she getting too famous now. She confide me also Betty husband have never stop her from get the modeling job but beauty standard in Chittagong not so high as rest country and Betty have never got any job whatsoever.

She say "What can I do? All best Charity is taken."

She walk around toss the head make you think many camera point on her. Then she get idea. "I must start own Charity." She suck on fingers and think for while. She say "As a mother I think would be best to start children Charity."

Betty is not yet mother. Lovely tell me she will start Charity for stopping the child worker. Which ones you will stop I asking to her. Oh she say all of them. The maid next door? I asking her this. She look surprise. But really she like daughter to them. The boys on roof who is now mend gutters sweep leaves? She look bit cross. That different she say. Which are the ones? The boy who come around sell butter? Lovely say are you washing that floor or not?

Something have bother Lovely too much. Instead lie down look magazine she walking around and around. Zaid say just keep her out of my kitchen. But she wander around everywhere. One day I helping her with dressing and she look in mirror and big big sighs come. "I wish I wasnt beautiful. I wish I didnt have all this beauty and nothing to be done with it. I wish I was plain like you."

Driver blowing horn and she go out take children for visit. When she gone I wander around house like her. Then go in guest room pull sheet down. Instead go out again I get inside the bed. This is such bed! Sheets all white cotton smooth and crispy. White lace on pillows. Many many pillows. Mattress hold me like lover. Few seconds I feel sleep will come but when close the eyes so many things I remember so long kept from mind.

I get up go in master bedroom. Sit at her table and present the face in mirror. It look like a stranger face to me. I take brush. Brush the hair. Take cream. Cream the cheek. Take kohl. Dark the eyes. Take earring. Dress the ear. Then I feel is someone watching. Zaid have creep up but he stay quiet this time. He look at me and I know this look.

Sister what shall I say? It as the poet did write.

My heart is not to my hearts liking.
I wish I knew
How to unite the two.

Some days Nazneen was so tired that she went back to bed, and the days were short and the nights were long. "She is convalescing," said Chanu on those days. Other days she was filled with a kind of brittle strength and spilled caustic words on her children and husband. "She mustn't overdo it," said Chanu on these days.

"I'm going to run away," moaned Shahana. "If he tries to get me on an aeroplane, I'll bite his hand and run."

"Better wear your training shoes, then," said Nazneen. And to Bibi, slack-jawed and watching, she said, "Your grandmother was also a saint."

When the girls were back at school, Karim came in the afternoon. His beard was thick. "My husband will be back soon," she told him. When he had gone, she lay for hours on the soiled sheets, smelling him. When you have fallen low, she told herself, what hurts is pretending you are high. She rolled herself up in the sheets and when the girls came back from school that was how they found her.

Chanu bought her an ivory comb. He bought a length of lilac silk with silver threads in the border pattern. She told him to take it back. He found a romantic Bengali novel and read to her in bed, and kept his interjections to a bare minimum of three or four per page. She told him to go back to his own books. One evening, he scanned the newspaper and discovered that there was ice skating on the other channel. "Your mother is a fan," he explained to Shahana. "When she was younger, she thought of taking it up herself." The girls knew he was joking, but they didn't dare to laugh. They made room on the sofa, and patted the cushion where she should sit. Nazneen looked at the couple on the television screen, the false smiles, the made-up faces, the demented illusion of freedom chasing around their enclosure. Turn it off, she said.

Mrs. Islam came, billowing Ralgex Heat Spray and self-pity. "Take it," said Nazneen, stuffing ten-pound notes into her hand. "Take everything. The righteous get their rewards." But she shrank a little under the hard black eyes.

She began to spend time at the window, as she had in those first few months in London, when it was still possible to look out across the dead grass and concrete and see nothing but jade-green fields, unable to imagine that the years would rub them away. Now she saw only the flats, piles of people loaded one on top of the other, a vast dump of people rotting away under a mean strip of sky, too small to reflect all those souls. She lowered the net curtain and watched the groups of boys who drove endlessly around the estate, even on the parts where cars were not supposed to go. There were faces she did not recognize. They got out of their cars and approached other cars. They formed in fours and fives and got back in their cars. They carried an air of violence with them, like a sort of breeding, good or bad, without ever displaying it. Sometimes she saw Tariq. He walked with his head down, and he did not get in the cars.

Razia came around and sat with her. "He says I should be grateful. He didn't take my bride's gold."

"Did he go to the doctor yet?"

Razia clamped her legs together and stiffened her back. She spoke in a whisper. "If the boy does not *want* to give up the drugs, that is his choice." It was a poor imitation. She lit up a cigarette and two smoke ropes hung from her nostrils. "The doctor has the English disease," she said. "If I have to lock him in his room then that is what I will do."

She smoked intensively, barely releasing the cigarette from her lip between drags. "I saw the boy—the middleman. He was coming down the stairwell."

A familiar heat began to kindle at the back of Nazneen's neck. It crept up around to her cheeks and flushed down her spine. "Yes," she said, "he was here." And she tingled with shame, a kind of pins and needles of the soul, roused again after a crooked sleep.

Feeling returned to her slowly, like blood beginning to circulate. Anxiety, which had been unable to bite through the blanket of her depression, began to maul and chew. *An eternity in hell,* she told herself. *That is already done.* She drew no comfort. Is there not a life to get through first? She thought she had been sharp with the children, and fussed over them until even Bibi pulled away. Chanu's corns had flourished. She sliced and scraped. His toenails had begun to curl over the ends of his toes. She clipped them. Chanu said, "She is feeling better," and presented his nasal hair for grooming.

She realized that the little bit of money she had put aside to send to Hasina had been used up for the payments to Mrs. Islam. She returned to her sewing and worked until her eyes swam. Chanu had said he would make a plan for Hasina, but had never mentioned her again. Hasina had gone the way of all his plans. Nazneen bent to her work, all her concentration for that moment pulled into a buttonhole.

Chanu slammed through the door as if he would take it off its hinges. This man, who would not sit if he could lie, would not stand if he could lean, moved faster than Nazneen had ever before witnessed.

"Quick. Be quick!" he shouts. "Put on the television."

He rages around the room looking for the remote control, passing the television several times. Eventually, he switches it on by pressing the button below the screen. "Oh God," he says. "The world has gone mad."

Nazneen glances over at the screen. The television shows a tall building against a blue sky. She looks at her husband.

"This is the start of the madness," says Chanu. He holds on to his stomach as if he is afraid that someone may snatch it away.

Nazneen moves closer. A thick bundle of black smoke is hanging outside the tower. It looks too heavy to hang there. An aeroplane comes in slow motion from the corner of the screen. It appears to be flying at the level of the buildings. Nazneen thinks she had better get on with her work.

"Oh God," shouts Chanu.

Nazneen sits down on the sofa, her hand on the shiny patch where Chanu's hair oil has mixed with the fabric. The scene plays over. Chanu squats on his haunches with his stomach between his knees and his arms wrapped around both. The television has enslaved him. He rocks around in a state of fearful excitement.

The aeroplane comes again. The television shows it again and again.

Nazneen leans forward, straining to comprehend. She works herself to the edge of the sofa. The words and phrases repeat and she begins to grasp them. Chanu covers his face with his hands and looks through his fingers. Nazneen realizes she has leaned so far forward she is doubled up. She straightens herself. She thinks she has understood, but she also thinks she must be mistaken.

The scene switches. "The Pentagon," says Chanu. "Do you know what it is? It's the *Pentagon.*"

The plane comes again and again. Nazneen and Chanu fall under its spell.

Now they see smoke: a pillar of smoke, collapsing. Nazneen and Chanu rise. They stay on their feet as they watch it a second, a third time. The image is at once mesmerizing and impenetrable; the more it plays, the more obscure it becomes until Nazneen feels she must shake herself out of a trance. Chanu limbers up his shoulders, holds out his arms and circles them. He blows hard. He says nothing.

When a knock comes at the door Chanu seems not to hear it. Nazneen lets Nazma in and asks her to sit down.

"I'm not staying," says Nazma, and stands in the middle of the room. "My husband's cousin's brother-in-law went to New York." After a silence she says, "But now he is in Boston."

Nazma is defined by roundness. It is not only her head that is ball-shaped. She is made up of a series of balls, some larger than others, none of them small. Even her arms are circular, like the arms that Bibi draws on her snowmen.

Nazneen looks over her neighbor's shoulder, at the screen.

"Anyway," says Nazma, as if Nazneen has been detaining her. "Anyway, I came to ask if you would mind the children tomorrow after school."

Nazneen agrees. On her way out, Nazma runs her hand over the sewing machine. "Still getting plenty of work?"

The glint in her eye makes Nazneen's stomach somersault.

The children come home and they all watch together. It is hard to keep looking at the television and it is impossible to look away. Shahana starts to ask questions but Chanu flaps his arm to keep her quiet. He has taken up his squatting position once again, part reverence, part subjugation. The girls sit on either side of Nazneen and they, too, become enthralled.

The room grows dark and nobody has moved. "You will see what happens now," says Chanu. Shahana kicks off her shoes and settles back in the sofa. Bibi winds a strand of hair around her finger and inserts another strand into her mouth. It feels to Nazneen as though they have survived something together, as a family. She goes into the kitchen to heat up some dal and boil a kettle for the rice. She turns the light on and has to shield her eyes for a moment. When she returns to the sitting room there is something new to see. A small figure leaning out of a window; high up, maybe a hundred floors in the air, he reaches out and he cannot be saved. Another figure jumps and at that moment it seems to Nazneen that hope and despair are nothing against the world and what it holds and what it holds for you.

That night she dreams of Gouripur. She stands at the edge of the village and looks out over the light-slaked fields, at the dark spots moving in the distance: men, doing what little they can.

A pinch of New York dust blew across the ocean and settled on the Dogwood Estate. Sorupa's daughter was the first, but not the only one. Walking in the street, on her way to college, she had her hijab pulled off. Razia wore her Union Jack sweatshirt and it was spat on. "Now you see what will happen," said Chanu. "Backlash." He entangled himself with newspapers and began to mutter and mumble. He no longer spoke to his audience.

Nazneen went to buy ghee and chapati flour. Four men leaned over the counter, studying a paper so closely that when they looked up she almost expected their eyeballs to be smudged with newsprint.

"It's very serious," said the eldest, and the rest looked grave.

Nazneen thought, My husband should come here and discuss with these men. He is too alone with his thoughts.

The old man ran his fingertips along the newspaper as if he were reading by touch. "The strike is planned for later next month."

There was a general sucking of teeth.

"What can we shopkeepers do?"

"We are at their mercy."

"Yes, if they don't collect the rubbish the whole of Brick Lane is going to stink like an elephant's arse."

But Chanu thought nothing of striking binmen. He worked long hours and he spent the rest of his time watching the news or reading in the newspapers of the air strikes planned against Afghanistan. "It's time to go," he told no one in particular and hitched up his stomach, girding himself for action. "Any day, any moment, life can end. There's been enough planning."

One day he began counting money. He held a pile of notes and sat blinking at it for a long time. "Wife, my wife," he said, "a wife does not keep anything from her husband."

Nazneen stroked his head briefly. Two hairs came away in her hand. She went to the kitchen, to the cupboard under the sink, and opened the Tupperware box.

"We just need a little bit more," said Chanu. "Enough will be enough, and we will not need any more than that."

He called the girls and Shahana revived her deep interest in the carpet. Bibi clenched her fists in concentration.

"From time to time, I have tried to teach you a little bit of something here and there." Shahana groaned. Chanu let it pass. "Maybe you don't remember any of these things. It doesn't matter. Let it go." His face, Nazneen saw, was unusually calm. "But I will teach you something now that you will not be able to forget, even if you try." He paused for a moment, and Nazneen thought he would clear his throat. But his throat was already clear. "There was a painter from Mymensingh. His name was Zainul Abedin. His work was shown all over the world and received many high accolades. Now, this man did not paint vases full of flowers or high-society portraits. His subject was the common people of Bangladesh. He showed life as it was. And he showed death. Just as it was."

Shahana lifted her head. She was wearing her new jeans. Chanu had stopped objecting to the tightness of her old jeans. The new ones were baggier than a pair of rice sacks, and she had cut the ends off and worked on them so that they frayed in exactly the right way.

Chanu went on. "This artist, Abedin—he painted the famine which came to our country in 1942 and '43. These famous paintings hang now in a museum in Dhaka. I will take you to see them. In the famine, there was life and there was death. The people of Bangladesh died and the crows and the vultures lived. Abedin shows it all: the child who is too weak to walk or even to crawl, and the fat, black crows—how patiently they wait by the child for their next feast.

"This is how it was. Three million people died because of starvation. Can you imagine that? You cannot. Can you imagine something else? While the crows and vultures stripped our bones, the British, our rulers, exported grain from the country. This is something that you cannot imagine, but now that you know it, you will never forget."

Chanu breathed deeply but his face remained still. "That's it," he said. "It will be time to go very soon."

* * *

Every day Chanu counted the money. His cheeks grew thin. "Are you driving that needle at all hours for love? Is there no money to be made in this damn place?"

Nazneen bowed her head. "Here. There is a little more here."

He looked at it. It was not much. "I'll speak to him."

"No!"

Chanu fanned the silence with his look. The silence gave off its fumes, and Nazneen's breath came short.

"Who?" said Chanu. "Who is it that you do not wish me to speak to?"

"No one. I'll speak to . . . No one. There's no one you shouldn't speak to."

"I'll talk to him, then."

"I'll do it."

"Do what?"

"Talk to him."

"Who?"

"Why are you doing this?"

Chanu shrugged. "Me? What am I doing?" He rubbed a finger on his chin. For a long time he looked somewhere, inside rather than outside himself. "Ask for at least fifty percent more. Explain that it will only be for a short time. Tell him that your husband has told you to ask, and tell him that it is lucky for you that your husband is an educated man."

One evening he said, "Children can adjust to anything. The place is immaterial. They will make their own place *within* the place."

"Shahana is growing up fast," she said.

Chanu meditated for a while. "Too soon ripe is too soon rotten."

He sat cross-legged in the middle of the bed wearing a yellow undershirt and checked blue lungi. Nazneen, in her nightdress, sat at the end and brushed her hair. She watched her husband in the mirror. She saw herself being watched by him, and there was no beginning or end to how they were caught up together. The brush traveled down the straight black lines of hair. Her forehead looked heavier than usual and she tried to stick her chin out to balance it.

She thought about her husband. So many years he had talked of going home. And now he was working himself up to do it. The history lessons: they were not, after all, about the past.

"Do you think they will be all right?" said Chanu.

"Only God knows the answer."

Chanu's face contorted, and for a moment Nazneen thought he was responding and then she saw it was pain.

"What is it?" she said.

"Ulcer is coming again."

She brushed vigorously on the right-hand side. Chanu watched her. "It's the right thing to do," he said. She put the brush down. Hair fell across her cheek. It was dense and rich as treacle and she dipped her fingers in it. Her lips parted and in the mirror she saw a man looking at a woman. The woman's face was soft and full of gentle curves, and though she was not beautiful there was something that would make a man keep looking.

"Are you happy to be going?" Chanu smiled. It made him look sad.

"If it is God's will."

Chanu shuffled down the bed. He put a hand on the small of her back. She smelled his hair oil and deodorant, absorbed the warmth of his hand. Over their heads, a toilet flushed, a door opened and closed, and bedsprings creaked.

"But you want to, don't you?" He rested his chin on her shoulder. Her hair made a curtain between their faces.

She thought, Would we sit like this in Dhaka? In a room like this? *And would we sit like this and would it feel just the same and would everything be the same but just in a different place?*

Chanu lifted his head from her shoulder. "But of course you want to go." He smiled again. "What kind of sister would you be if you did not? Of course you do want to go."

The projects stopped. There was only one project and that meant no unnecessary expense could be entertained. No more gadgets for the computer or the car. Even book expenditure was curtailed. Chanu drove for long hours and when he returned he was too tired to talk about the ignorant types who rode in the back. And he was too tired or his ulcer was too troubling for him to relish his meals. He ate a bowl of cereal standing up, or bread that he cut in cubes from a loaf, as if cutting a whole slice would be too much effort. "Just wait while I heat up the bhaji," said Nazneen. But she could not persuade him.

He wore the money belt that he had bought as part of his tourist outfit and took it off last thing at night. All the money had to be kept in it and Nazneen opened the door only after careful surveillance. Twice she heard Mrs. Islam flay the outer corridor with sharp words. Nazneen stood inside the hallway with her back pressed to the wall.

After a silence, Mrs. Islam began again, in her invalid's voice. "Just a small glass of water is all I beg of you. For an old woman who has climbed so many stairs to see a friend."

Nazneen stared at the crumbling plaster.

"I know you are in there."

Then it went quiet again.

Once, after a double shift, Chanu came home in the afternoon while Karim was using the computer.

"Salaam aleikhum," said Karim. He yawned and rubbed his eyes, after a long spell at the screen.

"Aleikhum a-salaam." Chanu put his keys down on top of the show-case. He stood with his arms dangling. His trousers had ridden up and his socks showed, one gray, one black.

Karim stretched his arms. For a few seconds he looked at the screen but then he set about yawning again, as if it were simply impossible to overstate just how tired and relaxed he was feeling. Nazneen dug her fingernails through her cotton sari into her thighs. If she dug hard enough she would be able to cry out and break the room in two. But no sound came from her mouth.

Chanu unzipped his anorak and took it off. Holding it out by the hood, he looked at it as if he had no idea what it was. Then he let go and it fell on the floor, hiding his shoe and his gray sock.

"Is it interesting?" he said.

Karim was in no rush to answer. First he scratched his ear, then he cracked his knuckles. "Yeah, brother. Islamic website." He covered his mouth for yet another yawn. "Hope you don't mind."

"Why should I mind?"

Karim shrugged. He looked at his fingernails.

"When I was a young man like you, do you know what I wanted to be? I wanted to be a British civil servant. I was going to sit all the exams and be a High Flyer, Top Earner, Head of Department, Permanent Secretary, Cabinet Secretary, Right-Hand Bloody Man of the Bloody Prime Minister." For the first time, Nazneen saw that his face was capable of growing as serious as his eyes. His face came together. "I saw no reason why not. That's the truth. Anything is possible."

Karim's foot jacked up and down, working an invisible pump.

"Anything is possible so everything I wanted was possible," Chanu went on. "But what about all the other possibilities? The ones we never see when we are young, but are there all along. One day you wake up and say to yourself, *I didn't choose this.* And then you spend a long time thinking, *But did I?*"

"I know what I want," said Karim. He stared at Chanu, but Chanu seemed to have forgotten him.

Chanu picked up his coat and his keys. He put the keys in his pocket and jangled them.

"I know what I want," said Karim.

"The thing about getting older," said Chanu, "is that you don't need everything to be possible anymore, you just need some things to be certain."

He put on his anorak and, though there was nowhere to go, went out again.

The mela was canceled. Karim said, "It don't look right. Think about it. The American president is preparing his crusade. And we're preparing to party? It's not on."

The girls were upset. Chanu took the news so philosophically that he did not even care to philosophize about it. In any case, he had stopped singing. He had even stopped humming. At first Shahana said, "Thank God he's put a sock in it." After a week or so, she said, "Is he sick or something?" Finally, she said, "It's going to happen, isn't it? He's going to kidnap us."

Chanu sat on the floor reading a newspaper.

Shahana approached of her own volition. "Do you want me to turn the page?"

"You are a clever girl. Go and study."

"Abba, how much money do you have now?"

He carried on reading.

"Because I was thinking, if you left me behind, me and Bibi, if she wants, then you wouldn't have to save as much. And we could be adopted, or just looked after by someone. Really, we could look after ourselves."

He didn't look up. "Do you want me to beat you?"

Shahana screwed up her face. She clawed the air. "Yes," she screamed. "Yes."

"Well, I won't beat you," he said quietly. "And I won't leave you behind either."

He chewed indigestion tablets, whole packets at a time, and still his stomach pained him.

"Go to the doctor," said Nazneen every day.

"It's a symptom," said Chanu. "I've got to tackle the cause."

Bibi tried to interest her father in her schoolbooks. "Good," he said. "Study." He patted her on the head, cautiously, as if she were made of chalk.

"Abba, do you want me to walk on your back?"

The girls hated walking on their father's back. Shahana refused outright and risked floggings; Bibi trod along the furrowed flesh with all the relish of a girl stepping in fresh cowpats.

"Back?" said Chanu. "No." As if he did not even possess such a thing.

Then Chanu made a purchase. He laid it on the sofa and they all lined up in front of it. Bibi bent over to touch it, to check if it was real. Shahana closed her eyes and her lips moved silently. Chanu unzipped it and lifted up the lid.

"Might as well make a start on the packing."

It was an unremarkable suitcase: shiny black nylon and two straps with silver buckles, like a pair of cheap raincoats stitched around a frame. Nazneen was astounded. That Chanu should buy a suitcase was not in itself surprising. All of his projects required equipment. But there was something different this time. Chanu made no speech. He did not clear his throat. He did not begin to speak about his plans for the Dhaka house, or the rural retreat. Peasant types and ignorant types were not mentioned. Of the immigrant tragedy, the clash of cultures and the lessons of history, nothing was said. There was no singing, no humming, and not a proverb in sight.

Nazneen thought, It is going to happen. We are going to Bangladesh.

Karim had a new style. The gold necklace vanished; the jeans, shirts, and trainers went as well. Some of the parents were telling their daughters to leave their headscarves at home. Karim put on panjabi pajama and a skullcap. He wore a sleeveless fleece and big boots with the laces left undone at the top. The fleece and the boots were expensive. Nazneen saw him running his finger over the labels. When he took off the fleece he laid it down with care. The boots had to be unlaced in just the right way, neither too high nor too low. Nazneen felt that Karim did not want her to mention the new clothes. The matter was either too trivial or else too important to be discussed.

There had been a laborer who worked on her father's land whose name was Arzoo. Besides his name he possessed very little. He had his arms and legs, tough as jute from his work in the fields, and he had two lungis and two undershirts. In cold weather he wore both undershirts at once and a sack with holes cut in it.

One day Arzoo caused a stir. He appeared in a jacket made of red wool with two patch pockets on the front and four brass buttons. Nobody could understand it.

"Hey, Arzoo! Joining the circus?"

"Quick, everyone run. Police inspector coming."

"Trousers coming next year, eh, Arzoo?"

Arzoo was dignified. He walked more slowly than before, giving everyone the chance to appreciate the jacket. And he sniffed with his nose held high.

"Something flavoring the air. Whoever thought jealousy stink so bad like that?"

As far as anyone knew, he never took the jacket off. He wore it in the fields and it became caked in mud. When he walked around he took to picking off lumps of dirt and he could never get enough of touching the jacket.

In the village, people had to make their own entertainment.

"In this day and age, a man doesn't need a wife to make love to. All he needs is a nice jacket."

"Oh, maharaja! Sahib! Can't you see that we are in need? What is a few lakh takas to a man like you?"

Arzoo ignored them all but he walked in an urgent way, and it seemed to Nazneen that he was trying to give his jacket the slip.

He came to collect his wages. Abba studied his undershirt and knotted shoulders.

"What has happened? Dacoits?"

The laborer lowered his head and looked glum. "If someone wanted to take my jacket they would have to kill me first. But I have finished with that jacket. Was nothing but trouble." His skin was as dark as dates and the only parts of him that were not dusty were the whites of his eyes. He widened them now. "You think that a clothing is just a clothing. But as a matter of fact it is not. In a place like this it is a serious thing."

Nazneen could not concentrate on her sewing. She watched the back of Karim's head, the strong lines his neck made. If she were to describe him to Hasina, what would she say?

That even when you knew you had not, you could end up believing you had said something that might change his life.

She would say that he knew so many things.

Chanu also knew many things but they only left him bewildered. If knowledge was food then while Karim grew strong on his intake, Chanu became only bloated, bilious, and pained. The way Karim made you feel was . . .

Casting around in her mind, she rejected all the words that came. How could she make Hasina understand? She meandered back into the village.

Tamizuddin Mizra Haque was Gouripur's barber. Beneath the shade of a moss-encrusted pipal tree he set up his shop with three or four stools, two buckets, special soaps and oils, cutlasslike razors, and his gleaming scissors, the cleanest and brightest object for miles around. A few feet behind, bamboo grew like a living wall, defining the space and investing it with an official quality. If you had to describe Tamizuddin Mizra Haque to someone who did not know him and was, nevertheless, intent on finding him in a gathering of men, you would simply tell them to look for the most important person in the room. Inevitably, they would gravitate towards the barber. For of all the men in Gouripur, if looks were kingmakers, it was the barber who would be crowned. It was not a matter of "handsome" or "beautiful." It was simply that Tamizuddin Mizra Haque had an important face. Even when he was working—and a barber's status was not high—he was undiminished. By his face alone you would guess that this man of influence had fallen suddenly on hard times, or was merely playing a role. Perhaps it was this quality that wrote the rule that everybody at all times addressed him as Tamizuddin Mizra Haque. It was not possible to shorten his name in any way, and though it was the custom to show respect by naming people Uncle or Brother or some other fictitious relative, it would have been frowned upon in this case.

Even when his wife came to call him, she said, "Tamizuddin Mizra Haque, would you kindly bring your miserable backside over here."

Nazneen and Hasina loved to play near the barber's shop. When a customer's face disappeared inside a cloud of white soap, it was thrilling to see the razor fly over the throat and cheeks and see how the skin beneath looked new and untouched. When the barber applied the lotions with a great slapping noise Nazneen felt her own skin tingle at the touch.

But the best thing about the barber's shop was the information. If you wanted to find out something about somebody, the best plan you could make would be to hang around near the pipal tree. Not too near because men would shoo children from their path as easily as ducks. But not too far either.

Eventually, one way or another—and learning a great deal in the meantime—you would have your information. For in this great establishment every topic under the sun and several which lay above, in heaven, was discussed not once, not twice, but many, many times. Men came for shaving and haircutting but most of all they came for talk. As a result Tamizuddin Mizra Haque was the greatest repository of information in the entire village.

Typically, two or more men would dispute something, anything. If there was nothing really to dispute, at least one man would take issue just out of politeness.

"Abdul Ali has bought his land, finally. Three and one-half hectares."

"I heard it was only two."

"Three and one-half hectares."

"That is what he was planning. But in the end he only bought two."

"As God is my witness, I swear—"

"May God strike me deaf, dumb, and blind if I lie, and shrivel my manhood like a dead woodlouse."

This would go on for some time while the scissors flashed like miniature lightning against dark heads. Detached and ineffably impressive, the barber took no part in debate. He bided his time.

Eventually, someone would say, "Tamizuddin Mizra Haque, settle this affair. How many hectares?"

And without hesitation the barber made his pronouncement.

"Three and one-half hectares."

Or, "Two hectares only."

Whatever the verdict, the opposing side immediately caved in. A man could be yellow and purple from his exhortations; he might have sworn on his honor, his children's lives, or even his testicles; he might have ranted in every emotional key, oozing sincerity, spitting with frustration or weeping with anger, but when Tamizuddin Mizra Haque pronounced, he would cave.

"Is it so, Tamizuddin Mizra Haque? Well, you know best."

Nazneen and Hasina delighted in this moment of transformation. Squeezing each other's hands, they squatted with their hems in the dirt and stared at the man who settled everything with a word or two. They were proud that a man like this, who knew all that there was to know, actually lived in Gouripur. That he should choose to live among them was a wondrous thing.

The girls said to each other, "What do you want to know? Let's go and ask Tamizuddin Mizra Haque."

Nazneen thought hard. Hasina said, "How high is the tallest mountain in the world? No, that's too easy. If a python swallowed a baby whole, could you cut open its tummy and take the baby out still alive? Who killed Auntie's mynah bird? That's what I'd ask him. No, what I really want to know is, who are we going to marry?" They often played this game but they never went to ask the barber anything. To actually ask him would spoil the anything-at-all-ness, which is what they liked.

Some of the children were not quite as enraptured. They shouted from a safe distance, "Tamizuddin Mizra Haque, what the president having for breakfast today, eh?"

Anyway, thought Nazneen, I should write to Hasina soon. Running a hand along the eggshell cracks of the pale green sewing machine, she realized she had scarcely begun on her work. And it would be better if Karim left soon. Another few minutes and the salaat alert would come on his mobile phone, and then he would stay for his prayer. She let the thought wash over her. It saturated her so heavily that she was unable to act on it.

From the set of his neck, Karim was intent on his work at the computer. Magazines, he had explained, could be radical. But the internet was where things got *really* radical.

Nazneen knew she would never write about him to Hasina. Her next letter, when she got around to it, would follow in the footsteps of the others. *We are all well. Shahana is getting top marks in her class, and Bibi has grown at least one inch. I tried again to make dhoie but it never comes out quite right, too much sugar I think, or not the right kind. I pray for your friend Monju and her boy.*

What a poor answer it would make. Hasina's letter had arrived yesterday.

I tell you about friend Monju. Acid melt cheekbone and nose and one eye. Other eye damage only with pain and very hate. Difficult thing how I make you describe? Is worse see this good eye. Is where hope should be but no hope is there.

Monju sister has take Khurshed in village. Boy has not see the mother. She will not allow. "Promise me." She say every time I go. Promise me the boy get his operation. What can I say? What to do?

Nazneen stood up and walked about the room. Perhaps she would mention Tamizuddin Mizra Haque to Hasina, ask how she remembered him. Of course, she thought, the barber did not know everything. That was only how it seemed to us as children. But about village affairs he knew a great deal, and everyone deferred to his knowledge. He could settle such matters very easily. Or perhaps it was just a way of ending the conversation. Maybe they were mocking him, and he knew so little that he did not know even when he was being mocked.

"Who benefits?" Karim got up so fast he kicked over his chair. "That's the key question, man. Who benefits?"

"From what?" It was obvious she should know what he was talking about.

But he didn't hear her. "I can tell you—no Arab nation benefits. No Muslim, anywhere in the world. We are the ones who're going to suffer. You got to ask, who benefits?"

Nazneen looked behind her and back again.

"Not that difficult to work it out," said Karim.

Nazneen thought, *What a lot of rubbish I have in my mind about barbers and pipal trees, as if there is nothing important to think about.* At the same time she thought, *Only my husband and this boy are thinking all the time about New York and terrorists and bombs. Everybody else just living their lives.*

Karim picked up the chair. "A devout Muslim, right, willing to sacrifice himself for his religion. Does he go to bars and watch naked girls and drink alcohol? What kind of Muslim takes his Qur'an into a bar? And *leaves* it there? These stories are made up by idiots. People who don't know nothing about Islam. Maybe a Christian carries his Bible around like a pack of cigarettes. He don't know how a Qur'an is treated."

Glancing up at the specially built high shelf, Nazneen regarded her own Qur'an in its cloth case.

"They're saying *another* Qur'an got left behind in a rental car by these so-called Islamic terrorists." He laughed without mirth. "All these devout men throwing away the Word of God like sweet papers."

"And a Muslim cannot commit suicide," said Nazneen. No matter how many times he explained about martyrs, it seemed to her incontrovertible.

He who kills himself with sword, or poison, or throws himself off a mountain will be tormented on the Day of Resurrection with that very thing.

"It's not as simple as that." Karim talked over her. "There's other stuff too. It don't add up. Listen. All four black boxes from the aeroplanes—that's where everything that went on is recorded—were destroyed. But have you heard about the magic passport? One of the hijackers' passports survived the fire—heat of over one thousand degrees Fahrenheit. Found in the rubble of the World Trade Center. What kind of fools does the FBI take us for?"

"Who did it then?"

He touched his skullcap briefly, as a woman might touch the hair coiled on her head to make sure it was still in place. "Ask the right question. Who benefits?"

It seemed to Nazneen that no one benefited.

She would not let him pray at her home again. Maybe it was not, officially, a sin. But it was not right. It was something she could stop, and if she could stop that then maybe she could end the rest of it too.

But she had tried and she had failed.

"It isn't right," she said, with his breath hot in her ear.

"I know," he moaned. "I'll fix it. Don't worry." And the weight of his body was all that she needed.

How could she tell him not to come anymore? What would it mean? That she had taken her pleasure and had enough? That what was between them was within her power to stop? That, controlling it, she need never have begun it?

For a while she pinned her hopes on Chanu. That day when he wandered in and Karim was using the computer, she thought, *He knows it all.* But he said nothing to her. Everyone else knew. Nazma—that glint in her eye when she ran her hand over the sewing machine. "Still getting plenty?" she had said. Razia showed no surprise at all when let in on the "Secret." How early had she guessed it? Who had not noticed the comings and goings?

Let my husband find out, Nazneen prayed. Let him kill me, she added.

Chanu was not so obliging. Can't you see what is going on under your nose, she demanded silently of him every day.

In the mornings she said her prayers and did housework and began her sewing and there was nothing inside her that demanded more. By lunchtime, when she looked for Karim out of the window, her stomach began to surge with excitement and dread and on the days when he did not come she had to leave the flat and walk around the streets for fear that she would wear out the remaining threads of carpet.

"Why do you like me?" she asked one day, hoping that the words came naturally, as if she had just thought of them.

He was in a playful mood. *"Keno tumake amar bhalo lage?"* Who says that I like you? His fingers touched the hollow of her throat.

"I do," she said in a firm way.

"I see." He kissed a trail from her throat to her armpit.

"I am not beautiful. I am not a young girl."

"Not young and not beautiful? Then I must be crazy."

"And you are young."

"What about beautiful?"

She was determined to be serious. "But you do not answer me."

Karim rolled onto his back. As he moved his hands up behind his head Nazneen watched the muscles in his arms tense and relax. His skin was golden, like honey. It looked like you could lick it off.

"Well, basically you've got two types. Make your choice. There's your Westernized girl, wears what she likes, all the makeup going on, short skirts and that soon as she's out of her father's sight. She's into going out, getting good jobs, having a laugh. Then there's your religious girl, wears the scarf or even the burkha. You'd think, right, they'd be good wife material. But they ain't. Because all they want to do is *argue.* And they always think they know best because they've been off to all these summer camps for Muslim sisters."

"What about me?"

He propped himself up on one elbow. She smelled his sweat and it stirred her. "Ah, you. *You* are the real thing."

"Real thing?"

"You can arrange for a girl from the village. Bring her over here." He was still setting out his options. "But then there's all the settling-in hassle. And you never know *what* you're going to get."

"I am the real thing?" A conversation overheard in the early days of her marriage came to her mind. She stood in her nightdress in the hallway while Chanu was on the telephone. *An unspoilt girl. From the village. All things considered, I am satisfied.*

Karim was getting out of bed. He had his back to her.

"My husband is taking us to Dhaka," she said.

She watched the curve of his spine to see if he had noticed: the emphasis in her voice had gotten out of control.

He straightened up but he did not turn.

She curled herself into a ball. The shush of air in her nostrils, the minute clicks of her skull, the wheeze of her chest, gurgles from her gut, blood thumping dully in her ears.

At last, he spoke. "When I went to Bradford, I went to see a girl. Selected for me. I turned her down. For you."

"What can I do?" Her face was hot and wet.

"What do you want to do?"

She had wanted to go. But now she did not know. The children would suffer; Chanu would face fresh agonies of disappointment; and she was not the girl from the village anymore. She was not the real thing.

Karim picked her up like a child and held her. "Don't be scared. Let your husband go. It's gonna be the best thing. Then you get a divorce because he's left you. Don't be scared. I'll sort it."

October arrived and with it Chanu's chilblains, colds and coughs for the girls, and condensation. Nazneen began her winter ritual of wiping the windows with a towel every morning. It helped with the damp. Two workmen blundered along to fix the toilet.

"How long's it been broken, darlin'?"

She told them.

"That's the council for you, darlin.'"

They poked around a bit and then cleared off.

"Got yourself a problem there, sweetheart. Shouldn't'a left it so long."

The suitcase stood on its little smart wheels at the bottom of the wardrobe, on top of Chanu's certificates. Nazneen tested the handle. It was heavy.

She gave up trying to persuade Chanu to eat and then she gave up cooking. The girls had burgers or baked beans or whatever they wanted. Once, when she got up in the night and pulled open the door to an empty fridge, she started making cauliflower curry, and as the spices hit the hot fat and burst their seams she thought she would waken everybody and they would eat together like a normal family. But it was two o'clock in the morning and she ate alone, standing up against the sink, watching the moon and wondering if she would ever eat a meal with her sister again.

The next day, the leaflet appeared through the letterbox.

MARCH AGAINST THE MULLAHS

Karim picked it up. He turned it over. "Yes!" he said. "We've got a date." He folded his arms and stood with his legs wide. "Let them come. We'll be ready."

When Chanu got home he picked up the leaflet and studied it for some time. Then he put it down, went into the bedroom, and closed the door.

Chapter Seventeen

The only thing on which everyone could agree was that the boy had been stabbed. Everything else was as hotly disputed as the price of brinjals on market day. Some said the fight was between two gangs, with as many as ten boys involved. Others said twenty or thirty or fifty, while their opponents maintained it was only two, the stabber and the stabbed. It was said that the gangs had a long history of rivalry, dating back to their schooldays when they had all bunked off to attend noontime raves in darkened warehouses, getting changed in the toilet, taking nips of whisky and drags of cigarettes and listening to Joi Bangla, Michael Jackson, James Brown, Amiruddin, and Abdul Gani, making up new dances and hostilities, inventing their lives in a way that no one—especially not their parents—had imagined for them. Between these two gangs there was always tension, and the only surprise was that someone had not been stabbed sooner.

But this was all lies. The boys involved were members of the same gang, and they had fallen out over a girl. More lies. The issue was drugs. Or it was money. Indeed, it was drug money. This, for a certain fact, was what led the boy to end up in hospital with a wound *this* deep in his thigh.

Some people were ignorant as donkeys! For the wound was to the chest, and he was not expected to live, although only Allah would decide and it was not up to anyone to be expecting or not expecting, but it was difficult not to expect this kind of thing to happen because what else were gangs for but trouble?

Of course, some people had only mustard plants growing between their ears and they would believe anything. As a matter of fact, and as the song said, in spite of their eyes they were blind. There were no gangs at all. The white press had made them up to give Bangladeshis a bad name. The *Tower Hamlets Bugle* was the worst offender (but all white newspapers were culprits); if you read that rubbish you'd think that our boys were getting as bad as the blacks. No, there weren't any gangs. Just boys who grew up together and hung around together.

The *Bugle* reported the identity of the victim as Haroon Zaman. The majority took issue with this report. The boy who lay at death's door—or on his right-hand side to protect his wounded left thigh—was actually *Jamal* Zaman. Or Jamal Shamser. Or, according to Razia, who got it from Tariq, it was somebody called Nonny. And nobody seemed to know Nonny's real name, although many people pretended to have heard of him and agreed that he was a violent character, just the type to be fighting, and many others felt sorry for Nonny because he was such a meek boy, just the type to be picked on.

Chanu said, "Do you know the problem with these boys?"

"Not enough studying," said Bibi smartly.

"Too much roaming around," said Shahana. "Like goats."

"Don't try to be clever."

"Tell us, Abba." Bibi stood up to speak.

"I don't know," said Chanu. "Apart from this: sometimes, when it seems that the world is against you, it is tempting to side with the world." He picked up his car keys and Shahana reached for the television remote. "Of course, if they studied more then they would be strong. Mental strength, that's the key." He took the remote control from his daughter and gave it to Nazneen. "They will sit with their books tonight."

Razia and Nazneen stood with a little group of mothers outside Alam's High Class Grocery shop on Bethnal Green Road. On a pair of wooden trestle tables beneath the windows was a box of tomatoes that had ripened to a point beyond red, darkening now like old bruises, a hairy pyramid of coconuts, a heap of dark green knobbly karela, bitter even to look at, and a large glass jar filled with neem twigs. Nazma poked a tomato and wiped her finger on the fake grass mat covering the table.

"High class?" she said, and a wobbling indignation set up in her cheeks. "In Bangladesh, a man calling his wares high class and selling rotten tomatoes would not be allowed to get away with it."

"Oh yes," said Sorupa. "There are laws against that kind of thing."

"Laws?" cried Nazma, as if she had never heard the word before. "A scoundrel like that would never get to see the inside of a court."

Sorupa was less sure now and, to compensate, spoke more emphatically. "Never."

"The people would take the affair in their own hand. One or two good thrashings is all you need. Is simple. Is quick. Is effective." Nazma went over to the table with the karela. Nazneen imagined her rolling along on little round feet. Nazma picked up a vegetable and pinched it. Judging from the expression on her face she had squeezed out at least a dozen caterpillars.

Sorupa had by now got the idea. "Is the best best system. Beat up the scoundrel on the double. No bribes to pay, no waiting around for police and lawyer and all that thing." She extolled the virtues of the village justice system. What she lacked in material she made up for in her willingness to repeat herself.

Nazma quickly grew bored. "I hear the boy who got himself stabbed has got punctured lung. I hear he getting involved in drugs." She looked at Razia and opened her eyes as wide as they would go; Nazneen could see the whites top and bottom.

Nazneen watched the two women. Nazma's breasts, high and round as footballs, heaved beneath her thin black coat. They emphasized the slackness of Razia's chest, hanging low beneath her sweater.

Razia looked at the coconuts. She picked one up and weighed it in her hand, selected another, and weighed that.

"Drugs," said Nazma. She said it the way a parent might say "monsters" to thrill a young child.

"Drugs," said Sorupa.

Nazma looked annoyed. She clicked her tongue at Sorupa, who pretended not to notice.

"Of course you hear all sorts about boys getting mix-up in drugs these days. The parents can't control and they bring shame on the family. Anyone who had any sense would send them back to Bangladesh."

Little light flakes, no bigger than Chanu's dandruff, began to fall on the tomatoes and other high-class items and on the women's heads. They landed and vanished without trace.

"Rain," said Razia to Nazneen. "We'd better go."

"Snow," said Nazma. "Of course, some people can't see what's beneath their own nose."

Sorupa brushed the air with her fingers, demonstrating clearly the fact of snow. "Right beneath their nose."

On Commercial Street there was a funeral procession. Four big black cars followed a hearse packed with lilies and chrysanthemums and presumably somewhere beneath them a coffin. Inside the cars, people were stuffed together as densely as the flowers. A red van with a picture of a pig on the side was caught up in the procession and kept swinging out into the other lane in an attempt to overtake. The pig sat as if on an invisible chair, with his fat little legs crossed, eating a pie. As Nazneen waited in the middle of the road she looked inside one of the funeral cars and a woman raised her head from checking her lipstick in a compact mirror and stared back at Nazneen. The woman had short blond hair cut in an efficient style around her jaw. She looked at Nazneen with a ready kindness, a half-smile on her lips, but in her eyes there was nothing. It was the way she might look at a familiar object, her keys that she had just found, the kitchen table as she wiped the juice her daughter had spilled, a blankness reserved for known quantities like pieces of furniture or brown women in saris who cooked rice and raised their children and obeyed their husbands. Nazneen lifted her hand and waved. The funeral procession pulled away with the red van trapped like a beating heart in a comatose body.

They walked over to Wentworth Street and Razia did not say a word all the way. Nazneen thought about Nazma and Sorupa and the little group outside Alam's. At the time she had not realized it, but none of the women had spoken to her. Had it been deliberate? Would she find that people hurried past her in the street? Would there be no more women popping around to borrow something for the kitchen, an eggcup's worth of misti jeera, a couple of sticks of cinnamon, just a pinch of saffron when an unexpected visitor stayed for dinner? It happened to other women. Only recently Hanufa had been frozen out when it was discovered she had been attending a massage course. It was un-Islamic behavior and, apparently, the imam at the Jamme Masjid had preached against that very thing. Hanufa protested that it was a women-only course and that she was practicing for the sake of her husband, who suffered with a bad back. But it was too late. "If she so damn proud of it, what the hell she creeping around behind our backs for?" Nazneen remembered that she, too, had not called on Hanufa, though she had not snubbed her deliberately. She turned this last thought over a few times, trying to decide if it was true. In the end she gave up and reflected that Hanufa would at least have the opportunity to snub her in return, Nazneen's crime being so much vaster than her own.

They walked along past the shoe stalls, where every shoe resembled an instrument of torture. At the fried chicken stand, a man patted chicken quarters with a kind of tenderness, as though he was trying to rub them back to life. Nazneen saw that he was coaxing spices into the skin. A group of African girls tried on shoes, twisting their backs to look down at the heels.

Nazneen wanted to ask Razia if she was getting the Hanufa treatment.

"Shall we go into Yellow Rose? Or Galaxy Textiles?"

Razia shrugged.

"Let's try this shop," said Nazneen, and pulled her arm.

They went inside and ran their hands over lengths of cherry-red silk, mauve and turquoise cottons, and peacock-blue satin. Razia said, "Maybe we should leave it for today." And she sounded so much like a person who could never be tempted by anything again that the sales assistant did not even attempt to delay them.

Although it was early it was beginning to get dark, and as they walked the lights went on in windows and pulled them up to the panes without them even willing it. They looked at trays of gold rings, rack upon rack winking lewdly under the spotlights. At Best Buy Trading Ltd they were arrested by three mannequins all draped in hot pink crepe de chine. The mannequins were posed like dancers, their arms bent in ways that suggested movement, gayness, maybe even abandon. But their faces remained detached, giving no clue to the ecstasy below. For the actions of their bodies, there was no accountability.

Nazneen longed for Razia to speak, to roll her eyes and begin *puff puff*-ing to turn herself into Nazma. She did an excellent imitation of Nazma. After every few words she inserted a *puff puff,* and though Nazma did not in fact puff, this lent an essence of Nazma to the speech: the bumptiousness of the woman and, somehow, the roundness. Sorupa she also had to perfection. The way she pressed her lips flat against her teeth in self-righteousness, and the way she nibbled them and looked away when Nazma slapped her down.

Nazneen wanted Razia to slip into these other voices, to become the old Razia once again. She studied her friend. Nothing lit up her eyes today. Not anger, not fear, not pain. How long had it been since mischief starred in those deep gold flecks?

She remembered another day when they had come shopping together for fabric and how bursting with secrets she had been. She blurted out everything about Mrs. Islam, and it had felt good and Razia said she would help, but now Razia was devoured by her own troubles and Nazneen could not say, But what about this help you said you would give to *me*? Everything she had suspected about Tariq, it was all true but what could be said about it now? Should they wring their hands and cry every time they met and poke around every little bit of pain?

Then there was Karim.

A few times she had imagined conversations with Razia. She played them out, reading both the parts, trying a new phrase here and there. *He will never give me up.* Razia tucking her feet under her bottom and leaning over to squeeze all the juice out of the story. *It consumes us. It's not something we can control.* Razia shaking her bony shoulders; the intensity—even at this remove—enough to make her shiver. *The most astonishing thing of all . . .* She never knew what she would say then, but the phrase kept coming to her. With narrowed eyes and her sideways look, Razia attempted to tease it from her. *The most astonishing thing of all . . .*

They did not speak of him. It was not possible.

With all those secrets between them, how easy it was to talk. Talk flowed like the Meghna: the fast-flowing gush of new gossip; the hiss and splash of their various moans and complaints; disturbances around the rocks of the more serious stuff, always family; a widening and a narrowing, running deep and coming shallow; even in silent stretches the currents between them never stopped and the whole vast outpouring tumbled endlessly into the sea of their friendship. And now the river had met a dam, built out of truth and knowledge and need. These things had stopped up their mouths.

They paused outside a new shop.

"Fusion Fashions," said Razia, reading out the name.

Inside, a white girl stood in front of a mirror turning this way and that in a black kameez top with white embroidered flowers and a sprinkling of pearls stitched near the throat. The trousers were not the usual baggy salwaar style but narrow-hipped and slightly flared at the bottom. The girl picked up a stack of green glass bangles from a shelf and attempted to get one over her hand.

"She'll never get it on like that," said Nazneen.

A similar outfit was displayed in the window, only this version was red with black embroidery and black beads. Razia looked at the price tag. She shook her head and sighed as if the evils of the world had been revealed to her.

"Look how much these English are paying for their kameez. And at the same time they are looking down on me. They are even happy to spit on their own flag, as long as I am inside it. What is wrong with them? What is wrong?"

* * *

Chanu was out, driving ignorant types and collecting parking fines. He had taken to keeping the penalty notices in an envelope addressed to the local council. On each of the slips he had written: Gone away to address unknown, return to issuer. The girls were sitting on the sofa and Bibi had the remote control on her lap. Every time she touched it Shahana kicked her on the ankle.

"Amma, Shahana keeps kicking me."

"Shahana, don't kick your sister."

"She keeps trying to change the channel."

"I haven't done anything."

"Just wait until you're in Bangladesh," said Shahana. "You'll be married off in no time."

Bibi said, "But . . . but . . ."

"And your husband will keep you locked up in a little smelly room and make you weave carpets all day long."

Bibi jumped up. "What about you? You're older than me. You will have a husband before me."

Shahana hugged her knees. "That's what you think."

Nazneen switched the television off. "But you would like to see where your mother grew up?"

The girls wriggled a bit and did not answer.

"You would like to see Mumtaz auntie?"

"Tell us a story about Mumtaz auntie," said Bibi. She sat cross-legged now on the sofa to show that she was ready.

"Only the one about the good jinni." Shahana pursed her sweet pink lips. "All the other stories are boring."

So Nazneen told about the good jinni.

Mumtaz had inherited the jinni from her father, who kept it in an empty medicine bottle with a lead stopper. On her father's death, the jinni agreed to become Mumtaz's jinni only on the condition that it was released from the bottle and allowed to live freely. Mumtaz covered the bottle with cheesecloth and smashed it with a hammer, crying, "O jinni, I give you freedom and you will give me wisdom."

At first it had seemed that the jinni had not kept its end of the bargain. Mumtaz called it and it did not answer. She went out and wandered among the banana trees, having learned as a child that jinn were partial to bananas. Still, it did not answer. She searched among the sugar cane, the elephant grass, and the chili plants. She stood beneath the plane trees and called. She looked in the cow pen, the well, and underneath the lily pads in the pond. The jinni had tricked her.

After checking inside her bedroll and among her jewelry boxes and shaking out her hair in case it had become caught in her tresses, she resigned herself to the loss. Perhaps, she thought, the jinni has given me wisdom after all: never trust a jinni.

Barsa came and the rains that year fell hard enough to split a grain of rice in two. Sarat turned the land to gold and the snowy cranes flew in from the north to stand on withered legs in the deep green paddy. One cantankerous old fellow took to walking around the village pond like a retired schoolteacher with his arms folded behind his back, keeping a beady eye on the children, little brown fish who splashed and screeched, and whom he would dearly love to discipline. Hemanto brought jasmine, lotus, water lilies and hyacinth, krishnachura, kadam, and magnolia, and everywhere the smell of drying rice stalks. That year one of the cows gave birth to three calves and it was taken as an auspicious sign and many marriages were hurried through even before their proper season.

It was Basanto before the jinni made itself known to Mumtaz. Cleaning a large and particularly bloody hilsha fish, she was thinking about a problem that one of the village women had set before her. The woman had three sons and five daughters and could scarcely feed so many mouths. Yet her husband still wanted to sleep with her and make more mouths, more empty bellies. What should she do? How could she deny her husband? And how could she magic more food from her cooking pot? Mumtaz gripped the fish guts and pulled. A spurt of blood landed on her sari. "What should I tell her?" she said aloud.

The jinni replied, "Tell her that she should gather together all her children, the oldest to the youngest, and stand them in a line before her husband. She should say to him, 'First you must choose which one will die. Kill the child and I will give you another. We cannot keep any more children alive, so you must choose the ones to die. For every child you kill, I will replace him.'"

Mumtaz was pleased with the answer and she decided at once to tell the woman exactly what the jinni had said. But she was cross with the jinni and berated it, saying, "Why did you go away from me?"

"But I did not go away," said the jinni. "It is only now you have decided to listen to me."

From that day, Mumtaz was able to call the jinni whenever she chose, and people came to consult her on many important matters. Although she claimed to converse with the jinni casually, just as a daughter chats to her mother while she is mixing cow dung and straw or lighting a fire, for these special sessions Mumtaz sat in a purified room and burned candles and incense. She dressed in white and put a white veil across her mouth and nose. And to draw the jinni to her she muttered some special charms, spoken at the speed of a butterfly's wing and impossible to decipher.

Nazneen begged to be told the charms but Mumtaz said only that first she must get her own jinni.

"Will I be elected to the council?"

"What should I name my child?"

"An enemy has sworn to put the evil eye on me. How can I protect myself?"

Mumtaz spoke her mantras and swayed around in her little white tent. When she gave the answer she suddenly lay down on her side and it was understood and accepted by all that, having channeled a spirit through her body, she should now be allowed to rest.

Everyone, that is, apart from Amma. "A fraud, nothing but a fraud." She sucked on her big teeth and wiped the corners of her mouth with her sari.

The girls were getting ready for bed. Nazneen went to the bathroom with them and sat on the edge of the bath.

Shahana pulled Chanu's daaton from the toothbrush mug. "In Bangladesh, you'll have to brush your teeth with a twig. They don't have toothbrushes."

Chanu had been delighted to find the neem twig in Alam's High Class Grocery. He chewed the end until it splayed, rubbed it vigorously around his mouth, and declared it to be excellent for massaging the gums.

"You know, Bibi, they don't have toilet paper either. You'll have to pour water on your bottom to clean it."

Bibi looked distressed. "What about you? You'll have to do it too."

Shahana put on her inscrutable face.

Then she attacked her sister with the daaton, trying to force it into her mouth.

Nazneen separated the girls and shooed them into the bedroom. She stood in the middle of their room like a referee while they got into bed. She was still thinking about jinn.

There was another story, which she had never told the children.

Nazneen was maybe eight or nine years old, just tall enough to look down the well without standing on tiptoe. This was the year that Amma became possessed by an evil jinni. The jinni prevented Amma from washing and made her smell like a goat. It arranged her hair in knots and tangles and mockingly inserted sprigs of jasmine behind her ears. For days at a time she did not speak. Worst of all, at the jinni's bidding, Amma began attacking her own husband, stabbing wildly at his eyes with bamboo sticks that she spent hours on end whittling to a fine point. Sometimes, when the jinni let his guard down or was perhaps sleeping, Amma was returned to her usual state. She took a bar of Sunlight down to the pond, swam, and washed. She began cooking again and resumed the endless litany of complaints against the servants. And she took up her usual commentary on life.

"What can I do? I have been put on this earth to suffer."

Abba said, "And she suffers so well."

"The jinni may come upon me again," said Amma. "Whenever he wishes, he uses up my body, my strength, my soul."

And Abba rolled his eyes. "Let us hope he does not wait too long."

But when the jinni returned he was ever more mischievous and before long Abba was compelled to call in the fakir.

Exorcisms were a spectator sport in the village. A crowd gathered and it was a bigger and more excitable crowd than formed even for Manzur Boyati, the most highly esteemed of storytellers. The fakir was an impressive sight. He was tall and straight as sugar cane and his beard was at least twenty inches long, twisted into two halves like a woman's braids. Immediately they arrived, his assistants commandeered the kerosene stove and set about boiling up potions which, in Nazneen's view, should have frightened the jinni away by their smell alone. The fakir examined Amma from a distance. Amma lay on her bedroll, spasms running obligingly through her arms and legs. The fakir seemed satisfied.

"Who is willing to help this cursed woman?" demanded the fakir. His eyes were as cloudy as old marbles and yet he seemed to focus on each person in the room, individually and all at once.

"I will be the volunteer," cried a servant boy from Nazneen's house, and he scrambled to the front. The crowd relaxed and there was much scratching of noses and backsides.

The servant was a moody young boy who kept a half-starved mongoose tied to a palm tree and amused himself by goading it to bite his hand. The mongoose, though essentially a pacifist, would sometimes be persuaded to play this game and was rewarded with a swift kick that lifted it several feet in the air.

"Sit," barked the fakir and pushed down on the boy's head.

The boy curled his upper lip but sat down on the ground with his legs crossed. The assistants daubed his head and shoulders with their emetic pastes. Then the exorcism began. As a warm-up exercise the fakir and his two helpers walked in circles around the servant boy, half singing and half speaking verses, words which locked into each other as tightly as bones in a hand, moving around, flexing and curling but never breaking the chain.

Ke Katha koyre, dekha deyna
Ke Katha koyre, dekha deyna
Node chode, hater kache

Faster and faster went the chanters, faster and faster flew the words. The white cloths tied around the fakir's waist and arms streamed behind him, making visible his huge energy with which he would fight the evil jinni.

Ke Katha koyre, dekha deyna
Who talks, not showing up
Who talks, not showing up
Moves about, near at hand

The servant boy disappeared in a vortex of wheeling limbs.

I search for him
In the sky and the earth
Myself, I do not know
I search for him
In the sky and the earth
Myself, I do not know
Who am I?
Who is he?
Who am I?
Who is he?

Abruptly the singing stopped. The assistants vanished and the fakir threw his arms wide and bellowed.

"O evil jinni, leave that woman's body! By the command of Allah, leave her. Sky! Water! Air! Fire!" He paused for a moment and added "Earth!" for good measure. "Torment her no longer."

He let his arms fall by his side. His belly heaved, moved around in strange shapes, as though a baby had shifted inside him.

All heads looked towards Amma, who now lay quietly on her mat with her face turned down.

At once the servant boy, who had volunteered his body as the jinni's next receptacle, began to grimace and leer. He let slip an obscenity and pressed his jaw and the top of his head. The fakir turned to him.

"Why did you abuse that poor woman?" the fakir said, addressing himself to the jinni.

The servant boy jumped to his feet. He bared his teeth like a frightened monkey and scratched the air. "She came out in the bushes," he said in a strangled voice. "She walked under the tamarind tree and stepped on my shadow."

The fakir rushed at the boy and wrestled him into a headlock. He was a big man, and the boy bent as easily as a dog's tail in his grip.

"Begone from this place," roared the fakir, and his glassy old eyes were terrifying. "If I see you around here again, I will destroy you."

"No need to get nasty," squeaked the boy, whose head was turning an impressive shade of purple.

"Out! Out! Out!" shouted the holy witch doctor. He released his victim, who fell unceremoniously to the floor.

The fakir adjusted the ends of his beard and yawned. The jinni saw his chance, and the boy sprang at his opponent, grabbed the two braids hanging from the fakir's chin, and wound each deftly around his fist.

"Come on then, you swine. You defiler of goats." He swung the fakir along by his beard, causing him to stumble and come to his knees. "Come on then, you shit-eating lover of corpses."

The fakir was suffering. His eyes were ready to pop and his brow shed water.

The crowd was impressed by the strength of the jinni. It promised to be a good show. Nobody even thought of talking, though many people nudged each other to ensure all aspects of the spectacle were being fully appreciated.

"He's faking," cried the fakir. "Somebody stop him." He got to his feet.

"You will never be rid of me," shrieked the boy. "She stepped on my shadow under the tamarind tree and disturbed my rest." He again whirled the fakir around by his beard and, as an innovation, flapped his tongue at the same time.

Nobody moved to intervene. The assistants squatted by the kerosene stove, smoking beedis and working strictly within their job descriptions.

"Are you going to let him kill me?" screamed the fakir.

"Don't blame the boy," called someone from the audience. "You put the jinni on him."

"He's faking," the fakir protested. "Can't you see he's faking?"

For a little while longer the servant boy tortured the holy man, until a delegation from the crowd separated them and sat on top of him. The boy began to shake his arms and legs and roll his head to and fro.

The fakir sought access to the boy, in an attempt to exorcise some of his own rather vengeful demons. This prompted much debate.

"Why do you think he was pretending?"

"Didn't you, just a few minutes ago, see that the jinni had possessed him?"

"If he is faking, let us tie him to a tree and thrash him. But don't expect money for exorcism that has failed."

It was dangerous ground for the fakir. At stake was this week's only income (and expenses had already been incurred), his pride, his desire to bash the boy's brains out, and his reputation.

For the boy, who feared he might have gone too far, the situation was also tricky. His chosen strategy was to foam at the mouth.

Amma lay completely forgotten and out of the way.

"Look," said a villager. "This boy is possessed. See how the bubbles come at his mouth."

Abba took a backseat in the proceedings. Although he had to be seen to do the right thing in calling the exorcism, he had an aversion to holy men who took his money and he preferred not to be involved.

Abba declined to give a verdict one way or the other. There was further discussion and very nearly a fight among the crowd. Eventually, however, a compromise was reached whereby the fakir was permitted to reengage the boy in a headlock in return for a solemn promise to rid him of the evil spirit.

The fakir was most thorough. Everyone agreed he threw himself into the job with great energy.

Amma did get better. There were no more days when she did not wash and she restricted herself to attacking her husband with only her sharpest of instruments, her tongue. At the time, Nazneen had been thrilled equally by the spectacular show and by her mother's recovery. Though she had heard later, eavesdropping near the barber's shop, that the servant boy had been boasting how he humiliated the big man, she still believed—of course—that the jinni had been vanquished from Amma. How it happened was a mystery, and it was not a mystery to be solved but merely treasured.

Now, as she folded away a pile of clean laundry, she began to wonder what had really happened that day, and why it was that Amma believed only in bad jinn and not in the good.

Of Karim she saw very little. He was busy regrouping the Bengal Tigers, planning the March Against the March Against the Mullahs, foreseeing catastrophe for the ummah (local and global), and taking religious instruction from his spiritual leader. When they did spend an hour or so together, Karim brought up wedding plans.

"Just a very small affair. Very small, but very, like, religious."

Nazneen smiled. It was so ridiculous.

"I'm finding out about divorce. How you do it properly."

She tightened the muscles of her pelvic floor, afraid all of a sudden that she would wet herself. If she stayed here, then what alternative would she have but to marry Karim? The thought flooded her with so many conflicting emotions it was a wonder she retained control of any of her bodily functions. She tried to single out a thought, any thought, and take charge of it. The children. How could she present the girls with a new father like that? And what would they think? How terribly it would scythe at their young minds, one question repeating itself over and over: By what means did our mother ensnare this boy?

The worst thing was, she did not know what would happen. What was the point in fearing this and that, if only *this* and not *that* would happen? If Chanu filled more suitcases and bought the tickets and bid her leave, then would that determine the end? Would Karim, set on his course, prevent her from going? What if going home turned out to be just another of Chanu's projects? A short while ago it seemed certain, but how could she be sure? She reminded herself: she had only to wait for everything to be revealed.

Instead of appeasing her as usual, this thought rankled. Why should she wait? She felt as strongly as if someone, standing beside her in the kitchen, had taken a piece of paper, written down the answers, and then set light to the page while she watched. She stood at the kitchen worktop making onion bhajis for the children, who would eat them smothered in tomato ketchup. In her frustration, she forgot she was in the middle of chopping chilies and rubbed her eye. Immediately a sensational pain exploded her eyeball. It was enough to make her cry out. She turned on the tap and twisted her head beneath it. To the curative powers of cold running water, the chili burn was immune. Nazneen gasped as the water ran up her nose.

She focused on the pain, rising up to meet it head on, boring into it, challenging it to do its worst. The burn was fierce and it unleashed in her an equal ferocity. Suddenly her entire being lit up with anger. *I will decide what to do. I will say what happens to me. I will be the one.* A charge ran through her body and she cried out again, this time out of sheer exhilaration.

The pain subsided slowly. A shadow of pain remained long into the night. The exhilaration also drained away, leaving only its ghosts behind. *What* would she decide? *What* did she want?

Her first thought was that she would go to Dhaka with her husband and her children. It would be the right thing to do, and she would be with Hasina again. Doubts assailed her on all sides. The children would be miserable. Shahana would never adjust. What would happen to Chanu in Dhaka? If his dreams fell apart, what net would catch them all? How would they live? How would they eat? Would it not be better to stay here and send more money to Hasina and help her that way? Maybe even bring her over here. But if Chanu went ahead and left without them, then what? Would she marry Karim? Did she want to marry him? It would be difficult for the girls. And it would be impossible simply to spurn him. Perhaps it would be best to go to Dhaka.

Unbidden, a memory of Karim came, entering her as he entered her, tearing apart her passive soul.

In the night, while her family slept, she performed wudu and took down the Qur'an. She read from the sura "The Merciful."

He has let loose the two oceans: they meet one another.

Yet between them stands a barrier which they cannot overrun. Which of your Lord's blessings would you deny?

Pearls and corals come from both. Which of your Lord's blessings would you deny?

She thought of her husband, sitting on the sofa that evening, serenely picking his toenails. When he had come home he had kissed her on the forehead and told her, "In all these years, I have never—not once—regretted my choice of bride." She thought of her daughters. What beautiful gifts from God. For once she felt calm. None of her Lord's blessings would she deny. She began to read again.

Mankind and jinn, We shall surely find the time to judge you! Which of your Lord's blessings would you deny?

The March Against the Mullahs was due to take place on October 27. Lion Hearts leaflets began fluttering through the letterbox (Nazneen "used them up" for shopping lists); they littered the courtyard and drifted over the grassy mound of Altab Ali Park.

> All over the country, our children are being taught that Islam is a great religion. But the truth is clear. Islam burns with hatred. It gives birth to evil mass murders abroad. In our own towns, it spawns vicious rioters.

Chanu read each leaflet with care. He remained calm.

Karim became excited. "Man, they are going to live to regret it. They don't even know what they're saying. Islam lays down clear rules of engagement for war. It ain't *permitted* to kill women, children, innocent men, or the elderly. It ain't *permitted* to kill other Muslims. How many Muslims died in New York?" He stood by Nazneen's net curtains and worked his legs as if limbering up for a race, or shaking out a cramp. His mobile phone rang. He looked at it and turned it off and Nazneen knew it was his father.

"They should get their facts straight." He folded his arms and looked beyond Nazneen. In his panjabi pajama, fleece, big boots, and skullcap he looked like he could be on his way to a mosque; or to a fight. "Islamic terrorists. Islamic terrorists. That's all you hear. You never hear Catholic terrorist, do you? Or Hindu terrorist? What about Jewish terrorist?" It seemed that just as Chanu had lost an invisible audience, Karim had gained one. He orated to the assembly. "But let's think about it. . . ."

Nazneen tried to, but she drowned in the sea of his anger. While her husband talked less and less, Karim talked more and more. The more he talked, the less sure he seemed.

"You know that lad who got stabbed?"

"Is he out of hospital?" said Nazneen.

"All these people going around talking about gangs, all they're doing is feeding the racists. The newspapers *love* it. But the truth is there are no gangs."

Nazneen opened her mouth and closed it. Not so long ago, Karim had used the word freely. And what about the boys who came to the meeting, didn't they nearly start a fight there? And every evening they patrolled the estate, "roaming around like goats," as Chanu said.

"It's just a bunch of lads, mucking around, playing up. All right, getting in a bit of trouble. But they're good lads. When we march, they'll show. Support us. When the Bengal Tigers march we're all on the same side. And if there's going to be any trouble we won't be the ones starting it, but we'll *finish* it all right."

September 2001

Allah have release her from suffering. Give thanks to Him the Most Merciful the Most Kind.

Sister I tell you how nice is this Lovely? She have prove her name. I went to her say how is plan for start Charity? She show me fingernails have paint little star on each say do they look all right? I know it meaning the Charity is not yet start. I say what this place have need is Charity for helping childrens catch by acid attack. Name is come to mind Acid Innocents. No hesitate whatsoever she asking name of Monjus boy. Within two three minute she ring newspaper give all details to newsman. Main important detail is Lovely her own self is pay for Khurshed operation.

I tell to Monju. Even face is melt still you see how it change her. She close good eye and rest for while. Almost is too much. Is like give feast to starving man.

When she open eye she say something I cannot hear. I must put ear against mouth. Before I go I must confess. She say this. Something so wrong I done and I never tell to anyone. This is what she say. I look inside the good eye and see she must speak or have no peace.

What she tell me when Khurshed two years old baby is scream and scream many hour and one time she losing all presence of mind and slap hard on legs. She say only week before was operation to leg region. Maybe is she who make leg damage need more further operating. She say this.

Have you ask doctor? I tell her. Have you ask doctor? I shout for her to hear me. No. She did not tell to anyone.

Then I go away and walk around hospital. I come back I put my face to hers and I shout. The doctor has say No. It is not for you but the acid has damage him.

The trouble go out of her eye. I see a bit like the old Monju. She whisper from very small mouth hole nearly close up now. These secret things will kill us. Do you have any secret? You want to tell to me? I keep it safe for you! I think she try for smiling.

Next day I go for telling her newspaper man come make photograph with Lovely. But that day sister my friend is gone.

Chapter Eighteen

A Bengal Tigers meeting was called for Friday, one week and one day before the march. Chanu said, "I think we will go to that meeting."

Nazneen dropped her scissors.

"Yes," said Chanu, "I think it will be interesting."

Nazneen retrieved her scissors and continued unpicking the stitching on a botched jacket lining. "You go. I have to work."

"Very well. But I think you'll find it interesting," said Chanu. He hid himself behind a newspaper.

All night, Nazneen imagined what he could mean. What did her husband intend to do at the meeting? If he knew about Karim (how many times had she willed him to know? He would not yield to her and yet he must know), had he chosen this venue to confront him? But surely he would not do anything in front of all those people? Did he intend to try to humiliate him in some way, challenge him to a public duel of intellects? Did he mean to take her along to humiliate her as well? Perhaps even to stone her, as was his right? What was Chanu going to do? She could think of no plausible answer.

The girls went off to school and Nazneen went with Chanu to the meeting. The preparations compelled her. Chanu donned his suit. It had a little white mark on the jacket collar which he rubbed with a flannel and turned into a bigger mark. The suit, dark blue serge, double-breasted, was old and the fabric had become a touch uncertain around the knees and the elbows. But Chanu had lost weight since the return of his ulcer and the fit was not bad. He could get all of the buttons on the jacket done up, which had never before been possible. He put on a salmon-colored tie belonging to his council days and slipped a packet of Rennies into his trouser pocket. From a folder marked "Speech," he took an A4 Premier Collection refill pad and flicked open the cover. Holding the pad in one hand, he made a sweeping gesture with the other and rocked on his heels. His lips moved but no words came out. After a while, he made a slight bow and closed the notebook. He cleared his throat. "I think we're ready."

She followed a step behind him across the estate and into the concrete valley that cradled the meeting hall. Chanu was eager to get there. To keep up, Nazneen had to trot. By the time they entered the building her heart had overpowered all other internal organs. It beat in her chest, in her stomach, in her ears, and in her head.

The secretary hung around by the doors. A boy in a dark purple tracksuit called to him. "Hey, get on the train of repentance, brother."

The secretary grinned. "It's already passed your station, brother."

They slapped each other on the arms.

The hall was about half full. There was none of the family atmosphere of the previous meeting. Most of those gathered were young men. A handful of girls of similar age clustered at the back of the room and several more in burkha gelled together at the front. The boys on the right-hand side of the aisle had broken the ranks of chairs to form a circle. Within the circle, some were sitting on their chairs, others were standing, and a few had perched with their feet on the seats and their bottoms on the chair backs. At the outer perimeter the boys stood on their chairs. They were listening to someone at the center. Above the general hubbub, Nazneen discerned a speech already in progress. She tried to interpret the voice, to hear Karim's tones within it, but the voice was unfamiliar and it slid away from her.

On the left-hand side, where Nazneen and Chanu took their places, the boys kept glancing over to the other side of the room and shaking their heads. One lad smashed a fist into his other palm and ground it around. Then he flicked his hand like a wet rag and the fingers made a snapping noise. His friends laughed and a finger-flicking tournament began. The boys wore jeans, or tracksuits with big check marks on them as if their clothing had been marked by a teacher who valued, above all else, conformity. A few were in traditional Bengali garb with a twist. Panjabi pajama customized with denim on the leg and sleeve cuffs, or worn with a black leather jacket, or with the trousers tucked into buckled knee-length boots. Only Chanu wore a suit. The elbows were really quite worn. He touched the knot of his tie over and over as if he were afraid it would choke him.

He took his pad out of the folder and turned to the front page. "I'll give you a taste," he said to Nazneen. "This is the title: 'Race and Class in the UK: A Short Thesis on the White Working Class, Race Hate, and Ways to Tackle the Issue.'"

So that was it. He would challenge Karim with words. And prove himself his equal. His better. During these past weeks, in which he had hardly spoken, he had been storing his words, stockpiling them for this battle, honing them for this: the fight to reclaim his wife.

The circle broke up and chairs were scraped back into position. The people on the left looked at the people on the right. Some people got to their feet to get a better look. Then the doors at the back of the hall closed and Karim bounded onto the stage. The secretary skipped on after him, carrying what seemed to be an old mango packing crate. He put the upturned crate on the stage and stood on it. "Order, order, order. I call the meeting to order."

Conversation was extinguished at a leisurely pace.

"Brothers and sisters," said Karim. "It's good to see so many of us—united in our stand against those scummy people who dare to come around here and slander our religion."

"Kick them out," yelled someone from the back.

"Send them back where they came from," shouted another.

Karim folded his arms. "Leave the cheap insults to the racists." He paused and looked over the whole audience, taking his time, making everyone feel his power to do this, to make them wait. "When we march, we'll show them how wrong they are about Islam. They'll see we are strong. And we will show them we are peaceful. That Islam is peace.

"What we need to discuss today is how we are going to spend every hour, minute, and second between now and the twenty-seventh getting people to pledge their support."

A hand shot up in the front row.

"Yes?" said the secretary. From his elevated position on the crate he no longer bounced on his toes. "State your question."

"Can we get a flatbed truck there? Hire one?"

"For people without legs?" said the secretary. "Or the very sick?"

"For a sound system, brother. Or if you like I could set up a keyboard and play live."

"Live music is un-Islamic," said the secretary, raking his beard.

"What?" said the musician. "What about devotional bands? What about all the Sufis? They're always, like, singing and dancing."

"Un-Islamic," said the official, quickly. "Move on."

Someone else spoke up from the audience. "That's why the Taliban banned it."

"What about recorded music?" said the musician.

"That's banned as well."

"Don't we have a spiritual leader here? Let's ask him what the Qur'an has to say."

The spiritual leader was located. The secretary stepped down to confer with him. The spiritual leader had put on a considerable amount of weight in a few months. The little conference on sharia did not interfere with his consumption of a very large, lavishly glazed pastry.

"It's settled," announced the secretary on his return to the stage. "All banned."

"Man!" said the musician.

"Move on. Move on," urged the secretary.

The musician stood up. He still wore his strange fingerless gloves. Maybe he didn't burn himself, thought Nazneen. Maybe he has some kind of skin disease.

"If everyone's going to sit there and tell me I'm un-Islamic, then I ain't staying."

"Sit down," said Karim. "It's all right. We'll talk about music later. Now, I've got a list of the local estates here and I want two organizers for every estate. . . ."

From the corner of the stage, a figure materialized.

Karim hesitated.

"Don't let me stop you," said the Questioner.

"You're not," said Karim.

"I've just got something to show people, when you're finished."

The audience emitted a low noise, like a pan of boiling water.

"Show it, then," Karim ordered.

"Well," said the Questioner. "If you say so." He reached into the lining of his jacket and took out a scroll of papers. He unrolled the sheets, rolled them up the other way, and did his best to make them hang flat. He held them against his chest so that only a blank page showed. "Our chairman is a man of peace. I am also a man of peace. Islam is a peaceful religion. But what do you do if someone comes to fight you? Do you run away?

"A few weeks ago, persons unknown launched an attack on American soil. Innocent people were killed. Civilians. Men, women, and children. The world wept and sent money. Now, America is taking her revenge and our brothers are being killed. Their children die with them. They are not any more or less innocent. But the world does not mourn them."

He turned his sheaf of papers around and held it out, gripping both top and bottom to prevent it from curling. The photograph showed a tiny girl dressed in rags, her leg blown off at the knee. "Some collateral damage," said the Questioner.

He showed the next photo.

"This is a just war." The boy was no more than six or seven.

He rolled the pictures up and put them away. "Our chairman says we must show our strength. What he means is we must walk together down the street. We mustn't do more than that."

"What shall we do, then?" called someone from the audience. The crowd rumbled a bit, as if the last words had been stolen from the tips of their tongues.

The Questioner shrugged. He put his hands in his pockets. "The most powerful nation on this planet attacks one of the most ravaged countries in the world. We are fit young men. There are no chains tying us to these walls. With a little planning, a little effort, we can cross continents." He shrugged again. "What can we do?"

Nazneen looked at Chanu. He had his head bowed. His cheeks hung like empty purses.

The black man, now the multicultural liaison officer, got to his feet. "I been reading up," he began. He blew hard to signify just how much effort this had cost him. "I been reading up, and it seems that being a Muslim brings many heavy responsibilities. Not just the praying, and laying off drinks and laying off bacon and women and laying off every other manner of thing. It also has it written in the Qur'an that every Muslim should work towards one unified Islamic state across the world. It is written, Khilafah is fard." He thumped a huge hand against the snowy expanse of robe that covered his great chest. "Now, what are we all doing about that?"

"Good question, brother," said the Questioner.

Karim stepped in front of him. "Listen to me. Let's not get distracted—"

A couple of seats to the right of Chanu, a girl jumped up and shouted over him. The sharp lines of her hijab emphasized the fine bones of her cheeks. "According to United Nations statistics, there was another big tragedy on September eleventh. On that day thirty-five thousand children also died through hunger." The girl looked straight at Karim as she spoke. Karim folded his arms. He looked straight back at her. The girl was barely out of her teens. She had large, long-lashed eyes, not too close together. The dark headscarf framed her forehead to perfection. "What do we know about this tragedy?" the girl continued. She looked down at the piece of paper in her hand. "Victims: thirty-five thousand. Location: the poorest countries in the world. Special news reports: none. Appeals for the victims and their families: none. Messages from heads of state: none. Candlelight vigils: none. Minutes' silence: none. Calls for the perpetrators to be called to justice . . ." The girl looked up. Her face grew flushed with emotion. "None." She sat down quickly.

Karim let his gaze travel over the audience. He saw Nazneen, and Chanu with his head bent, and for a brief moment his eyebrows knitted together.

Nazneen wondered how he would look at her if she jumped up now and began to make a speech.

"How many were Muslims?" called a voice from the front of the hall. It was a woman's voice, emanating from somewhere in the region of the burkhas. "How many of the thirty-five thousand were Muslims?"

What does it matter? thought Nazneen. Those who were not Muslims, would they be any less dead?

"People, people, let's get around to our business." Karim paced up and down across the front of the stage. His elbow knocked against the Questioner, but Karim appeared not to notice. "Out there, right now, are people who are twisted with hatred for us and for Islam. They are planning to march right on our doorsteps, and we are not going to let them get away with it. Let's show the Lion Hearts that Bangla Town is defended. Tigers will take on Lions any day of the week." He strode over to the secretary and procured a sheet of paper from the clipboard. "Right. The list of estates. We need volunteers for organizers. First one: Berners Estate."

Over on the right-hand side of the aisle, two lads rose to their feet. "That's ours."

Immediately, three boys jumped up on the opposite side of the aisle. "It's ours, and you know it."

"It doesn't belong to you."

"Come here and say that."

"You come here."

The boys regarded each other with distinct and yet lazy menace, as if they knew there was much more in the way of menacing to be done and they did not wish to exhaust themselves.

"In here," said Karim, "and out there, as Bengal Tigers, that's the only group we belong to. Get it? No one owns any estate. Leave everything else out of it. OK?" He looked from one group to the other. "OK, lads?"

Karim assigned people to the estates. He issued instructions for canvassing, targets to be met, reports to be filed, dates for the organizers to convene, plans for stewarding the march itself. He kept up a constant flow of talk, and all the time he talked he moved about the stage, filling it with his personality. Nobody objected to his allocated role. He eased each one into a slot, with a "You'll be good at this, Khaled," or "This is just made for you, Monzur." "The Women's Committee I'm putting in charge of the banners."

Nazneen kept glancing at her husband to see when he would make his move. Chanu did not look at her. His neck curved closer and closer to his body until it appeared he was examining his chest rather than his writing pad. Nazneen moved her legs slightly so that her knee pressed against his. She elicited no response.

For a while, as she watched Karim, she lost track of his words and witnessed only the tension in his body as he traced and retraced a path across the stage.

It was supposed to be her. She was supposed to be the one who could not think about the world, who had a head so filled with herself, her week, her day, her hour, that the big things would not fit. But she looked at Karim now: how absorbed he was in his maneuverings. If the Questioner had talked about the Lion Hearts, Karim would have talked of Afghanistan. If he said black, Karim would say white. And she felt misery rise like steam from Chanu at her side, and knew that he was lost in his own private torment; Race, Class, and Short Theses did not touch him there.

But what was the good of aching for the world if she offered no balm to her own husband?

"Let's go," she said. He did not hear. She pushed her knee against his and his leg swung away from her.

The meeting wound up. Chanu cleared his throat and tucked his speech inside his folder. "Better save this for another day," he said and smiled while his eyes danced on hot coals, darting everywhere and flinching from everything.

"Anyone who is interested in what I was saying, come and see me now," called the Questioner.

A few boys gathered around him. Nazneen saw Sorupa's eldest among them.

"Insh'Allah, we all stand together," shouted Karim as people began to file out of the hall.

But God is not willing, thought Nazneen. Oh, Karim, why do you see only what you want to see?

There was no escaping Mrs. Islam this time. As Nazneen stepped over the threshold of the butcher's shop she practically stood on the great lady's toes.

"Ah, to be young again and walk around in a dream," said Mrs. Islam.

Nazneen inquired as politely as possible after her health.

Mrs. Islam ignored her. "Dreaming of home? But not long to wait now."

The smell of meat was intense. Entering the shop was like wandering into a giant intestine. A huge stack of plucked chickens filled the window. It was a plain old massacre, nothing like the polite displays of cellophaned body parts in the English supermarkets. Behind the high counter the men wore white coats, honestly and decently covered in blood. Inside the counter was every cut of mutton and all the cuts were jumbled together. Sides of beef coated in yellow fat hung from ceiling hooks. At the back, a solitary chill cabinet contained only an empty ice-cream tub, placed there to collect drips when the cabinet was unplugged after a brief and never-to-be-repeated term of service. The chill cabinet never caught on. Nobody wanted to buy meat that had been hidden away in there for who knows how long.

The meaty smell was so thick that when Nazneen opened her mouth it felt like she had licked a raw and fatty chop.

"You are looking very well today, Mrs. Islam," said Nazneen.

Mrs. Islam fumbled in her cardigan sleeve. She took out a pink lace-edged handkerchief and coughed into it. It was the first time Nazneen had heard her cough. Maybe she had run out of Benylin Chesty Coughs.

Mrs. Islam stuffed the handkerchief back into her sleeve. Both sleeves bulged massively, as if she had elephantiasis of the arms.

"I am dying," she snapped. "Perhaps you think it suits me." Her little black eyes glittered and raged.

Nazneen studied her as closely as she dared. It was true that Mrs. Islam seemed a little different today: not in any obvious way, but lacking somehow in substance, as if she had begun to fade out. Nazneen tried to pinpoint it. Had she lost weight?

"So, your husband will have bought the tickets by now," said Mrs. Islam. "Run home and start packing."

"What tickets?"

Without warning, Mrs. Islam grabbed Nazneen by the chin. Her fingers felt crispy, like dried leaves. "Such an honest face. All the better to lie with!"

It occurred to Nazneen that, even at such close quarters, beneath the blood-heavy air she could not smell Mrs. Islam's sickroom smell. This was what she had lost.

"I don't know what you're talking about," said Nazneen. She held Mrs. Islam's hand and gently removed it from her face.

"You don't? Of course, such an innocent creature as Mrs. Ahmed hardly knows a thing. You don't know that your husband went crying to Dr. Azad and Dr. Azad gave him the money to make his escape?" Her breathing became labored. She swayed on her feet and Nazneen had to restrain herself from putting her arms out to steady her. "Dr. Azad is a fool. He will never get his money back. I told him, but who listens to an old woman who has reached the end of her life?"

Nazneen stepped back. The doorway was not far behind. She turned her head to see how close it was. She had an urgent desire to get away from this woman.

Reading her mind, Mrs. Islam snatched Nazneen's hand and rubbed it between her papery fingers. She sweetened her voice as much as possible; it was like mixing chilies with sugar, an inadequate disguise. "I would let you go, my child, give you my money and my blessing—but how would it look to all the others? Let one slip through and they all slip through. I have my sons to think about. Just give what you owe."

"But it's impossible," cried Nazneen. "Whatever we give, it's not enough."

Mrs. Islam let go of Nazneen's hand. "God always provides a way," she said, and smiled humbly as she spoke. "You just have to find it."

Chanu drove until the early hours of the morning but Nazneen was ready for him when he walked through the door.

"Is this true?" she demanded as if she had already laid everything out before him.

"It's a good question," said Chanu. "It is, perhaps, the best of all questions."

"I want to know. . . ."

"Wait then," said Chanu. "Wait a minute. Didn't I just step inside a second ago? I still have my coat on." He tugged at his anorak to ward off denials. "Isn't it fair to say that you hate it when I come inside and forget to take it off? Isn't it fair to say that you would rather suck a cockroach than watch me eat with my coat still on?"

Her mouth became dry. How did he know that? She had been so careful to hide her feelings.

"Yes," said Chanu. "You see, I am not totally blind." He made no move from the hallway. The lightbulb hung over his head. It was a feeble lightbulb, the wrong kind. It didn't get rid of the dark; it swept it into the corners, and into the crevices of Chanu's face.

For a while, Chanu just stood there and Nazneen began to fill up with dread, not at anything he might say or do but at what he saw when he looked at her.

"Is this true?" He weighed each word. "It's a question I like very much. A student of philosophy must inquire all the time: Is this the real nature of the world? But so must a student of physics, of history, of literature even and art, for only art which is true is worthy of the name." He stopped and unzipped his anorak. It immediately slid off the slopes of his shoulders. He picked it up and patted it. "Whenever we are told something, before we receive it into our minds and hearts, we must put it to the test. We open a book, we turn a newspaper page, we allow the television and the radio to come into our homes. All the things we are told every day—are they true?"

She waited for him to continue.

"When the imam speaks, it is not the word of God. Does he speak true? It is easier to believe than not believe. Just think about gossip. The things our mothers told us, that fill our bones like marrow. We learned them before we learned to question.

"All this. All this, and more. Because it is possible for a man to lie to himself. And a woman, too." Chanu looked away from her. He spoke to his coat. "A heart says this and that, it shouts and makes a big scene. But put it to the test and sometimes you will find it out for what it is: a big and hollow noise. When you feel something so strongly that it can't be questioned, you *have* to ask yourself—is this true?"

For a few seconds they remained frozen, unable to end the moment.

Then Chanu rubbed his nose with the palm of his hand and shook his cheeks like a man who has just dipped his head in a bowl of water. "Let's go inside at least, and I'll show you the tickets."

Nazneen examined the sloping red letters of the Biman Airlines logo on the ticket wallet. She ran her fingers over each ticket and was surprised how flimsy they were, how lacking in substance.

"Twenty-seventh of October. Five more days," said Chanu. "There is a lot to do."

"But we will never be ready. What about the flat? We can't just leave it."

"Dr. Azad has come to our aid once more. He has agreed to deal with everything. Rent it out for us, or hand it over to the council—whatever I instruct from Dhaka."

Nazneen moved around the room. She touched the trolley, the corner cabinet, the glass showcase, the dining table, the coffee table, and the bookcase. She stood behind the dung-colored sofa and gripped the top. Her little finger popped through the fabric and into the stuffing.

"But what will you do in Dhaka? How will we live?"

Chanu patted his stomach. "Do you think that my stomach will go long without being fed? When I went to the doctor, I went for medicine, not money. Don't worry. The ulcer will soon be gone and I don't plan to live on water alone. There's nothing to worry about. I am going into the soap business." He cleared his throat prodigiously but there was nothing waiting to get out.

She sat on Razia's windowsill with a big bubble of panic caught in her mouth. Slices of gray sky wedged themselves between the blocks of flats. How small they were. How mean. In Gouripur, when she looked up she saw that the sky reached to the very ends of the earth. Here she could measure it simply by spreading her fingers.

The bubble moved to her chest and lodged just beneath her collarbone. She sat very still. If she moved, the bubble might get into one of her lungs and burst it. A rhythmic knocking came from the bedroom door.

Razia lay on the floor. Her hair, filled with static from the carpet, lifted around her head like a great gray sea anemone.

Nazneen said, "Shall I see what he wants?"

"No," said Razia. "Only one thing he wants."

There were three more days to go. Three more days to take action, if any action was to be taken. Chanu had bought more suitcases. The girls and Nazneen gathered around them as at a graveside.

The knocking grew louder. It became a pounding.

Razia got up. She rubbed her arthritic knees. Approaching the door, she walked against an unseen drag, as if wading in chest-high water.

Nazneen felt the bubble expand. Her collarbone would snap. She breathed carefully.

Razia stooped and examined the iron bar across the bottom of the door. Then she checked the top bar.

Only three more days to go and then all this would pass. She felt the bubble subside a little. Having won this advantage, Nazneen pressed for more. They would get on the plane and go.

An enormous bang shook the door. Tariq must have thrown himself at it.

Now it was quiet. Perhaps he had knocked himself out.

Razia turned around and back again, like a cat about to curl up. Then she lay down on her side and closed her eyes.

And it was right to go with her husband. Chanu was the one who needed her. Children must have a father. There was no choice but to go.

"You think you're doing what's best for your children," said Razia, still with her eyes closed. "But you can never go back and do it a different way and see if that would have been better."

"How long has he been in there?"

"Two days." Razia opened her eyes. "Look at all this space," she said, as if she had just noticed the furniture had gone. "It was his idea—the bars, the locking in. He said, 'Even if I am calling you all the names under the sun, don't let me out until it is finished, OK-Ma?' And I promised him. Son, your OK-Ma will not let you out."

Hasina stood by the pond and shook her hair down over her shoulders. "Come on," she called to Nazneen. "Let's jump." She didn't wait. She never waited. She ran and jumped, disappeared and resurfaced. Her hair streamed behind her, catching little gems of water and sunlight.

Three more days and she could go and find Hasina. She pressed the tips of her fingers together and brought them to her lips. Nazneen tried to conjure an image of her sister that did not belong to yesterday. She tried to see her as a woman with all the scars of her life. All she could see was a girl with pomegranate-pink lips, a face that made your breath catch, and a flick of her shoulders that said she would not wait.

"Ma! Ma!" Tariq sounded like someone who had made an exciting discovery and wished to share it.

Razia, who was scratching her thigh, stayed her hand.

"Come and talk to me, Ma. It's boring in here."

"What is it?" said Razia, unwilling to be drawn.

"Just come near to me. I don't want to shout."

"I can hear you very well. No need for shouting."

Tariq was quiet.

She would not say goodbye to Karim. He was busy with the march. If she was lucky he would not come again. When he did come it would be too late. She imagined him knocking at the flat, then pounding the door, finally breaking it with his shoulder. He raged and he wept. Nazneen gave Razia a rueful little smile.

"Hey, Ma, listen. I'm feeling a lot better. Really a lot better."

"Good," said Razia.

"It's all down to you, Ma. I think we've done it now. I think we've cracked it."

"Good," said Razia.

"Honestly, honestly, honestly, I could walk out of here now and never touch the stuff again."

"Good," said Razia.

"Ma? Why don't you just open up the door for a minute and we'll have a nice cup of tea, you and me."

"No," said Razia.

"It's all right. I'll go back in my room afterwards. I don't want to take any risks."

"I promised you," said Razia.

"Yeah, Ma. Look, you've done really well. I couldn't have done it without you. Now just open the door."

Razia drew her legs up so her knees touched her face. She wrapped her arms around them.

Would he find solace, thought Nazneen, with someone else? She pictured Karim falling into a girl's arms and burying his face inside her bosom. Who would it be? She tried to give the girl a face. Perhaps it would be the girl from the meeting, the one who knew everything about the thirty-five thousand children who would never have justice done in their names. She was the kind of girl that Karim *ought* to be with.

Behind the door, Tariq whistled softly as if he had just woken to a bright and beautiful dawn.

Karim kissed his new girl.

Tariq whistled louder.

Karim began to unwind the sari.

Nazneen jumped up and turned to face the window. Karim wrapped the sari around the girl's shoulders and draped it over her head. That was better.

The whistling dropped any pretense of a tune. It became demented.

A thousand thoughts crushed into Nazneen's skull. Dhaka would be a disaster. Shahana would never forgive her. Chanu would be finished. It was not even going home. She had never been there. Hasina was in Dhaka, but the city of her letters was an ugly place, full of dangers. And there was Karim. If she could leave him so easily, if it was as easy as that, then why did she ever begin it?

"Open the door, you bitch!"

Razia held on to her legs.

"Ma! Ma! I'm dying."

The panic in Tariq's voice made Nazneen's heart thump.

"Aah, aah, it's these cramps. Let me out and rub my leg. It's killing me."

By the light of day, and by the dark of night, your Lord has not forsaken you, nor does He abhor you.

The life to come holds a richer prize for you than this present life. You shall be gratified with what your Lord will give you.

"Ma, I've been sick in the bin. The bucket is full and it stinks. Let me out to empty it."

Nazneen clung to her lifeline. What would be would be. It was not of her making.

"Are you there? Can you hear me?" Tariq talked fast, the words running into each other like raindrops down a windowpane. "I think we're rushing it. It's not good. It's not right. It means I might have a relapse. I just need a little fix now. Let me out for an hour. I'll be back in an hour and I'll be a lot stronger then. Just let me out. Come on, Ma, let me out."

It was not of her making. It was not of her making.

"One five-pound wrap," screamed Tariq. "That's all I need. You bitch."

For a few moments all was quiet. Then Tariq began to cry.

She stood in the kitchen with Razia and sipped a cup of tea. The walls were tiled, blue and green squares right up to the ceiling. A narrow tabletop, painted white, was squeezed in between the fridge and the door. Razia called it a "breakfast bar" and lined up cereal packets like ceremonial soldiers along the back. When her husband was alive, when the flat was filled with junk, every spare pound (and many that were not spare at all) went back home to buy another brick for the new mosque. After he died, Razia spent her money on her children, and on her flat. She never talked about going home. "Tell me this," she said with her oblique smile. "If everything back home is so damn wonderful, what are all these crazy people doing queuing up for a visa?" And she would get out her new British passport and bend it between thumb and forefinger.

Nazneen perched on a stool at the breakfast bar. The seat was molded plastic, two parted indentations to fit the buttocks. She wondered how much it would cost to put little tiles all over her kitchen.

"So," said Razia. "You are leaving your old friend."

"Dr. Azad lent some money, and Chanu had some saved up."

"Have you told the boy?"

Nazneen gazed at Razia and mouthed the word *no.* She looked down at her tea. Tears gathered in the corners of her eyes and escaped down the bridge of her nose.

"Come on. Tell me. Take my mind off—other things."

So Nazneen began the conversation she had already rehearsed by herself, and still she played both parts. Razia, who had not learned her lines, stayed quiet.

"He lifts me up inside. It's the difference between . . ." She cast around. "I don't know. It's like you're watching the television in black and white and someone comes along and switches on the colors."

Razia said, "Mmm."

"And then they pull you right inside the screen, so you're not watching anymore, you're part of it."

"Mmm," said Razia again.

Nazneen thought about what she had said. She was pleased. It was not an easy thing to describe.

"Is called *in love,* no?" said Razia.

Nazneen sighed. "It is too difficult. It is ridiculous."

"But you want this?"

"Everything goes against it. Family, duty, everything."

Razia rolled her big bony shoulders. She was tired. Even her shoulders were too heavy for her today. *"In love,"* she said. "It is the English style."

Nazneen lost a sandal and slid off the stool to retrieve it. She felt her friend looking at her but she would not return the look. How irritating Razia could be sometimes! Who was it who made herself so English, anyway? With her British passport and tracksuit and Union Jack sweatshirt. Who was the one almost getting like the queen herself? She would not ask for Razia's opinion now. She would do as she pleased.

A knock came at the front door.

"It will be the doctor," said Razia, "come to give Tariq his medicine." Razia let the doctor in. He had come with a helper, deployed just outside the bedroom door to discourage any idea of escape. Razia went to and fro, emptying slops, throwing away food that looked untouched and replacing it with fresh.

Nazneen sat on the stool in the kitchen and watched a pigeon walk the window ledge. The pigeon stood on the brink, ducked its head, and walked back along the ledge.

Dr. Azad entered the kitchen. "Ah, good, good," he said. He found a glass and filled it with water.

She should show her gratitude, for the money. "How is the boy?" she said.

"There is a lot of pain for him," said the doctor. "A lot, a lot of pain."

"Will he get better?"

"Maybe. If that's what he decides."

He drank the water down quickly and refilled the glass. Then he pulled something out of his suit pocket. "I brought this for Tariq. I'll go and give it to him now." But the doctor did not move. He shook up the snowstorm and watched the tiny blizzard whip around miniature castle turrets. He tapped the blue glass dome. "It's calming, don't you think?" Another shake. "Watching everything settle back down."

Nazneen assented.

"You know, actually my wife gave me this particular one." The corners of his mouth turned down and his eyebrows lifted into his peculiar smile and met his thick black fringe. "Back in the early days, we used to give each other gifts, only little things like this because money was scarce. We lived on rice and dal, rice and dal. But my wife told you that. We lived on a cup of rice, a bowl of dal, and the love we did not measure." The doctor drank his second glass of water. He checked his cuffs and ensured they were perfectly aligned, peeping virginally from his jacket sleeves. Nazneen thought, he will not continue. He would like to swallow his words with the water. But the doctor had gone too far to stop now. "We thought that the love would never run out. It was like a magic rice sack that you could keep scooping into and never get to the bottom." He let the snowstorm tip between his fingers and dangle upside down. "It was a 'love' marriage, you see." The puffy gray skin around his eyes seemed to grow, as if he had shed tears on the inside. "What I did not know—I was a young man—is that there are two kinds of love. The kind that starts off big and slowly wears away, that seems you can never use it up and then one day is finished. And the kind that you don't notice at first, but which adds a little bit to itself every day, like an oyster makes a pearl, grain by grain, a jewel from the sand." He put the snowstorm back in his pocket. He rinsed his glass and stood it upside down on the draining board. Then he wiped his hands and inspected his fingernails. "Yes, well, I will see the patient, and then I have a lunch to attend. Good, ah, good."

He clicked his heels together as if in salute and made to leave. At the door, he turned. "All the little irritations," he said. "Who would think they could add up to anything?"

Nazneen dreamed of Gouripur. She sat cross-legged on a choki and Amma sat behind her and plaited her hair. Hands that smelled of garlic and ginger tugged at her hair and lifted her scalp till it pinched.

"When you were born, I put you to my breast and you did not feed."

She loved to hear the story. But a part of her was guilty. From the day she was born she had caused trouble.

"How many days, Amma?"

"Many, many days." Amma tied a ribbon at the end of one plait. "You looked like a chick fallen out of the nest."

"Then what happened?"

Amma sucked on her teeth. "Everyone came to look and advise. Take the child to a hospital, they said, or she will be dead by morning." She began on the second plait, dividing the hair in three, yanking so hard that Nazneen put her head back. Amma pushed her head straight again. "What could I do? I am only a woman and everyone was against me. But I told them, 'No, I will leave the child alone. If she is meant to die, then it is already done. If she is meant to live, then the doctors will only mess it up.' When they saw that I was firm, they went away."

Amma worked on the plait. The pinches on Nazneen's skull stung like ant bites.

"And so I was left to my Fate," said Nazneen. This was the part she liked. It sounded so important.

"And so you were left to your Fate," said Amma. "And that is why you are here with me now."

"What shall I do now, Amma? Amma?" Nazneen turned around. There was no one there. A black dog loped across the courtyard. She decided to go and look for her mother and began to uncross her legs. As soon as she moved, the smooth wood of the choki turned to glue and stuck to her thighs. She tried to free herself but sticky tendrils lashed around her legs. In her struggle she overbalanced and ended on her back. Thick fronds whipped around her stomach and arms, warm and wet as mucus and tough as vines. She tried to move her arms but they were locked against her sides. She bucked her body but the more she struggled the more the fronds lashed at her until they covered her chest, her neck, her face. She tried to cry out but her mouth was filled with sticky fibers that bore into her throat and down and down.

Nazneen woke up and felt the wet on the pillowcase. Was it possible to cry in your sleep?

She went through to the sitting room and sat at the sewing machine. She rested her head on the cool plastic.

"What shall I do now, Amma?" she said out loud.

Amma walked through the door wearing her best sari. Her Dhaka sari, in green and gold. "You modern girls. You'll do what you like." She had kohl around her eyes and her thick gold necklace that weighed as much as a baby. "But you should remember one thing, at least."

"What's that?" Nazneen closed her eyes. Now that Amma had come, she wanted her to go away again.

There was no reply.

Nazneen opened her eyes.

"That's better," said Amma, and she smiled with her hand over her mouth. "Your son. You seem to have forgotten him."

"No. Not forgotten."

"All those things you said to yourself, I heard every one of them."

"What things?"

"Oh! Oh!" cried Amma, so loudly that Nazneen feared the girls would wake. "She has forgotten. This woman, who calls herself a mother, has forgotten."

"Where are you going?" said Nazneen suddenly. "Why are you dressed up?"

Amma tilted her head. "I don't think that is really any of your business. Now let me remind you of a few things. When your son, your true blessing from God, was lying in that hospital I heard every word you said."

"You already told me that," said Nazneen, and marveled at the casual way she spoke to her dead mother.

"Don't think I wasn't watching you," Amma snapped. A little ooze of red ran out of the corner of her mouth. Still a secret pan chewer, thought

Nazneen. "You thought it was you who had the power. You thought you would keep him alive. You decided you would be the one to choose." She began to spit the words out and drops of red flew with them. "When you stood between your son and his Fate, you robbed him of any chance." Amma walked towards her. She held her hands over her chest. The red spurted from between them. "Now say this to yourself, and say it out loud, 'I killed my son. I killed my son.'"

"No!" screamed Nazneen.

"Say it. Say it."

"No. No. No!"

Chanu's face hovered over her, loose with gravity and tense with worry. "Just a dream," he said. "Wake up and tell it to me. When you chase it with words it will run away."

Chapter Nineteen

DHANMONDI, DHAKA

October 2001

Sister I do not know which way to go. Now I have unquiet mind. It do not leave alone but must give question at all and every time. Morning time children play in hallway. Little Jimmy push car inch and inch along tiles to door. Inch and inch he push it back. Then he begin again. Baby Daisy roll ball down two stair. Pick it up and roll. I dusting all glass frame photo hang on wall. These photo Lovely lean on tree Lovely lie on couch Lovely blow kiss Lovely look shock fingers spreading out. Children whole body mind both inside the game. I wish was same for me wipe the glass. How long I stay here? Big house it good house. But one room house feel big if belong in fact to you.

Amma always say we are women what can we do? If she here now I know what she say I know it too well. But I am not like her. Waiting around. Suffering around. She wrong. So many ways. At the end only she act. She who think all path is closed for her. She take the only one forbidden.

Forgive me sister I must tell you now this secret so long held inside me.

You remember in our house the store hut how it build with tin roof and bamboo wall squash shape like two big arm hug it tight? But how you forget? It there Mumtaz auntie find her. I see so clear the day. Sky is red and purple hang down on us. We wait for rain so late that year. I have new shoe black leather shine bright as buckle. I in love for those shoe. Amma say they for best but I cannot keep my foot from out those shoe. I walk around look down all the times. Every few step I bend down and put the dust off. Then I start game with the chickens and I forget the shoe. I try to make the chickens fly but they too hot and fat and lazy. Like better the cooking pot to stretch the wing. I make some special insults for them and then I see how brown and scratchy the shoe have come. I sit down and spit the leather. Then I see her. Amma have Dhaka sari on. I want to run to her and call Hai, Amma where it is you going? But I worry for the shoe. If she see them I getting red stripes on back the leg.

I follow her but I keep from sight. She walk very quick and she not looking around only in front the nose. We go past Mumtaz auntie ghar. I remember I scrape the side of shoe on wall. I want clay to stick on side. I think to make the toe look less bad. Amma go past kitchen. No one is there. She go into store room. One two moment I stand outside. Then I go in stand behind the kalshis they stack tall up near to ceiling. You remember those kalshis how beautiful each one paint with flower?

I am bandit stand there rob her secret.

She take spear and test on the finger. She take another and put it back. And third one she take before is happy. When she move the rice sacks she grunt a bit but she never look around. Another sack I think is chickpea but inside the light is weak and I never go again to look.

I think then maybe Amma not go out anywhere but someone is coming for visit today is why she have put on fineries. I dont know why but I run away then. Is it that she look around? Is it just I get bored? I go back to chickens or I go to find you. I dont remember. But I go away from her then.

May Allah forgive her. It she who leave.

May Allah show His Mercy onto her. She see no other way.

Sister I sitting in my electric light room write to you and I asking Him to put light in my heart so I see more clear the ways.

Chapter Twenty

The paper was pale blue and light as a baby's breath. Nazneen looked at the outline of her fingers beneath the letter. She held her hand open, flat. Hasina's letter lifted at the ends, cleaving to its folds. Breathless, she watched it flicker and held it by her fascination alone, like a butterfly that alights from nowhere and, weightless, displaces the world.

Nazneen curled her fingers. She pinched along the creases and clapped the letter between her palms. There was no escape. Turning the letter deftly between the heel of one hand and the hollow of the other, she worked it around and around. Then she tucked it into the drawstrings of her underskirt at the place where she had pleated her sari.

The plane left tomorrow and she would not be on it. She opened a drawer, took out a pile of Bibi's undershirts and pants, and put them into a suitcase. From the cupboard she pulled down an armful of salwaar kameez and flung them on top. It would not do. She knelt down and began to disengage the metal hangers. Down on the floor she looked at the shelves beneath the girls' desks. The books were tumbled and askew, and the corners dented by feet. She looked up at the wallpaper, shyly turning in on itself. Nothing would stick to those walls. They would have to be scraped clean and begun afresh. Three, four, five, six kameez folded. What else to pack?

She stood by Shahana's desk. A cracked mug bearing a picture of a thatch-roofed cottage and a mouse in trousers leaning on the gatepost. It was a picture of England. Roses around the door. Nazneen had never seen this England but now, idly, the idea formed that she would visit it. The mug held pens, a gnawed ruler, hairclips, and two lipsticks. Nazneen pulled the lid off a lipstick and it gave way with a satisfying pop. On the back of her hand, the color showed like dried blood. She saw Shahana's pink mouth turn to black.

She recapped the lipstick and put it back in the mug. There was a lot to be done. It would look best, she had decided, if most of the packing was finished by this evening. Or Chanu would find a way to make her change her mind. The children were distorted with anxiety, but she could not help it. Not yet. When they left for school—for the last time, as far as they knew—Shahana had stamped on her foot. "Be careful," said Nazneen, swallowing a scream.

"I hope it's broken," said Shahana. She cracked her thumb joint.

Bibi ducked away, and dodged a kiss. She did her own plaits before Nazneen had even risen. They were tight and straight and without need of a mother's hands.

Nazneen worked quickly. The clothes went into the suitcases with room to spare. The gaps made everything more unhappy and she rearranged until they disappeared. Then she fished the books from beneath the desks and piled them into boxes. How little time it took. Nazneen left the room without looking around.

The rest of the packing could wait awhile. There was something she had to do now. The sitting room was half packed. The computer sat inside an old nappy box. A pink-and-white baby reached its little fist out from the side. Brown cardboard boxes, full of Chanu's papers and files, were stacked up on the trolley. The door of the corner cabinet was open and the only thing inside was yellowing newspaper, lining the shelves. What had been in there? When was the last time she had opened it? Inside the glass showcase the pottery tigers, lions, and elephants still roamed freely, hampered only by dust and lack of will. The shelves had been cleared of books. Only the Qur'an floated above on its special ledge. Nazneen went to the trolley and opened up one of the brown boxes. She searched through, looking for Chanu's address book. She knew the name of the street where Mrs. Islam lived. She knew the house by sight, but she did not know the number.

For some reason, it was impossible to go out on her mission without arming herself with this knowledge. She wished she had something else to take with her. A piece of paper, a letter with official stamps and powerfully illegible signatures, an amulet to hang around her neck. She felt the letter at her hip, and removed it to the table. Then she lifted a corner of the sewing machine and slipped it beneath the flat metal.

There was somebody at the door. Nazneen touched her hair: the temples, across the forehead, the crown, and the bun at her nape. She went to the hallway and caught the cloying smell of medicine and the high lift of mints.

"I was on my way to see you," Nazneen told Mrs. Islam.

It was impossible for Mrs. Islam's face to register surprise. Her eyebrows lifted but they could say nothing more than "I disapprove."

"Indeed?" Mrs. Islam rolled into the hallway, massaging the top of her thigh. Two wide shapes swung into view and overlapped in the doorway, like a pair of ill-fitting double doors. "What are you dawdling around there for? Get along now, for the love of God." She didn't bother to look over her shoulder. Her sons walked behind her, one toting the black bag, the other clutching a can of Ralgex Heat Spray.

Nazneen went to make tea. All but two of the mugs were packed. While the kettle boiled she pinched the air out of bubbles in the plastic wrapping.

When she returned to the sitting room, Mrs. Islam was lying on the sofa, feet on one armrest, head on the other.

"Not long now." Her voice was small but still sharp around the edges.

"Tomorrow," said Nazneen.

"Tomorrow?" snapped Mrs. Islam. "I don't have long, but I can assure you I will live out this day and the next." She snorted. "God willing," she added.

"What I thought you meant . . ."

"Yes, yes. What you thought I meant. I know. But how is it that young people these days never listen to their elders?"

Son Number One and Son Number Two stood behind the sofa. Son Number One wore a round-necked peach sweater and a collar of chest hair. The distance between his nostrils and his upper lip was unusually small. As a result he appeared constantly offended. He looked like he was making up insults. And failing. By contrast, his brother looked like a genius. He had a politician's face: alert, eager, sensitive, cunning. His eyes twinkled with a love of his fellow man, and his mouth was a cast of sympathy. How galling it must be for Mrs. Islam. How often did she look at Son Number Two, let hope triumph over experience, and expect from him what his face so patently promised?

Mrs. Islam regarded her sons. She closed her eyes.

Nazneen poured tea.

Upstairs the television was on. An audience applauded. Two faint pings, some mumbling, more applause.

"I have brought something for the girls," said Mrs. Islam. She opened her eyes and fluttered her hand at Son Number One.

Son Number One opened the big black bag. "They're here." He closed the bag.

His mother mouthed some terrible and soundless curse. She pushed her hand against her forehead.

"Make her give the money first." Son Number One's mouth appeared to brush his nose as he spoke.

"Idiot! Stupid! Imbecile!" Mrs. Islam blew the words from her mouth like poison darts. "First you must get a brain, *then* you can use it." She began to cough. Each cough lifted her feet off the armrest.

Son Number One looked straight ahead, his face as immobile as his brain.

Son Number Two seized the medicine bag. He fished out two little brown-glass bottles with white prescription labels. Mrs. Islam took the pills and chewed them slowly. Her teeth clacked together. She washed down the bitter powders with a swig of Benylin Chesty Coughs.

"The girls," she said to Son Number Two.

Son Number Two drew two sets of ankle bells from his mother's bag. He shook them next to one ear and then the other.

Mrs. Islam gave him a look.

"Just a small thing. A gift between friends." She spoke in short gasps and held her chest as though that would stop it heaving. "How are the girls? Don't tell me. They don't want to go. I know how it is. Giving you plenty of worry. And it never stops." She gave birth to a long-gestated sigh. "Believe me, it never stops."

Nazneen said, "I was coming to see you."

But Mrs. Islam was still circling her own thought. Her hair was coming loose as it rubbed on the sofa. It was tied in a loose white bundle. The hair looked so dry it was a wonder it did not simply crumble.

"You'll miss the march, then," said Son Number Two. He turned his intelligent face to Nazneen.

"Yes. The flight is later, but yes." Nazneen looked around. "So much to do."

"We'll be there," said Son Number One. "It's going to be good."

"I reckon," said Son Number Two. He wagged his finger and looked sure to produce some insight of stunning acuity. "It's going to be a laugh."

"Laugh? I'll tell you what's funny." Mrs. Islam lifted her head and propped herself on her elbows. "All our boys going around, march, march, march. They have nothing better to do. Who is going to go and march against them? One or two troublemakers sticking dirty leaflets through our door. Why not catch them and give them a good once-for-all beating? Why go to all this bother, march, march, march. I will tell you something now." She paused awhile. "I will tell you something. Not more than ten white people will turn up tomorrow. Not more than ten."

She rested her head again. Nazneen could hear her breathe. Each breath came so unwillingly, how many more could come? How brave it will be, thought Nazneen, to stand up to this dying woman.

"I'll tell you something else," said Mrs. Islam, speaking to the ceiling. "The rest will not come because they are too busy. When there is money to be made, why should they care about anything else? No. They will not come because they are not afraid. They have no respect for us. How can they fear us?"

She began to rub her hip and Son Number Two, proving no slouch, handed her the Ralgex. Mrs. Islam sprayed her sari indiscriminately.

"Now, if we had money," she went on, "then you would see the difference. The block off Adler Street, the council sold it off. Do you know how many flats inside there now? Eight! Each one the size of a cricket pitch. Only one or two people living in each flat. How are they going to respect us, living ten to one room? They will not march. It is too much trouble. If they want us out of here, they can buy us out."

Son Number One said, "Not *us* though, eh? We'll buy them out first."

Mrs. Islam pulled a handkerchief from her sleeve and spat into it.

Son Number Two said, "Didn't she tell you to keep quiet?"

Nazneen looked at the brothers. There was a rumor that they owned a pub in Stepney. There was another rumor that on Sunday mornings a woman danced in the pub and took all her clothes off. It was said that this was an English tradition. That the men went to the pub on Sunday morning, sent by wives who wanted to cook and clean while the husbands were out of the way, looking at another woman's breasts. Son Number One pushed his lips farther up his face, working really hard on an insult. There was a rumor that Son Number One had a white girlfriend and two buttermilk children. There was a rumor that Son Number Two had been in prison for assault, or fraud, or both.

Rumor surrounded them but it did not touch them.

"Two hundred pounds, to settle the debt," said Mrs. Islam, still talking to the ceiling.

Footsteps traced the length of the room above.

The only thing that people did not talk about was this: the money-lending.

Son Number Two came out from behind the sofa. He stood by the showcase with his hands behind his back.

"How much did my husband borrow?"

"What?" said Mrs. Islam as faintly as she could. "Oh, two hundred will settle it."

Nazneen looked down at her hands. "Because I worked it out. And unless I made a mistake, then we've paid it all back."

Mrs. Islam's breath rattled the windowpanes. She coughed so much that her shoulders and her feet lifted and she sort of folded in the middle. "Whenever God decides, I am ready," she rasped.

"We paid it all back, and some more as well."

"I am an old woman now. Do as you like. The money is for the madrassa, but what does it matter to you? I am an old woman now." Mrs. Islam took a spotted handkerchief from her stores and dabbed it over her face.

The sound of breaking glass shot like iced water down Nazneen's spine. She looked up.

"You're upsetting my mother," said Son Number Two. "When she gets upset, I get upset. Sometimes I break things."

The top of the showcase was caved in. A little cloud of glass dust showered the pottery figures.

"Sometimes I break things as well," said Son Number One.

Mrs. Islam panted. She motioned to Nazneen to get moving. "Quick. Two hundred pounds and settle it."

Nazneen's blood thickened. Her heart strained to push it around her body. "No."

Son Number Two had conjured a cricket bat from somewhere. As he lifted it over his head, Nazneen wondered if it had been inside the black bag.

The bat came down on the showcase and smashed through two shelves. The noise was terrific. Son Number Two turned around. He had flecks of blood on his cheek, glassed by splinters. His expression was both analytical and concerned, and entirely pleasant.

"Wooo!" said Son Number One. He tickled his chest hairs and tried to tuck them down his sweater.

"We paid what we owed," said Nazneen. Her voice clogged up her ears. "We paid at least three hundred pounds on top of that. I am not going to pay any more . . ." She hesitated. "Any more *riba*."

"You bitch," said Son Number One. "Should I make her pay?" He looked at his mother with great hope in his little eyes.

"Riba," whispered Mrs. Islam. *"Riba,* she says." Her head lolled

around as if the word had given her fever. "Do you think, before God, that I would charge interest? Am I a moneylender? A usurer? Is this how I am repaid for helping a friend in need?"

"No?" said Nazneen. She thought she might be shouting, but she really could not help it. "Not interest? Not a usurer? Let's see then. Swear it." She ran across to where the Book was kept. Glass crunched beneath her sandals. "Swear on the Qur'an. And I'll give you the two hundred."

Mrs. Islam was perfectly still. Nazneen listened for her breath, but all she could hear was her own.

Son Number One stirred. "I'm going to break . . ."

"My arm," shouted Nazneen. "Break my arm. Break them both." She held her arms out, until she began to feel foolish.

Slowly, Mrs. Islam swung her feet down and sat up on the sofa. Her hair had been dragged apart and it hung in thick swaths around her neck. She glared at Nazneen with her hot-coal eyes. Nazneen took it and she turned it around. A minute passed. The television crowd applauded with muffled enthusiasm. Music came and went, and the lunatic scramble of advertisements. Mrs. Islam stood up.

"There are some things a wife does not want a husband to know."

Nazneen burned. She did not look away.

"Fresh start," said Mrs. Islam. "New life, back home. You don't want anything to spoil it."

"My husband," said Nazneen slowly, "knows everything. He'll come soon. Why don't you ask him?"

The impossible happened. Mrs. Islam looked surprised.

Nazneen, strengthened, said, "Swear on the Qur'an. That's all you have to do."

Mrs. Islam picked up the ankle bells from the back of the sofa. She placed them on the coffee table. "For the girls," she said.

She walked over to Son Number Two and picked up her bag.

Son Number Two nodded, as if everything had happened just as he expected.

"Let's go," he said. "They paid too much anyway." He gave a good-natured laugh.

Mrs. Islam let out a cry, a low animal noise of despair. With both hands she raised her medicine bag and swung it at her son's shoulder. It bounced off. She swung at his head and missed. She made another cry; shrill this time, as if she had been cut. Son Number Two moved leisurely towards the door. He put his hands up to shield his head. Mrs. Islam followed. As she passed, Nazneen saw the tears flood her eyes and pour down her cheeks. She wielded the bag once more and struck Son Number Two on the back. She made a sound in the back of her throat that Nazneen remembered for days.

Son Number One was still at his station behind the sofa. He looked around, trying to decide something. Then he walked over to the ruins of the showcase and leveled a kick at the one remaining door. The door twanged and vibrated and came to rest intact. Son Number One shrugged. With the tip of his shoe he toppled a few boxes, and then he left.

Nazneen fetched the dustpan and brush. She wrapped the large pieces of glass in newspaper and began to sweep up the rest. Nothing at all came to her mind. As she squatted in the debris, everything inside was peaceful. She stopped working and slipped into the moment like a hot bath. Gradually, a thought began to form. God provided a way. Nazneen smiled. God provided a way, and I found it.

She walked down Brick Lane to get to the tube station at Whitechapel. Days of the Raj restaurant had a new statue in the window: Ganesh seated against a rising sun, his trunk curling playfully on his breast. The Lancer already displayed Radha-Krishna; Popadum went with Saraswati; and Sweet Lassi covered all the options with a black-tongued, evil-eyed Kali and a torpid soapstone Buddha. "Hindus?" said Nazneen when the trend first started. "Here?"

Chanu patted his stomach. "Not Hindus. Marketing. Biggest god of all." The white people liked to see the gods. "For authenticity," said Chanu.

Outside the station a little lad, maybe ten or twelve years old, walked back and forth across the entrance. He had headphones around his neck and springs in his heels. A boy came galloping up the steps and banged into him.

"Watch it," said the little lad.

"You all right? Didn't see you there." The boy was older; old enough perhaps that he called himself a man.

"Clear off," said the small one. "Or else."

"Or else?" The boy was amused. "Or else what, little brother?"

"You fucking-bloody-bastard," said the lad calmly.

The boy raised his hands, smiling. He shook his head. "Shouldn't you be at school?"

No answer. The little brother put his headphones on.

The boy began to walk away, still shaking his head.

"Don't come around here again," the little one shouted. "If I see you again, you're dead."

Nazneen reached the entrance. She stopped in front of the little brother and pulled off his headphones. "Fanu Rahman! Does your mother know where you are? Get yourself off to school this second."

As she bought her ticket, she wondered what she should tell Nazma about her fifth and most precious son. Then she remembered that Nazma was not speaking to her.

There were two other people on the platform. Nazneen stood close to the edge, watching the mice twitch in and out of the tracks and looking out for the eye of the train in the black tunnel. She willed the train to come. Two hours ago, she had dialed his number and felt her skin prickle at the sound of his voice. Since then, she wanted to knock down walls, banish distance, abolish time, to get to him. What she had to say to him could not wait. The electronic notice board said four minutes until the next train. Then it blinked and added another couple of minutes.

Somebody passed behind her on the platform. She turned around. A young woman in high-heeled boots and jeans, a denim jacket pegged on her fingers and slung over her shoulder, stalked towards the free bench. Her footsteps rang like declarations.

Nazneen fell in line behind her. The way the woman walked was fascinating. Nazneen watched her and stepped as she stepped. How much could it say? One step in front of the other. Could it say, *I am this* and *I am not this*? Could a walk tell lies? Could it change you?

The woman reached the bench. Nazneen almost collided with her. "Sorry," said the woman. "Sorry," said Nazneen. They both sat down.

The train took her to King's Cross. She had to change to the Piccadilly Line. Karim had explained it all. She got lost and walked for miles through tunnels and up steps and down escalators, across ticket halls, past shops and barriers, and through more tunnels. A couple of times she was close to tears. She challenged the tears to come and they backed down. Eventually, she found the platform and entered the train. By the time she sat down she was sweating. She tried to think about what she would say to Karim. The urgency inside her began to fade. Only three more stations to go. There was not enough time.

A picture of him came into her mind. Karim in his jeans and trainers, sitting at her table, bouncing his leg. Karim with a magazine, feeding her slices of the world. Karim in his white shirt, rubbing his smooth jaw, telling her all the things that lay hidden just outside her window. He always knew. He knew about the world and his place in the world. That was how she liked to remember him.

It was never so. Apart from where it mattered, in her head. He was who he was. Question and answer. The same as her. Maybe not even that. Karim had never even been to Bangladesh. Nazneen felt a stab of pity. Karim was born a foreigner. When he spoke in Bengali, he stammered. Why had it puzzled her? She saw only what she wanted to see. Karim did not have his place in the world. That was why he defended it.

At Covent Garden the carriage emptied. Nazneen rode in the lift. She saw Karim across the street immediately she came out. He waited by a clothes shop, as they had arranged. She did not pass the barrier but stood to the side and watched. A burger van greased the air with fatty smells. Cars jammed the road and people weaved in and out. On a plinth, a man who seemed to have been dipped in white paint stood still as a rock while a child poked his leg and was pulled away by her mother. A gaggle of girls walked with their arms folded beneath their breasts, clutching their purses and cackling at each other. As they walked they knocked shoulders, a friendship ritual. Two men came out of a pub and made a show of tucking their shirts into their trousers, trying to get back into shape after a long lunch. Nazneen watched Karim watching the people. He leaned against a strip of wall between two shop windows and rested a foot up against the brickwork. Behind the plate glass white lights heated the faceless mannequins. It had rained, and the slick brown pavements bore a liquid print of the light inside and carried it down to the gutter.

People passed in front of Karim. The street was busy. All day long, people passed each other. Nobody spared a glance for the boy in the panjabi pajama and expensive brown fleece. Karim bounced his leg. He looked at his watch. She had seen what she wanted to see. She had looked at him and seen only his possibilities. Now she looked again and saw that the disappointments of his life, which would shape him, had yet to happen. It gave her pain. She almost changed her mind.

"What is it?" he said, as soon as she came near. "I've got about one thousand things to do."

"Let's walk." He still smelled of limes. It made saliva come into her mouth. It made her feel that before she had been sleepy, and now she was awake.

They went towards the market and turned right into the square. A juggler collected his batons from the ground while a small group of Japanese clapped in a half-hearted way.

"Shall we watch?" said Nazneen. It occurred to her that they could have done this before.

"Are you going to tell me?"

"Yes," she said. But she looked ahead, and said nothing more. It had been Karim's idea to meet here when she said she had to see him. Chanu was going to be at home. "We'll have to go out of the village," Karim had said. He sounded almost like her husband.

"Well." He looked at his watch. He pulled his phone out of his pocket and looked at that. "I've got to go now." He began to turn.

She put her hand on his arm. He did not pull free but his arm was tense against her hand, as if he meant to move.

"My husband bought the tickets. The flight is tomorrow."

His arm went slack. She took her hand away.

"All right," said Karim. He watched the juggler. The juggler threw gold hoops in the air. Every few seconds he caught one around his neck and his assistant passed him another.

"But I am not going," said Nazneen. It occurred to her that *she* could have done this before. What kept her tied to the corner of the room? "The children are not going."

"All right," Karim said again. "We can talk again after the march. I've got ten thousand things to do."

"I know. I had to tell you."

The juggler caught his last three hoops about his neck and flung his arms out to receive his ovation. He was a thin man with an enormous mouth. The mouth never stopped smiling.

"Call me on the mobile," said Karim. "We shouldn't see each other again before the wedding."

The mouth was still smiling. It reached all the way up to his ears. He had no coat, just a thin shirt and plum velvet trousers and suspenders. The juggler spoke to his assistant and shivered. Nazneen wondered if he stopped smiling when he finished the performance. She imagined him at home, sitting in the dark in front of the television, smiling.

"We can't get married."

"Not straight away," said Karim.

He shivered as well. Or perhaps it was just a yawn.

"Not ever."

"What do you mean 'not ever'?" He sounded irritated. He kicked his boot against the ground.

"I don't want to marry you," said Nazneen, looking at the juggler. "That's what I mean."

He stood in front of her and took hold of both her hands. "Look at me," he said. "Look at me now." She looked at him. The triangle of hair that stood up at the front of his head, his beautiful long-lashed eyes, his straight nose, the beard that buried the little mole on his chin. "If you mean it, you must tell me again, while you look at me."

"I don't want to marry you."

She squeezed at the pain, trying to make it hers, trying to keep it from him.

He let go of her hands.

"Karim—"

"You really don't?"

"It's not that I—"

He put his hands on his hips and leaned his head right back, as if he had a sudden nosebleed. It was unbearable. It was the worst thing she had ever done.

Karim brought his head down. He blew out, long and hard.

"Right," he said. "Right, right, right." He rubbed his hands together. Was there a little bit of a smile around his lips?

"Why do you keep saying 'right'? How many times are you going to just keep saying it?"

"You don't *want* to marry me?"

"Don't you have ten thousand things to do? Didn't I just tell you the answer?"

She curbed herself. She had to remember she had hurt him.

"Right," said Karim. He blew hard. The juggler took up three blazing clubs from his assistant. Karim clapped wildly, as though the man had suddenly become his hero.

"It would be too difficult," said Nazneen, "for us to be together. So I think we had better stop now."

Karim began to say "right" again, but caught himself. "Yes, I see what you mean. With the children and everything."

"I have to think of them first."

"Exactly," said Karim. He sighed.

Nazneen began to understand: how much she had lightened his load.

They watched the show for a while. Nazneen wondered if the man's cheeks ached. She wondered how his face looked when he stopped smiling, whether he looked sad, or just indifferent like everyone else.

"There's a café inside the market," said Karim. "Let's go and sit down."

Nazneen wanted a baked potato, though there was no reason to be eating in the middle of the afternoon. The potato was enormous and covered in melted cheese.

"I've never seen you eat before," said Karim. He put his elbows on the table and leaned over.

"Sit up straight," she said. "I'm not part of the show."

She ate half the potato and worried about the waste of it. "You eat it," she told him, and pushed it across.

"It's going to be a good turnout tomorrow. Come if you can. Bring the kids." He talked about the march, how many would come, what he planned to say in his speech, the route they would take. As he talked, Nazneen realized that, though he was speaking Bengali, he was not hesitating. She thought about it and tried to remember if he had stammered the last time she saw him, or the time before that. She wasn't sure. Had he lost his stammer? He had gained control of his speech, but she had lost control of hers. She blurted out, "But you're not stammering anymore?"

He widened his eyes, pretending to be shocked at being so rudely cut off. "When I was a kid, I stammered. Now it only happens when I'm very nervous."

"Nervous?"

"Yeah, you know, *nervous.*" He trembled his hands. "Like when I met you."

She laughed. "Me? I made you nervous?"

"What's so funny? You made me nervous."

Nazneen rocked in her seat. She tried to quell her laughter, but it spurted out everywhere. She put her hand over her mouth, but the laugh came down her nose, out of her ears, through her eyes, from her pores. "Oh, oh, that's the funniest thing I've ever heard." She tried to compose herself. "But do you only get nervous in Bengali? Why don't you stammer in English?"

He raised his eyebrows. He stroked his beard. "But I do. Maybe you don't notice in English."

Nazneen wiped her eyes with a napkin. She smoothed her hair and checked her bun. Was it true? Did she not notice in English? Well, why would he say it if it was not true? She straightened up the salt and pepper. People said all sorts of things that were not true. But it seemed possible that she simply had not noticed, or—more than that—had decided not to know.

Karim leaned across to her again. "What's the real reason? Why do you not want me?"

A waitress came to clear the table. She stacked the cups on top of the plate. Then she wiped the surface in long smooth strokes, each one perfectly placed so there was no wastage. Not an inch of the table felt the cloth twice. The blue-green veins on her hands stood up proud and the skin on her knuckles was rough. On her right hand, she wore a ring shaped like a beetle. The nails of her ring finger and her little finger had been filed to a pretty shape and the cuticles pushed down to reveal little white crescents below the pink. The other nails were ragged. On her forefinger, just below the nail, there was a hard lump of skin. When Chanu had begun his art history course and taken notes all day and long into the night—so many notes that Nazneen knew he was copying out entire books—he had developed a lump exactly like that. The waitress moved on to the next table.

Karim waited for her answer.

How did Karim see her? The real thing, he'd said. She was his real thing. A Bengali wife. A Bengali mother. An idea of home. An idea of himself that he found in her. The waitress stood by the counter. In her right hand she held a pen. Between her thumb and forefinger, she rolled the pen around and around. She spoke to a customer. The pen kept rolling.

How had she made him? She did not know. She had patched him together, working in the dark. She had made a quilt out of pieces of silk, scraps of velvet, and now that she held it up to the light the stitches showed up large and crude, and they cut across everything.

"I think I know." Karim regarded her with great sympathy, as if she were a child, suddenly orphaned. "If you were with me you'd never be able to forget what we did, when it all started. Technically, yeah, it was a *sin*. It bothered me, too. So it's for the best. Really. Pray like hell. That's what I'm going to do. Allah forgives. 'O My servants, who have transgressed against their own souls! Do not despair of the mercy of God, for Allah forgives all sins.'" He nodded. He seemed to want her to join in. "Is that what it is?" he said. "The sin of it?"

She touched his hand for the last time. "Oh Karim, that we have already done. But always there was a problem between us. How can I explain? I wasn't me, and you weren't you. From the very beginning to the very end, we didn't see things. What we did—we made each other up."

* * *

At eight o'clock, when the bags were packed and the tension in the flat ran so strong that you could reach out and pluck it like a sitar string, Nazneen went downstairs to see Razia. She descended two flights, paused at Razia's level, and carried on down.

There were no boys in the stairwell. A blister of paint from the metal banister came off on Nazneen's hand. She stepped over an empty cigarette carton, a brick, and a syringe. Outside, the estate was dead. A pile of turf squares stood on the scrubby grass at the center of the courtyard. They had been delivered in summer. Then, they were bright and even. Soon enough, they blended into the environment. There were no kids out this evening. Nazneen walked around the courtyard and into the center of Dogwood. Where did everybody go? Now that she had decided to stay, had everybody else packed up and left? Windows were lit; the air was dense with curry smells, but not a single body in the courtyard. The cars in the car park were not revving. Where were the boys who drove in and out, in and out, and played that music with the big, bulging beats? It seemed that everyone had fled, evacuated in an emergency of which she alone was ignorant. Where were the little lads who sat on the edge of the raised beds that once held lavender and rosemary and now cradled old cans and dog shit, where had they gone to smoke and duck their heads like old hens?

She walked past the concrete valley that sheltered the meeting hut, past the destitute playground, over the car park, along by the raised beds, and back to the foot of Seasalter House. When Dr. Azad greeted her, she screeched.

"I've been to see Tariq," he said quickly, as though she would reprimand him. "He's getting along, I'd say."

"Yes," said Nazneen. "I was just . . . walking."

"Good, good," said the doctor. "Excellent," he added, having considered the matter thoroughly. He stood so stiffly, as if it cost him something dearer than money to bend a joint. His black shoes shone. The coat he wore was long and heavy. His shirt collar scratched the underside of his chin.

Nazneen resisted the urge to reach over and undo a button.

"I'm going to Razia's now," she said.

"She needs the support. Until, of course, you"—here he coughed discreetly, as if the matter were a delicate one—"um, go."

Nazneen sucked the soft walls of her cheeks between her teeth and chewed them. Why had Dr. Azad lent the money? Did he expect to get it back? She would return the girls' tickets and her own and take him whatever she could get for them. As far as he knew, they were all going away. Why did he lend the money? Was it a cure? For that special Tower Hamlets disease that he had discovered and named and which would never get into the medical books. What had he called it? Going Home Syndrome. Did he, with his own marriage broken, want to save another marriage where he could? Did he simply want to get rid of Chanu? Get rid of this ridiculous man who claimed him for a kindred spirit?

"Dr. Azad, did your wife leave you?"

A shadow passed over his face.

Wasn't it obvious enough long ago that she had left? Nazneen bit into her tongue.

"No," he said softly. "She is still there. In a manner of speaking."

"Of course," said Nazneen. "Yes."

A wind blew in over the courtyard and fetched up a crisp packet at her feet.

"Dr. Azad," she said. "Why did you give my husband that money?"

The end of his nose was pitted with age, his cheeks had given way to jowls, pockets of air puffed the skin around his eyes, when he smiled the corners of his mouth turned down, and it was a big, generous smile. "It's very simple. Because he is my friend. My very good friend."

The day had come. Nazneen sat on Bibi's bed. The girls stood by Shahana's desk looking as though they were waiting to be shot. Nazneen had not heard Shahana speak since yesterday morning. All her features seemed to be pulled together at the center of her face, as if by a drawstring. Everything was locked up. Her face had shut down. Bibi had gone beyond desolation, to indifference. On the broad canvas of her face nothing was written.

"Shall I tell you a story? Which one would you like to hear?"

Bibi lifted her shoulders slightly and dropped them. Shahana remained frozen.

"Shahana, Bibi, listen to me." Nazneen stopped. What could she tell them? If she revealed everything now, how could they hide it?

The flight went at two o'clock in the morning. Chanu had calculated that they would have to leave at ten. Nazneen decided on nine o'clock as the time to tell him. It would give them an hour to talk things over, to say goodbye.

"Sometimes things don't turn out so badly. Sometimes the bad things that you think are coming don't come at all. You just have to wait and see."

If he knew now, he would work on her.

He could not sway her.

She would not take the risk.

"I'll make things right. Be patient. Don't make yourselves upset."

He would go and the girls would stay with her.

It was possible that *he* would be the one to change his mind: put the tickets away and start unpacking.

It was his one last dream. He would not rip it up.

"Shall I tell you that story? Which one did you want?"

If he stayed they would unpack together, man and wife, and the long night through lie on the bed and stare at the ceiling and forever after that avoid each other's eye and the reflection of what was in it, what was true: that for both of them the time had gone and it was too late now, too late.

Nazneen got up. "I don't feel like a story either," she said.

As she went past the desk, Shahana kicked her on the shin. "Wait and bloody see," she cried. "How long have you waited? What have you seen? What about if this little memsahib is sick of it? What are you going to do about that?" Nazneen moved out of reach. Shahana kicked the chair. She kicked the desk. Then she turned around and kicked her sister.

Chanu was in the bedroom. He wrote on a label and stuck it on the wardrobe door.

"Very good of the doctor to deal with all this. The wardrobe—I thought we should sell it, rather than ship it. Do you agree?"

"Oh, sell it," said Nazneen. "Definitely. Get rid of it."

Chanu looked at her.

"How overjoyed your sister will be to see you! Imagine it. Such joy!"

"Yes," said Nazneen. It was inadequate. "I have imagined it many times. Over many years."

He opened the wardrobe and the doors hid him.

After a while, his voice came again. "All my certificates here." He closed the doors. He made a jolly face. "Shall we sell those, too?"

"Take them with you. Take one or two at least."

He inspected her closely. His eyebrows tangled together. In his hand he had one of his framed certificates. "Can't get mangoes from the amra tree," he said. Then he sat down on the bed and held his knees.

She went close to him. Maybe an hour wasn't long enough.

"Haah," he said, winded. "Pheeooo-oo."

Last night, when they went to sleep, he had wrapped his arm around her, molded his body around her back, shaped himself to her. When she woke, he was still there.

"I haven't been what you could call a perfect-type husband," he told his knees. "Nor a perfect-type father."

He had shrunk. Not just his cheeks and his belly, but all of him. His voice, his words, his temper, his projects, his plans. He had shrunk. And now he was just too small to send out all alone.

"But I haven't been a bad husband. Would you say? Not bad." Chanu looked up at her and squinted as if her face was too bright to behold directly. "Some of our women, they never go out. Her." He motioned upstairs with his head. "She never goes out. You never see her out, do you? Many aren't allowed to work. You know how it is. Village attitudes. The woman gets some money, she starts feeling she is as good as the man and she can do as she likes." He smiled and his little eyes nearly disappeared. "That's how they think. They are not modern. Not like me."

"It was lucky for me"—her heart swelled as she spoke—"that my father chose an educated man."

Chanu grew a little. "All this talk. We should be doing. Let's go into the sitting room and see what else needs to be done."

Nazneen rolled up the rugs. Chanu stood and watched. After a while he lifted his shirt and peered at his belly. He turned to present his profile to Nazneen. "What do you think? Very streamline, eh?"

His stomach no longer looked like a nine-month pregnancy. Now it was closer to six. He patted it affectionately. "Willpower," he said. "And ulcer," he conceded.

"Hup," he declared and sucked the belly in. He viewed it again, now with some uncertainty. "Gone too damn far. Does this look like respectable-type? Does it look like soap factory manager, or like rickshaw wallah?"

"It's big enough," said Nazneen. She wondered if she would keep the rugs or throw them away.

"I might go for samosas. Pack a few for the aeroplane. And I have to see Dr. Azad about administrative matters, before he leaves the surgery." Chanu let go of his shirt. It didn't occur to him to tuck it back into his trousers. At the remains of the showcase, he paused. "But what were you doing trying to lift the computer onto a glass cabinet?"

"Too many boxes on the floor. Just tidying up."

Chanu twinkled at her. "My wife, tidying up! And making more trouble for herself. Never mind, it doesn't matter. But next time there's a big job to be done—leave it to me."

He went to attend to samosas, administration, and other matters pertaining.

Nazneen finished with the rugs. She took stock of the sitting room. She did a circuit. The boxes of Chanu's papers were labeled *Ship.* The coffee table had been tagged *Auction.* On the back of the sofa was another label: *Charitable Foundation.*

Only the sewing machine remained to be packed. She sat in front of it for a while. The letter was still beneath the machine. She left it and moved to the window.

A rudimentary stage had been erected out of wooden pallets in the courtyard. Around the stage a handful of youths talked into mobile phones. A steady stream of young men filed into the courtyard from both sides of the estate. They, too, gathered around the stage. Everyone checked what was happening. Nothing was happening. Everyone checked again. One or two ran on the spot and jumped up and down. A boy with a red-and-green scarf knotted around his forehead carried what looked like a bundled-up old sheet. He put it on the ground and spread it out. It was a Bengal Tigers banner, hand-painted.

"Amma," said Bibi from the doorway.

"Bibi," said Nazneen, without turning. "Bibi?" She looked around.

Bibi chewed on the end of her plait.

"Are you hungry? Do you want lunch?"

"No."

"What is it?"

"Nothing. I was just coming to see you."

Nazneen held out her arm. "Come."

"It's OK," said Bibi, backing out. "I've seen you."

People were pouring into the courtyard now. They came thick and fast. It was as if a couple of blocks of flats had been tipped on their side and all the people came helter-skelter out into the street and landed up in the middle of Dogwood. There were women among the crowd, and girls. A white banner with black and gold letters proclaimed *Bethnal Green Islamic Girls' Group.*

Nazneen saw Sorupa, Jorina, Nazma, and Hanufa. Hanufa was back in favor. She looked for Karim.

The boys outnumbered the girls and the women, but they were all outnumbered by the older men. They came with their green and brown herringbone overcoats buttoned over baggy trousers. They walked in knots of three or four, and ignored those they walked with and shouted across to others. White beards tinged with nicotine, skullcaps and missing teeth. Dark, polished faces and watchful eyes. A few wore lungis; others carried walking sticks. They came with plastic Iceland bags and moved along like hospital patients. Nazneen wondered if Karim's father was among them.

There was another group: white people. They were the smallest of the clans but they were the most active. They buzzed around the older men, giving out cardboard signs mounted on wooden poles. The white people wore trousers with pockets all over them. They had pockets at the thigh, the knee, down on their shins. All their clothes had little tabs and toggles, zips and flaps and fasteners. It was as if they had dressed themselves in tents and to settle for the night they would simply insert a few poles and lie down. They moved among the crowd and began to hand out something (badges? stickers? sweets?) to the lads. Finding themselves rebuffed, they retrenched a generation or two. The Bangladeshi patriarchs dangled their placards along with the Iceland bags. A white girl with tiny silver-framed glasses held up her placard and jabbed it in the air. She wedged it between her knees and began a little mime. Clasped her hands together. Pointed to the sky. Palms out to the patriarchs. Rub and a pat on the cardboard sign. Hold. Up. Your. Placards.

The patriarchs "listened" politely. Then they discussed it among themselves.

Nazneen examined the faces near the stage. Karim would be there. He would stand up on the stage and speak. It was his big day.

It was her big day as well.

Somewhere, down there, he was preparing his speech. Adding the finishing touches.

She had not yet made a start on hers.

A chant was setting up among the demonstrators. Nazneen could not make out the words. She opened the window. The white people moved among the patriarchs. They were the chanters, these two groups. The bespectacled girl and her friends made pistons of their arms: *go, go, go.* The patriarchs stowed their Iceland bags on top of their feet, turned up their collars, and buttoned their coats beneath their chins. They chanted along with their new friends.

"What fresh hell is this?"

She had not noticed Chanu come in.

"It's a massacre out there. Three hundred and five people have stood on my toes. 'Mind out,' I said. 'Man with corns coming through. Man with chilblains.' Nobody listened."

He came to the window.

"What are they saying?" asked Nazneen. "Something about Gurkhas? Or burkhas?"

"Workers. That is the cry which they have taken up. 'Workers! United!' It's a myth, of course. Those white people are from the Workers United Front. When I was passing through, they were attempting to get a longer chant going. 'Workers. United. Will never be defeated.' They gave it up for a bad job."

Chanu eased his shoes off. He lifted a foot, rested it on his knee, and began to massage it through the sock.

He cleared his throat. "Ahem. Hem. What they are doing, you see, is coopting these immigrants into their grand political schemata in which all oppressed minorities combine in the overthrow of the state and live happily ever after in a communal paradise. This theory fails to take account of culture clash, bourgeois immigrant aspirations, the hatred of the Hindu for the Muslim, the Bangladeshi for the Pakistani, and so on and so forth. In all reality, it is doomed to failure."

He switched feet.

"See those people down there, chanting? All aged about—what?—forty-five to sixty-five. Workers united? They are not even workers! Ninety-nine percent, they are unemployed."

"What about the other march?"

"Lion Hearts? I didn't see anything. Maybe they canceled."

Nazneen remembered Mrs. Islam's words. *Not more than ten will come.*

Karim mounted the stage. He held a megaphone to his lips.

Chanu closed the window. "What is going to happen to our people here?" He took her hand and led her away. Karim's voice was indistinct, a radio playing out of tune in the background.

"The young ones," said Chanu, "they'll be the ones to decide. Do you know how many immigrant populations have been here before us? In the eighteenth century the French Protestants fled here, escaping Catholic persecution. They were silk weavers. They made good. One hundred years later, the Jews came. They thrived. At the same time, the Chinese came as merchants. The Chinese are doing very well." Chanu still had hold of her hand. "Which way is it going to go?"

"Shefali is going to university. Sorupa's nephew is going to Oxford."

"And Tariq? What is he doing?"

Nazneen reclaimed her hand.

Chanu motioned with his head towards the window. "What are they doing out there? What are they marching for?"

"Because the others, who have a wrong idea about our religion, are going to march against Islam."

"Islam," said Chanu, turning the word over carefully. "It could be about Islam. But I don't think so. I don't think it is." He entered his own private world of theory and refutation, striving and puzzlement.

Then he plumped up his cheeks and his hopes. "But when we're back home, we won't need to think about these things. Back home we'll really know what's what."

When the courtyard had cleared, Chanu went out again. He was going to a shop called Liberty's to buy soap. His briefcase had been transformed into a sample carrier. Already it was full of bars of Lux, Fairy, Dove, Palmolive, Imperial Leather, Pears, Neutrogena, Zest, Cuticura, and Camay Classic. "First rule of management," said Chanu. "Know the competition." At Liberty's he would stock up on the "refined-end soap market." He had plans for the factory. When they came to fruition, he would move the family to a bungalow in Gulshan, with a guest cottage at the bottom of the garden. To start with, they could have a couple of rooms above the office. "Second rule of management," said Chanu. "Think big, act small. Then the rewards will come."

Nazneen went to the bedroom and lay down on the bare mattress. She slept a dreamless sleep. When she woke it was dark outside. She checked the time. Six o'clock. A vision rose before her. Chanu sitting on an aeroplane, trying to peer out of the window. No matter how he struggled, he could not reach the window. He was too small. Just a baby-sized Chanu, and his legs did not reach the end of the seat. Nazneen lifted him up and put him on her knee. She looked out of the window and saw the runway lights. But they were not on the runway! The lights were lampposts and houses, office blocks and tower blocks, and they were pulling down and away, shrinking, sinking, into the black.

"Amma." Bibi stood against the wall with her hands behind her back.

"Yes, Bibi. Were you waiting for me? You could have woken me."

Bibi slid down the wall and straightened up, slid down again.

"Let's go to the kitchen. We'll get something to eat."

"Amma."

"Go and tell your sister. You can give me a hand, both of you."

Bibi slipped right down the wall and sat on her bottom.

Nazneen went to her and felt her forehead. "Are you ill? Shall I get the doctor?"

"She's gone," said Bibi. She began to cry. "She's run away."

Chapter Twenty-one

Bibi was sworn to secrecy. Between big sobs she explained this to her mother, and then she told her the rest. Shahana had gone to meet Nishi at the Shalimar Café. They were going to have a kebab and a banana lassi and possibly a jelabee and then they would catch the train to a place called Paignton. In Paignton, Nishi said, there were no Bangladeshis and they could do as they pleased. Nishi's sister, who was sixteen years old, had gone for a "holiday" in Sylhet and returned six months later with a husband and a swelling belly. Nishi, strong on forward-planning skills, was taking evasive action: she was going on a holiday of her own and she would return when she was twenty-five. At that ancient age the danger of marriage was over.

"Which Shalimar Café?" said Nazneen.

"The one on Cannon Street," said Bibi. "I think it's the Brick Lane one."

"You're sure? Brick Lane."

Bibi nodded. Then shook her head. "No. I don't think so. Cannon Street."

"Think, Bibi! Think!"

"Cannon Street." She said it with the air of a game-show contestant, hovering in suspense, waiting to be affirmed.

"Wait here," said Nazneen. "Don't go anywhere. Whatever you do, don't move."

Nazneen ran. Down Bethnal Green Road. Turned at Vallance Road. Jogged down New Road. Stitch in her side on Cannon Street.

The door of the Shalimar Café had a sprung hinge. It swung back and hit her on the shoulder. The solitary customer lifted his head. His sweater was unraveling at many different places; it straggled like a pubescent beard. He went back to his chapatis.

"Has a girl been in here?" Nazneen held her side where it was splitting. "Twelve years old. Blue kameez. Yellow here and here. Two girls together."

The man behind the counter was peeling carrots. He dropped the peelings into a steel basin and the carrots into a plastic tub of water.

"How old the other girl?"

"Thirteen," said Nazneen. "But she looks older, more like fourteen, fifteen."

The man put his carrot down. He removed a little something from his nostril. The seconds came and went and infuriated Nazneen.

The man wiped his finger on his apron. "What she wearing?"

"I don't know." She looked over the tables and under them. What was she looking for? Would they leave a trail behind them? "Look," she said. "Have you seen them, or not?"

"Today?" said the man. "No. No customers today. Only this one." He pointed with a carrot.

The George Estate was covered in scaffolding. Dense green netting ran between the poles. It looked as if the entire building had been hunted down and taken captive, the people with it. Nazneen crossed over Cable Street and passed under the railway bridge. The Falstaff pub was boarded up, the forecourt choked with weeds and grass and a bathtub filled with traffic cones, rubble, and mossy cushions. She had to walk, to let her breath come back to her. A shopkeeper came out on the pavement and emptied a bucket of foul-smelling water into the gutter. Nazneen turned her head. Through an open door, down a flight of concrete stairs, she glimpsed a row of sewing machines beneath a low yellow ceiling. A woman stood up to stretch and touched the ceiling with her palms. Nazneen pressed on, past the Sylhet Cash and Carry, the International Cheap Calls Centre, the open jaws of a butcher's shop, the corner building run to ruin and bearing the faded legend of a time gone by, Schultz Famous Salt Beef.

She turned into the Berners Estate. Here, every type of cheap hope for cheap housing lived side by side in a monument to false economy. The low-rises crouched like wounded monsters along concrete banks. In the gullies, beach-hut fabrications clung anxiously to the hard terrain, weathered and beaten by unknown storms. A desolate building, gouged-out eyes in place of windows, announced "Tenants' Association: Hall for Hire." Nazneen looked up to the balconies. A woman in a dark blue burkha hung a prayer mat over the railing, and withdrew. A small child trundled a red plastic truck along a balcony and back, over and over again. At the end, near the sick orange light of a lamppost, two black children sat behind bars, watching their new world. Where had they come from? What had they escaped? Nazneen had learned to recognize the face of a refugee child: that traumatized stillness, the need they had, to learn to play again.

Out of the estate and onto Commercial Road, past the clothes wholesaler's, up Adler Street, and left onto the brief green respite of Altab Ali Park, where the neat, pale-faced block of flats had picture windows and a gated entrance, from which the City boys could stroll to work. Nazneen ran down the slope and caught the green man at the crossing on Whitechapel Road.

A row of police vans covered the mouth of Osborn Street. Behind them a legion of policemen stood with arms folded and feet turned out. A length of tangerine-and-white-striped tape stuck the sides of the street together.

"Let me through," said Nazneen.

"The street is closed, madam. Go back." The policeman sounded friendly but decisive. He seemed to think the conversation was finished.

"I have to go to Shalimar Café and find my daughter."

The policeman looked ahead, as if she had not spoken. Nazneen glanced down the line at the black-suited men, all of them braced against an invisible force. What was happening in Brick Lane? Could they have closed it just for the Bengal Tigers to march? Wasn't this the last place on Karim's route? But it was dark, it was late. By now the marches would be over.

"Why I can't go through?" said Nazneen. She put her face right up to the policeman's face. *Do you see me now? Do you hear me?*

"Disturbances," said the policeman. She felt the warmth of his breath and drew her head back.

"My daughter is there."

The policeman shook his head. "Madam, she isn't. We cleared everyone out who wanted to come out. There's only the waiters and restaurant owners left. They didn't want to come away. Unless your daughter is participating in the disturbance, she has taken herself back home. I suggest you do the same thing."

Without seeming to move, the policeman filled her space so that she was forced to step back.

But Shahana would not be at home. And if a policeman came to get her, and the other runaway, what would she think? What would she do?

Nazneen looked beyond the cordon towards the neck of Brick Lane. It revealed nothing. The electrical shops were shuttered, the stonemason's dark, the sandwich-shop window showed empty trays and a naked glass counter, and only the steps and the awning of the Capital City hotel were lit up.

Inside her, the thoughts ebbed and flowed. Shahana had cleared out long ago. She was at the station, buying a ticket to Paignton. Shahana was still at the Shalimar, trapped by looters or her own fear, cowering in the toilets with Nishi. If she was at the station, it was too late. But if she was on Brick Lane . . .

Panic hit Nazneen like an asthma attack. For a few moments she felt she would expire then and there, into the policeman's folded arms.

A white couple came up to the cordon and asked something. They looked disappointed. They wanted curry. More people were arriving, expecting curry and lager. Nazneen's policeman spoke to a woman with wattled neck and a strident voice.

"Can I suggest that you consult a restaurant guide, madam."

Nazneen slipped around the back of him. She hoisted her sari and hurdled over the orange-and-white tape. Someone thumped her on the back. She turned her head, but there was no one behind her. It was only her heart playing tricks. She stuck close to the walls and shadows, crossed a side street with its little vein of houses, and entered the main artery of Brick Lane.

Across the way, formed in a semicircle, was a row of Perspex shields, and behind the shields an arc of policemen with bulging jackets. A group of lads stood on the pavement and in the road, hoods pulled up, scarves around their faces, as though they had entered a manly purdah. It was quiet.

Nazneen passed behind the boys. They paid her no attention. In lighted windows, waiters pressed their foreheads to the glass. Restaurant owners stood by, nerves flickering across important faces. All the mixed-blood vitality of the street had been drained. Something coursed down the artery, like a bubble in the bloodstream.

A police car was parked at a crazy angle in the road, the front doors wide open and the interior abandoned. The car rocked. A door swung shut. It rocked again. Nazneen looked at the boys pushing it. They worked quickly and quietly, as though this was a task they had been assigned to do and they wanted to make a good job of it. The car went over and suddenly a noise licked around Brick Lane like a flame, crackling from every corner.

"Bengal Tigers, *zindabad*!" went the cry. Long live the Bengal Tigers.

As the boys whooped, Nazneen began to run again. A tall dark shape smashed the windows of the police car with a stick. Another hurled something through the hole. It whizzed through the air and exploded with a dull thud. From behind the black municipal bins, out of doorways, around corners, and up from car bonnets, more and more people appeared, ejected by this simple purgative. Nazneen ran past the car. A figure dressed in white was crumpled on the ground by the rear wheel. She turned around. The figure rose and fell again, toppled by a large and heavy head. It was the multicultural liaison officer, and he was praying. Nazneen sprinted towards the car. She got hold of the man's flappy white sleeve and pulled it.

"Please," she said. "Get up."

He turned his face towards her and the whites of his eyes showed clearer than his robe in the dark. "Ah, sister, how many rakahs for the isha prayer?"

"Are you mad? Get up. Run."

"What? I is praying to Allah to save all these boys. Can't get up now."

"Allah," said Nazneen, heaving at the neck of his robe, "does not want your prayer now. He wants you to save yourself." The cotton ripped and she let go.

"Damn," said the multicultural liaison officer. He got on his knees. "Shit. You made me swear."

Nazneen pulled his arm. "You can make du'a later. Run. Now. Run."

A siren wail smacked the sky and showered their heads. They ran down the road. Nazneen's feet hit the pavement so hard she felt it in her teeth. At the corner of Hanbury Street she stopped and looked over her shoulder. The police car belched a little black smoke, and burst into a ball of fire.

"Yea, though I walk through the valley of the shadow of death—"

The Shalimar was three blocks up. Nazneen said, "Let's go. Come on."

The multicultural liaison officer raised his arms. "I will fear no evil: for thou art with me."

"I can't wait for you."

"Thy rod and thy staff comfort me." He turned to Nazneen. "In these circumstances, better safe than sorry." He lifted his face to heaven.

She left him and walked close to the shops, brushing the walls with her arm. Ahead, eight or ten boys gathered behind a municipal bin. The large black container stood at shoulder height. Two lads darted out to the side and made an overarm bowling motion. They hurled themselves behind the bin and all the lads crouched down. Nazneen stopped moving. A lighted window was at her back. She wished she had picked a better place to be, during this sinister game of hide-and-seek. There were no white people here at all. These boys were fighting themselves. A dizziness came over her and she leaned against the glass. How long, she thought, how long it has taken me to get this far.

Missiles rained across the road. Empty bottles, full cans, a brick, a chair, a winged stick. A bottle smashed at Nazneen's feet. She decided to run again. But which way? Towards the Shalimar and the source of the missiles? Or back up the road to take shelter? She turned around and back and around and suddenly she was not sure which way the café was. She recognized nothing. Silhouettes across the way, substantial as shadows, but solid enough to smash through windows. Crouching shapes and whirling arms, the pale streak of trainers on the black ground that had gone soft beneath her feet. The buildings curved away from her, shrinking from the violent pavement. The light came in crackling twists of red that stabbed at the dark and did not lift it, as though a devil had danced through with his blazing torch. Nazneen tried to focus on a window and take refuge in the clean white light, but when she looked the light burned her eyes. In the middle of the road, a coiled snake of tires flamed with acrid fury and shed skins, thick, black, choking, to the wind. Shop alarms rang, *clang, clang, clang,* more frightened than warning. Back up the road, an ambulance crawled stubbornly along, its twirling blue eye sending out a terrible, keening lament.

Nazneen got her legs to move. She walked with her arms in front of her, as if she did not trust her eyes. Gradually, she came back to herself. She had the sensation that she had fainted, and now the world was forming again. The light steadied itself. She recognized shapes for what they were and sensed the bodies that filled the dark, people-shaped outlines. A fire engine slashed across the tarmac. She passed the burning tires and for a while her eyes became useless again. When she stepped out of that smoky infestation, she saw a figure standing alone in the middle of the road. His face was covered by a megaphone, but even then, even in the twisted light, he had a spare look about him. There was not an inch of waste. His jacket hung from his shoulders as from a coat hanger, no unnecessary flesh covering the bones.

"Brothers," he said, and his voice was familiar. "Brothers, why are you fighting yourselves, Mussulman against Mussulman?"

Another winged stick flew through the air and clattered on the pavement next to Nazneen. She bent down to look at it. It was a placard and it read: STOP THE WAR.

"Is this what happens when Islam goes on the march?" said the Questioner.

Nazneen hurried on. The megaphone competed with the screech of car brakes, car doors slamming, the clanging of shop alarms, a high-pitched whistle blown by a hooded youth as he raced past on a bicycle.

"The police are laughing at you, my friends. They are waiting for you to finish each other off."

A boy ran into the road, beckoning with two hands wide, *come on, come on.* Within seconds, five others jumped on him and he fell to the ground. Another three piled on top. And then came the waiters, black-trousered, white-shirted, brandishing skewers and carving knives and chests pumped with outrage. *"You bloody bastards,"* they screamed. *"What the hell you shitting on our doorsteps for? Go to Oxford Street! Go to Piccadilly Circus! Go to hell!"*

The heap of boys scrambled up and disappeared into the bowels of Brick Lane. "Right now, let me tell you, the world is watching." The Questioner turned slowly around with his megaphone, speaking his next words to the whole three hundred and sixty degrees. "Right now, you should know, George Bush is laughing at you."

Out of the dark, a woman with a microphone ran up to him. He lowered the megaphone. A white man shouldered a camera and swung it in his direction. The woman spoke to the Questioner and the Questioner replied, but Nazneen could no longer hear him.

Ahead of her now were a blazing car and two dozen heels turned up in flight. She began to hope that Shahana was on the train, or in Paignton, anywhere but here. She tried to run with the crowd but she could not keep up. The next instant, something caught her around the chest and she lashed out at the air.

"Get in here," said Karim. He dragged her into a doorway.

Nazneen tried to speak but her breath fought against it.

"What are you doing here?"

"Shahana." It was all she could manage.

"Go home. You shouldn't be here."

"Shahana. I think she's here."

Karim held her by the shoulders. There was thunder in his face. He looked as if he wanted to shake her. Then he softened. "All right. Tell me."

She told him as quickly as she could. Karim peered both ways and signaled for her to step out and follow him.

"What is happening?" she asked, as they walked past a shattered shopfront. She remembered his words. *Insh'Allah, we all stand together.*

"Jamal Zaman got out of hospital today. You know, that lad they call Nonny."

She trotted to keep up. "So what is this?" But she knew already, had seen it at the last meeting.

"It's revenge. And revenge for the revenge." He turned around. "Man, what it is, it's a mess! It's not even *about* anything anymore. It's just about what it is. Put anything in front of them now and they'll fight it. A police car, a shop window, anything."

"And the march?"

He shrugged. "We marched. So what, really?"

"The Lion Hearts, did they come?"

"About twenty or thirty. They weren't anything."

The pavement was blocked by a hillock of clothing, loot half desired and hastily abandoned. They ran in the road.

"They weren't anything?"

"Not here. Not yet. People only take a job on for themselves when their leaders aren't doing it for them. Do you understand?"

They reached the Shalimar. The lights were off. Each table, laid for dinner, had a little pot of plastic flowers next to the triple tin dishes of chutney, chopped onion, and raita. Nazneen looked at Karim.

"Go home," he said.

She put her face up to the glass and cupped her hands to the sides.

"She'll be back by morning."

She looked across from the toilet doors at the back of the room to the counter stacked with kebabs, tandoori chicken, bhajis, puris, trays of rice and vegetables, milky sweets, sugar-shined ladoos, the faintly sparkling jelabees.

"I'll take you up to the corner. You'll be all right from there."

Then she saw them. Three waiters with their backs and arms pressed to the wall, and behind them two smaller figures, holding hands.

She pounded on the glass and yelled. "Shahana. Shahana. It's me. I'm here. Amma's come."

Chanu knew what she was going to say. That was why he could not stop talking. He talked over the television. Nazneen stared at the screen. The picture was just in red and black; even the Questioner's face was shades of red and black. His words were lost once more. Chanu sat on the arm of the sofa, swaying slightly as if he might fly off in either direction at any moment. He talked with his hands, his arms, his eyes, eyebrows, cheeks, and nose as well as his lips. All were in constant motion. His legs swung now and then to show just how animated he had become, how full of life, and possibility, and promise. "Just a reminder," he said, waving lavishly at the screen. "Just a reminder of what we leave behind. Of course, Shahana was a bundle of nerves and she is very highly strung and it's not surprising that she decided, as it were, to show her heels, but look where it got her and where we are going. . . ."

Shahana was taking a bath and Bibi was sitting on the side of the bath, keeping an eye on her sister.

Nazneen looked at her husband. He smiled at her as he talked, but he would not halt the words.

"A colleague from Kempton Kars is coming to collect us. At first when I met him I considered him what you could call an ignorant type, and actually he is, more or less, ignorant-type but he is a good-hearted man. As they say in English, *salt of the earth.* Do you know what it is?"

"It's very close to the time. . . ."

His face bubbled and dimpled. "I know, I know, how exciting it is! Shall we check the tickets and the passports for the last time? We'll check them again at the airport, I expect, and then they will put stamps all over them and . . ."

"I should have said this before." Nazneen looked at her hands.

Chanu stood up. He dusted down his trousers, his best blue polyester-cotton mix that came with the pale-blue-and-beige toned-in belt. He walked over to the television. His steps were light and quick; more hop and skip than walk. "Let's turn it off. Essentially, watching that is looking backwards. Let us look forwards from now on. When we move to the bungalow, your sister will come to live with us. Would you like that?" He replaced the label on the television screen: *Auction.* He crossed the room again. Now he was practically dancing. "Of course you would. Think of it! Reunited with Hasina, the girls with their aunt, holidays in Cox's Bazaar, maybe the girls would like a little trip to the Sundarbans. They could see a real Bengal Tiger. Ha! Ha, ha. Nazneen? Ha!"

She stood up and went to him and they were very close, there in the channel between the sofa and the armchair. She lifted her hand and placed it on his cheek. He pushed his face against her palm and kissed it with great and very grave tenderness. His neck began to wilt and inch by inch his head drooped lower. She held his face, hard, as if stanching a wound, and put her other arm around him.

"You see," he said, and he mumbled it inside her palm. "All these years I dreamed of going home a Big Man. Only now, when it's nearly finished for me, I realized what is important. As long as I have my family with me, my wife, my daughters, I am as strong as any man alive."

He rested his forehead on her shoulder. A sigh shook his body. She pulled him in a little closer.

"What is all this Big Man?" She whispered in his ear. Sadness crushed her chest. It pressed everything out of her and filled the hollows of her bones. "What is all this Strong Man? Do you think that is why I love you? Is that what there is in you, to be loved?"

His tears scarred her hand.

"You're coming with me, then? You'll come?"

"No," she breathed. She lifted his head and looked into his face. It was dented and swollen, almost out of recognition. "I can't go with you," she said.

"I can't stay," said Chanu, and they clung to each other inside a sadness that went beyond words and tears, beyond that place, those causes and consequences, and became a part of their breath, their marrow, to travel with them from now to wherever they went.

She could not sleep. She got up in the night and went to the kitchen. Inside a box marked *Dr. Azad* was all the food they had not eaten up. Nazneen searched for the chopping board. She found her frying pan, a saucepan, knives, spices, onions, and red lentils. She washed the lentils, fished out the stones, covered them with water, and set the pan to boil. The ladle had vanished, but she retrieved a large spoon and skimmed off the froth and poured it into the sink. She chopped onion, garlic, and ginger, dropped a portion into the lentils, and put the rest in the frying pan with some oil. A teaspoon of cumin, a pinch of turmeric, and some chili went into the pot. When the onion started to turn, she split eight cardamoms with her teeth to release the little black seeds, and threw them into the frying pan. She sprinkled on a few cloves, three bay leaves, and some coriander seeds. The spices began to catch and gave off their round and intricate smell. It was a scent that made all others flat; it existed in spheres, the others in thin circles. Nazneen leaned over the frying pan. The coriander seeds began to jump. She lowered the heat. She pushed aside a box to make more space on the work surface, and there was the photograph.

Chanu with his stringy calves sticking out from oversized red shorts which dangled beneath an outsize belly. The girls tucked up in his armpits. Shahana in her dark green kameez and Bibi in pink, their expressions somewhere between Dutiful Daughter and Hostage.

Nazneen rested the picture against the tiles. She looked at the clock. She looked out of the window.

Chanu had called his daughters. "There has been a change of plan." He rubbed his face with his palms, getting the blood to flow again. "I have suggested, and your mother has agreed, that the three of you come later." He weighed his stomach and slapped it around a little. He cleared his throat and this time the obstruction seemed genuine; it brought tears to his eyes. "I'll go on ahead now, clear—ahem—the path."

The girls looked at Nazneen. They saw that it was true. Bibi chewed the ends of both her plaits. Shahana went to her father and put her arms around his neck. "But who will cook for you, Abba?"

"Who will cut your corns?" said Bibi.

Chanu tickled Shahana under the arms. "What? Do you not know? I am a better cook than your mother. And look, Bibi, my stomach has gone flatter than a paratha. I can reach my own toes now." He bent down to prove it. Then he began to rearrange bags and money, tickets and passports. He clicked on his money belt and tested the catch. "Be good girls, do as your mother tells you, finish your homework every night, don't waste time on television and all that rubbish, read Tagore (I recommend *Gitanjali*), don't think that there's anything you're not good enough for, remember that—" He broke off. "Yes, well. That should do for now."

Nazneen stirred the dal.

"We're hungry as well," said Shahana.

The girls came into the kitchen and began the hunt for the rice.

They took their plates into the sitting room and made space on the table.

"When will we go to Dhaka?" said Bibi.

"*If* we go," said Shahana. "We don't have to go. Do we, Amma?"

"What about Abba?" said Bibi quickly. "We can't just leave him on his own."

"He could come back," explained Shahana. "I bet he'll come back. And when he comes back he'll be a lot happier."

"Why will he be happier?"

Shahana shrugged. "He just will. I'm telling you."

"So are we not going, Amma?"

"Just wait and—" Nazneen interrupted herself. She took more rice. She took more dal. She offered more to her daughters. "We'll talk about it tomorrow, or later, and we'll decide what to do. Staying or going, it's up to us three."

MARCH 2002

Razia took off her glasses. She held the sketch up to her face, almost touching her long nose. "No problem," she said. "We can do this very, very easy." She put her glasses back on. "But it's going to cost them more. Do you see all this beading?" She offered the paper to Hanufa. "Five pounds extra per piece. They can take it or leave it."

Hanufa passed the drawing to Nazneen. The trousers sat low on the hips, without a waistband, and the bodice cut away above the belly button. The detail indicated gold and diamanté dhakba work and the ends of the dupatta were beaded in a cobweb design. The swatch attached was ice-blue silk.

"What about white organza for the scarf?" said Nazneen. "Nice contrast."

"They don't pay us to design as well," said Razia. She got up and pressed her hands into the small of her back. "This sofa is an old bitch. It's more broken down than me."

The sofa came from a junk shop. It was pretend leather, dyed an uncertain purple, the color of pigeon shit. It was so plastic that if your skin touched it, you received some kind of static shock to the teeth.

"Why not?" said Nazneen.

Razia looked at her sidelong, through narrowed eyes.

"They can pay extra for it."

"Do it then. You make a design. I'll sell it."

Razia had been the one to set it up. Walked into Fusion Fashions, bold as a mynah bird, and asked for work. She cleared out of the sweatshop. She got on the bus and went to distant lands: Tooting, Ealing, Southall, Wembley. She came back with orders, swatches, samples, patterns, beads, laces, feather trims, leather trims, fake fur, rubber, and crystals. "These young girls"—she sucked in her lips and sprayed her words like lead shot—"they'll put anything on a piece of cloth and call it an outfit. They'll be sewing kettles on their pants before you can say 'lengha.'" She laughed, and her laugh clattered around the room like a couple of saucepans dropped from a great height.

Hanufa gasped. "Oh, poor Mrs. Islam. Haven't you heard? She is very ill. She is not even coming out of her house. I am keeping her in my prayers."

"The old faker," said Razia. "She'll outlive us all."

"The doctors can't find what is wrong with her. She has baffled them all. Do you know, they called a fellow from Manchester. Another came from Scotland. And a third was flown from India. It's a terrible thing."

"Oh, yes, terrible thing. They can't find anything wrong, do you say?" Razia lay down on the floor. She had got used to the floor and now she thought it was better for her back.

Hanufa opened her eyes a little wider. "There's a special clinic in Switzerland. Probably she is going there to recuperate. In fact, she is thinking of taking her entire family with her."

"Her entire family," said Razia. "And all her bank accounts."

The bedroom door opened and Jorina tiptoed out. She wore a cherry-blossom-pink outfit of appliquéd chiffon, with shoestring shoulder straps and trousers slashed to the thigh to reveal the translucent pink silk churidar beneath.

"Oh, my God." Razia rolled onto her side. "What has this Bollywood Beauty done with our Jorina?"

Jorina twirled around, still on tiptoe. "Look! It fits me so perfectly. Do you think I should keep it? It's like it was made for me."

"We took your measurements for the pattern," said Razia. "You are Mrs. Average Shape. Don't get carried away. Are you going to wear it for frying onions? Listen, let us build up the trade first, then we can start dressing like film stars." She reached over for her accounts book and chewed on the end of a pen while she studied the figures. "Hanufa, I'm going to pay you today. Nazneen and Jorina, you wait until tomorrow because I get another payment in then. OK with everybody?"

It was.

Razia parceled out the work. She had a brief conference with Jorina about the stretch in a woolen jersey fabric destined for a salwaar kameez. She made some calculations and gave Hanufa her money. Nazneen watched her friend, Razia, the businesswoman. In her head, she began work on the new designs.

"How is your son?" Hanufa asked Razia. "His studies and—everything."

"Studies are OK-Ma. Everything is OK-Ma." Razia put her hand on Hanufa's wrist. She leaned in close. "I thought I lost my Tariq. I thought, 'He does not want to live this life I made for him.'"

Jorina said, "But that is our problem—making lives for our children. They want to make them for themselves."

"Yes," said Razia. "They will do that. Even if it kills them."

Nazneen dropped her work off at the flat. She collected her bag and headed out again to the shops to pick up some lace trimmings. From the edge of the courtyard she glanced up to see how the window boxes looked from down here. Over the edge of the long white tubs a few dark green leaves were visible. She had bought winter pansies and they would soon be in flower. Razia had her washing out on a line tied between an overflow pipe and an iron hook. Her Union Jack sweatshirt flapped against the double glazing.

Nazneen turned left, going towards the back streets behind Columbia Road. She hurried because she wanted to be home again before the girls came back from school. When Chanu went home, Bibi turned into a little owl. Nazneen would wake to find her sitting on the edge of the bed, her knees tucked up inside her white nightdress. Or she went to check on the girls and Bibi would be on a chair, keeping watch over her sister. In the daytime she was silent, black-eyed, and sleepy. By night she was on guard, alert to the slightest movement.

Only now was she beginning to relax. Nazneen found her curled up by the bedroom door, or asleep on the floor next to Shahana's bed.

"I'm not going anywhere without you," Nazneen told her.

"I know that," said Bibi. "You won't, will you?"

She always asked for stories. She wanted the words because the words stitched her mother close.

"Tell us the one about How You Were Left to Your Fate."

"Not that one," groaned Shahana. "It's boring."

"True," said Nazneen. "I'll tell you a better one."

Nazneen walked through the car park, over the playground, and onto the tarmac hill that bounded the concrete valley. She checked her purse: nearly twenty pounds. Maybe she would buy some chocolate for the girls. Nazneen gave silent thanks. Without Razia there would be no money at all, because Karim had disappeared. She had no middleman, no contact for the factory, no work for her needle, no means to support the children. She prayed to God, but He had already given her what she needed: Razia.

A couple of workmen tried to maneuver a walnut-legged table with a green baize top through the doors of the community hut. Another rolled thick cream paint over the graffiti on the dull red brick. The long, low sloping roof had been replaced and it was black as melted midnight against the watery blue sky. A sign had been erected above the doors, in English and in Bengali: "Dogwood Estate Youth Club."

The table squeezed through the doors and a thin young man walked out into the pale spring sun.

After the riot, everything was going to change.

Politicians came and walked around the estate with their hands behind their backs to show that they were not responsible, leaning forward slightly to indicate that they were looking forward to the future. A councillor in a corduroy jacket and round-necked shirt came to Nazneen's flat and looked at the hallway where the plaster had come off. He had a reporter and a photographer with him. The photographer took a picture of the councillor with his hand against the bricks.

"How long has it been like this?" said the councillor, dispensing his words one by one.

"Seven, eight years," said Nazneen.

"Are you finding it hard to cope?" asked the councillor.

"No," said Nazneen.

"How many children do you have?"

"Two," said Nazneen.

The councillor looked disappointed. He went away.

Television crews came in the afternoon. There was nothing to film, so they filmed each other. They returned after dark and filmed the boys riding around in cars. They found the disused flats where the addicts gathered to socialize with their addictions, and filmed the grotty mattresses and the bits of silver foil. It was a sensation. It was on the local news.

Three dealers were arrested. Job opportunities opened up.

A Tower Hamlets Task Force was established to look into "Youth Deprivation and Social Cohesion." In two years' time it would deliver its verdict.

In the meantime, reporters equipped with notebooks and tape recorders roamed the estate looking for gang members. They accosted Tariq. "Where are the gangs? Are you a member?"

"No," he said. "There are no gangs here."

"Fundamentalist, then. Are you one of those?"

On Brick Lane scabs formed quickly over the wounds. Band-Aids were applied. There was nothing that would not heal, and after a few weeks, when the wooden boards and the Band-Aids came off, it was as if nothing had happened. There were no visible scars.

Nazneen descended the steps into the concrete basin. The thin young man walked over the flagstones, away from her. She quickened her pace.

"Salaam aleikhum."

He turned around. "Aleikhum a-salaam."

"Do you know," she asked him, "what has happened to the Bengal Tigers?"

He regarded her with a devouring interest. His nose, large, pestle-shaped, became inquisitorial. "It was disbanded. The chairman went away."

"Oh," said Nazneen, looking down. "Where did he go?"

"Karim? He went to Bangladesh."

"I see. Yes."

"Or he joined the caravan. That's what some people say."

Nazneen had a vision: Karim in his jeans and white shirt, a thin gold chain at his neck and a bale of dresses over his shoulder; Karim in a mountain cave, surrounded by men in turbans wielding machine guns.

"But I think he went to Bangladesh."

"Yes," said Nazneen.

"Anyway," said the boy, "*I* wouldn't go for jihad in some faraway place. There's enough to do here."

Nazneen glanced at the youth club sign.

"Yes, exactly. They are looking for organizers. And I'm starting a new group. You know, I never approved of allowing women in the Bengal Tigers. It was supposed to be an Islamic group! It was a mixed-up idea. Not my idea." He gave her a look that said, We both know whose idea. "My group, it's not religious, anyway. It's going to be a political organization. Local politics. You should come along."

If it was his group, then he would become the chairman. The Questioner was moving on. That left a vacancy.

"I'll come. I'd like to, though I only went to a few of the other meetings," said Nazneen. An aeroplane passed overhead. She looked up. The plane climbed steadily. The higher it climbed, the deeper the sky. It rode up. And it went on. Nazneen stopped watching. She said, "But that was before I knew what I could do."

She put the chocolate in the fridge, went into the sitting room, and turned on the radio. The radio was tuned to one of Shahana's stations. A man sang about love and leaving, rain and tears. He sang of loss and perhaps—the words were not clear—of death. He sounded inexorably happy, bounced along by the drums and the tune. Nazneen took a pen and paper and sat down at the table. She began to sketch out a design. The sun warmed her hands. It poured into a glass of water and spilled golden rings on the dark tabletop.

Razia would pay her tomorrow. Tomorrow she would go to Sonali Bank and send money to Hasina. There had been no letter from Hasina for more than two months now.

Chanu wrote every week. Sometimes there was a gap of three weeks and then all three letters arrived at once. Then, especially then, it was easy to see that it was always the same letter that he wrote. He wrote this and that about the weather. It was hot. It was cooler now. And now very hot. He was sweating very much, or not so much. He was looking forward to the rain. He wrote about food: his breakfast, his lunch, his dinner. She knew the contents of his stomach as intimately as ever. He mentioned soap, management, strides forward, little setbacks. The Big Boss was either "encouraging" or "encouraging but cautious." These lines gave little away. It was as if the censor's pen hovered over them, ready to strike out any material fact. Other aspects of his new life Chanu detailed with precision. He had embarked on an exercise regime and reported faithfully the week's program. Twenty-five sit-ups and thirty press-ups on Monday, forty press-ups and fifty squats on Tuesday, and so on. And week by week he constructed a word map of his new home. Living area twenty feet by ten feet, kitchen area six feet by four feet, nearest barber two hundred and fifty yards, nearest butcher six hundred yards, nearest bank approximately one mile. Week after week he sent the information. Everything else he kept to himself. He wrote on thick yellow paper and filled one side, right to the end. He never stopped short of the end of the page. Sometimes he reported twice on the weather, simply to fill the space.

Once a month or so, he telephoned.

"How are things with you? Shall I send money?"

"No," she said. "We are all right."

"The girls are studying?"

"Getting good marks. Shahana is starting French lessons."

"Well. It's all right then."

The line crackled conveniently. Their voices echoed down the wire. It was difficult to talk.

One time she asked him, "Is it how you expected? Is it what you wanted?"

White noise filled the earpiece, like a gale caught in the telephone. Then the line cleared.

"The English have a saying: You can't step into the same river twice. Do you know it? Do you know what it means?"

She knew.

Another time he called and said, "I've seen her."

"Hasina!"

"The family she is with is a respectable-type family. But it would be better if she had her own living accommodation."

"How did she seem?"

"She seemed . . ." Chanu paused. "Unbroken."

"What did she say? How did she look?"

"We must send some money. Will you send to her?"

The first wage that Razia paid was not much. All month they ate rice and dal, rice and dal. And at the end of the month there was five pounds left to send to Hasina. Next month there was more.

Nazneen put down her pen. It was not working. She was not ready. She had thought it would be a matter of trying. Now she realized that the work would come later. First she had to imagine.

A new song came on the radio.

Weeeeeeeeeeeeeelll

A woman's voice, half singing, half screeching.

You know you make me wanna shout

She went to the radio and turned it up. The singer jumped off her cliff of expectation and cavorted in an ecstatic sea.

Nazneen moved her head to the song. Her hips went from side to side. She tapped her right foot, then the other. She raised her arms and moved her chest. The music broke in waves over her entire body.

She waved her arms, threw back her head, and danced around the table. *Shout!* She sang along, filling her lungs from the bottom, letting it all go loose, feeling her hair shake out down her neck and around her shoulders, abandoning her feet to the rhythm, threading her hips through the air. She swooped down and tucked her sari up into the band of her underskirt. *Shout!*

Nazneen put her hands on her waist and kicked her legs high. She turned and kicked, turned and kicked, jumped and kicked, and her foot went over her head.

The phone rang. Nazneen ran to the radio and switched it off.

"Hello." She was panting.

"What's wrong?" It was Chanu.

"No. Nothing. Just running for the phone."

"Your sister has vanished."

Nazneen's chest hurt. She pushed it with her hand. "Oh, God, what has happened?"

"Her employer came to see me. She has vanished with the cook. They have run away together."

"Oh," said Nazneen. "I thought something terrible . . ."

"Something terrible *has* happened. The cook is only a young boy. How soon before he gets tired of her? Remember what happened the last time."

The line was clear but Chanu, out of emotion or force of habit, shouted.

"When did she leave?"

"A week or two ago. I don't know. There was hell to pay with the employer. Good cooks don't grow on trees, as he kept reminding me."

"Did you see him, the cook? What was he like?"

"Don't expect me to go chasing after her. There's more to this soap business than meets the eye. I can't go running around all over the town on your wild-goose chase."

Nazneen imagined him nursing his belly.

"I know," she said.

"Why did she do it? Why does she do these things?"

Nazneen glanced down and was surprised to see her legs. "Because," she said, "she isn't going to give up."

Chanu was quiet. The line played a static tune.

"I've been thinking," said Chanu. "Maybe you could come for a holiday, you and the girls."

"What about school?"

"Oh," he said and was very casual about it, "oh, come whenever it's possible."

"Yes," she told him. "We'd like that."

The miles did not matter. She saw him beam. His eyes disappeared in crinkles. His cheeks were ready to burst. His voice, when it came, was unsteady. "I'd like that too. That is the thing I'd like most in the world."

"Where are we going?" Nazneen asked again. "Give me a clue."

They were on the bus, heading towards Liverpool Street. That was all she knew.

"A clue. A clue," said Razia, with her best sideways look.

"No," cried Shahana. "Stop it."

"It's a surprise," Bibi explained, with the patience of angels.

"I'll guess, then. We're going to the zoo."

"No."

"The cinema."

"No."

"The fair. The circus. The end of the earth."

"No more guessing," said Shahana. She took a Tupperware box out of her bag and lifted the lid. She had made the sandwiches herself, cream cheese spread with mango pickle. "There's two each. Who wants one now?"

Shahana and Bibi had half a sandwich each.

The conductor came upstairs and told them theirs was the next stop.

As they got off the bus, the girls took hold of Nazneen's hands. "Close your eyes," they told her.

She obeyed.

They tugged her hands. "Come on. Walk."

She opened her eyes.

"Walk with your eyes closed."

She felt the breeze against her skin, the warmth of the sun against her eyelids, the hair that tickled her cheek. As she walked she was aware of each step, testing out the mechanics of her legs.

"We're here," said Bibi.

"Hush," said Shahana. Her hand covered Nazneen's eyes. "Tie your scarf around, Bibi, or she'll cheat."

"I hope you don't expect too much of me," said Razia. "Remember I'm an old lady. Old and arthritic."

"Hush," said Shahana. "You'll give it away."

The girls guided Nazneen along with one hand on hers and the other in the small of her back. Nazneen heard voices, the ones that passed her and the ones that melted far away. She heard music played on strings and piped from on high. There were thuds, too, like boots having the mud knocked off them. And a faint whooshing that came and went like the wind in a tunnel.

"Where are we?"

"You sit here with Razia. We'll organize everything."

"Shall I peep?" she said to Razia, when she could tell that the girls had gone.

"You could try," said Razia, "but then I'll have to poke your bloody eyes out."

Nazneen rested her arms on a table. She could smell fried food, old leather, the warm, used smell of air that has been in countless nostrils, a hint of talcum powder, furniture polish, and the sharp skin of limes. She breathed deeply. It was the furniture polish that smelled of limes.

"We're ready. We're ready," said Bibi.

They stood her up and turned her around. Shahana untied the knot at the back of her head.

"Go on. Open them."

She opened her eyes.

In front of her was a huge white circle, bounded by four-foot-high boards. Glinting, dazzling, enchanting ice. She looked at the ice and slowly it revealed itself. The criss-cross patterns of a thousand surface scars, the colors that shifted and changed in the lights, the unchanging nature of what lay beneath. A woman swooped by on one leg. No sequins, no short skirt. She wore jeans. She raced on, on two legs.

"Here are your boots, Amma."

Nazneen turned around. To get on the ice physically—it hardly seemed to matter. In her mind she was already there.

She said, "But you can't skate in a sari."

Razia was already lacing her boots. "This is England," she said. "You can do whatever you like."

Acknowledgments

I am deeply grateful to Naila Kabeer, from whose study of Bangladeshi women garment workers in London and Dhaka (*The Power to Choose*) I drew inspiration. Thank you to Naila for her comments on the manuscript, and also for lunch.

I would like to thank Nan Graham for being brilliant, Nicole Aragi for wisdom (provided) and wonders (performed), and Mari Roberts for getting things under way. Colin Robinson and Grant and Wendy Bardsley gave me encouragement at all the necessary moments and valuable observations on the manuscript. I am indebted to my parents and my brother for many discussions over the years, and to my father in particular for handing down stories. Syful, Sofia, Naema, Ali, Shofiur, and everyone else who gave up time to talk to me—thank you. To Simon I owe special thanks for being my first and most patient reader.

About the Author

Monica Ali was born in Dhaka, Bangladesh, and grew up in England. She lives in London with her husband and two young children.